OUTLAWS

OUTLAWS

EDMUND FAIRFAX

BOKOS
TORONTO

ISBN 978-0-9952965-0-3

Published by Bokos (Toronto, Canada)
www.edmundfairfax.com

WARNING

The wayward "laws" of English spelling—is it *boyfriend,
boy-friend,* or *boy friend?*—are betrodden in the following.

THE NAKED TRUTH

How it tears so easily, naked unshielded flesh. And what blood is spilled as thew and sinew are ripped asunder, and as limbs are wrenched out of shape and out of body. Do but ask Actaeon, if you can find him, that wretched huntsman who had seen altogether too much flesh, and he will tell you, "Beware the eye of a priggish goddess, for she will make a beast of you and tear your heart out!" And yet ask not, for you will not find him. Besides, what good would it do? For what do rosecheeked youths care about Artemis Agrotera? What is Artemis Agrotera before hearts flushed with the stirrings of early spring?

And spring had come early this year, hot and panting, like an untimely guest to winter's wake, long cheerless as a Puritan's lenten meal. But this was, after all, the year of 1645, when war, with his bedfellows of dearth and death, stalked abroad: in Germany war, in the Netherlands war, and in England inland war, wars begun over kings' *prérogatives* and kings' prayerbooks.

But what were *prérogatives* and prayerbooks to the rosecheeked youths who now hastened across field and meadow, in the nearness of little Kingswood, a mere stone's throw from Bristol? Coming upon an old stonen hurdle, which lay athwart their path, this lad and lass stopped short and stole a quick reckless kiss. Oswin then, as if the master of unclipped wings, overlept the hurdle and dashed off, borne along by the underlay of spring's unruly growth. And Maddy stood on and watched awhile, and then taken by an afterthought, she called out, "Take care, brother!" But he was already well out of earshot. And then she turned her back and hastened off too.

Not far away there was another lad no less eager to take leave of folk for an afternoon romp, a young Godwin, followed hard upon by his younger brother Charles, the highborn sons of one Lord Drighten. Coming to a sudden stop by a littletrodden path, Godwin meant to take hasty leave, yet as he was about to spur on, his brother reached over and, with the deftness of a puppeteer, took a hold of Godwin's rein, and said, "Don't be late. You know how it upsets father."

"I'll be on time," he said grudgingly and galloped off, not stopping his flight until he came to where lowly Oswin stood stripping himself at water's edge.

"What, here?" Godwin called out from the lee of the nearest stand of trees.

"The day's warm, and I'm hot."

"But—"

The naked one dived in and began splashing and hooting, and then called out, "What are you waiting for?"

At length Godwin got down, stripped himself, and came to the edge, where he stood gawking at the brownish green water (or was it grey?). It did not look that clean, he thought, and—well, he had never been much of a swimmer. All until Oswin swam up, and in reaching up, took a hold of his arm and pulled him in, making a big splash.

And after a spell of swimming, they came back up onto the belly of the sunny bank and lay there in the open. And thinking themselves to be alone and unseen, they drew towards each other, touch answering touch.

But not far away, two girls, daughters of a butcher in Kingswood, were out scampering, in flight from father and Sunday boredom. And so it happened that in time they unwittingly came within eyeshot of Oswin and Godwin. Wide-eyed and dropchinned, unseen and unheard behind shielding bushes, the two wondered at the sight below.

"What are they doing?" the younger whispered and then laid hands to mouth to hold in giggles.

"What silly things grownups do!" whispered back the other.

Enough! The two dashed down the backside of the hillock, trying to outrun their giggles, as if wishing to dodge clear of damning touch in a game of blindman's bluff. Wait till Mary hears about this! She'll split her sides and topple over into the gutter! Onwards they were driven until they came to a breathless stop, a fair landspan away.

But now they heard a woman's voice nearby. What, was everybody out in the woods today? Doing more silly things? Well, how else could it be? They hastened soundwards but grew warier the nearer they drew, for these sounds became cries and screams. And then they saw a young woman lying facedown, with her arms caught behind her back, and a young man over her.

They watched but a little and then dashed off again. Homewards, yes, homewards, but which way was that? Good God! They had somehow lost their bearings! Curse these wayward woods and meadows! Great was the maze of snarling clawing growth that hindered their headlong homing, threatening to tear them asunder! Great was the need to be back on *terra cognita!* And when they reached Kingswood, and its crush of sweaty black-clad bodies, they found themselves altogether tonguetied, as much from breathlessness as from unknowningness. A wordless shedding of tears and pointing of little white fingers was enough to upset a mother into inklings of something somewhere all awry.

The mere handful at the butcher's threshold swelled to a rabble by town's edge, bristling here and there with broomsticks and walkingsticks, with whips and clubs. Into the woods this Samaritan band footslogged warmanlike. At every stride, head upon head sketched forth one hellscape after another, one more gruesome than the other, and with as many thoughts as heads about what was to be or not to be done.

And as Oswin and Godwin lay dreamily carefree upon the green, seemingly far from the madding crowd, the world around them shifted. The shouting of a roving rabble in their nearness jarred them into wakefulness. They threw on their clothes and in no time were come upon by the forefront of the throng. It was somewhat of a tossup who was the more startled to find whom in the woods thus. Indeed, the rabble, hoping to find knaves afoot, found here only neighbours abroad, seemingly lawabiding even if a little guiltylooking. Well, one could always turn a blind eye to a little foxy poaching in times of need.

"Some evil's astir," upspoke one townsman. "Someone's in need hereabouts. Will you make one with us and help?" Without thinking, Oswin nidnodded. And so swept along by time and place, Oswin and Godwin became part of the hunt.

What a shock it was for the youth, not long thereafter, to come upon his own sister in sorry fettle, her clothes ripped, her body bruised, her look crazed, her frame shaken. Forsaking his mates, Oswin ran ahead to enfold within his arms this wretch of his blood. And little answer he got for all his asking, for no sooner seen but the shamed girl gave herself up to the bitterest of weeping and wordless blubbering.

But an answer did come, only when nearly the whole band had caught up, among which stood Godwin somewhat off and aloof. How the sight of *him* ruffled the weeper, such that, with an outstretched finger, she blubbered a mangled "His brother!" For many, however, the finger proved to be mightier than the word; indeed, most had failed to make out her words altogether. So here, after all, was the knave in their very midst! What a swine to illhandle a slip of a girl thus! By God! They would take it out of his hide here and now!

Cries of "Get him!" came from those furthest away, and the mob thronged towards Godwin, halfshielded by his horse, which at once grew skittish and unruly in the enfolding hubbub. Rearing and veering, the beast pulled Godwin to-and-fro, as he held reins in one hand and fought besetters with the other. And the foremost of the rabble yawed no less, all greatly hindered in their scuffling.

Coming between the strokes and the stricken, Oswin tried to enlighten, only to find himself no less battered under aimless blows. But somehow Godwin horsed himself and galloped off. In his madcap flight, Godwin overshouldered one glance after another at the tailing mob, some even sprinting along behind, and he wondered if they meant to follow him right to his own doorstep! Indeed, the crowd had deemed it fitting and needful that blood should answer for blood, here and now or yonder and later, although none had been spilled, leastwise not yet.

Time had ticked away on Godwin. He had overstayed in the wilds and was sure to home too late, to a father's cold cheer, with unwelcome tidings as a cold sauce to a cooling meal. With evening falling, amidst shadows lengthening, Godwin rode on heavyhearted. In time, he found himself upon hometurf again, his horse growing ever more sluggish, until lastly it halted before the Drighten greathouse. Topped with the *Semper-Immotus*-besloganed Drighten blazon, which showed St. George trampling into the earth a writhing drake, the foredoor to this lordly abode swallowed Godwin as he hastened within.

"You're late! And father's upset with you!"

"Where is he?"

"Where else would he be?"

Godwin hastened to the wonted stead of their father, enwalled with many lawbooks and ledgers topped by downgazing busts of lofty Roman statesmen. And there, amongst the leatherbound and goldstamped, aslouch over a heavy ledger, sat Charles Drighten the elder, father and widower, lord and landlord, alderman and magistrate, the leading hand in Bristol's *Fellowship of Fartraders,* and the thumbs and fingers of even more farflung tradingbodies outside the hub of Bristol.

As panting rosecheeked Godwin stood wide-eyed before his father's desk waiting for leave to speak, the old man's stiff quill scratched on, the fingerends of his bloodless right hand blackened from much writing with a sputtering tool. The taskful quill took its ease, allowing the careworn coughridden man to look up.

"Why are you standing there like some sniveling hoyden?" asked the magistrate, who had long ago reached the years wherein the weary mind more readily lingers upon old letdowns than upon old hopes.

"There was a great upset this afternoon among the townsfolk, and one—"

"I care little about what passes in the byres and barnyards of England, but I do care about timeliness, and meals in this house are to be taken on time! Is that understood?"

"Yes, father. But this afternoon—"

"To table!" rang out, at the ledger's clapping-to.

Godwin willynillied along behind, to where the sty's yield awaited them, to wit, Lord Drighten's pet dish of porkpie, which was timehallowed upon the Sunday table. As the lord lustily fell to chewing, Godwin picked at what lay before him, but then, one man's food is another man's poison—and the gristlier, the grislier it was for Godwin! All the while, through the youth's brain there wheeled and whirled thoughts of that afternoon's happenings, raising worries about how the day would end. And before long, a worried footman came with untimely tidings of a rabble heading boldly for the house.

The magistrate was greatly taken aback by the sudden show of angry bawling faces, flailing arms fisticuffsready, and brandished sticks and cudgels, all forgathered in a writhing heap at the foot of his steps. Coming out into the open and standing upon the topstep, Lord Drighten towered above the crowd *Colossus*-like, with Charles at the right hand of his father, and Godwin at the left and well to the rear.

"What is the meaning of this?"

At once, the mob fell still and speechless, one mouth sheepishly waiting for another to say something. Then Oswin, pushing himself to the forefront and cheekily climbing up a few of the steps, fingered out Charles and shouted,

"That thing, your son, has laid hands upon my sister!" Bodies shifted aside, showing forth the shamed girl in tears and tatters.

Godwin breathed more easily, in the knowledge that the throng had lastly been enlightened about his guiltlessness—in this business leastwise. But Charles smirked, half under his breath, "Likely the wench is unhappy with her fee."

"How dare you make this shameful ruckus before my house, like so many drunken swine!" At this, the throng began to stir and din again, all riotready. The magistrate, seeing that he had misreckoned, straightway shifted to a more soothing asking, "What proof is there of any wrongdoing?"

"The sworn word of two witnesses and my sister, and if you cannot see the harm to her body, then you are as bloodblind as any other crooked lordling!" frothed Oswin. The mob began to rabble again, even more cheekily than before.

Oh, these were fightingwords, riskladen for the lowranked! And so Godwin spoke out, "Take care! You go too far!" even if outdinned and unheard, and unflabbergastingly so, since he had barely raised his voice.

Mindful that tomorrow happened to be the start of the courtsittings, the magistrate boomed forth again, "If you wish to have a hearing, you must show yourselves tomorrow morning at the *Sessions* in Bristol, ready, with your witnesses, to lay forth your case."

"And he's to run free until brought to trial?" asked a nameless voice.

"He's in my keeping until tried."

Little likelihood there was that one outstretched finger would unhouse this son of a lord for a turnkey's grimy hole. Yet loath to think that they had come this far all hotheaded only to leave now sadly emptyhanded, the throng fell again to whining and writhing.

"This is not the way of the law, as you well know! Right will be done only in its rightful place. All of you leave now and leave this business in the hands of those whose business it is. Begone before more are made to answer!"

Having stopped short at the threshold, the many, in meeting the one, now melted away as one meek and biddable body.

In turning about, Charles leered at Godwin and asked, "Why the siding with bumpkindom, brother?"

"I, I meant only to keep peace!"

The lord had not taken kindly to the upstartswain cheekily dirtying the

Drighten steps at mealtime with his rowdy hickbacked mudslinging, and the magistrate would not easily forget these bygones. In abouting, he snapped at Godwin, "Why did you not tell me that this was afoot?"

"I tried, but—"

The magistrate was over the threshold and beyond earshot. Godwin stood on, shillyshallying, whether he should out or in. Out or in.

At length, he turned his back and went inside, where he could hear high words behind shut doors, yet not so high as to overhear. And idling in the forehall, like some waiting caller unsure of a welcome, he mindplayed the father-to-son utterings within, yet he had heard and beheard them all before, or so he thought.

When he had quickly wearied of these timeworn thoughts, seated as he was upon a hardbottomed backstool, his eyes fell upon the great plaque screwed to the wall across from him, which showed the familytree, with bough upon bough, all trimmed and straightened, reaching backwards and forwards and sideways, binding one kinsman to another across time and tide. In gazing at the blankness that yawned beneath his own name, his mind grew numb and his bottom sore. And a weakling of a thought padded unseen through his mind, that, yes, this was Sunday, another day of lordly rest and rant.

With the belts and wheels of law having been set aturning in the Drighten household, the sun laid its dizzy head to rest in enfolding darkness, leaving Oswin and Maddy benighted for the better part of their homeward trudge. But herein, they were not alone, for a handful from the rabble, those who were nearby neighbours, stayed with the two for most of the trek. And such clubbiness stemmed seemingly from keenness to heartsoothe the girl, or perhaps more from eagerness to share words of wisdom.

Goodman Sowerbutts bemoaned that "Long has the everyman been the plaything of the rich, but a day of reckoning will come—and not soon enough!—when the high are made low and the low high. Until such day, we are chaff under the flail!"

"How can a girl from the field stand against a lord in all his robes?" said Goodwife Hardy. "And what good will it do now? Law or no law, her shame will be longlived, for who'll want the young'un now, stained as she is?"

Goodman Dashwood threatened, "If any lord had done such to my daughter, I'd blaze his way to Hell in a mighty bonfire and burn his damned house down with him still in it!"

"And you'd go up in smoke along with him!' gainsaid Goodman Bracebridge. "No, you must go to court to drop a king, and to court the girl must go!"

"Everlasting shame upon those who kiss the rod and carry coals!" were Goodman Sowerbutts' last words before he took unseen leave of the dwindling cluster.

All these high words, and many more of the same, wantoned through Oswin's brain in the emboldening darkness, mixing mindfulness of new hurts with that of old, until the angry young man said, "You may be sure that my sister and I will not let this pass fightlessly, and tomorrow morning we shall see wrong righted."

"Then you're a bigger fool than I ever thought!" blurted Goodwife Hardy. "Many a handled girl has come before a magistrate only to leave a laughingstock. What makes you think the lamb will fare any better?"

"Why should we cower when right's on our side? And there are even witnesses!"

"Many the slip 'twixt cup and lip. If you take on your betters, you'll live to rue it. Mark my words!" And with that, Goodwife Hardy and the last of their fellow trudgers went their ways, leaving Oswin and Maddy alone in the dark but a short stretch from home.

For much of this trek, tightlipped Maddy had struggled to keep herself coldly aloof to the day's happenings, but now with the last of the meddling crowd gone, she gave into her pain as freely as any child, for she was barely out of childhood herself, having only latterly turned sixteen.

"Bear up, sister! I swear to you that this wrong will not go unrighted!" begged Oswin, eager to heartsoothe this the last of his kind—only a halfsister at that—in a bloodline as scattered as harvestchaff. Yet such flimsiness of tie strengthened all the more their kinshipbond, in Oswin's mind leastwise, and now further hardened his setmindedness to see a rightsome reckoning.

"I fear we'll come away the worse for it, and he may yet do me more harm!"

"I'll never let that happen! Trust me, sister, all will turn out well if we only fight! Our family has put up with more than its share for too easily giving in."

"I don't want my shame the talk of the town!"

"Where there's no guilt, there's no shame, and all but the wicked will see that."

Maddy was lastly overswayed into not letting this business lie. Yet it seemed to her that with no money to hire a lawyer, and neither of them ever having been to court before, or even to Bristol, winnership in such an undertaking was unlikely to come easily. Nonetheless, she yielded.

Thoughts of yesterday and tomorrow unsettled the foresleep of more than one weary head that night. As he lay upon his wobbly bed, in his tumbledown hovel of a crofter's cottage upon land that was not his own, Oswin's dimming wakefulness drifted back to a bitter past, wilfully lingering on thoughts of a lost father, pressganged into a warlike death upon some faraway strand; a lost stepfather, taken off by hunger and sickness; a lost mother, overworked into her grave; a lost childhood, wherein the burden of raising himself and a halfsister fell upon his own shoulders.

Yet little did Oswin know that sleep came no more readily to the Drighten household that night or indeed other nights. Charles tossed within his binding sheets: why a mere tumble-in-the-hay should upshoot in such a tiresome to-do was beyond his fathoming. The magistrate squirmed no less, his unhappy greying head warring with its pillow, the latter as hard as ledgers that would not balance themselves. Godwin lay still, even if his thoughts could not, which drifted off to a time thereafter only to dash back to the now all affrighted, to what seemed the lesser of two evils, to a time of stolen happiness not yet stolen away, but unlike others, he soon slumbered off and then slept like a baby. But thralls to the cock's throat, the Drighten and Underhill households rose betimes and headed for nearby Bristol.

Great was the throng of townsfolk teeming through the mazy streets. Great was the stench from its open gutters steaming in the untimely sweltering weather. And great was the blend of worry and hope in Oswin and Maddy, as they hastened wide-eyed and breathless through this hitherto-unknown world of stony narrow lanes and uneven cobbled streets, of too many bodies jockeying and hustling, of too many marketbound wagons crossing and blocking.

And somewhere amidst this enwalled sprawl of overbuilt land and overbefolked throughways, swollen with the king's idling soldiery, stood the courthouse wherein Oswin and Maddy were sure to see wrong righted that day, if they could but find the building! And they had almost not found the town itself, for in their earlymorning footslog, they somehow lost their bearings and overshot their goal, ending up westward of the town, and thus needed to wend back, belatedly finding inlet, greatly strapped for time.

When they reached Justitia's abode, a guard stood ready at the door to turn them away, for the courthouse was overfilled to bursting that morning, and no more bodies were to be let in. And it was more by dint of stronghand than softtalk that Oswin inned, shoving through and dragging behind a halfhearted sister clad in shabby red and white. And what a hellish airless hothouse they found! Enough to take one's breath away! Sweltering as much from the heat of the day as from the crush of overmany sweaty bodies, bodies of seemingly boundless shapes and sizes all busying and fidgeting in their keenness to witness the workings of the law.

Hardly had they time to take in this new setting when they heard Maddy's name spoken forth by the crownlawyer, one Richard Hooker, a little man with a great taste for task, no less than the churchman who was his namesake, for this our Hooker was—hook, line, and sinker—a staunch Puritan and a hardcore belonger to the *Brethrenship for the Bettering of Morals.*

As Charles Drighten the younger, with the bearing of a man slighted, swore himself not guilty to the burden-of-blame spoken forth, it lastly dawned on Oswin and Maddy that none other than Charles Drighten the elder himself was to oversit as doomsman in this his own son's trial, for the grimlooking man did not yield up his seat to any new placetaker. Nor did fear of any unevenhandedness owing to kinshipties seem to overcloud the foundins, who, uneasily twilighted between breakfast and lunch, were keen to get down to the nittygritty.

However much Oswin had striven that morning to build unbending backbone in the green girl, she found herself altogether overawed. Indeed, the swiftness with which the business was brought to trial had hardly left any time merely to overcome the shock, let alone gather thoughts, all without the needed help of a lawyer.

Once called to the stand, Maddy faltered forth thus, in this her maiden-speech before a lawcourt: "I was out, with my brother, gathering flowers, he left, alone then I was, gathering flowers, and he came upon me, with his horse, he who sits there, he rode around me, many times, again and again, as the hand goes about the clock, blocking my way, and said, 'What have we here, a fair maid gathering rosebuds while she may?' I asked him to let me be, he would not, I asked what he wanted, he said, 'Whatever sweets of countryliving you might have,' I said, 'I have none to give you,' he said he thought otherwise, I asked him again to let me be, but he would not, I tried to run away, but he rode his horse against me and knocked me down." A gush of tears, apish blubberings and gasps, more freeflowing than the needed words, and then, "I was hurt in falling and couldn't get up at first. He got down." Sobs and blubberings. "He knew me." Sobs and blubberings.

How downletting this, little more than a wishywashy fingerwag, with much left unsaid. So thought many of the foundins.

"Do you have anything further to say?"

A tearful naying headshake.

"Do you have any witnesses to call?"

"They've already been asked to come."

"Do you mean to sift the witnesses?"

"They've already been asked about it."

Seeing that girl had not the slightest understanding of lawing, the magistrate had Maddy stand down and Hooker take over. Of the two eyewitnesses, the butcher of Kingswood's two daughters, only one was called up.

"My sister and I, we often play in the woods when the weather's fair, and we were there yesterday. We set about making garlands, crowns for our heads. We were princesses who had to flee and then try to get home without being caught by soldiers, and—"

"How is it that you came to see the two together?"

"After running awhile, we saw two men, but they didn't see us. They were as naked as God made them, and one lay more or less on top of the other, all shaking with his body, as if taken by some great laugh, and it looked as funny as the groans sounded, the groans they made while he quivered so, and yet it didn't seem to bring any pain to either of them, all that pushing of his part into the bottom of the other. I've seen father and mother do the same, at times when they thought I wasn't home. And then we—"

If breath wholly failed many, the heart nearly failed Hooker. The witness meant to go on, but Hooker could not let this blatant bearding of law and godliness go unchecked, even if the matter was beside the point here.

"What 'part' did he push?"

"The part that men always hide if they can."

"Are you sure? Are you sure that it was his 'part,' as you say, that was pushed into the 'bottom,' as you say, of the other?"

"Yes."

Hooker could not at all forbear now, for it was not enough to know whether some fellow's manhood had found its way into another man. Why? No less farreaching was how deeply such a "part" had went its way within, for the matter of a few inches or more meant as much as life or death. How so? Such was commonlaw at this time that if more than two inches of manhood had made its way within, what was otherwise a mere *misdemeanour* now became a hanging-*felony*. Hooker was bound to ask further.

"And how much of his 'part,' as you say, was taken into the other?"

"Most of it, as far as I could tell."

But how much was "most of it"? fretted Hooker, for he very well knew that not all men were born with bodies of like girth or limbs of like length. Oh, how could one be sure here, when law clearly called for, nay, stood upon clearcutness? Alack, alack, that so many things dance upon the earth like so many hazy notes wavering upon the fretless fingerboard of that more and more faddish instrument the fiddle, which the French are so keen about these days, with all their lewd gambling about thereto, with faddishly crooked feet—one pointing south and the other north—not unlike the two parts of a cloven hoof! Trust the French to spread the taste for such an instrument—along with the pox—one that needs much playing before the fingers fall into their fitting places without thinking and bring forth an unmingled sound!

Now, where was he? Ah, yes. Still keen to get to the bottom of this lewdness, Hooker, in his lawyerlike thoroughness, held up his right forefinger, and marking off from the tip what was surely two inches, he asked, "This much or more?"

"More. I don't know how his friend could have taken so much in, for it looked very big, much bigger than my father's. Have I said something wrong?"

"No child, it is not you who is guilty of wrongdoing. And now you must tell me, who were these two men that you saw thus?"

What an upstir followed when the witness fingered out Oswin and Godwin! What hell broke loose when Hooker uttered hard upon, "Oh, how this misdeed stinks to heaven high and cries out for the lash of law!"

The magistrate, who had always prided himself on his coolheadedness, found himself now dumbstricken beyond belief, but then, how could he have foreseen this, one further pitfall to the Drighten weal? Oh, why did he let Hooker run on thus? Damn that fool Hooker! Nor did his asking looks to Godwin, which met with guilty looks, do much to bring him to himself. And as the crowd whipped itself into an eddy of dinning unruliness, the magistrate sat there, milled about by a rabble of rearing thoughts and jostling fears, which strongarmed him into a dozy deedlessness.

Heeding Hooker's call for the "lash of law," a few bysitters took it upon themselves to flog the devil out of Oswin, but the latter, unchary of standing his ground, foot-and-fisted back. As the courtroom brinked upon outright lawlessness, the magistrate lastly mastered himself and called forth the guards. Once a handful of the rowdies were taken into grips and led off, order tiptoed back into Justitia's abode.

Hooker stood most sheepishly biddable, all too well aware now of how he, in his keenness to ferret out lewdness, had worsened the magistrate's lot, for Lord Drighten was bound yet again to have a son lawtaken. The too-deep-scratching lawyer would have much to make up for now.

Oswin and Godwin were forthwith taken into grips, under the blame-burden of sodomy, and led away, in the magistrate's doddering hope that out-of-sight would be out-of-mind. But this unforeseenness was to leave the courtroom in an ugly mood and sour the rest of the trial. The magistrate now ordered the young witness to speak of the matter in hand, and only the matter in hand.

"We watched until we could no longer hold back our giggles and then ran off. We kept running until out of breath, and we had to stop. Then we heard cries nearby, and we drew near. We saw her there and that man there doing the same. Yet something seemed wrong, for—"

"Was the girl tied up?" asked Hooker quickly.

"No."

"Did you see her try to flee?"

"No."

"Did you see him strike or threaten her?"

"No."

"We often weep when we're sorrowful or pained, but sometimes we weep when we're happy. Have you ever wept for happiness?"

"Yes."

"You said that you heard the girl crying. Do you know why she was crying?"

"No."

"Do you know, child, what they were truly doing?"

"I guess I don't."

The girl was told to stand down, and Charles was called up.

"Charles Drighten, did you have dealings with Maddy Underhill Sunday last?"

"Yes."

"Did you lie with her, as the girl and the child have witnessed?"

"Yes."

"Did she ask you to lie with her?"

"Yes."

"And what were her words?"

"She playfully spoke none."

"Then how could you have known her will?"

"She at length fell upon her back and lifted her skirts. It was clear that the loose wench was keen to feel my edge."

The courtroom broke out into muttered and halfmuttered spare-the-rod-and-spoil-the-child screeds, to the shaking of heads filled with thoughts of how shamelessly awash with rank lewdness the world had grown, until thwarted by the magistrate's call-to-order.

"How is it then that the witness heard the girl cry?"

"The wench was hardset to lodge me. 'Tis known I'm a pretty piece of flesh." This teased forth an unfewness of merry sniggers, although no-one thought to ask for proof.

"How came she then to be bruised?"

"She liked her lovemaking rough, as illbred women are wont to have it. In the end, she was well paid for her pains."

"You paid the girl?"

"It's run-of-the-mill that wenches who have dealings with men look to be paid. I did but follow the times. And by the way, she was no maiden."

"How do you know that?"

"There was no blood upon my blade."

"She's a hedgesidewhore then?"

"For all I know, yes."

Maddy rose up and bellowed, "Liar! Liar!" and carried on wildly black-guarding the magistrate's son. To many, this outburst brought to mind an old fishwife bemoaning the loss of some stale haddock, and not a few began to jeer and bleat in mockery.

With the backing of law-and-order, Charles was told to step down and Maddy to stand forth again, for the law was not yet done with her.

"Is it true that you have been known by other men?" asked Hooker.

"What does that have to do with his illhandling of me?"

"Answer as bidden," ordered the magistrate. For some time, she sat there tightlipped—it was none of their damned business, and why should I damn myself before all these folk? The magistrate most roughly ordered her again to answer.

At length and at a loss, she brought forth a mousy "Yes," a truthful answer not altogether true, for with "men" she had not lain, but rather with only one other lad, who had stolen her heart and maidenhood. And it was while waiting to tryst with this unnamed youth that Charles happened upon her instead.

"Is it true that you were paid?"

Again, she sat tightlipped awhile, until roughly ordered to answer. She uttered another mousy truthful "Yes" that belied the truth. What a clever stroke it had been on Charles' part to sow one further wild seed, after having ploughed the girl, for before leaving her, he had dropped a handful of coin upon her back as she lay whimpering. This let him reap well later, that is to say, let him speak truthfully of dirty money having passed hands, in the unlikelihood of his ever having to answer for his deed. And she did indeed take the money—as atoning payback and not as earned pay. But who there would believe that?

Now she felt the earth beneath her shift, as if long tired of sitting still, like a fidgeting child too long seated in a hard pew. She was no more of a match at the bar than she had been upon the bed of stony earth the day before. And now what shame! To have been stripped bare thus, before all these gawkers, and then pitchblackened into a whore! To have been laughed at! Her pain laughed at! And now, beyond belief, to hear the magistrate freespeak his son of any wrongdoing, to the smug nidnods of these found-ins! She could bear it no more. Overwhelmed with bitterness, the girl fell to cursing and crying, flailing and blubbering, wrecking mayhem with nail and tongue upon all who dared to come near.

As she was manhandled out by the guards, the magistrate toyed with the thought of not letting this *outrage à la Cour* pass—and he was in his rights here. But then, he bethought himself again, he had had his fill of the wench already and furthermore did not wish to seem overly grudgeful. Besides, if she had been seeded by one or other of her bucks, he would see her soon enough for the unlawry of bringing forth a bastard.

It was some time that day before Oswin, who had been lodged in the filth of lockup, was to learn of the trial's outcome. And when his tearful sister came to stand before him, on the other side of the bars, the unhappy upshot seemed all too clear, yet he asked nonetheless, "What did they do to you, sister?"

"What they would."

"I'm so sorry!" Then stiffening and darkening, "They didn't harm you, did they?"

"How could they have harmed me more? I'm a whore to as many as know me, and no man will have anything to do with me now!"

"Why should you care what others think? Let them look with sticks-and-stones! And what do you need other men for, when you have one who loves you so?"

"His love didn't outlast the court's laughs, for he was there too, and afterwards he stopped me in the street and said, 'I have done with you!' and turned his back and went his way."

"Damn the bastards! The bastards! Curse them all! I swear to you, sister, these blackguards will be made to answer as soon as I'm free?"

"Free?! They say that you're likely to be hanged if found guilty! Little good your high words will do you at the end of a rope! And how then am I to run the croft by myself?"

"I've done nothing wrong, nor will I lie nor grovel before these highhands!"

"Can you not see? To them, the truth is but a lie not yet unhidden!"

"And truth will always out, for all their cunning!"

"Oh, you fool! What a mess you've made! Why did I ever listen to you? Go and be hanged then, for all I care! I've done with you! Better a dead brother than half a one!" And in a fresh outburst of tears, she turned her back and hastened out, heedless of Oswin's calls. And for a long while thereafter, the brother stood stiffly on, with the bars gripped in his whiteknuckled fists, as if they might tumble down should he let them go.

Godwin had fared somewhat better, having been locked up in the same building albeit, but lodged up in the higher rooms, where, for a handsome fee, a wrongdoer might be not unhandsomely stowed, far from the stench below in the unwholesome nethergloom. But then there are fouler things in this world than rats and bodywaste underfoot, as the youth well knew. And he had spent not even an hour there but was bailed out only to be straightway mewed up in the Drighten townhouse, where he was to be kept under watchful eye.

In the stillness of his room, he idled away, long gazing out at the leaded window, blankly watching the townsfolk below bustle by on their ways. His mind grew overclouded with dread of his father's homecoming after a long grueling magistratical day, and of the bitter chiding that was sure to follow hard thereupon. Wayward thoughts broke in, weak straggling sunbeams from sunnier days of carefree wantoning. And at length a weakling of a thought padded through his mind and whispered into his ear, how much better things would have turned out had he stood his ground and more wisely stood upon finding less open ground for sporting.

And this thought was soon fellowed by an even bolder one, that nothing stood now between him up in his room and the open street down below but a daring walk down the stairs to the foredoor and thence out onto the crowded street and then out of sight and reach and, hopefully with time, out of mind, there being no bonds, no bars, no bolts to hold him back, as he thought to himself. Indeed, there was hardly anyone at home. Now was the time to make thought deed, and now darted his mind about the room, searching for things that he would need to take along, ways to get clear of the town. And as time ticked away, he strove to forethink of every hurdle that he might come upon in his mindplayed flight into the unknown.

Having at last worked himself up to a pitch of boldness and setminded-ness, he was startled by the sight of his brother at the door, who said, "You are wanted below." With his father at home now, all thought of flight fled Godwin. And down the two went as one, until they came to stand before their father, who was seated at his desk.

Guilty looks from the son forthwith met with chiding looks from the father, who, more magistrate now than father, well knew as magistrate the look of guilt and the sound of lies, he having been so long at home amidst such in his many years as lawkeeper. And thus on the strength of outward seeming alone, he did not need to bother himself with asking for the truth. "What in the name of God were you thinking? Have you taken utter leave of your mind?"

An unlooked-for halt in this onslaught seemed to mean that Godwin was to say something on his own behalf, and so he began falteringly, "I didn't think—"

"Bloody right you didn't think! You've made a laughingstock of this family! And for what? Playing in the gutter? By God, I have half a mind to turn you out of doors and leave you in the gutter, where you belong! Do you know how hard this will be to patch up? If this gets to Antwerp? And what thanks do I hear for the pains I must take on your behalf?"

Again, a break in the rant seemed to call for some answer, and Godwin began, "I'm sorry—"

"Ay, a sorry piece-of-work you are! Had I known your mother would spawn such a limp wretch, I would have had her whipped out of town before she were ever bedded! I'm ashamed to say I have sons when I see only halfwits!"

Godwin stood there and took all this in his stride, as he had done since time out of mind, for he had learnt to be out of mind when under the brunt of such tonguelashings. As his eyes began to glaze over, the magistrate, in seeing his words seemingly fall upon deaf ears and his glares meet with glossy eyes, grew even more wrathful, such that he bolted to his feet, altogether beside himself, and slapped Godwin in the face, so strongly that the youth turned his cheek.

"How you sicken me! Get out of my sight! The pair of you!"

Godwin had outgrown the age to be sent up to his room, yet to his room he went nonetheless, glad at bottom to be shut up from such ranting, and glad to have been slapped only once. Back to the leaded window. It was not long, however, before he was called back down, not so much to be tonguelashed again but to be enlightened on how to ready himself against the morrow. That is to say, how to speak and answer, or better said, how to whiffle and wheedle such that a father might not be openly ashamed of his son, even if the latter ought to be of himself.

And the morrow came soon enough. However hellishly hot the fore-going day had been, this day was to be even more sweltering. But Hell or high water, nothing could keep away the throngs of townsfolk, those who hankered to hear the nittygritty of the lewd business that was the trial of magistrate Drighten's son, those who now elbowed and shoved and bickered and scuffled for sitting- or standing-room in the bursting courtroom. To the indwellership of Bristol, this was to be a trial to overshadow all others.

The crownlawyer was again that same Puritan Richard Hooker, who trod forth now upon a very short limb indeed, given that this case, no less if not more than yesterday's, reached high and touched the high. Yet for Hooker, as a hardcore belonger to the *Brethrenship for the Bettering of Morals*, this outcrop of rank sodomy was a hateful thorn all too deeply embedded. And the longer it bristled there unplucked, the more it festered to his eye and reeked in his nose—more than any wench's lost maidenhood. And yet any overreaching on his part, in the name of godly right, at odds with lordly might, could well unlodge him from his lofty perch.

At long last, the sodomites were brought forth. And what a sight the lowly swain made in his near rags, thoroughly dirty from the filth of lockup. But he cared not. Let them look and gawk until their eyes fall out! He would hold his head high. The unsightliness of the outward man hardly matched the ugliness of the inward, for with an unfilled belly and unbeslumbered head all hotly mindful of yesterday's wrongs, Oswin was in the foulest of moods. And the foulness deepened when in scanning the rabble, with their mouths whispering and muttering and hands pointing, he did not see his sister anywhere. As before, there had been no wherewithal to hire a lawyer, and without one, Oswin had not a leg to stand upon, or so it seemed.

"Oswin Underhill, you stand under the burden-of-blame for the hateful misdeed of sodomy, a sin and a misdeed against the law of the king both heavenly and earthly. How do you answer?"

"I've done nothing wrong," smirked Oswin and glowered back.

"Answer as bidden," snapped the magistrate.

Hooker began afresh, "Did you—"

"If you mean 'Did we sport?' then yes."

The room hubbubbed. Few, least of all the magistrate and the crownlawyer, had reckoned upon meeting with such selfdamning unabashed truthfulness. A veering wind to trouble the wrong shoulder of a sail.

"By these your own words then, you are guilty!"

"There's no wrong in doing what I wish with my own body."

"God's law does not allow you to do as you wish with your body."

"Then to Hell with God's law!"

The magistrate's calls-to-order were hardly heard above the din, but Hooker could not forbear and so went on, well before full hush backed. "What you call 'sport' is an enfilthening of nature, an overturning of the Godgiven order of this world wherein man is above woman, and a man who gives himself to a man is no more than a woman, by whom came evil into this world."

"What evil did my sister bring into this world? No, it's your law that's 'enfilthening,' if it winks at true wrongs and kicks at the guiltless!"

The hearing, which had barely started, was now at its end, for the magistrate took the floor to end all. "The court has heard enough, indeed too much. Oswin Underhill, your guilt has been clearly shown."

Then shortwhiles, the magistrate fell speechless. This was not how he had foreseen or wished to see the trial unfold. And in his speechlessness, he waited Abrahamwise for an inrunning thought to give him some ground to stay the harsh hand-of-law, or leastwise find its more softfisted lookalike. And forthwith a way out of this bind offered itself huggermugger.

"Oswin Underhill, I hereby rule that you be taken from this court, and at the earliest, crossshipped to Virginia where you shall drudge for the length of your life, until the filth of your wrongs be washed away by the sweat of your brow. Nor shall your scouting of court, and of law and faith, pass scathelessly. I further rule that you be taken from this court and, before your shipping, set in the pillory for one hour, where you shall be rightly laid bare to the wrath of all. God take ruth upon your Godless soul."

In damning himself thus, Oswin had also damned the magistrate's son, for such was the law at this time that two witnesses in such cases were enough to prove guilt, and both Oswin and the butcher's daughter had spoken against Godwin. And so without even taking the stand, Godwin was likewise damned out-of-hand to a lifetime of drudgery in Virginia. But what else could the magistrate do, for was not the law the law, and was not the law one law, and was not the one law for one and all? As Godwin had not spoken against law and faith—indeed, he had not been allowed to speak at all—he was spared the dreaded pillory.

Nor had it been lost on some that the law's sternness had been softened here, for the ruling, while not unknown at this time, was nonetheless uncommon in cases of sodomy—that is, those going beyond two full inches—where mosttimes hangings were meted out. But sending Oswin to his death would have meant as much as sending his own son to the same end, a son for whom he had other far weightier plans.

WATER AND WINE

T HE STENCH OF FILTH is hard to wash away. Scrub as you will—why, even shower in Niobe's tears or bathe in Pluto's Lethe—and still there lingers a stink in the nose. How true, how true this was for young unscrubbed Oswin! Following yet another illslumbered night in the grime of lockup, he awoke this morn with a stink in his nose, on this now-sunny-now-cloudy day, the first day of his reckoning and reckonings-to-come. But of the latter, the youth knew nothing as yet, sitting and stewing in a little cart parked between gate and inlet to the jail. No, he had thoughts only for what lay ahead of him this day and more so for what lay behind him, that which seemingly got him to this day.

At first, he hardly marked or minded the two other inmates who sat to either side. The slightest had grown most fidgety, as they waited thus. "All this for snitching a sheepshank!" he whined at last. It was not the first time that he had come before the magistrate to answer for thievery, and as before, the takings were as unlofty as the man's cravings. But while he had gotten off lightly time and time before, he had the illluck of standing trial on a day of Drighten spleen and now was to pay for his full belly of stolen sheepshank with a costly stint in the pillory.

Feeling a little selfsorry, the thief nudged Oswin and in a show of would-be fellowship asked, "What was your misdeed, mate?"

"Sodomy."

This straightway robbed the thief of his chumsy smile. And just as suddenly there came a splatter of spittle on Oswin's face, shot forth from the third inmate. In glowering back, Oswin fancied scuffling with the burly spitter, but fettered and shackled as they were, there was little opening for that.

In this, happenstance was happily on Oswin's side, for here, indeed, was a man not to meddle with. Amongst his many bespeckled deeds, this rough-hewn wharfworker had only latterly trashed a whole inn during a drunken brawl, set abroach by a Roundhead oath, and he had gravely laid up not a few of his fellows. When brought before the magistrate, the brawler at one point made at one of the witnesses in a fit of anger, grappling with him and biting off a snatch of his ear. But the coming stint in the pillory this day owed more to the brawler's bold wish shouted at the magistrate—"Stuff yourself with your bloody gavel!"—during one of Lord Drighten's begaveled calls-to-order, when the brawler was barely wrestled to the floor by four guards.

The sheepish thief deemed it best to turn away from Oswin as much as he could and, in doing so, became aware now of the muffled rumble coming from beyond the high stonen wall. "I can hear them now!" he halfwhimpered to himself. This brought Oswin and his brawler out of themselves even as quickly.

Heard before seen, the throng was great indeed, with body upon body all cheek-to-jowl along the path to the pillory. Yes, Oswin's trial had been of such unheard-of lewdness and surliness that not a soul in town—or nearly so—had failed to hear of it, and it seemed now that not a soul in town would hear of missing out.

When the gates to the jailyard were thrown open, the hitherto scarcely heard rumble became at once a deafening angry roar, and into the teeth of this hulking gathering, the sorry threesome trundled forth in their creaking flimsy cartlet. "My God!" stammered Oswin to himself, in beholding streetsides and windows and doorways and rooftops all bristling-bursting with untold writhing bodies and countless limbs, like so many gullwings, wildly flailing in and out of time to a burthen of hissing and hooting, jeering and catcalling.

No sooner had the cart pushed itself through the gates but those bystanders within a stone's throw began to hurl all manner of filth: mud and dung, rotting kitchenwaste, more mud and dung, bloody offal from butchershops, more mud and dung, even dead rats and cats, more mud and dung, and—most harmful of all—brickbats. So great was the hail that, to spare themselves, the threesome bowed down in the cart, as cravenly low as any fearful heathen groveling before the scowling mug of some graven thundergod. For Oswin at least, there was little point in gawking now: he had taken a hit to the right eye, and it was something of a struggle to see clearly.

Yes, by God! The time had come to make the crooked straight! And so swept along by time and place, the crowd, too swollen for so coopy a place as Bristol's narrow streets, shoved and pushed, jostling and jockeying amongst itself for the best spots to throw unhamperedly.

Amidst this mayhem there stood two crones, whom the cart was yet to pass. As these *twa corbies* waited, Goodwife Kirkland—so the one was called—shouted to her sidekick, "Many's the time that me and my ol' granny stood here. Watching the rogues, we'd be, yes, watching the rogues go by, like today. My ol' gran—God rest her soul!—before the rogues would go by, my ol' gran would always be telling me about all those great happenings from Queen Mary's time, how all those hairyticks were burnt at the stake. Oh, how their flesh would crackle in the fire, she'd say! Crackling and yelling and wriggling! But things like that, we don't see anymore. Gone they are. And gone is Mary."

"Come again," shouted Goodwife Hewitt, squinting and holding up a great brazen horn to one of her ears.

"I said, gone is Mary."

"Ay, so she is. The Lord giveth, and the Lord taketh away."

"If only my old knees were what they were once! But the Good Lord's seen fit to make me stooped and ricketykneed, and I must bow down before His will."

"What was that?" shouted Hewitt, still holding up her horn and thrusting her head forwards.

"I said—" but by this time, the cart was nearly before them, and so Goodwife Kirkland shrieked into the horn instead, "See where the rogues come!" And she gawked amazed, wondering, "How black these devils look!"

"Don't be shy, my dear! Cast away before they pass!" shrieked Goodwife Hewitt, who fell lustily to casting her shot as best she could. But it was not long before she stepped back, having winded herself, or so she thought at first, until it struck her that she had indeed fallen backwards, having taken a staggering hit to the forehead from a rogue brickbat.

Such mishaps were far from uncommon, for in all the wildness to hurl and hit, little thought was given to careful aiming. Indeed, most flung away hit-or-miss until not a few fellow pelters were hurt by rogue brickbats and only belatedly saw the need to keep well back from the cart, lest they be struck by the peltings from the other side of the street. And when the wounded fell back or pushed back against their mates, others behind them were in turn shunted back, some stepping or even stumbling into the foulness of the open gutters.

Even if lacking the heavy iron cladding of the turnkeys, Goodwife Hewitt was, nonetheless, made of sterner unflinching stuff, even if outmanned here. In no time she was back on her feet, but not before that oddish blur of blackness had dimmed away out of sight, beyond her shotspan.

"Do you know, my dear, what those rogues did?" puffed Kirkland.

"Come again."

"What did they do?" shouted Kirkland into the horn.

"Oh, I don't know. I'll ask."

Onwards trundled the cart. And it was only now that Oswin, wincing under the brunt of it all, began to understand what the sheepshankthief had meant before by "all this," for the youth had never been to a pillorying before. And the brawler's earlier spittle seemed but a weak foretaste of what was now in hand. Before the heavy weight of numbers, there was little that he could do but cringe and groan and curse and grit his teeth, in this slow painful ride to the townsquare, where the pillory had been set up in the long shadow of the churchtower.

After what seemed to Oswin an endlessness, the cart halted, as did the hurlings. Oswin opened his gummy eyes and straightened up, his besplattered body smarting from the many hits and aching from overhunching. Indeed, had he curled down any further inside the cart, he would have been nearly upsidedown. Having thus reached the pillory, the three were dragged up onto the scaffold, where they were yoked into a great wheeling crossbeam that was bolted to an even greater turning upright.

Once they were fastlocked therein, with head and hands thrust through, one of the ironsides gave Oswin a push to have these bondlings begin their slow hard footslog about the pole. And round about they plodded, as if dwarflike drudges turning a huge key to wind up a giant's clock. The mighty spring to this timepiece, which seemed to lie buried beneath the townsquare, was hard and unyielding, and the more they struggled to tighten it, the more the crowd grew enlivened.

And all the while a further hail came down upon them, to shouts and cheers, and curses and cusses, far more thickly now, it seemed, than before while acart. Here in the open, before the many, there was no hiding at all, no cloak to cast around, no great blanket to overlay.

Oswin would have most readily stopped and stood his ground against the mob and backcast, however outnumbered he was. But he well knew that to stand still here was to make of oneself an easy target, and that to shift ground was to stay alive, however cravenly it felt. And however much he made shift to keep shifting, time nonetheless seemed to stand still, as if its gears had become dirtclogged and its hands tightlocked. And so the hourlong stint in the pillory seemed to Oswin no shorter than the passing of a whole day.

To the crowd, however, the hour came and went all too quickly. When the three were unyoked, calls could be heard, "Up! Up! Have them rise and do another jig about the Maypole!" So peeved were some that a scuffle broke out between a few mobbers and the turnkeys, the former wishing to take over and bring the rogues back to the pillory.

With the cart loaded again, the sorry band headed back to lockup, along the same path as before. By this time, however, most of the muck to be thrown had already been cast, and so the flight from the pillory was ruthfully far less scathing. But there was only so much that filthmongers could bring forth, those who had spared a good many throwers the messy task of gathering together things castworthy. Most of the hurlings had been brought well beforehand, by push-and-go keeners, who sold the lot for a pretty penny to those oversqueamish about lifting foundthings straight out of the gutter.

And dirty work it had been, with dirty hands and even dirtier streets to show for it. So caked were the carted ones with pelted muck that it seemed as if these black blackguards had perhaps fallen into a bog and only now had been pulled out. And there was no telling the one from the other.

Never had anyone been so gladdened to find himself again within the grim walls of a jailyard as Oswin, who now thought his ordeal at last ended. Yet no sooner was he taken down off the cart but the cartdriver, rather miffed at being robbed of the freedom to take part in the free-for-all, twice struck Oswin hard with his horsewhip as the youth staggered past dazed, as if to waken him again from some slumber, although by this time, Oswin's flesh was nearly beyond feeling.

Far more startling were the pailfuls of cold salted water thrown upon them. Slowly they began to look like men again, as their slough of caked filth was stripped away with each dousing. And the aftermath of the battery began to show itself: through the openings of their shredded clothes peeped forth manifold bruises and cuts, which the bearers now felt with renewed feeling at each onslaught of salted water. Yes, Oswin's body burned like a witch's bonfire. As none of the three had the wherewithal to afford a leech, none was called for, and none came. And so following their washup, or washdown, the three were led back down into the filthy maw of the jail—or rather two of them were, for the sheepshankthief had been so weakened by the ordeal that he needed to be halfdragged along.

As he trudged through the gloom to the rattle of fetters and shackles, Oswin inwardly plodded forth through a snarling maze of twisting thoughts and bewildering feelings, with no unwinding clew for him to follow back along. He had not in the least reckoned upon meeting with such bloody-mindedness from everyday folk and now found himself at a loss to understand his own lot. True, he had always been an outsider and had fisticuffed his fair share throughout his boyhood, bludgeoned yet never bested. But—Hell!—he would never have been so cowardly, he swore to himself then and there, as to fight two or more against one, or to kick a man when down. And be damned if he could fathom how upstanding men, women, and even children could have only now stooped so low to this unmanly cravenness. By the Dickens, this was wrong! he swore. He had been wronged!

Yet it had not crossed his mind that the thief and the brawler, in sharing the pillory, had drawn away a good deal of the pelting that would otherwise have been meant for him alone and would surely have been the death of him had he been alone—he had, as it were, been partly lost in the crowd. In truth, the thief, who had lost an eye in the morning's hail of brickbats, later that day lost his life, as he inwardly bled to death.

But sundry and manifold are life's sorrows, as Lord Drighten himself could well witness. Yes, the magistrate had his own sorrows and felt that his hopes had now reached bedrock, thanks to those wayward sons of his and their naughty bedfellowships. By God! The man had grounds to be upset, did he not? If only earlier he could have found some misty middleground wherein the whole messy business of lawing might have been sideslipped! But he nowise could chide himself. No, no, he was in his rights. How hard he had groped, amidst a welter of dreads and forefears—as if trying to grasp some great eel that had slipped out of a trap by oversight—to find a happy outcome.

Such was the law at this time that wrongdoers shipped off to the New World were at bottom salegoods, to be bought and sold at wharfside as bondsmen. At no cost to the realm, these outbounders were entrusted into the hands of any willing shipmaster, who could pocket a handsome ten pounds for a healthy unskilled body and even twentyfive for a skilled one. And this would more than easily offset any shippingcosts and leave the skipper with a tidy gain. If it so happened, however, that kith or kinfolk with wherewithal were to outbid any other bidder and buy back outlawed loved ones and thereby spare the latter from their sorry plight, the law would not, nay, could not thwart them. Justitia could not very well look each bidder up and down and ask after their whence and wherefore. So long as these outlanded lawbreakers did not back to the homeland before their time of outlawry was up, why should anyone niggle over who ended up with the lot?

For the magistrate then, the way-out seemed straightforward enough: as long as a fullpocketed somebody was at wharfside when and where and if Godwin made landfall in Virginia and as long as that somebody outbid all other bidders when the youth was sold, his son would not be lost after all. Although Lord Drighten was too old and sickly to lay himself open to the great risks of such a seacrossing, he did have a spare offshoot, for this father had not been so careless and stinting as to sow his seed only once. And now he meant to reap in some way what he had sown. And so the baby-of-the-family was called forth and enlightened about his forthcoming role in the history of the Drighten line.

"The time has come for you to show me that you're not the sorry thing I see before me. Tomorrow you will set sail aboard *The Coinon* for Virginia, along with that brother of yours. Upon landing there, you will buy his freedom. You will then set sail again for the Spanish Netherlands, upon the next ship with the next fair wind."

"It'll be a breeze, I'm sure, Papa."

"By God, this is no laughingmatter! Much hangs upon this business, more than the pair of you are worth together! If only Cruikshank were back! But as it is, I must trust you not to foul up. Cruikshank will meet up with you in Antwerp. And you are not to leave the shores of Virginia without your brother! Do I make myself clear?"

"Yes, father."

"Now off with you and get packing. You leave first thing in the morning."

Off to his room Charles tramped and set footmen packing. What a lot of baggage one has when leaving home, even shortwhiles! And then he turned in early. A fitful squirmy sleep it was beneath heavy Drighten bedding, until it was no sleep at all, rather a bothered stare into darkness.

What a bloody fuss owing to a brother! Two twomonth seacrossings! Putting up with the dampness and the seasickness and the wretched food and the boredom was one thing, but outliving the nasty threats from scurvy or shipfever or other suchlike illnesses, and even worse, freebooters or shipwreck, was altogether another. At best, the odds were one-in-five that he, like anyone else, would die before ever reaching the shores of the New World, not to speak of the odds against him for yet another trip back to Europe. All this for the bequestling!

But oh, how the boot chafes the sore heel! And how the spur upon that boot galls the steed's flank! And this bitplayer dug his heels in and balked at the thought of his dotty father's dotty plan. What cringing curlikeness! To be skulking aboard a stinking deathtrap, at the whim of every passing tooth-and-claw. Seacrossing be damned! He was enough of his father's son to know that there were roundabout ins-and-outs to all things. Besides, the old man had seen better days, and surely his mind was not as unaddled as it might have once been.

And so this younger fresher blood—having the why and needing only the how—was taken by a daring kickseywinsey, which he fancied would set him down handsomely in the old man's good books. He could see it all now, even pinch it!

His head big with brainchild, he rose up, kicking off those heavy bed-clothes, dudded himself, gathered together whatever helps he would need to hand, and hurtled off into the early foredawn, while others slept. Soon enough, he reached the jail, the latter already astir with the forereadyings against the shipping of outbound jailbirds.

Once inside the main inlet, Charles, like all highborn folk who find themselves inside such a smelly hole, held to his nose a fine lacy hanky *parfumé*, with *C.D.* embroidered off in one aloof corner. And there he stood, with a bundle under his left arm, stymied at the unmanned desk in the forehall, for his way further into the building was blocked by a grill of bars. Where was the blasted turnkey? *Maudite bureaucratie!*

It then struck Charles that the place was understaffed. Why, bless that whore Fortuna, with her come-hither looks, for having drawn him hither even now when the law's guard was down! He would not need to watch his back so narrowly after all, it seemed. He would have his way freely with the wench! But first he had to get inside, and so he bellowed and browbeat the forehall a bit, until one dragheel underling, with dropped chin and tired eyes, came to sight, fumbling keys at the grill.

"Beggin' your forgiveness, Sir," drawled this keeper of the law and minder of the lawless, "but Jibber's been called away, and I'm left to see to his job here, on my own, but I too was called away for a bit, carried away by nature herself, so to speak," the man chuckled lazily to himself, rubbing his halfwet hands up and down his shirtfront, the latter once white, now gray, on its way to black.

"I'm here to call upon the magistrate's son, Godwin Drighten."

"The magistrate's son, you say! Indeed, it's not everyday that we get such calls. Now where's that pen?" muttered the turnkey as he rifled through loose papers and books strewn upon the desk.

"Look here, you, I'm squeezed for time, so on your feet and lead on now!"

"In good time, good Sir. Be not overhasty! We're awful busy this morning, what with all the—"

Charles reached over, grasped the man by the neck, and pulled him up onto the desktop, sending papers and books to the floor. "You're a blackhead on a booby's bottom, and if you speak to me again like that, I will squeeze the filth out of you!" Thereupon he thrust the man back down behind the desk, who took more papers and books to the floor with him, but not before he knocked over the inkhorn and spilled bookblack everywhere, with a blackened shirt to match a bluish mug.

"Beggin' your forgiveness, kind Sir!" The man fumbled to his knees, with hand athroat, hardly able to speak. "I could find no pen! You must write your name in the book before I can let you in!"

With a few strokes of a gloved hand, Charles swept more inky papers to the floor, until the guestbook showed itself, with the missing pen hidden inside. At bottom, this guestbook was no more than a ledger, a bookkeeper's

tool now used as a lawkeeper's, or better said, a jailbirdkeeper's doddery way
of tabskeeping amidst all the bodily income and outgo.

Before the turnkey could get to his feet, Charles slickly wrote into the
ledger "Parson Rideout," in what he thought looked like his brother's hand.
Then beneath it he wrote his own name, or rather his own for the next hour,
to wit, "Elias Wylie, Esq.," and quickly blotted.

By now, the turnkey—Onslow was his name—had risen, still rubbing
throat and dabbing body, in the hope of freeing himself from inky stain.
He checked the ledger with a dropchinned squint, to see that Charles had
indeed written in something fitting. As the turnkey slowly mouthed the
letters of the name one by one, Charles said, as he fingered the name above
his own, "Ah, I see Parson Rideout's already here."

This was an overload of letters and sounds for Onslow, who said, "Come
again, kind Sir."

"I see Parson Rideout's already here. He was to meet me here so that
together we might call upon the magistrate's son, but he has overtaken me,
it seems. The earlybird gets his worm, or so they say."

Onslow mouthed the letters, then said, "Parson Rideout?"

"Parson Rideout, so it says."

"Never heard of him."

"'Never heard of him'?! What a ninny you are!"

"Maybe he came earlier when Jibber was here."

"Maybe he did, indeed."

Onslow was in no mood to pettifog, nor to ask for any guestfee to be
paid, nor to ask about what was in that bundle under Charles' arm—surely
clean underwear or the like. It had struck the turnkey only belatedly that
this hothead was highborn, maybe even one of the magistrate's men, and
he would do well not to ruffle suchlike. And so Onslow said, "Right, Sir,
be so good as to come along then." Turning his back on the great unorder
of order that lay strewn upon the floor, the inky one shambled to the grill,
unlocked it, and let Charles in. And thus they began their climb to the top.

"What a reckless fool you are, breathing in the unwholesome air here,
when jailfever is rife. You should do as I do."

"Do as you? Ah! A hanky to the nose to keep fever away. Does it work?"

"'Does it work'?! Have you ever known a man to die of jailfever behind
a hanky?"

"A man behind a hanky?" Onslow rooted in his pockets to see if such a thing haply lay therein. "Can't say that I have, Sir."

"Well, I will run no risks, what with the magistrate's son having fallen ill."

"Ill, you say?" and a hand groped again in Onslow's pocket. "He seemed fit enough yesterday."

"Fit enough to fall ill, as any man is."

They reached the cell, where Onslow unbolted. They peered in and beheld a seemingly lifeless inmate abed, but then the hour was still early.

"Look, where the wretch lies low," whispered a sorrowful Charles, who then suddenly found himself without any shielding hanky. "Alack! I must have dropped my hanky on the way-up. Be a good man and fetch it for me now." He drew forth a coinbag and held it out to the turnkey, "Here's for your pains."

"Most beholden to you, kind Sir!"

But as the turnkey now meant to lock in Charles before loping off, Charles held the door ajar and said, "There's a good chap and leave the door unbolted. Surely Parson Rideout is about and will show up soon enough. No need to keep him locked out."

Onslow was torn. The rules said that turnkeys must lock up behind themselves, leaving no doors unbolted, yet having taken the man's money, he felt he could not rightly naysay now.

"Have no fear. As you well know, there's no leaving the building without a turnkey's help, and I fear we've already come too late for yon dust and ashes."

True enough, it was not unknown for men-of-the-cloth to be found wandering the hallways of a jail, stopping here and halting there, soulsoothing or browbeating the black sheep stuck in this wrongfold, and always bothering turnkeys to open up here and shut up there. And true enough, the inmate over there did not look so well, lying there so stilly. And true enough, even if the inmate were to sneak out of his cell, he would not get far, not without a turnkey to open up the maingate. So there was, all said-and-done, little risk in leaving the celldoor unbolted, and only for a short while too, for he would be back in no time, with the hanky. And so lastly, Onslow nidnodded and hastened off without bolting the door.

All this whispering and dithering at the door had by now wakened Godwin. Charles shut the door and flung at his brother the bundle that he had been carrying under his arm.

"Quick! Put these on! We've no time to spare!" ordered Charles, who stood by the door, peering out so as not to be taken unawares.

In rising from his cot and unbinding the bundle, groggy Godwin found inside a set of clothes, an old getup—he knew it again—a parson's stiff frock, broadbrimmed hat, and silly wig, one of the many such getups from home. Yes, it was ballgarb from happier times when their gruff father had been less gruff, outwardly at least, and seemed to care more about how others felt and thought, outwardly at least, and threw fancy masked balls to endear himself amongst his like, outwardly at least. And this was one guise among others with which these two sons had been wont to deck themselves out in their childhoodplay.

"What are you waiting for? Put them on!"

"To what end?"

"What a booby you are! It's a smokescreen to keep you out of Hellfire." A blank stare from Godwin. "A way to get you out of this hole and spare us the good many hassles that you've brought upon us."

"You'd have me sneak out of this stronghold as a parson! Brother, you've been reading too many crackpottales filled with hackneyed tricks. No-one would fall for this!"

"There you're wrong, brother. The looked-for is always the least looked-for, and the oddball always ends up in a bold footnote. That's why you're in here, and I'm not." Indeed, the Duke of York would, in a few months' time, be sprung from bondage clad as girl.

"And who's to take my place here if I walk away as a parson?"

"Your empty duds and all the bedding stuffed under the blanket. The turnkeys here are none too bright, and if browbeaten enough, they will do as they're told. Oh, come on, shift your clothes!"

"No, I will not be party to such daftness and end up in an even greater mess!"

"Why must you always be a bur under the saddle? This is what father wants, and you know how raving upset he'll be if you blunder yet again. I would not want to be in your shoes when he brings you to book."

Godwin had earlier settled upon playing by the book, that is, going with the flow and standing fast by sitting tight and waiting to find his freedom in Virginia, far from the long reach of his magistratical father. But now the near deadhand of the latter, as it were, made him begin to dillydally and shillyshally, until he looked down only to see his fingers busily unbuttoning his doublet for him.

"This'll never work! I must be out of my mind!"

"Make haste! We've little time!"

Having doffed his duds and donned the parson's, Godwin padded the cot with whatever was to hand to make a dummy of himself, which he buried under a great blanket.

"It will easily pass for you, brother," said Charles of the cotlump. Then he pulled out his hanky and held it to his face once again. Godwin aped his brother and tried to hide as much of his face as he could, even as Onslow showed up.

"Stay back! The inmate has jailfever! Parson Rideout and I must away and find a doctor!"

"Beggin' your forgiveness, Sir, but I could find no hanky."

"No matter. We must be off. Well, don't stand there, you fool, lead on!"

"Right, good Sir." And mousily glancing at the cotlump, the turnkey locked the door and led on.

"Make haste, clubfoot! We need to hunt up a doctor." As the Drighten brothers followed along behind, Charles leaned over and said under his breath, "Watch and learn, my dear bumpkin brother, watch and learn."

But before the three had gotten too far, they were met by a sobbing woman altogether beside herself, who rushed up to Godwin, and stopping him with a wrestler's handgrip, begged him to come now to her dying husband and give him the "last rites" before he gave up the ghost. Godwin was wholly fazed by this unforeseen buttonholing, and before such tearful bemoaning of looming loss, his heart gave way. Having donned the duds of a parson, he now felt somehow beholden to play the part and could not bring himself to—coldly, coolly, or even warmly—naysay.

The woman towed the fightless parson along to where her husband lay adying. A sorry sight it was: a man outstretched upon a cot, gurgling and gasping, his eyes swimming, his body struggling not to drown within its own skin. Seated at his side was some other turnkey, grasping the dying man's right hand, as if to hold him fast lest he should somehow unallowedly sink away or fly off. The steadfast-to-the-last wife sat by, sobbing and whimpering, she too gripping the man's other hand, as if to keep him from the rot of death.

And there too stood our parson, nearly unmanned, as looming loss spoke strongly to him, and altogether untongued, for long years of daydreaming in church, or wherever else ghostly fathers haunt, had upshot in a shocking knowledgelessness about churchways on his part. No matter how hard he strove to find that patter of faith that all men-of-the-cloth could utter faultlessly, sleeping or waking, the sad truth was that he altogether lacked the needful words.

Looking the parson up and down, the jailer at bedside asked, somewhat taken aback, "Where's your gear?" by which he meant the tools of faith, such as holybooks and so forth.

"I have none on me," stammered Godwin.

"None? Beats me why a parson would go about without such," said the jailer half to himself.

With all eyes hopeful upon the speechless parson, a peeved and worried Charles trod forth beside his brother and whispered through his hanky, "We have no time for this foolishness! Let us be gone!"

"A parson cannot walk away without helping!" whispered back the man-of-the-cloth through his hanky.

"But you're not a bloody parson!"

"But they don't know that! And if I leave now without saying something, they'll know that there's something wrong!"

"Then say the damned words quickly, and let us go!"

"I don't know what to say!"

"If you love your freedom, you'll say something, be it ever so foolish, and say it quickly!"

The parson stalled further by hemming and coughing, but the longer he dithered, the more untrusting grew everyone around him. At length, Charles leaned over and whispered into the parson's ear words that seemed fitting: "We beseech thee, Almighty God the Father,"

"We beseech thee, Almighty God the Father," afterworded the parson.

"We the sheep of your own fold,"

"We the sheep of your own fold,"

"Look down upon this man,"

"Look down upon this man,"

"Lying in great weakness,"

"Lying in great weakness,"

"And set him free from every bond,"
"And set him free from every bond,"
"That he may rest in everlasting bliss,"
"That he may rest in everlasting bliss,"
"With the Father and the Son,"
"With the Father and the Son."

However workable had been Charles' plan at the outset, its hackneyed-ness notwithstanding, the world had in the betweentime shifted, making the timeproven unworkable, and making the looked-for now the looked-for. Godwin's fumbling patter of faith and his overall shabby showing as a parson had spawned misgivings in Onslow's mind. Why, shouldn't a parson be able to patter away his prayers and suchlike as freely as a moneylender can rattle off numbers? And who was this frumpy parson anyways? Something was wrong. Yes, something was wrong.

Slipping out unseen, Onslow hastened back to the cell and peered in through the spyhole. Seemed odd that the man would lie there so still, all hidden away without even his head showing. And the body looked awfully flat, and even if sick, the frame could not have wasted away that quickly.

Onslow let himself in, and shielding his mug in his dirty sleeve, crept up to the cot where he drew back the heavy blanket. Knowledge breached the turnkey's brow belatedly. Better late than never, and not too late, blushed the man.

Off rushed Onslow to the dying man's cot. And quickly rushed blood to the turnkey's head. Dang them! What did they take him for? Onslow burst in amidst the last of the mangled last rites, hastened up to Godwin and pulled hat and wig from his head and hanky from his face. "A wolf in parson's clothing, is it?" And grasping Godwin by the wrist, he said further, "Back to the cell with you!"

But Onslow got not a stride nearer the door, for with a mighty blow from Charles, he teetered into a daze and then downslumped meekly against the wall. The other burlier turnkey straightway upped and made at Charles, and the two then struggled away. But Charles quickly gained the upperhand. In no time he had floored the man and bestrode his buttocks. Then pulling out a dagger, cleverly hidden aboot, he thrust the blade into the turnkey, again and again, until the man gave up all tokens of struggle.

Charles rose, and Godwin gasped, "What have you done?"

"How dare the rogue make bold with me!"

"You've murdered him!"

"And he has no-one to thank for it but you!"

At this, the woman, who, like Onslow, had hitherto watched on as if unseen behind shielding bushes, began to weep and wail.

"Shut up, bitch, or you'll lie next to him!" shouted Charles.

The woman started at this threat and clapped both hands to mouth in order to stopple up any sound that might leak out against her will, while her eyes above neared bursting. And Onslow cringed stilly against the wall.

"We must fly!" said Charles, who reached down and took the ring of keys.

The Drighten sons took to their heels, but not before Charles had threatened to cut out the tongues of the turnkey and woman, should they squeal. And then he locked the two guiltless ones in with the dying wrongdoer, the latter even now giving up the ghost. Soon enough, the two found themselves down at the great grill, where turnkey Jibber, who had only now backed to his post, opened up for the hankywielding Elias Wylie, Esq. and Parson Rideout. He had them scribble themselves out—a scrawl in the book—and he did not so much as look them up and down, for the peeved man had eyes only for the great inky mess left behind by Onslow. A quick jaunt through the jailyard, and the Drighten sons became one with the bustlers of earlymorning Bristol.

FLOTSAM AND JETSAM

T HE SMELL OF SEA, the smell of open boundless sea, how it stings in the nose of the landlubber, and even more so in the nostrils of the squeamish townlubber, fullwonted to his cobblestones and keystones and headstones. Ay, Neptune's tangy *cologne*-water is not for everyone, not the nosesweet whiff of highlife. Best left it is to saltstained seadogs and smelly riffraff and other wishywashy unwanted unwashed. Such, at least, was the standpoint of the lawmen standing lordily upon Bristol's wharf this forenoon, those of Bristol's best who had forgathered betimes to oversee the outshipping of Bristol's worst.

Amongst the latter was Oswin, who had been brought forth from lockup early, carted through the streets again, and dumped here, where *The Coinon* lay moored, the ship that was to oversea him to Virginia. The latter, by-the-by, had been so-named to flatter Elizabeth I, the great queen who had kept her maidenhood to keep her queenly might, or at least, so the story went.

But Oswin knew nothing about such storied honeying of a spinstery queen, held up as he was amidst the straightrunning lineups, in the tiresome waiting to board—held up indeed, for he stood chainganged at the right ankle, linked to others of his ilk. And these fledgeling and hardbitten lawbreakers, young, old, inbetween, were not the only shipmates standing ready to find their allotted place in the emptybellied *Coinon*. Here as well were pelf- and land-keen outsettlers; and blackclad Bibleclutchers New-Jerusalem-bound; and outnumbering throngs of luckless souls, the "indentured," to be sold in the New World as cheap workers.

Amidst the welter of thronging bodies beshoved and betugged, and angry shouts and curses from roughtumble seamen, and untold boxes and barrels of freight ever aloading, Oswin hoped to catch sight of Godwin, who, he thought, was also to be aboard. Yet for all Oswin's scanning, the youth was nowhere to be seen. But then, this was hardly flabbergasting: too many were the inmates, and too few the wagons on hand to cart them all.

A tricky business this was, making one's way over a narrow landingplank and then through the tight gangways, while yet linked to all the unsteady lumbering before and behind. And so it befell that the lad to Oswin's fore, who must have been only a year younger than Oswin's sister, or so it seemed to the brother, lost his footing on the landingplank and nearly dragged Oswin overboard.

"Lift your bloody hooves, doltling!" barked shipman Holding and thwacked the youth, who was already in the early throes of jailfever.

"Let the lad be! He meant no harm!" snapped Oswin.

Holding backed off, grudgingly, for now at least, and the chaingang trampled on. Oswin took one last outlook at the wharf, still teeming with bodies yet to board, still swarming with wellwishing kith and kin seeing off kith and kin. There was no Godwin, and there was no farewellbidding sister.

But shipbusiness soon overshadowed thought. All needed to keep sharp and mind their feet while wending through the gloomy underworld, with its stench of moulder. Having reached bottom, Oswin and his mates were herded into one hold, where their chain was fastened here and there along the wall. The next chaingang was brought in, and their chain was fastened to rings running along the floor, and more of the same darningwise, until the hole was patched up. This cheek-to-jowl hovel would be their home for the next eight-to-twelve weeks, or even longer, God or Sea willing, whichever were the lordlier.

Then upon all the hellish rumblings and bangings and curses and groans and shouts, hush fell in a clap, as if hit with the uncanny still that foregoes a storm. All hands had forgathered on deck, where they stood meekly bare-headed, straightrowed, with eyes and noses towards the poop. And upon the latter towered a man-of-the-cloth, ready to bestow God's blessings. With their overeasy belief in things eerie and otherworldly, all these seamen prayed—nay, begged fullheartedly—that nothing untoward would befall them. Why, there was never any telling when the sea might turn against a man, what with her freebooters and storms and whales and krakens and other shuddersome freaks of the deep. Indeed, shipwreck and watery death shadowed all who bolded forth over her surftops. Himself none too keen on the sea's whorish sway of broad hips, the churchman unshipped himself, and the craft set out with the fairest of winds.

After an hour of good swift headway, the hitherto-not-altogether-biddable sea began to roughhouse more earnestly, and some of the unseaworthy began to grow most queasy. As the main heaved and heaved, the unwell youth to Oswin's side, the same who earlier had nearly dragged Oswin down, at length retched and fetched up the little within him, and so powerfully that some of it went splashing upon the back before him. Curses comes from those sitting nearest, and laughs from those furthest. And those next to the boy tried their best to shift themselves away.

But it took more than a twinkling for the inmate with the befouled backside to twig that he was the laughingstock. The man slowly overshouldered a look, glimpsed the misdeed done behind his back, then felt his dirty backside with his right paw, and his mug darkened at the feel of it and darkened even more as the laughter sharpened. "Gutterling, I'll wipe the floor with you!"

"The lad's greatly ill! Can't you see?" snapped Oswin.

"And who are you, his nanny?" The great man suddenly froze, peering at Oswin, and then uttered, "You, the sodomite!" The cackling all about died away. "Ay, a nanny and a nancy, and a ninny to boot! Now I've got one-and-a-half rags to the wipe the floor with."

"You'd best play maid somewhere else!" sneered Oswin, who knew the man again. Yes, it was the spitting scarface with whom he had shared the pillory.

The backjibe stung the man unforgivingly, and with a snarl, he leapt at Oswin, and the two began to grapple most fiendishly, as much as bonds and seatoss would allow. Hoots, cheers, hollers rose from the watchership, and this ruckus quickly drew to the barred inlet a handful of shipmen, who likewise watched on merrily. How keen Oswin had been, the day of his pillorying, to scrap with the man who had spit in his face. But now, as he was worsted, Oswin would fain have shaken hands and walked away, for this Goliath was beyond even a David.

The foregone ending was that Goliath altogether overwhelmed Oswin and began to throttle the life out of him. This would surely have been Oswin's end were it not for the timely coming of Perce, the master's mate.

"Why are you rats standing here while they brawl? It'll be twenty pound lost if one of them should die, and forty if both. In and part them, or the loss'll come out of your wages!"

In they rushed and strove to keep their pay. But this was no easy task. How tightly huddled together were the inmates and how wildly thrown to-and-fro was the ship, such that man fell upon man fell upon man. And how hardset were they all to make out who was who in the murky hurlyburly. Lastly it took four of them to wrestle the brawler down and jackknife him, cuffing him hands to feet, while Oswin was unhoused.

As the battered limpling was dragged into the halflight of the gangway, one of the shipmen gasped, "He's all bloody!"

A flurry of worried looks, broken then by the mate's order, "Staunch the bleeding, then burn the rags."

"Shall we throw him overboard, Sir?" asked another, nearly shaking.

"Nothing's thrown overboard without the skipper's orders! Shackle his feet and stow him in the freighthold. Keep him out of sight. And not a word of this to anyone! Is that understood?" Grudging nidnods. "Again, not a word! Now back to work!"

They brisked off under the mate's watchful eye, while shipmen Holding and Kettell dragged Oswin along.

"What's all this fuss about?" asked Holding.

"You don't know, man? Ah, right, your maidensail! A greenhorn you are!" said Kettell in a nearwhisper. "Wellknown 'tis to hardened seafolk that the landarm of Seven Heads—it lies out yonder on the southern shore of Ireland—be the home of a most wicked thing. They call her the 'Seawitch of Seven Heads,' and they say she dwells in an underwater cliffhollow, at the gnarly fingertip of the landarm. A blackhearted and bloodthirsty hag she be, with ten crooked horns on her head. And whenever blood be spilt on a ship in her nearness and the smell of that blood be upon the air, she wakens from her nasty slumber beneath the waters, and she rises up from the sea with mischief in mind. How shuddersome she be, says those who've seen her and lived to tell the tale. How tasty be manblood to her! Some even say that she be the Pope's bastard, that she were brought northwards by the great Spanish fleet of old but were shipwrecked and washed up on the Popish Irish shores, where she now dwells as a bane to all Godfearing seamen of England. So some say, but that seems a little farfetched to me.

More likely she be the daughter of the Devil himself, and the mother of all our hardships at home."

Holding blanched and began to wipe and dab away the blood, most hothandedly. The bloody stuff! Why must it leak out? Good God! Things are never happy unless they go awry!

A nightmarish trek now, through the narrowest of dimlit lurching gangways, until the right hold was reached, where Oswin was stuffed into a chink, a chink between the straight rows of lashed-together freightboxes. An overtight squeeze it was, an airless clasp, and here he was left, in utter darkness.

When at length he felt something crawling about his ankles—rats! bloody rats!—he began to stamp wildly, but this only upshot in the shacklecuffs mangling his ankles, for so short was the chain that he nearly lost his footing with each lift of a foot. And the rawer his ankles became, the more of a draw it was for other bloodsmelling rats. Lodged thus in this Goliath's crush, warring against rats underfoot—how long would he be locked up here? He would not last an hour here, let alone weeks!—he would surely go mad!

Yet however uncosy, the narrow bind of his lodging had something of an upside to it, amidst the ship's madcap uppings and downings, for he was spared much of the pitchabout that bedeviled his less tethered shipmates. And things were yet to worsen. Indeed, in this roughing forestorm, a cross-running sea—no purling runnel of Pan this!—had gone far already toward toppling the squeamish little *Coinon*. But now, beneath the bluster of an everblackening sky, it was high time for the high sea to show its mettle.

As if angrily awakened from an unsettled slumber, billowing waves, in any line but that straight, rose aloft, and then curving and curling downwards, thrust themselves into the depths below. Again and again, surly wave upon cheeky wave rose on high to be one with the clouds, and having kissed the heavens, these upwellings, in headlonging downwards, enclasped all that lay upon the breast of the sea. Heaved and heaved, again unrestingly heaved the sea, and with it *The Coinon* flimsy.

And in time, the watery up- and down-rushes were overshadowed by waterspouts, which were more wayward than any witch in a whirlwind. These whirlpools upsidedown hopped and skipped and loped along, lifting their petticoats, as it were, only to drop them heavily beyond some yawning hollow, where they again brushed along over the breast of the sea, or by turns raised their skirts so high that the garb nearly wisped away altogether, leaving the airrush in nakedness unseen. And all seemed lost when one of these flirting waterwhirls made her way towards *The Coinon*. But by the time the hoyden came within a stone's throw or so of trysting with the ship, her fickle eye was drawn by something unseen beyond, and she veered off.

To the bugaboofearing sailors, it all seemed as if the Seawitch, the Irish hag herself, was astir again. Ay, does the Lord not write forth His will—be it blight or blessing—even in the fall of a leaf, or the droop of a bud, or the shift of a pebble? And so in the tiny and seldom lulls of the storm, more than one shipman crossed himself or kissed a roodlet dangling at the bottom of a neckchain, in the hope that the heavens might turn the other cheek and show meekheartedness. Yet the wind and the sea would not peace. But then, who can harness wayward heaven's blasts and gusts, or steady spray and scud above upstirrèd sea? Who can still the upwhelmings of nature's unsounded depths?

In time, it became clear that the ship had lost ground, or rather, had gained ground in losing sea, for the crew could see land to starboard, Irish land, land that they had passed earlier. By Jesus, the storm meant to dash them against Irish boulder and beach! And as mutterings of a jinxed sail spread freely, Holding, who had not forgotten Kettell's words, could not overmaster his wayward tongue, for all Perce's warning. So it befell that word of spilt blood passed quickly from sailor to sailor. Yes, the truth was out: they had awakened the Seawitch, and she was coming for them. God help them now!

But Holding was loath to wait for the help of a dragheel god and so settled upon helping himself, at least until the good Lord found the time to show up and put things aright himself. Didn't the Good Book say, after all, that God helps those who help themselves?

As briny uprush was met now by heavy downpour in the twilight, Holding sought out Kettell and whispered—as well as any man could in the shrieking wind—whispered his thoughts on how best to spare all. What aghastness Kettell showed upon hearing such plotful talk! But it took only one great swamping and neardeadly billow breaking upon the deck to bring the man to a nidnod. And so the twain slunk off, down to the jinxed mote.

"Come on, draff, shake a leg to topdeck!" But this took more shift than Oswin could make, given the shortness of his chain and the hurt done to his body in the brawl. And so in their great haste the two sailors halfdragged him along.

What a shock upon reaching topdeck, in seeing *The Coinon* so hardset in its struggle to stay afloat! Oswin had never thought sea and sky could be so wildly set upon undoing the handiwork of man. So overwhelmed was he by the frightfulness of it all that he failed to mark—once the three of them were out of sight by a lifeboat—how Kettell and Holding quickly bent down, grasped his shackles, and in standing up again, thrust the chain aloft, and with it Oswin's feet.

For a twinkling, the youth hung upsidedown narrowly beyond the gunnel. An oddish eyetwink this, as the brains of the two mavericks were darkened belatedly by the sudden fear of some kind of fallout. But then both were struck by the same brainwave at the same time: if called up, they would say that they had done nothing but toss overboard a body already dead to this world, for the battered youth had in the meantime given in to his wounds—a handy heal-all fib. Then they let go, and Oswin fell headfirst into the sea. Let the seahag batten awhile on that measly offering! Amen.

No sooner dragged down but Oswin fought his way up for air again, where he was able to keep his nose above angry water fitfully. He shouted out for help until his lungs nearly burst. Hell! He would be heard! But all were deaf to his bellowing, for the crew could hear only the shrieks and howls of that keening banshee the wind, and the frightful groans of shivering timbers. As the ship was drawn further and further away, Oswin, with tears in his eyes, screamed out, "Bastards! You bastards! Be cursed all of you!"

What was he to do now? He could not last long in such a sea. He looked all about him and, like his former shipmates, quickly caught sight of the Irish shoreline, which was not so greatly far away. And so he strove landwards. But oh, how the sea toyed and trifled with him, hurling him dozens of yards towards land only to yank him heartlessly back, and down, and up, and over, so near and yet too far! Then he reached the end of all strength and all willpower. And so he made his peace with the warring world.

As he let himself drop like a stone, the mightiest of billows, as if out-of-nowhere, thrust him back up and so far forward that he felt the burn of sand along his forehead and cheek in skidding to a halt. He had reached the shore after all. There he lay, overcome with pain and weariness, barely beyond the reach of the everclawing stormwaters. There he lay uncaring, the wind and the rain beating upon his back. He could no more. His eyes shut. Wakefulness slipped away.

As the Lord maketh the rain to fall and the sun to shine upon those deemed good as well as wicked, so it was that the stormcloudy heavens were no less behindhand in offloading their heavy wares upon the western shores of England, no less than they had been in unshipping upon the seaboard of Ireland. Down came the rain on Bristol and the nearlying, washing away the hardedged caught in turf and earth.

Amidst all the swirling twistywisty rainsheets, there came thundering knocks on the foredoor to the Drighten greathouse, knocks heralding the coming of a sheriff from Bristol. When this sheriff came to stand before Lord Drighten, the latter seated at his desk shrewn with papers and books, the dripping man spoke. "Forgive my coming thus on so foul an evening, your Lordship, but I bring unhappy tidings. It seems that your Lordship's younger son has helped your Lordship's elder boy break out this morning, before the ship was to sail."

"'Seems?' What, do you not know rightly?"

"It is suremost, your Lordship. And before fleeing they murdered one of the turnkeys. They were last seen heading eastwards of Bristol, and I thought it most likely that they were set upon a stealthy homecoming. I take it that this is the first your Lordship has heard?"

"What's been done thus far?"

"I've gathered together a small band of horsemen to ride in search of them. We've called here in the hope of getting further waymarks as to what should be done."

"You've lost their trail then in all this rain?"

"Yes, your Lordship, spoors of any kind have been wholly washed away in the cloudburst, and we've heard of no further sightings since leaving Bristol. Shall we give it over then?"

"No, no, by no means. You must head northwards to Chester. We have land there, a likely place to hide out. If that proves bootless, then we must give over the manhunt."

"Very well, your Lordship."

And with that, the soggy muddy sheriff from Bristol, together with his manhuntmates, set off Chesterbound, and unavailingly, it would turn out, as the magistrate well aforeknew.

Straightway, Lord Drighten ordered a footman to go upstairs and tell "those gutless sons" of his to "get their asses down here." Yes, the Drighten sons had not slunk off to Chester, but had hurtled home right after the breakout, where they were tonguelashed and then sent up to their rooms, where they were to keep themselves out of all sight.

A little heartlightened the magistrate was that the manhunt at least had been shunted off after a jinkful trackless wildgoose. What a godsend this timely unweather! There was a god after all, it seemed. He had, however, lost little of his earlier overwroughtness. Why, what a shambles the Drighten line was now! Good God! Wherefore must he suffer so? What had he ever done to earn all this? Whence had come such wretched offspring? Bad blood from that bitch of a mother of theirs, surely. And likely, the rod had been spared far too often, but then, what good was there in flogging dead horses? Horses? God no! Fiends!

And speak of the devil. "So what's next, father?" asked Charles, as if an aloof outsider.

"We bloody well go down with the ship if there's another foolish blunder like this!"

"See what hardship you've brought upon us all," said Charles to his brother.

"*I've* brought?! I was not the one who raped a girl and murdered a turnkey!"

"And what nancy got himself locked up, and for whose buggering sake was the churl bumped off? Without a word of thanks, by the way."

"Oh, shut up, you feckless ninnies! Green countrygirls would not have botched this as badly as you have! Useless as tits on a goose, the pair of you! Godiva and Charlotte would have been more fitting names for the sniveling daughters that my sons have turned out to be!"

"Shall I, your Lordship?" spoke a hemming mousy voice from one murky corner of the room, a voice that belonged to one Peter Cruikshank, Lord Drighten's do-all. A blazeless man this Cruikshank was, one who could be trusted to plod away at his given work faithfully and unaskingly, like a blinkered gelding that daily clipclops along before its wonted heavy cartload of beerkegs, unsettled by bustle unseen. Or better said, Cruikshank was an old broom that still swept the best for Drighten, and this trusty tool of cleanup, only newly back from abroad, had been fetched from Bristol shortly after the guilty twosome had found their way home.

At a nod from his master, Cruikshank stood up, came forward, and took the floor, right where the sheriff had stood, still dabbled with watery mud. "His Lordship, your father, has entrusted me with the task of putting in order the business in hand. You are both now on the outside of English law, hunted most doggedly, high and low, even as I speak. In view whereof, his Lordship has settled hereupon, that you lie low here for a few days, most carefully out of all sight, until some of the fuss dies down, and then, under my wardership, hasten to Antwerp in all stealth, where, without a word of these lattertime mishappenings, Mr. Godwin will wed the Leeuwenhok girl with all speed, as forelaid."

"But I do not wish to wed the girl!"

"And what's wrong with her now?" snapped the magistrate.

"Nothing, I should think."

"Then why the whining?"

"I, I feel nothing towards her!"

"Feel?! How can you 'feel' anything when you don't even know the girl? Feelings come later, if they come at all."

"But what if I don't like her?"

"You will like her, or you will lump her in the fullness of time, as other wedded men before you have done with their wives. Good Lord! One wench is as good as another! What little sets them apart in the beginning soon fades away. What, do you think it's better to be a puppet dangling from the ends of maudlin heartstrings? What do you know of the world? What do you know of your best interests? You've always been as clueless as headstrong!"

"But why must I wed at all?"

"You owe it to your family and the great name you bear. The Drighten line is a mighty one and a lofty one, stretching back unfalteringly to the time of the Lionheart. By Jesus! Many would lie, cheat, steal, even murder to be linked to such a birthline! And its history will not be cut short owing to some childish kickseywinsey, from one of the least of its afterspring. It's the least you can do in return for everything your father and family have done on your behalf. In short, it is the way of the Drightens, and even the Holybook says that a man must go forth and sow his seed."

"But the Leeuwenhok girl will surely be deadset against wedding herself to an outlaw, such as me, or so I'm now said to be."

"Hence the need for you to wed the girl with all speed, before knowledge of your blunders reaches Antwerp. If the Leeuwenhoks find out later, it matters not, for all ties and bonds will be fastknotted by then, and they'll be stuck with you."

"Why can't Charles wed her in my stead?"

"He's the younger, and only the spare, and a paltry one at that. You've been groomed for this task."

"But—"

"Look you, I will not put up with any moping. You will go to Antwerp and you will wed and bed the girl, and I will hear nothing further on this head, other than belated thanks—should I be so lucky!—when you see what a ninny you were at the outset. And I warn you, should you take it into your head not to do as bidden, I'll pack you off to the sheriff in Bristol, where you will answer for your lawbreaking."

Godwin had run out of counterwords. And so it seemed that, sob-or-smile, there stood before him but one great unchoice. Yet there was perhaps some truthfulness in all the said, he bethought himself, that in time, all women choicelessly turn out to be more or less the same. He himself had marked how daughters all too often grew into the likeness of their mothers. And he sheepishly owned up that he was still wet behind the ears, for he had been not yet twenty years in this world. And as to feelings—Good Lord!—behind what door did they dwell, and what tongue did they speak, and what garb did they wear?

Thus sagging under the downweight of beholdenness, he unwavered himself into leastwise going abroad and giving it a shot. He could always say no, yes? Time would tell, wouldn't it? Yes, yes, it was all a matter of time now. Besides, he dimly felt that, with his years, it was time for him to make a clean breakaway from the Drighten household (as when heads of cheese tumble out their overturned moulds). And surely a wife was less bothersome than a father. And where else was a hunted outlaw such as himself to go now?

Oswin might have asked himself the same, for he was altogether witless of his own whereabouts. And some were at a loss to know whether he were in or out of life, such as the mews winging above his seemingly lifeless body. At length the gulls gave the wastrel up for dead, and one plucky rascal alighted on his head and pecked boldly at the deathly face, narrowly above the right eye. This pricking goaded Oswin into groggy wakefulness, and he clouted back angrily, making the scavenger take flight. A headlift off dank sand and an outgaze into enshrouding mist showed that he lay upon some seashore, together with strewn shipwreckage and scattered bodies.

He meant to find his legs, but body stubbornly withstood will. Racked he was with pain, and so down he slumped again and lay awhile. But he could not bide there, and warring against weightedness, he began to crawl, grimly clawing his way forwards in the sand. At length he found strength enough to rise up, up onto his legs, which still bore their shackles.

He looked about. Here, it seemed, lay *The Coinon,* or rather what was left of it. Indeed, the pains taken by sailors Holding and Kettell to spare ship and crew had come to naught after all, for little did they know, the Seawitch had had a nose only for the stench of shiprot, and she would not rest until that one boat had been made manifold in a hurling scatter of wreckage. And however much shipsmithers had lustily frisked and frolicked upon the sea in their newfound freedom, and however much the shipmen, having risen up out of the ship's belly, wantonly bobbed off to the ending beats of The Grim Reaper's cheeky wooingdance, a good deal of this scatter would not let the outcast youth be but had followed him up onto this strand, bitmeal and stitchmeal, like so much lost baggage backing to a naked wayfarer.

Now began a halfhopeful search through the wreckage for anything that might have broadly passed for food, water, or tokens of life. What an unlikely hodgepodge of things the sea had chosen to cast up here: now a ragamuffinly doll, whose seams had burst as its inner straw swelled with seawater; now crockshards caked here and there with the soggy bits of shipman's hardtack; now a handsome leather binding entangled in seaweed; now shackles still gripping the leg of its missing owner.

But what went most to Oswin's heart was a wretched huddle of bodies still chainganged together, like forsaken beggarchildren asleep by the wayside, now no more than grub for gulls and worms. He picked up flinders of shipwreckage and hurled them at the mews, which flapped up, cackling and overcrowing. The dirty bastards!

His heart nearly burst in seeing a facedown body sporting a shock of flaxen hair. Rushing up, he turned over the body only to see that it was not Godwin's. Driven now, he hobbled from one body to the next in mad search, all the while casting flinders of shipwreckage at plaguing fowl. He must have trodden a quartermile of strand before lastly slumping down, fullfacing the sea, and wearily leaned back against a chunk of hull. There was no Godwin. Dead and drowned then was Godwin.

He caught sight of something near his head, something hanging from the jagged edge of the wreckage. A bag it turned out to be, snagged on a hook. He yanked free the pouch and, opening it, found it to be a coinbag, still filled with its silver crowns. Like many of their mates, these coins had formerly been handsome silverware meant to brighten a lordly table but, since taken as plunder or grudging gift, had been melted down and stamped with the king's name, all to back his war against Parliament.

By rights, the pouch should have sunk to seabottom. Why of all things should this bag of silver, so useless to anyone here, have made it up onto the shore? These crowns, this bloody money! He rose up and, with a snarl, cast the coins to the winds, even though the pieces came down only a little ways off, like heavy stones, scattered and halfburied in the sand.

As a child, like nearly any other youth, Oswin had heard gripping, even if at times farfetched, tales wherein some luckless wretch was bereft of all his few havings in this world, but Oswin had never thought that suchlike could truly befall. Yet within less than a week, his world had been turned upsidedown. And for all his hardy squirming, his pockets had been shaken empty, as he dangled helplessly from his heels, fastheld by dandling Fortuna. And not unlike one of those storybookish wretches, Oswin found himself washed up on some stretch of forsaken shoreline, he alone having outlived the storm, anklebound, haveless, alone. So this was life: to be mated to hardship and want, to be bullied and outcast, to be no more than the plaything of unright.

Fullyielding to his heartbreak, he ranted and he wailed and he cursed this world, which had given so little and taken so much. And then with all the hopelessness of a fordoomed man, overwrought, overstrained, overwearied, the sobber slumped down beneath the flickering cries of jockeying mews and buried his face into the dank sand, little caring whether it should ever rise thence again.

No such teardrops, no such drooping eyes, no such downcast head, wetted, bewept, beweighted the stealthy farewell at the Drighten greathouse a few days later, when Godwin hastened forth into the misty foredawn alone. He had risen early and slipped out, leaving behind baggage packed to bursting in readiness for the trip to the mainland that day. Fatherly behest be damned! The would-not-be Drighten groom had cut and run. Yes, no sooner out the foredoor but he took to his heels.

Onwards he loped, setting breadth between himself and the towering house, until he stopped short, a fair landspan from the housegrounds, and standing his ground, he said to himself that no, he would not run away cravenheartedly. To Hell! He would walk away proudly! And after a last gaze at the Drighten home, he aboutfaced and walked on.

Whitherbound this cheeky turncoat? He himself was none too sure. In the shortrun, he thought his best bet was to hold out at Oswin's sister's for a bit. Surely if anyone were to open a door to him, it would be the sister of a friend. In time he reached the tumbledown cottage. Inside he found the sister stuffing her few havings into a tatty bag.

"What do you want here?" she asked coldly.

"Sorry to come upon you thus, but I've run away from my family, and I'm not sure where to go. I thought I might stay here for a little."

"'Run away'?! You'll need to do better than that! You're still on Drighten land for all your running-away." Godwin blushed. (He had been unaware that this measly bit of hardscrabble lay on the very edge of Lord Drighten's widespread landholdings.) "I'm the one who's being run off. And I fancy that's what you've come for: to see me off today, so keen you are to be rid of me."

"'Run off'?"

"That's what I said. But what would you care? Beggarly folk are nothing to your kind!"

"Run off by whom, upon what grounds?"

"By your father, the landlord, the same magistrate who damned me and my brother for the sake of his own kind."

"I had no hand in that business, and I'm as greatly saddened by—"

"Don't you talk to me of sadness! What would you know about it, about being illhandled and outcast, while the wrongdoer goes scotfree? What would you know of a brother wrongly sent to his death while another goes scotfree?" She began to weep.

"Take heart! Oswin hasn't been sent to his death. My brother was to buy my freedom in Virginia, but I meant to buy Oswin's freedom there as well. But everything went awry. But it's not too late. I have little money to my name, albeit, but I mean to find the wherewithal somehow to buy his freedom."

"Little good your money will do the fool now! He was lost at sea!"

"What?"

"As I said."

"But where?"

"Does it matter? One sea is as good as another. The ship went down, and lost-and-gone is lost-and-gone. And he would not be food for fish now, and I left all alone without any help, if it had not been for the likes of you! You lords, with all your money and your greathouses and your laws, you think you can ride roughshod over whoever you like! This shack will be yours soon enough, but you might at least let me be, for the little time left that I have a roof over my head. Haven't you done enough already? Now get out! Get out!"

What could Godwin do but leave? How could he have known that he would meet with such handling and with such tidings about the loss of *The Coinon,* sorrowful news which reached Bristol and its nearlying only the day before? It was only when he reached the yardgate that he became aware of horsemen blocking his path, horsemen who turned out to be warder, brother, and Drighten footmen.

"Well, well, one lost brother come to hand again," smirked Charles.

"Come along now, Mr. Godwin," said Cruikshank kindly. "We are belated enough as it is."

Little did Godwin know that his missing had been marked within minutes of his leaving the house that morning. He had not slipped away as soundlessly as he had thought, and then he had been spotted heading off while still within eyeshot of the house, only to be followed and now overtaken.

Back to the Drighten household it was, where, yes, a nasty fatherly tonguelashing awaited him, long or short enough to fill up the time while an overmuchness of baggage was loaded onto the coaches. And then following hurried tearless farewells, the wayfarers set out with all speed.

As forelaid, Cruikshank was entrusted with the task of seeing to it that the magistrate's flesh-and-blood would not moulder away in some kind of soggy unoverseenness. Or in the man's own words, "See to it that these backboneless bitchdogs stay akennel." And if they were somehow to get out of hand, for such was the way of youth—see what weeds upsprout when the gardener lays down his hoe!—he should "kick their asses into next week," for "there was nothing that a good clout would not mend." But such roughhanded forthrightness was not Cruikshank's manner. More given to slackhand than to asskick he was, for he believed that broadly, and more gainfully, a way could always be wormed through the most trying of binds. Yet, lest he should fall afoul of his master, he had nidnodded, halfheartedly.

Before setting out, Godwin, Cruikshank, and Charles were, by fatherly behest, locked inside their coach. Be damned if he would have his son go missing again! But none of this was marked by Godwin, who sat slumped within, dead to the world. In a way, it all seemed meaningless now anyways. It mattered not where he went or what he did. He would go along becomingly, without any armtwisting. Yes, he would go along hushfully, with a heart full of unwordable loss and sorrow.

WASHUP

FIGHT AS IT MAY, the head must in the end downflop upon the belly of a pillow, where, freed by godlike Hypnos from the hard havetos of day, it may do in dream what ought not to be by light of day, even if only to awaken again and lie no more as bedbound thrall to bodily need. Indeed, when the mind be overthrown by that lawless devil Shuteye, and when the body be left free as plaything to the world, there is no telling in whose bed one might awaken.

And there was no such telling for Oswin this day, as sleep turned its back on him, leaving him in a bed wherein he had not laid himself down. His eyes strove to unblur themselves, and the world began to show itself in ghostly splotches of black and white, which turned out to be a womanly twosome sitting across.

"*Conas atá tú?*"* said one, seemingly in a show of would-be fellowship.

To Oswin, that was but muffled gabble, but now as his mind sharpened a little, he asked, "Who are you?" and weakly looking around, "Where am I?"

Such an answer, or rather such an answer of askings, straightway robbed these two women of their hopeful looks. The unsettled elder quickly upspoke again, "*An Éireannach tú?*"† but in seeing her words meet again with only a blankmugged stare, she leerily, grudgingly shifted to a broguish "You are English, not Irish?"

"Yes. Are you Irish?"

---

* 'How are you?'

† 'Are you Irish?'

There followed a bout of uneasy speechfulness in some outlandish other-landish tongue well beyond his ken, but all that ended with a backslip into a curtish but prideful English, "We are."

Awkward stillness, this laying-bare of crisscrossing clan- and land-ties spawned, with asker and answerer eyeing each other warily. In all his greenhornhood, Oswin had never before come across the Irish. And he was somewhat taken aback now in beholding them not dyed with Pictish blue, for he had been led to believe back home that the wild Gaels, in all their ogrish uncouthness, wontedly stained themselves an inky hue, to the end of frightening their hapless boundmen out of their wits before eating them alive, one offwrenched limb at a time. Yet here he lay in a snuggish hobbitish cottage, before a brace of not unhandsome women with a lofty bearing, however outlandish their garb.

Feeling less cosy now, he asked, "How did I come to lie here?"

"In our combing of the shore for driftwood and washup, after the storm of late, we came upon you lying in the sand, amid the shipwreckage, not far from here. There you lay lifeless, and finding you so, I spoke forth before my daughter, as she herself will witness, 'Cast an eye upon these bruises, and these cuts, and these swellings, brought upon this fair broth of a boy! Cast an eye upon these shackles yet about his legs! And again cast an eye more narrowly, and tell me if this is not downtrodden _Éire*_ itself! The silk of the kine wronged by the English, for who else but the English would badfellow a man so? Let us take him up and bring him home with us and undo what the backstabbing English have done!' So thinking you to be one of us, we did carry you here, and here in my home have you lain now for nearly two days. But had I known that you were English, you would have surely fared little better than the other Englishmen whom we have found upon our strand."

How oddball it all was, this easyflowing, even lofty English—the heavy brogue notwithstanding—and this hatred of the English, in one and the same mouth! Feeling hardly cosy at all now, Oswin asked warily, nearly afraid of what he might learn, "What happened to the other Englishmen you came across?"

"Bring down the jar, daughter!" the Irish mother uttered. And as the daughter went about doing as bidden, Oswin for the first time became aware of this cottage's innards, which were crammed with all manner of things

---

* 'Ireland.'

that had been washed up by the sea and taken home by the woman and her daughter, this great whitewashed storehouse of flotsam and jetsam offcast by a choosy seagod. Here were shelves cramful, jugs jampacked, drawers chockful, trunks fullstuffed, crocks brimful, chinks and nooks chockablock with a gallimaufry of all kinds of havings that the world could yield up, a hodgepodge from the four corners of the world, all packed together now willynilly in the skimpyroomed oneness of this cottage.

From one of the upper shelves, the highreaching daughter, with the help of a footstool, brought down a great glazen jar and set it down heavily upon the lone table of the cottage, so all might see. To Oswin's aghastness, it was filled with eyes, gawking out from their bath of pickling brine, these the eyes taken from hapless English castups that had fallen into the hands of this twosome.

"For everything there is a fitting place. Does the Holy Writ not say, 'If an eye slight thee, pluck it out'? So here, you see, is an eye for an eye, an English eye for an Irish eye. And if the eels or gulls get to them first, we take the man's stones instead, stones for stones unrightfully thrown. This is how we deal with English skulduggery and Protestant blindness."

Oswin was wholly overcome with fear for his life. He began to struggle weakly with his binding sheets, to the end of readying himself for the worst, surely a scuffle with these she-trolls. And then it bore in upon him that he lay there with his heavy English shackles still about his legs and without a stitch of clothing on.

Yet the looked-for onslaught did not befall. The Irishwoman sat stilly unsettled, shackled, as it were, by churning thoughts that had strongarmed her into this dozy deedlessness. More than a few years back, a most holy oath she had sworn, that it would be a stern fastheld law of hers to do all that she could, in her own teensy way, to right English wrongdoing: all those years upon years wherein the English had slashed and burned, and plundered and taken, in their roguery of landgrabbing and oversettling of Irish lands, which had led to the bitter loss of beloved kinsfolk. Oh yes, she knew her history, for she had read the *Leabhar Gabhála* (or *The Book of Inroads*). If only she could somehow stop the onward rush of the clock's hand, if not turn it back! Oh, she would not be caught dead sparing an Englishman caught alive in Ireland! So she had sworn.

But oh, how the nearness of a handsome wellbuilt man thrills unseen through a woman's being like a cordial taken in stealth, bringing blush to bloodless cheeks, however fresh or weathered they be! And the woman had overlived more years of manlessness than she cared to bring to mind. Her heart had long ago wearied of all those mourningsongs crooned from the height of a beetling cliffbrow that overglowered open boundless sea, all those wistful strains of *sean-nós** newmade yearly in steadfast unforgetfulness of a lost husband.

And now she found herself helpless before this helpless Adonis from abroad. Oh, alackaday! Things never pan out as they ought! But the ways of the world are wonderfully odd and make unlikely bedfellows of us all, or nearly so. And even St. Patrick himself had first come to Ireland as an outland thrall, and this, even the Irishwoman knew. And so it was that the handsome and heartsome Oswin, luckless and homeless, altogether melted her sternheartedness without him so much as stirring to do so.

She came to herself and upped briskly, as if a doorman at the ready, neared the bedside and said, "Your shackles witness that there has been little love lost between you and English law. A foe to England is a friend to Ireland. You are welcome to my hearth, English. You may find a spot here for yourself."

No less stunned than the daughter, Oswin could utter no more than "Thank you," even though havenseeking at this outpost had not crossed his mind. Indeed, what he would make of his life in the forwardtime was at best a blur to him. Nonetheless, he was for the nonce heartlightened by the knowledge that part of him had not found a home, after all, in that great glazen jar, which was lifted back up to its fitting spot.

"We must get those legirons off. Fetch the tools, daughter." In folding back the sheets at the foot of the bed, the woman eyed him with something nearing a smile. "Your scars become you, English. They will set many a girl's heart afire!" And with a workmanlike handiness that would have shamed no locksmith, she in no time had the heavy shackles off his badly cut and bruised ankles.

"Now we must get you clothed. Those old tattered rags of yours will not do." From a great cupboard, she brought forth a set of clothes cut in an old manner. "Here, put these on. They are my late husband's. And what a man of a man he was! God bless his soul! A fine soldier who never said die! And he died a manly death, in the last ditch."

---

* 'Old style (song).'

Having put on the shirt, he now meant to rise from the cot to don the rest, but once up, he was somewhat hardset to keep his legs, so weak he was from all his lattertime hardship. And oddly enough, even though the shackles were off, he could still feel them about his ankles, and it would be weeks before the afterfeeling of them were to forsake him. This ghostfeeling fleetingly put him in mind of what he had once heard said, that when a man loses a leg, he can still feel thereafter the limb right down to the toes.

Once he had donned the deadman's clothes, which illfit him, the Irishwoman said, "And now you need to eat something. Sit, English. Daughter, lay forth the meal." After a muttered thanksgiving in Erse to a most Catholic God of rightwiseness, the threesome fell to, in this little would-be *broch* of a cottage upon a would-be *crannog* of a croft.

"Now we must settle you in, English," she said after their meal. He was led out to a nearby outbuilding, a somewhat tumbledown cote, in whose roughness a fitting place was found and a makeshift cot set up. "Now rest, English." She aboutfaced and walked away with the daughter, leaving him to himself. Uneasy speechfulness in Irish that quickly faded away, hush now, lonely hush.

For the first time in an overlengthy time, he felt that he had come near to a kind of motherly care. A lump rose in his throat. What was he to do now? His former life seemed hopelessly gone, and he would have to begin anew somewhere. Why not here? Here was not any worse than anywhere else he had been, and so far, a good deal better than what he had known latterly. Why not stay? Who knows? He might very well find happiness here; he might very well find peace here. With eyelids heavy and sight blurring, he groggily settled upon sticking it out, at least for a while. Then—fight as he might—sleep enfolded him, deep, deep sleep.

But morning comes soon enough to the battered soul and the weary body, and Oswin awoke to a rather rough shaking. "Up, English, up on your feet! We'll have no lieabouts here! There's work to be done, and you must earn your keep!"

And so, in the yet murky foredawn, on this the first day of his new life, Oswin rose breakfastless to a sleugh of much and mickle that needed to be done about his home-to-be, his home-to-be for the now leastwise. He soldiered on with his many chores, even if ready to drop like a stone. The greater part of his day was taken up with work on a new stonen hurdle, a breastwork stout enough to hearten any fighter. The Irishwoman had been hardshipbound latterly to sell part of a field—parting with it did not come easily—and the leftover land needed to be set off from its better half. This backbreaking work fell to Oswin, for as he well knew, that was rightly men's work, and he readily overtook this burden to spare the womenfolk.

Thus began Oswin's unbroken deedfulness about toft and croft, in the care of cottage, cote, and field. And by the sweat of his brow, he began the earning of his keep. As he settled willingly into all this sweaty busyness over the following days, it seemed in a way that he had never truly left his former home, that he had somehow won back some of the carefreeness that he had known before, some of the ease of his old life, if one might call it that, however grinding the unwealth and lowly the standing. But then, he would not let himself find the time to unforget those lattertime happenings in his life, for surely that was the way of a loser.

This did not come without a struggle against the world around, for all this swinking and sweating happened before a backdrop that was starkly stripped of any bedizening. The barren heartscape of the bereaved it might have been, long harried by ghosting wisps of things that once were. Ever aftersounding upon the heaths, thrown and battered back-and-forth unrestingly between the counterset walls of unyielding glens, one could hear, it seemed, the pangful cries of those who fell in clanstrife, from foretimes long out of mind, amidst all the clatter of gory swords beneath the cries of goading slogans, amidst the hubbub of quelled uprisings and quashed waylayings. Here was no beeloud glade but only a skimpy growth of green upon a back of hardscrabble, a stinting overlay of life upon seabegirt rock, such that the island, or rather this part thereof, was like a hardedged emerald caught in a seagod's crown.

But Oswin stuck to his guns, as it were, and plodded on. And all this hard work, day in and day out, did not go unseen by the Irishwoman, who was more given now to mutter *maith thú,** more so than in the last while. And her eye was taken ever more and ever more by the youth's sturdy wellshaped body, the glintfulness of his eye, and above all his doggedness. For what could be more handsome than a hunky fighter's iron will, and what could be more loathsome than a want of stiff manly backbone? At least, so it seemed to this onetime would-be banshee to the house of the Stuarts.

---

* 'Well done.'

Indeed, so taken was she that in no time a lighter, even merrier mood began to hold sway in the cottage, where once a heavyhanded Spartanness had been wont to override all things. And thus it was not out of keeping with the new order that one evening, while the threesome were still at table, the Irishwoman and her daughter broke out into lively lighthearted song with handclapping. So carried away was the Irishwoman that in a twinkling she got up onto the tabletop and began to jig away nimbly.

"By Jesus, English, have you ever seen a colleen so handy with her feet? If only you could have laid your eyes upon me in my youth! I was held one of the finest dancers to be seen then, more fleetfooted than any outlawed kern or gallowglass lurking up in the hills. No footloose colleen could be found nimbler!" Quickly she winded herself and grudgingly let herself down. "In my younger days, we would smear fat on the smooth top of a treestump and dance on it and see who could stay on top the longest before slipping and falling to the ground. And nearly always, winnership fell to me, even if I went home with a broken brow. Now it's your turn, English."

"Me?! But I can't dance! I never learnt how."

"Up, English, up! Dance for us now! We'll have no standers-down, no givers-up, around here! Up, on your feet! Rise up, man, and dance to our singing!" she said, taking him by the hands and pulling him up off his stool.

"Oh, mother, let him be! He says he cannot!" But as soon as the thwarted mother unhanded him, the daughter in a flash took up her own hold and said, "Come, English. I will show you how." And with the same nimbleness that the mother had foreshown, the daughter footed away before him so that he might follow and learn, she all the while keeping his hands tightly nestled in hers.

For all her good will, he was all left feet here, but he manfully bumbled and stumbled along for a while until he stopped. "I'm lame at this. You can't teach an old dog new tricks."

"'Old dog'!" hooted the Irishwoman, glad to take over from the daughter. "You are the sweetest whelp that I've clapped eyes on in years!"

As dance proved to be a deadend, the rest of evening was given over to the telling of tales, mostly tall—if not outrightly ogrish in height—unforgetworthy tales of high doings from bygone days, and then right before bedtime, tales of headstrong ghosts and fleshhungry werewolves.

But after the candle had been snuffed out and sheets drawn back, at least one soul in this backcorner of Ireland struggled unavailingly to let the day pass. As the hours ticked away, the Irishwoman tossed and turned, haunted by the feel of Oswin's strong hands in hers that evening, and earlier that day, the sight of his shirtless chest glistening with sweat in the sunlight, as he cast stone after stone up into the heap that was to be her breastwork against the world.

Her sleeplessness would surely have been much worse had her eyes been sharper that evening. Little did she know that she had a counterscuffler when it came to things touching the *Sasanach* (or her 'Englishman'). That same night, the daughter tossed and turned between her sweaty sheets and was no less harried by recalled sights of manliness unfimbled and unfondled. And this heavy burden was maybe even worse for the daughter, given her younger hotter waywarder blood. But to any of these understirrings, Oswin was wholly blinkered, and he slept like a bear in the wintry woods.

The following morning found the Irish twosome stymied in a kind of unsettling inbetweenworld, such that neither seemed to know what she was about. Indeed, the mother had gone half the day before seeing that she had put her shift on backwards. But for the daughter, the brunt of hotbloodedness, worsened by sleeploss and mugginess, was overwhelming, and she feared that her body would turn into a firebrand if she did not find some way to cool her flesh.

Later that day, a storm began to threaten, and Oswin forsook the field early. Upon reaching the yard, he found the daughter queerly standing alone in the gateway, almost fully blocking his way-in, and showing no willingness to shift ground.

Marking her halfcrazed eyes and halfopened stays, he thought that she was perhaps under the weather and asked, "Are you unwell?"

"I'm burning up."

"Yes, I'm very hot myself. I'll be happy to get these sweaty clothes off. The weather will break soon, though, I think. See, a storm's coming."

"I feel I could strip myself naked and lie beneath the coming downpour. Do you not feel the same?"

"I'd best get in now."

"Ay." But still she made no show to shift ground. After a bout of speechlessness and awkward stillstanding, she said, "The gate to the cottage is narrow. You'll need to push hard to get through."

Oswin was at a loss to understand what she meant by all this. Taking her at her word and thinking that she would not yield, he turned his back towards her and pushed his way through the narrow opening, between girl and gatepost. His greater strength and setmindedness to get beyond upshot in her being shunted aside rather roughly, wherein for a twinkling she lost her footing and stumbled to the side. And in a flash, it seemed, he was gone.

She did not follow but lingered by the gate for some time. The sad truth homethrust itself upon her now, that she had misreckonend. Yes, she had misreckoned. Oh, she had misreckoned! No, in all her unawareness she had not reckoned upon him coldshouldering her thus. No, in all her callowness she had not reckoned upon feeling all this shame and heartbreak. But then, what would a green landward wench of barely sixteen years, here at the back of the beyond, know about rosy Love's thorny ways?

"Damn that English bastard's eyes!" she whimpered to herself and began to weep. It was only a thunderclap and the opening drops of a downpour that brought her back to herself. And so it was that a drenching from on high brought the overheated maiden the wished-for cooling-off of the flesh.

The soggy weather, the Irishwoman's sleeploss, and the jilted daughter's seemingly unbottomed glumness made for a gloomy evening in the cottage. Feeling a little uneasy, Oswin deemed it best to withdraw early and left the cottage to the two women.

"The English are queer folk, mother."

"That is what comes of Protestantry, daughter."

"Do you think it was wise to let the Englishman bide here, mother?"

"What an asking, daughter! Have you fallen on your head? Do you not see how much work is getting done about the ol' place? And do you not see how much merrier we are? No, there is no harm in having a strapping young lusty buck around."

"But he is English, mother! The English who have murdered our own kind and stolen Irish land!"

"Well then, we will make a true Irishman of him, one that will out-Brian-Boru all of us! Was not St. Patrick himself from over the sea?"

"But, mother, this is against—"

"Enough blarney, daughter! I have given my word that he may stay, and I mean to keep it. I will hear no more about it!"

This wordsparring soured the mood a good deal more, and it was not long thereafter that they turned in wordlessly.

And that night, like the foregoing, turncoat Shuteye wantonly jinked past the Irishwoman, and again she tossed and turned, bedeviled by the evening's harsh words: He is English ... was not St. Patrick ... against ... against ... was it wise ... out-Brian-Boru ... St. Patrick ... across the sea ... stolen land ... Irishman of him yet ... enough ... enough ... blarney ... no more ... blarney. Yes, Brian Boru, an Irishman, why not? The bard's tongue, yes, the tongue, the tongue's the thing. Why did she not before?

What is bred in the bone comes out in the flesh, or so they say. Like mother, rather often like daughter, sadly enough. And the Irishwoman's flesh-and-blood likewise squirmed and stirred, twilighted between waking and sleeping, and no less haunted by the day's happenings. But in her wishfulness to unpain herself, Love's smouldering fire, loath to be smothered out, upflashed instead into something altogether other.

Scarcely had Oswin come forth from his cote the next morning when the Irishwoman came up to him, rope and bucket in hand, and said, "You must learn to speak the bard's tongue, English."

This was something of a takeaback, since Oswin thought that he already spoke such, for back home the selfsame wordcluster always betokened English. But it quickly became clear that she had something else in mind, to wit, her own dearheld Erse. (Had the Irishwoman known her wordhistory, she most surely would have underscored that the English word *bard* itself was a borrowing—if not a theft—from the Gaels!)

That morning then saw the beginning of a painful stint of daily schooling in "the bard's tongue" for Oswin. And what a great to-do to be in this tongue, moaned the learner in no time, with its *táim, nílim, an bhfuilim, bím, ní bhím, an mbím,* and then *bheinn, ní bheinn, an mbeinn,* or leastwise something not unlike such, and even more suchlike.* But on he plodded, even if his heart was not in it, for he had given his word, and that, he did not do lightly.

All this unscamping on Oswin's part, however painful the little headway, seemed nevertheless to hearten the Irishwoman greatly. To the daughter, however, this was too much! One more bloody inroad on the part of the

---

* 'I am, I am not, am I?, I am wont, I am not wont, am I wont? . . . I would be, I would not be, would I be?'

meddling English! Not only had the *Sasanaigh* taken Irish land but now the dratted reavers were taking over the Irish tongue as well! In her wild heart, hidden illwill towards Oswin began to stir like grub beneath the turf, illwill against him who had unwittingly snubbed her. And she swore that there would be a reckoning. Yes, there would be a reckoning. Oh, there would be a reckoning!

Given that her own dear mother had been shabbily hoodwinked—nay, blinded!—by the cunning *Sasanach*—what is bred in the bone must come out in the flesh, mustn't it?—and given that any further pesky needling on her own part was sure to prove bootless, leastwise for now, the daughter fancied that she would have to be more cunning and deedful herself. And so she craftily whelped a plan of stealthily undoing Oswin's work, to the end of undermining his all too cosy place and of winning back her own lost mother. Now, oddly enough, filled buckets were somehow unfilled, shut gates were somehow unshut, stowed-away gear was somehow unstowed-away, and stacked wood was somehow unstacked, not to speak of other doings and undoings.

At first, the Irishwoman was kindly given to the thought that such amiss-ness was the handiwork of mischiefmaking fairyfolk. But it was bound to happen soon enough that even she would begin to have misgivings about her *Sasanach*. And within days, the daughter was greatly heartened to overhear her mother upbraid him, "English, you are beginning to scamp your work! Take greater care!"

A few days later, another blisteringly hot day nettled forth another angry rainstorm that lasted well into the night. As the rain pelted roof and drummed against wall unforgivingly, as if drilling soldiers, the daughter rose up while others slept, slipped out to the goatfold, unlatched the gate, and scattered the beasts into the sodden night, before stealing back into her bed, unseen and unheard.

When daybreak came and the goats were not to be found in their fitting place, a cross cussing Irishwoman blamed and blackguarded all that stood within her path, for this untrifling slipup. Each straightway set out other-wards on this sour morning—how glad to be out of each other's hair!—in order to round up the missing flock.

But oh, how these little critters, in being freed from the oneness of their fold, had scattered themselves higgedlypiggedly throughout the night and early morning! And what work it was to gather them back together and make them stick together that morning! Why, it seemed that every outnook and cranny in the landscape would, with a bit of prying, yield up some wayward flockless goat. And thus Oswin was not in the least taken aback when he came across one helpless kid up to her hams in mud, at the bottom of a knoll.

It was clear that the wee waif could not get out on her own, and so he trod forth into this muddy patch to free her. But no sooner was he almost within reach but his own legs whisked out of sight beneath him, as he sunk to his knees in quicksand. There was no mistaking: he had unthinkingly trodden into a bog, one of many hereabouts known to suck whole heads of livestock down to a muddy death. Indeed, such bogs dotted the land roundabout as blebs and warts mar a measly hag's mug.

He began at once to fight against the downward pull and to call out. But the more he struggled, the more enmired he became. And the further down he sank, the more he lost his head. By the time he was breasthigh in mud, the kid had already gone under.

The daughter had by now and by happenstance worked her way to within earshot of Oswin's calls. Quickly climbing to the top of the knoll, she saw him squirming below. And there she stood, casting her gaze down from her height, snug behind shielding bushes, and she knew that it was only a matter of time before that great eye of mud would blink and shut in upon him. "The way to Hell is broad, English. You will need to pray hard to get yourself out of this bind," she said to herself. And with a smirk, she turned her back and walked away, down the backside of the hillock, thinking all the while how fitting it was that the *Sasanach* should be swallowed up whole by an Irish bog, all through his own foolish blunder of treading into where he did not belong.

But before she reached the bottom of the knoll, she heard a woman calling from the other side. She scrambled back up to the top, whence she saw that her mother only now reached the edge of the bog. How downheartening it was for the daughter to watch her own flesh-and-blood hold out a crooked shillelagh to Oswin, who in grasping it was slowly pulled out in the nick of time. And worse, how her mother then enclasped that dirty bogling, like a longlost lover. This near loss of life seemingly undid all the undoing that the daughter had hitherto done. Even more so now, she felt like an outsider in her own home and in her own homeland.

When at length the flock had been gathered together again and brought home, the Irishwoman straightway ordered the daughter to heat water for Oswin's washup, or rather washdown, for he was mudcaked from neck to toe, and from afar might have passed for some scrawny blackbear baitingring-bound. And to the tumbledown cote, the girl lugged a bucket of scalding hot water, which she plunked down midfloor, such that the water sloshed to-and-fro over the rim. She tossed the scrubbrush into the water, cheekily saying, "Take care not to drown in it, English!" And she trod off.

Unaware of how hot the water was, he nearly scalded his hand in pulling out the scrubbrush. Yet another of these hotheaded Irish days, he thought.

With the daughter busy elsewhere, the Irishwoman fidgeted and pottered away for a bit, alone in the cottage, until lastly those restless thoughts hovering about the *Sasanach* drew her helplessly out to the cote. By the wall, her heart began to quicken at the sound of splashing water, and going up to a chink in the wall, she peered in Thisbelike, unseen and unheard. Oh, no more than a wee peeplet to see how he is faring. Beyond, through the open door, she could see him, under the lee of the shed, standing upon the green and glistening in the sunlight, as naked as God made him, with most of the mud scrubbed from his body.

And oh, what a body! She nearly swooned as her gaze wantoned from sturdy limb to sturdy limb, from handsome top to handsome bottom, and lingered upon all that lay between. True, she had seen him in the buff before, when they had cleanscrubbed his saltstained body, as he lay abed, still shackled and dead to the world, the day they found him. And even then she wondered breathlessly at the sightliness of his manly shape. But that was nothing beside the onrush of heartflushes she felt now. And as her headlands were lashed by these heaving billows, her hands found her breasts and began, as best they could, to stroke and rub playfully the swelling knobbles. "Oh, God help me!" she sighed within.

But this dreamlike sweetness was doomed to be soured. Before long, she felt the oneness of a twosome of eyes burning themselves into her back, like searing whorebranding irons. She overshouldered a thief's look, only to freeze and then overblush in seeing her daughter standing behind her akimbo. In a twinkling, the Irishwoman's hands dropped to her sides, and her body aboutfaced and headed back to the cottage. In passing her daughter, she said still blushful, "Is he not the pink of a man?"

But the daughter could overmaster her tongue no more and said, as she followed along behind, "Ay, mother, the pink of a *young* man, the pink of an *Englishman,* who washed up on our shore in shackles. Even his own kind would have nothing of him but saw fit to pack him off in a ship to God-knows-where. And blindly you've let this unknowner into our midst, and never once have you asked him what he did to earn those legirons. For all we know, he could be a raper and throttler of helpless women, all to enliven his dull hours. By Jesus, it's a wonder that we're still whole and alive! And it's a wonder how, in the hindtime, you could swear a holy oath to fight against our wrongdoers, only to cast it to the winds out of a shameful weakness for some outland castup! I thank God that I have more steadfastness than that!"

"How dare you speak to me like that! My father is turning in his grave from hearing his own daughter slighted so! What a shame you are to this family!" She turned her back and headed off again.

"No, mother, you are! Shame on you, leering cowardly through a wallchink to eye a mongrel's tail! And if you mean to lie down with dogs, I will have none of your fleas! No, I would sooner beg by the wayside and die in a ditch than bow my head so as to dwell within an English brothel and be reckoned among the Stuarts' drabs! And then at least I will go to my grave knowing that I was no turncoat whore as my mother was!"

The Irishwoman stopped short, turned, and clouted this her own flesh-and-blood, with a hefty wallop to the right eye. In a shriek, the daughter lost her footing and tumbled aground, as clumsily lifeless as an unstrung puppet. Lest she should somehow fail to overmaster her burning wish to claw out the girl's eyes, the mother stormed off to the cottage, leaving her wounded daughter wailing on the ground.

Within the stillness of the cottage, the nearly bedeviled woman sat awhile, but after greedily downswigging a glass of strengthening homebrew, she little-by-little regained her selfhold. And as her mind sharpened, it bore in upon her, albeit willynilly, that there was perhaps some truthfulness in the daughter's hasty words, however heartlessly worded. A holy oath cast to the winds, it was said. Had she then forgotten herself? Had she? Oh, how the heart plays tricks on our wits! Good Lord! Better to be without a heart lest it scramble the mind and warp all that is rightwise!

And true, she had never once asked the *Sasanach* why he had fallen afoul of English law, or of any other law, for all that. Why had he not been forthcoming about such murky bygones? What was he hiding? Had she needlessly risked the lives—why, even the name—of her family? Had she truly bungled here?

After a good bit of such mulling, the time came, and like a doorman at the ready, she upped and stalked out to the cote, where Oswin had stayed idling after his scrubdown, for he had partly heard and seen the catfight, although he understood naught thereof, given that it had been shrieked in Erse. And he had struggled with himself over whether to stay aloof or take things in hand and settle the business.

Before him, the Irishwoman came to stand, akimbo, with all the stiff upper lip that she could muster. "You never told us, English. What did you do to earn those legirons? What misdeed did you do in the land of the Stuarts that they should want to be rid of you so?"

"Sodomy, although hardly a 'misdeed,' as you call it."

"'Sodomy'? With a beast??"

"With a man. Does it matter?"

Such an answer, and answer of asking, straightway robbed the woman of whatever hopefulness had lingered in her heart. *Och*, what sickening shame! With a man, for Christ sake! Such foul unmanliness! Such lowly cowardliness! Here was no ironsided Brian Boru after all, proudly swashing upon Clontarf's killingfield! Where had her head been? Why had she not left him to the stinking bog, or why had she earlier not cut his throat and plucked out his eyes upon the strand? Here was nothing but faithbreach. "By daybreak tomorrow, you will be off my land. God help you if you ever show yourself here again!" And with that, she aboutfaced and stormed off.

There was no eveningmeal that day: none was looked for; none was readied. And it was not until after nightfall that the daughter, who had earlier wisped away into thin air, showed herself again in the dimlit cottage. In the betweentime, she had mulled over the day's happenings and lastly had unwavered herself into going her own way. Her mother had always been a stick-in-the-mud, but now—alack!—one forlornly enmired in the wrong sludge.

But before the daughter could say that she had come only to gather together a few things and bid farewell in the morning, the mother, hitherto downslumped in thought, said, "Sit down, daughter." And the latter did as bidden, as she had long been wont to do—blood being thicker than mud in the end, leastwise in this cottage. "Tomorrow early, you will go out into the woods and gather some toadstools, enough for a meal, as it were. And in the evening, you will cook the Englishman a handsome meal. Do you understand, daughter?"

"Ay, mother, I do."

"You go out now and in stealth bring in the axe and any other tools that might be turned against us, so that no mischief befall us tonight while we sleep. And tomorrow, daughter, we will bring down the jar." The daughter smiled.

And when those tools of mischief had been stowed within and all was made lockfast before the *Sasanach* lurking somewhere outside in the dark, mother and daughter turned in.

The next morning, after a night of unsettled shuteye, the elder woman, who had said nothing to the younger about her ordering Oswin off the land by sunrise, went out straight to the shed to see if the *Sasanach* was indeed gone. There she beheld, lying upon the makeshift cot, her dead husband's set of clothes, tidily folded. No Englishman was to be found. But calls from the daughter came now to the mother's ears, and the Irishwoman made one with the caller in gazing out. Together they aftereyed a young man, clad in his own hardworn duds, a good landspan from the cottage, seemingly heading for the sea.

The Irishwoman picked up a stone and cast it after the outbound *Sasanach*, as he overlept the stonen hurdle that his own hands had started. The stone fell far short of its target, as she well knew it would. "Once an Englishman, always an Englishman! Never trust an Englishman! May the curse of crows lie upon the back of him and every other Englishman!"

"Are we not going to chevy after the turncoat blarneyer, mother?" asked the daughter, keen that blood should have blood, either at the first or at the last, even though none had been spilled.

"No, daughter, we will never catch such a man as that now. Let us thank God that we have seen the backside of him! Come, daughter, there is work to be done!" with one last lingering outgaze at her onetime English.

The daughter could live with this. The *Sasanach* was at least gone and out of their hair, even if his eyes had not found haven in the great glazen jar. And everything was again as it ought to be, everything in its fitting place: filled buckets were filled, shut gates were shut, stowed-away gear was stowed-away, and stacked wood was stacked. It was as if everything had never been otherwise, and that was all that mattered.

What was to have been Oswin's new life then had lasted barely a few weeks, and it was with some heavyheartedness that he trudged along. It greatly saddened him that so many things he had known in this world thus far had fallen by the wayside before hardly or ever truly getting off the ground.

He had worked unscampingly—like a dog!—for the Irishwoman, and he had gotten not a penny for all his drudging, which worthwise far outstripped the cost of his keeping. Why he should have been so illmeeded, he could not fathom. Why they should have turncoated, he could not grasp. Whence did this upflare of doggery come? Was it that he would not, that once, dance for them atabletop? Was it that he did not work hard enough at the Irish tongue? Surely not the loss of the kid in the bog. Perhaps it would have been better if he had cravenly lied about his runin with English law. But, oh, how sickening the thought of such toadeatership! And the answers to these askings fled by him jinkingly, however much he bethought himself. Queer as folk it all was!

Not knowing what to do or where to go—he did not even know where rightly in Ireland he was—he bumbled along driftlessly until he found himself once again on the strand where he had earlier been washed up. Bits of shipwreckage still lay scattered here and there, that which scavengers could not haul or could not be bothered to haul away as their own.

At this deadend, at this fraying selvedge of the world, he slumped down on the sand and stared out blankly at the sea. His hand began to play lifelessly in the sand until it grazed something halfburied there: a coin it turned out to be, an English coin, bearing a king's head.

Thoughts of bygones, grim thoughts of lost life and lost love, of sorrow and sadness, of hurt and harm, thronged and swirled in roughly upon him now, like salty gushes over open wounds. In a flush of bitterness he hurled the coin at the outflowing tidewater, at the sea that had spit him forth upon this Godforsaken shore. How sweet and yet how sour the unforgetting. How overpowering the longing, for only the losing makes the heart feel how great was the having.

He knew it now: he must back to England, even if a man with a price on his head. There were things that needed to be set aright there. Yes, there would be a reckoning, some kind of a reckoning, although he knew not what.

He would rise up now and go back to England and turn his back upon this wretched makeshift noncelife.

Getting to his feet, he found his legs, as quickly as a nearly overturned boat righting itself. No sooner up, however, but he choicelessly stood down, as it were, down to his knees, and began to sift through the sand around him for more coins perhaps yet unearthed. Penniless as he was, he would need some kind of wherewithal, no matter what lay before him. As he grubbed away in the sand, it dawned on him that the coins he began to unearth now were those that he had earlier scattered to the wind in a fit of anger and which still lay in the sand where they had fallen. How rather odd it was, it seemed, to be undoing his former deed, but it was, he told himself soothingly, only to the end of undoing earlier wrongdoing. And once he had grubbed up all the coins he could find, he rose up and set off, back to where he started.

SEMPER AUGUSTUS

S WOLLENBELLIED WERE THE SAILS—from panting Boreas' tireless thrusting and heaving—which bore this shiplet over the briny underlay that was Proteus' world. Onwards bobbed and bowed *The Simia*, in her overreaching of shifty water that bridged and yet unbridged the shores of England and the Spanish Netherlands. And aboard was one landlubber, our young Godwin, swaying between queasiness and sleep.

Yes, the wayfaring Drighten bevy—warder, outlawed wards, and overmany flunkeys—had flitted and snaked their hushhush way from Drighten household to English seashore without any mishap, and had boarded *The Simia* in the forenoon without any to-do, and had crossed the English Channel in one piece, and had reached the mouth of the Scheldt in good time. And now, on this last seafaringleg, the craft met with smoother sailing, letting Godwin at last doze off into a snooze that would hopefully settle his innards.

Yet it seemed as if he had hardly shut his eyes when he was shaken awake by a breathless Cruikshank, "Wake up, Mr. Godwin, wake up! We've reached Antwerp! We must unship ourselves forthwith!" So here at last was the longawaited and yet longdreaded burg.

"Antwerp. Good Lord! What a name!" muttered Godwin to his queasy self, scarcely off the boat. He shambled along the busy straightrunning wharf, trying to find his landlegs, while yet eyeing the great bouncer of a stonen wall that begirt the town. He tried not to straggle too far behind leadsmanlike Cruikshank and Charles, with their many tailing flunkeys, while at the same time Godwin's own footmanmob struggled along in their master's wake, lugging all his baggage. Ay, what a name, indeed, this *Antwerp.*

But what's in a name? Being neither hand nor foot nor any other part belonging to a man, or to a town, any dud of a name one might doff and instead take all of another's. Ay, any humdinger of a dubbing, if bespeaking worth and thus worth speaking, one might keenly don, if for the donning, and proudly flaunt. And most happy indeed he who is spared this hassle of doffing and donning, he who can sport a handsome tag botherlessly his own by birthright, such as our own young Godwin!

But what was in the name of *Antwerp?* The everydayfolk believed that their town lay where once a giant named Druon Antigoön had dwelt, who was wont to cut off the hands of the Scheldt's boatmen whenever they would not pay his stiff tolls, all until a Roman warman benamed Silvius Brabo—or Strabo—dared him to the fight. And this outlander ended up cutting off one of the giant's hands and flinging it into the Scheldt, thereby ending the giant's gainful stranglehold over the waterway. The unlearned thought that this gruesome happening of eld had given the town its name, for to them, *Antwerpen,* to give the Flemish form, must have stemmed from *Handwerpen,* 'handthrowing,' hence the townsblazon showing a stronghold flanked by a lone hand to either side.

The learned bookman Franciscus Junius, however, held that Silvius had not driven off Druon, but rather that Druon had forsaken his watery haunt in angry search of Silvius, who choicelessly fled before the wrath of the onehanded giant. Junius saw the town's name as stemming from another, much earlier, noun in Early Frankish, to wit, **Andawerpjum,* to give what was thought to be the *dativus pluralis,* meaning bit-for-bit '(at the) countercasters.' According to Junius, Druon, in his eagerness to strike back, had hurled at the fleeing Silvius many of the offcut hands that he had uphoarded, leavings from the once cheeky bearding boatmen, who, owing to their unwillingness to tow the giant's line, as it were, now all lay handless and unseen at the bottom of the Scheldt.

Such fanciful speech- and folk-lore was beyond the ken of Cruikshank and his wards, who had not bothered to lay their hands on and thumb through any sightseer's handbook. And such background would have been of no interest to Charles: for all he cared, the name *Antwerp* meant as much as *twerp.* Indeed, no sooner had Charles set foot in this little realm but he was straightway overcome with abiding illwill towards "these boggy upstarts" in their "midgety backwater of dikes and drains." Yet little did he know that such sniff- and snoot-iness, fitting for one of his standing, stood him in good stead to be altogether at home in this town.

Even if set in the Spanish king's crown, Antwerp was still a dazzling little jewel and easily outshone Bristol or any other place that Godwin had ever seen in England. And so, having now found inlet through the mighty begirding wall, he was greatly wowed by Antwerp's handsome townsights, as seen in their happy-go-lucky coachride, through burgherswollen streets, past girthswollen homes.

The streetfronts of these buildings were bedecked with all manner of eyecandy, with their grillwise entangling strapwork and scrollwork and scallopwork of brittle stucco or carved stone, which overlay hidden roughedged uneven brickwork. And such toppings were the outward marks of plumpening pelf. Indeed, these snuggeries of trade-enwealthied burghers and ledgerlords boasted even greater blazery within, larded and encrusted with *bric-à-brac* bought up hotcakewise, with pilfererish keenness, *coûte que coûte,** amidst warring seesaw bouts of openhanded outlay and hammerfisted thrift. Nor were middling households unposh, and even the lowliest abodes strove to a kind of unmeekish swank and snazziness, making do with pennypinching pinchbeck gotten *de bric et de broc.*†

With evening falling, amidst shadows lengthening, the coaches came to a stop before a townhouse most handsome, built of smooth gleaming stone. By all outward seeming, here was an abode fit for nothing less than a lord of lords, a dwelling outshining all its nearby neighbours most kenspeckly. When the newcome came to stand before the shut opening, crowned by a kind of would-be coat-of-arms blazoning forth the slogan *Luctor et Emergo*, the door below opened briskly, as if selfwilled, before any sluggish finger could so much as smudge the great knocker. And the latter, in all its backshine, was no less lookingglasslike than the door's many clinching nails and clinging hinges, so brightened by elbowgreasy spick-and-spanning that the hurdle seemed nothing less than diamondstudded.

There came to sight a great strapping Lowland lass, who, eyeing them from head to toe, said in the king's English, before Cruikshank could utter

---

* 'At any cost.'

† 'In any ol' way.'

a word, "You are wanted in the eatingroom." Cruikshank and his wards were somewhat dumbfounded by the girl's foreknowledge and overawed by her great size and sturdiness. A thickwristed housemaid, they guessed.

"Why do you stand there? You are wanted in the eatingroom!"

They snapped to life and made their way inside. Yet no sooner were they across the threshold but Machteld—so the housemaid was called—stopped them short. Taking hold of Cruikshank's arms, she hoisted him upon her broad thickset shoulders and set forth thus down the length of the forehall until she reached the end. There she set her lading down and had him sit on a backstool, stripping him of his streetshoes and stuffing his feet into houseslippers.

Leaving him there, she backed to the foredoor, sailing past her bucket and mop still bristling midfloor, for she had only shortly before ended all her daily scrubbing and scouring, washing and mopping, rinsing and rubbing, of the stately forehall's cool-under-foot marble floor.

Godwin could not help but think that the maiden looked as if she latterly had somehow tumbled out of a Rubensish unstilllife. Fed up with the chilling draft upon her naked buxomness, which had been long beset by windily sighing would-be or has-been ravishers, the girl had since bedecked herself in weeds of ironsided black, like any sturdy little she-Puritan. Indeed, with a tiller of a mop in hand, its bottom thrust into the murky froth yet in her bucket, she might have been skipper of some great ship of Puritan fathers tossled upon the high sea, keeneyedly in search of the land, ground, and dirt of a new and spotless Salem.

Then Charles and Godwin, each in his turn, were likewise borne across, with their dangling feet never once touching the clammy underlay. And once across, they too were set down and outfitted with illfitting embroidered houseslippers, the household's own hand-me-downs, as it were. Thereupon they set forth again, all as one.

In climbing the stairs, Charles said to Godwin, "That must've been the first time you've ever ridden a wench."

"That must've been your first time without spurs."

Charles was taken aback, for this was not in keeping with his brother's wonted behaviour. He would let it pass, for now. When the cat's away, the mouse will play.

At length they reached the eatingroom, where they were met by an oversize fleshy burgher, with a rugged seaman's mug badly scarred, seemingly in earlier days of hardship. This bloke stood forth clad in a glossy black silken doublet, which strained to hide his great barrelchest, and in even blacker breeches, which fell unfurled about his hulking thighs. To the man's starboard stood a beribboned and bebaubled chit, swathed in the costliest of silverywhite silks. Lacking her sidekick's heavyweightedness, she yet was not underfed, however winsomely slender, nay, hungrylooking she may have seemed.

The guesthappy man, jittery and overblithe, trod forth boldly to the newcome. Standing overnigh and uttering "Welcome, welcome!" again and again, he nearly shook off their hands in mighty handquakes, as if heartily clinching some bargain awharf.

The Drighten bevy had not reckoned upon meeting with such a seemingly unslick man. They stiffened uneasily and then answered with a bow, *comme il fallait,* while Charles, *naturellement,** met the man's *faux pas* with a smirk. Showing more fitting buckram in her manners, the missikin hemmed ablush and bobbed back, all this making the fumbler aware now of his bumpkinish oversight. He quickly yielded more berth and drew the amissful hand behind his back, in the doddering hope that out-of-sight would be out-of-mind. Scraping a foot, he too lolloped over in a tottery bow.

Before Cruikshank and his wards could rightly foreword themselves, the man blurted out, "You are right welcome to this my home! You must be hungry after all your wayfaring. We have held off in the hope that you would be here to eat this evening. Come, let us sit at once!"

To outlandish barks of orders, the footmen snapped to life, and the threesome were seated, benapkined, foredolloped with food. With this sudden shift to ungraspable Flemish, and with a newsprung feeling of outsiderhood, Godwin and his fellows wondered at their guestmaster's easyflowing—albeit heavily brogued—English, which had upped and offed, and then wondered if they had indeed come to the right house, since not one name had been spoken since finding inlet.

Before any opening arose for Cruikshank to say who they were and whence they came, and further to ask before whom they now sat, the Fleming found his English tongue again and, amidst all his hardy striving to meld chewing with talking, at last said, "Be not shy, Cruikshank, my

---

* 'As was fitting, . . . needless-to-say.'

good fellow, eat!" In hearing this, the Drighten bevy breathed a sigh. This then was indeed father of the bride-to-be, and master-of-the-household, one Karol Leeuwenhok. And that then must be the bride-to-be, and lady-of-the-household, one Henrietta Leeuwenhok. Yes, the threesome were unwrong to think themselves in the right place.

In all his lightheartedness, the great man, seated as he was upon a great gold and purple cushion, as plumply swollen as buxom Fortuna's bosom or bottom, which let him sit a little higher than everyone else in the room, and let his feet dangle a little above the cool marble underlay, the great man, I say, forgot himself again and again, losing his English and slipping back into Flemish, in order to thunder further orders at his footmen, who snappily brought forth and took away one handsome plate and platter after another.

Yet for all the blazery and finery of the setting, a kind of cold cheer nonetheless held sway atable, or at least so it seemed to hungry Godwin's tastebuds. Stacks of chilled ham and souse and jellied hocks and other such coldcuts together with baconed salads seemingly were to be had only, allowing Leeuwenhok to partake of seconds and thirds, but leaving Godwin to make shift with bread and water and with whatever little else was to hand there that did not smack of the sty.

Leeuwenhok now held forth lengthily on one of his most beloved talkhubs. "Think how all this goodly fare set before us here so greatly hinges upon those stouthearted sutlers to king and kingdom, the Cortezes of boursefloor and tradeship, by which I mean all those featful businessmen who daily risk life and limb in their hunt for goods, on every hand, in places where even levelheaded angels would rightly fear to tread. What sweets of life they wrench from Mother Earth's clenched fists! What deathful risks they run in homing their wares, as great as any that a soldier meets when foodhunting in the field! They are the very backbone and crown of man's happiness! And what great thankfulness is owing to them, no matter how low or high they be! I read only this morning—where is that good book of mine?"

A bark in Flemish set footmen astir to find the book, to wit, Nicolas Faret's *L'honnête homme, ou l'art de plaire à la cour*, snippets of which Leeuwenhok had latterly taken to scoffing down with his morninggruel. "Yes, here it stands written: *'La vertu n'a point de condition affectée, et les exemples* *sont assez communs de ceux qui d'une basse naissance se sont élevés à des actions héroïques et des grandeurs illustres.""**

All this highspeaking of a brave new world for gatherers and gainers fell sundrywise upon the ears of its hearers. What with all the bustle of newness, and the businessman's unbroken spate of pelfpuffery and tradeballyhoo, not to speak of his own unfed hunger, Godwin had hardly found time to take any meaningful note of the Leeuwenhok daughter, the set end of all this to-do. As he picked at his plate, his eyes at length roamed leerily sideways to where Henrietta had been seated, very much in keeping with the laws of righteating.

He had been blind to how the girl came to life upon seeing her groom-to-be in the flesh. She had already taken a great shine to the face of the likeness in small that had been aforesent weeks earlier, after a flurry of writing between Lord Drighten and *meneer*† Leeuwenhok touching upon the maybehood of wedlock between son and daughter. And Henrietta was now overgladdened to behold the face of the youth himself far outshining that of his limning. Indeed, ever since the likeness had come by mailboat, the girl woke to Godwin, spoke of Godwin, night- and day-dreamed of Godwin. In few, she ate, drank, and slept Godwin. Godwin, Godwin, Godwin! By God, Leeuwenhok nearly sickened at the name before the youth ever showed himself! And here before her now sat the very lad, this mailorderhusband-to-be! Surely a dancer's, swordman's, Adonis's foot, hand, face, and more!

"Oh, father, we have heard enough of inky tradeledgers! Let us hear from our guests!"

"Why, yes, yes, my dolly," said the reddened father.

"Do tell us, how was your crossing? Were you beset by seareavers and strained to make a bold stand? How rousing would be such a tale! I have heard that lately the Seabeggars have been busy looting, killing, and raping."

Godwin was somewhat taken aback to find that the daughter, no less than the father, spoke a most easyflowing English. How heartlightening to know that the wooing-to-come would not needfully stoop to cavemanlike grunts and wordless handwaves.

"I believe such things belong in storybooks." said Godwin. "We met with

---

* 'A stout heart is not something that one takes up, and it is not at all unheard-of for the lowborn to rise to heroic deeds and outstanding greatness.'

† 'Mister.'

no reavers, unless it was the sea itself, for one of the seamen from our rather unseaworthy ship was knocked into the water by mishap and drowned."

"How shuddersome!" sighed Henrietta.

"The most trying part of all was having to set out so early, for fear we might be caught by—"

"Caught by the rain!" blurted Cruikshank, his knife griding over the plate. "What with the weather's great waywardness of late, we feared that muddy roads from a clap cloudburst might belate us and make us miss our ship."

"There's nothing wrong in being late for a ship, unless one is a rogue on the run!" skylarked Leeuwenhok, which set Cruikshank into jittery giggles.

"I fear my landlubber of a brother is illset to speak of our tousled crossing since he slept through most of it fearlessly."

"Happy is he," said Leeuwenhok, after the bout of laughter at Godwin's cost, "who puts out of mind all unhappy bygones. Let us leave the past in the past. A lad with a lofty name and background such as his need not fret himself. My God, the elder son of the thirteenth Earl of Etenheighte! That is nothing to laugh at!"

"But you haven't yet told us anything bloodcurdling!" whined Henrietta.

"I fear then that our coming will be something of a letdown, for nothing truly untoward happened, other than the drowning and a good deal of tossing-about," said Godwin.

"Indeed, I believe the guts of my unseaworthy brother, our gutsy fighter of seawolves here, tossed about more than the waves themselves," said Charles, to further chuckles.

"As was said, swaggering freebooters and buried goldhoards are the stuff of storybooks," said Godwin, miffed.

"Oh, but you are wrong," said Henrietta. "Only lately, a Spanish duke showed up here in Antwerp. Having run up great owings, the man, who turned out to be a chimneysweep's bastard from Brabant, fled by night, and many businessmen who had dealings with him now find themselves out of money."

"The swine should have been strung up by the thumbs and left to rot!" muttered Leeuwenhok.

"Does that not belong to the world of freebooting and buried goldhoards? And Geert Laps, one of the most heartless of the Seabeggars, is said to eat his boundmen alive, one offwrenched limb after the other, hand and foot," said Henrietta, smugly in the know.

"Surely hearsay, if not outright old wives' tales," smirked Godwin.

"Hearsay or truth, it works out to be the same in the end, for few seaman who have fallen into Geert Laps' hands have overlived it," said Henrietta.

"Oh, let us not dwell upon such unhappy bygones. Eat, my men, drink!" interloped Leeuwenhok.

And now while aboveboard there held sway burbling tabletalk and hubblebubbly crosstalk on every head, belowboard there upsprung a rather bold play-of-foot, wherein Henrietta, freed from loosefitting houseslippers, began to footsie wantonly about Godwin's ankles, shins, and calves, in undertable huggermugger. Startled Godwin had only ever read of such comeabouts in silly hackneyed lovestories, those, it seemed to him, that bore few tokens of lifelikeness. Yet here was that same mindspun hackneyedness in living flesh-and-blood brushing roughly up against him now, in this, highlife's artful aping of low art. And he kicked himself, as it were, that he could not recall how the cleverer more deepfeeling youths of lovestory had unfettered themselves from such a bind.

Was it by will or mishap—he himself could not tell—that under the brunt of busy footwork, Godwin foozled his grip, and the glass popped out his hand, like a seaman jolted overboard, alighting in Henrietta's silvery-white lap, which turned bloodred with wine? At once she got up and began dabbing hothandedly.

What Godwin had thought to be some outlandish carving of a little "blackamoor," almost lost amidst the glut of roomfrippery, now came to life, and forsaking his standingplace by the wall, he drew near to offer his own hanky. Godwin marked that the beturbaned houseboy sported a diamond-studded golden neckring engraved with *Zwartenbok*, seemingly the name of this wordless thrallkin. Godwin had heard of this same folkway in England, that in more upmarkety households, these costly havings of black bondsmen were often fitted out with bejeweled neckrings showing the bearer's name.

There would be no easy getting rid of this stain, and so Henrietta withdrew to shift clothes. Keen to find his own boon herein, Godwin himself rose, shortly after her withdrawal, and saying his sorries and forgoing the aftersweets not yet brought forth, he too left the meal, such as it was, notwithstanding beseechings to stay. He betook himself to his room, now as frowzy as an old cask from the untimely hot weather.

What a day this had turned out to be! A botched skedaddle from home, sorrowful tidings, flight through the forenoon as a wanted outlaw, a sickening rocky crossing in a deathtrap of a boat, an ungutworthy meal at the table of a hamfisted *Laughing Cavalier*, a near mauling by a lovesick wench, and now a splitting headache. Hopefully all this was but roughcast to a finer topcoat-to-come. If not, God help him!

Brainfag set in. He lay down in the darkness. He battened down his heart. He fightlessly slumbered off, bestridden by the nightmarish goblin of muggy air and stifling heat.

The morrow came soon enough, and rising late, as late as he could, he idled and dawdled bedroombound, but he knew he would have to go down. And so he decked himself out in a most handsome outfit of red and white silk, as if the very Rose of England itself, the one hue warring with the other to outdazzle. Something truly upperhanded was needed, and a seamster's fanciful rendering of such a lordly bloom could not hurt.

Down he went, to a longsuffering breakfast that had long awaited him. He found Cruikshank and Leeuwenhok still atable heartily lengthening breakfast into early lunch. Straightway he was told, with most knowing hintful looks, that the young lady-of-the-household awaited him in the *cabinet des curiosités,** down beneath the eatingroom.

She was there alright, clad in a great flowing housecoat, like all fadfollowing ladies, who at this time of day, and in households such as this, were keen to be *oisives* and *négligentes.*† She was alone, apart from everwordless Zwartenbok. The sudden sight of Godwin filliped her out of daydreaming, and she rushed up to him.

"I trust, my young lord slept tight last night?"

"Tight enough, yes, thank you."

"Even if slow to rise, you come most handsomely, I see. *Bienvenu à mon cabinet des curiosités!*‡ This is where I keep many of my prettiest and costliest things. And what better place could there be to meet a handsome young man?"

"Out in the woods, perhaps, or on the green."

"Oh, let us leave the outdoors to the uncouth! Nature is always prettiest when preened, or brightened with the brush of a skillful master." There followed an awkward bout of speechless overnearness.

---

* 'Wonderroom.'

† 'Idle . . . laid-back.'

‡ 'Welcome to my wonderroom!'

Groping for aught to utter, he said, "And masters amany you have here!" He eyed the walls about him, behung as they were with stilllives, and starchy gatherings and broadviews of shipwrecks, and what-not-else.

He was then suddenly thrown into a great fright by the feel of a clawful hurryscurrying up his back and by the chatter of gnashing teeth about his nape. He backclawed wildly and blindly, in order to clutch and offlift the unseen beastly something gripping his shoulders, only to feel sharp teeth and then a downward scurrying-off.

"*Tiens-toi bien, Montauciel, tu monstre!*"*

Looking about himself, he caught sight of this Montauciel—Henietta's pet monkey it turned out to be—as it chatterfully scampered across the room and then clambered up a richly carved spindle, one upholding a lofty perch for a twosome of now cackling wingflapping parrots. The climber made good its offflight by springing further onto the top of a nearstanding cupboard, where it sat safely out of the reach of those beneath him.

"Blast your poxy ape! It bit me!"

"He's altogether harmless, if you let him do what he wants. Come. I have things to show you."

And so with a throbbing forefinger, Godwin was led about the room, to the burthen of Montauciel's chatter. Here was a great hold groaning under the weight of its lading: chests and boxes, cases and cupboards, shelves and ledges, filled and loaded to the utmost with all manner of whimwhams and knickknacks and keepsakes, with all manner of goodly gear and handsome belongings and other things haveworthy, each stowed away carefully in its fitting place. Here were seen countless coins of great seldomhood, sporting the heads of kings, all brightly burnished and outlaid in plushlined glasslidded boxes, which besheltered these pieces from grimy prying fingers. Here were great pieces of Ming pottery, like upended bells, so outsize that a man's body could easily be hidden away inside. Here were hueshot Turkey carpets, wantonly overlaying and softening not tabletops, as was the wont in these parts, but rather floortiles. Here were amazing beasts taken from faroff steamy jungles, harmlessly tame now behind glass, their outlandish bodies filled out with wax and wire and straw and sawdust. (And in passing these, Godwin thought that he would fain see that monkey there as well).

In short, here was upheapt plunder, brought from the four aloof corners

---

* 'Montauciel, behave yourself, you little rogue!'

of the world, all given by a doting Leeuwenhok to his beloved "dolly," all gotten in one bingebuyingsquandercraze after another. And all this plunder was manifolded as it backbeamed off the face of the heavy giltframed lookingglasses that somehow found room enough on the cluttered walls to downgaze upon this costly hoard. And at each stop in their ramblings, Henrietta held forth upon the whatness and whenceness, and the wherewithal outlaid to lay hold thereof.

Lastly they came to a great black cupboard, the outside of which showed here and there ladies of the East lost in a kind of lofty idleness, with their bowlined bodies swathed in lengths of silk, and their heads looking backwards over a shoulder, to see if seen. This cupboard, enholding her most prized havings, was now unlocked, and in a worshipful hushedness, she laid bare the hoard within.

"Are they cloves?" he asked, hoping not to have misspoken himself.

"No, tulipbulbs! Owning tulipbulbs is the height of fashion now," she said proudly in the know. Indeed, the craze for such bulbs had reached the height of folly only eight years earlier, in 1637, when it seemed that none was spared the wish to see bulbs wonderfully turned into gold. When the wild guesstrading ended in the crash of 1637, Flora and Fortuna had by then led an unfew from rags to riches and back again. This notwithstanding, the will-to-clink from "cloves" had not truly withered since, even if savings had.

"Do you mean to grow them?"

"Why no, if you let them grow, they become worthless!"

"I see."

"This is a *Semper Augustus,* the prince of tulips. The bulb is worth more than three thousand guilders!" she said with pride of ownership, as she cradled it in the lap of her cupped hands. The growthling was indeed princely when in full bloom, its crownleaves handsomely sporting reddish streaks on white, like drops of sluggish blood artfully brushed into fresh snow. Such outward dapperness was the outgrowth of careful breeding and weeding, setting the *Semper Augustus* head and shoulders above the lesser ranks of other tulips. Yet upon this earthless slumberling, neither of the two gawkers was allowed too long a gaze, lest they should somehow unsettle its cosy but costly sleep, for in no time she had the bulb tightly locked away again in her great black cupboard.

A few Flemish words from her sent Zwartenbok out of the room. And there awhile they stood wordlessly, at the end of all that stocktaking. And what was to be said now? For the time had come for Godwin to get down to the brass tacks of wiving. But what was to be said? Words needed to be spoken, even though no words needed to be spoken. But what was to be said? For at the beginning of all things starkly stood the be-all-and-end-all word, the living *logos* itself. What was to be said?

He screwed himself to the stickingplace. "As you must know, our two families have latterly been much taken with the thought of forming nearer ties, or bonds, one might say, the kind that come from a linking-together of houses and birthlines. And there is believed to be no downside to such a linkup. At least, I think that such is the viewpoint of your father and mine, and perhaps still others, although I cannot speak for everyone. And it is befitting that folk of our years should seek to find their place within the broader fellowship of mankind, as it were. So it is written, I believe. And perhaps it is the case that, we being roughly the same in years, you being a woman and I a man, we might over time come to think highly of some other wight, that a nearer bond might be not altogether irksome for folk like us. I myself, I must own, may well be not the best choice for many others seeking nearer ties, and many others not the best choice for me, but there must come a time when the many must be sifted through, to find one not altogether irksome to one's self."

On he fumbled, seeking, like some great Italian *castrato*, to warble forth flights of *passaggi* and *trilli*, anything to fill up the skimpy-to-empty bars of his *serenata*. And amidst all this aboutspeech, Godwin told—nay, begged—himself, 'Do but say the word and you shall be new born!' But the empowering word found no uttering, and having run out of padding, he could bring forth no more than "I, I lack the words."

Before he could go on—and he was unsure whether he would—she laid a forefinger to his lips and said, "I care little about words right now." And the lifting-off of this finger was followed by a laying-on of lips, which fell to a hearty mouthing of some unspoken words upon his dumb lips, as if he were to find the missing text of his *libretto d'amore* by aping her mouthshapes.

Such overhelpfulness struck him as rather forward, but then he had heard said back home that Lowland girls were mightily bold, if not outrightly loose—*andere Länder, andere Sitten!** What was he to do now? Try fumbling

---

* 'Other lands, other folkways.'

words again, he thought, as soon as she stops for air. Until then, he would show a stiff upper lip. But he failed to grasp how thoroughgoingly he had quickened this handful of sixteen years.

She took unmawkish hold of him and, with the knack of a wrestler, pushed him down. He thought at first that she wanted him to get down on bended knee, but there was scant opening for that once she had fullfloored him and bestrode him. Indeed, he had hurtled down like a churchbell cut loose in the belfry.

Having breached his mouth, her tongue swirled wildly over his. And having overcome the breastwork of his clothes, yank by yank and rip by rip, her hands swarmed over his flesh, grasping and gripping in their roundroving after longwished-for riches. And it was not long before the wench, emboldened by her steady gains running stepwise from a toehold to a foothold to a bridgehead, hand-over-hand, had tossed aside that flowing housecoat, her only cladding this midmorning, in all her *négligence*.

And as to body, it was the first time that he had ever beheld a naked woman in the flesh. He found her handsome yet somehow unwomanly, like some fair youth who, not yet out of boyhood, had been newly unmanned, and instead of the missing member, there was a great open unhealing wound that yawned hungrily before him, while her laddish chest lay yet sunken in a kind of wintry ungrowth. All this made Godwin wonder whether Henrietta were some kind of a man-of-a-woman or woman-of-a-man, an unwoman or unman. It seemed to him that only the weeds in a way fullmade the woman here, and that topping was no more than castaway now.

And it could not but happen, that that aforespoken wound—a kind of one-eye from the hitherto unbeknown netherworld of underskirts—fell to battening upon his mauled manhood, as if so much toothsome sweetmeat. And here, he felt that she had gone too far. Surely this was not the way hereabouts for a *chevalier* to woo a Flemish lady, or for a Flemish lady to deal with a *chevalier*. But he was stumped about what to do.

It was clear from the enfathoming groundswells flooding forth from her netherspring that it would be no easy task to overpower those pawing hands and now joggling hips, yet he was unwishful to harm her in withstanding her. And so setting his hands upon her shoulders, he strove to kidglove her off, but this only met with nasty bits to his wrists. And so he unhanded her straightway.

Should he let her have her way then? Hadn't fatherly behest been to "wed and bed the wench"? Did it matter if bedding came before wedding? No-one had enlightened him about how he was rightly to handle himself in this business. And yet, bedding her he was not, since it was she who had floored him and, truth-be-told, he would fain have been elsewhere.

With things thus being unspelled-out for him, he wondered further now if this was even lawful. As everyone well knew, it was against the law for a man to rape a woman, but what did the letter of the law say about a woman raping a man? What is good for the gander ought to be good for the goose, one might think. Yet in all the years that he had dwelt within a magistrate's house, where lawtalk was commonplace, he had never once overheard anything like, and he mindplayed that suchlike would meet only with laughter. And further, what if he hurt the girl in stopping her? Would he then be blamed, or might she illwillfully backlash, truthlessly calling him the highhanded one?

And so unable to stop the maiden or to settle his misgivings about the law- or unlaw-fulness of it all, he unwavered himself into leaving well enough alone, or better said, into putting-up and shutting-up. And he knew he could be a masterhand at that. Anyways, if nobody were to find out, what would it matter in the longrun? Besides, it was not as if he were in any pain—far from it indeed. And luckily for Henrietta, it was owing wholly to her very boyish shape that Godwin was able to bear up manfully and keep her busyness blissful.

And so on and away, she worked her will, while the knobbles of her laddish chest above heaved and heaved and tirelessly heaved. So wildly did she howl and groan in all this boarding and grappling that any eavesdropper at the door would have fancied that the room were the setting of some seawolvery or *auto-da-fé*. And Godwin greatly feared that all this would draw prying eyes and angry fists to the *cabinet des curiosités*, and he would find himself in yet another bind of some kind. But he underreckoned by far how truly muffling the stout walls of the Leeuwenhok townhouse were. Why, a man could be racked and wringed in the cellar, and no passer-by without would be the wiser for it.

She rode out this storm, with a wellgrounded boldness and steadiness and setmindedness that would not let her forbear until, in all her crazed deep delving, she at last struck gold, only to downslump lifelessly upon his bescratched and bebitten chest, the bourse of her body, as it were, having suffered a kind of stockcrash.

The rough wooing without soft nothings had come to an end. She came to herself and said, "Oh, we shall go well together, my pet." She got up and donned her housecoat.

Somewhat at a loss, Godwin lay for a bit on the floor, bloody from this first skirmish in the mainstream wars of Venus. Yet this manhandling, or rather womanhandling, had been for him in all his greenhornhood neither blustery squall nor squeamish breeze, neither windstorm nor doldrums. And for all the mugginess of her many enclaspings, he was left partnered with nothing more than the oddish afterfeelings of her cold hands and colder feet, and some unwordable ghostfeeling of loss and missing. And so it was that a weakling of a *petite mort* passed through his body.

He too rose to his feet and sought to do up his once handsome set of clothes. Seeing the shambles that she had made of his duds, she said, "Don't fret about the tears and rips. I will swaddle you in silk, as snugly as a silkworm, my love. Until lunch then!" And with that, she took her leave.

He trod off to his room listlessly, and in climbing the flights of stairs, he feared that he had blundered yet again, as he always seemed to do, no matter what he turned his hand to. Godiva. Godiva indeed! He wished that he had not held his hand but had stood up and stood his ground. But it had all happened so quickly. And worse, he feared that such roughness was a foretoken of things-to-come.

He felt dirty, altogether dirty. He could not wait to reach his room and scrub himself raw. He filled the washbasin with a rough sea of water. He stripped and scrubbed away. But even in this, he would not be left to himself, for kenkeen Charles broke in upon him and was not slow to mark all the telltale tokens of lovemaking: the ripped clothes cast aside, and those everreddening scratches and bitemarks, and a scrubkeen but rather sheepishlooking brother. If anyone could spot Cupid's spoors, it was Charles.

"Why, my dear buggering brother, you are the very darling of Lady Luck, bedded in satin and nibbled on by quim, with the bitemarks to prove it! I never would have thought it, but I see clearly you've risen to the task. What, did you daydream about one of the pretty houseboys while swiving the wench?"

In likewise trod Cruikshank, with his wonted cringing step, who now asked with bated breath, "Well, Mr. Godwin, how did the wooing go?"

"I do not wish to wed."

"My dear lad, we've been through this before! Indeed, you know that this match is your family's wish and your father's bidding. And I hasten to say that such a match is wholly boonful to your own fine self. What a pretty bewitching girl the Miss Henrietta is! Such manners, such graces! And I have seen how she is greatly taken with you, as is the father. And what a handsome house in such a fine town! And the family is rich beyond belief. You shall never want for anything!"

"Indeed, I swear, this great fat Dutchman, like the goose of fairytale, shits gold by the cartload," said Charles.

"But is this right? Misleading the Leeuwenhoks?" asked Godwin, who had stopped his scrubbing.

"My dear lad, your birthline is so lofty that it will sweeten even the sourest dish! Oh, do not fret yourself. Others before you, of your same standing and breeding, have misstepped as well, and perhaps even more greatly, but they outlived a deed that in time was forgotten. Gossip comes, and gossip goes. But such a handsome lad as yourself, with your youth and breeding and background, will surely come to be at the tiptop of townlife here, the apple of every eye."

"You fret too much, Cruikshank. Give no heed to what he says. The business is nearly clapped up by now anyways. He's already bedded the wench."

Cruikshank's eyes began to swirl and whirl, as if lost in whirlpools. And they caught sight of those same telltale tokens of lovemaking. "What! You, you have lain with the girl already??" A guilty look from Godwin was enough of an answer. "Good God, man! If the father should find out!" Cruikshank slumped down. "Mr. Leeuwenhok is not a man to trifle with! If you have lain with the girl, you have no choice now! You must wed her with all haste!"

"But she pushed me into it!"

"There can be no turning back now! What is done is done. There can be no undoing! We must push for a wedding as soon as happenable. And this rueful mishap, we must, with the greatest of care, keep hidden from everyone. And I warn you most earnestly, Mr. Godwin, that if you should foolishly fail to go along, we all will need more help than God can ever give! Forsaking the girl now would be the greatest harm thinkable to Mr. Leeuwenhok!"

Godwin set down his scrubbrush and gave a hopeless shrug.

Cruikshank hastened off, with happy tidings, down to a waiting would-be father-in-law. Was ever a man more overgladdened? Was ever a—why, nearly skipping—heavyweight more lighthearted? Leeuwenhok dragged Cruikshank—the latter nearly gagging from the tight handgrasp upon his collar—into the readingroom, enwalled with books upon books, all neatly enrowed and all nearly all unread. And there the two men, with their finetoothed combs, went over the *contrat de mariage,* which had been handily drafted beforehand—*en français* no less—so as to be ready to hand, *tout de suite.* It was something of a folkway here that wedlock was handled with all the earnestness of trade, with its bonds and writs and the like, such that both parties were lawfully bound by paperwork to keep their sworn word in a most businessmanlike manner, on pain of costly lawing. Ay, the Lowland Cupid brandished a quillpen no less skillfully than a bow!

Once the two men had reached onemanship about the nittygritty of the dowry, Henrietta, Godwin, and Charles were called down to the bookroom, where the *contrat de mariage* was read aloud to everyone, by Leeuwenhok himself, who was most careful in highlighting given weighty parts, underscoring the looked-for outcomes, should such-and-such befall or not befall. A hardnosedness he betrayed herein, which showed him to be—notwithstanding all his wonted jolliness—underlyingly unfain to footle or boondoggle. But no-one could have called him stinting: the dowry was of such greatness that it might buy handfuls of earlships back in cashless wartorn England. The pelfheap was, however, to be handed not to Godwin outright but rather forwarded, by way of Cruikshank, to the father, who was to have and hold the money until the son's twentyfirst birthday.

Henrietta and then Godwin were asked to come forth and underwrite their names to the aforesaid *contrat,* the which was witnessed by a smirking Charles and an almost giggly Cruikshank—how keen the latter was to have this ward off his hands! And then, when its ink had been hothandedly dryblotted, the writ was whisked away into safekeeping.

To Godwin, it all seemed a rather unmaudlinish workaday way to go about wedding. And he had never even asked Henrietta to be his wife, even though she were as good as one now, by dint of paperwork. But no-one else boggled at it, so why should he?

Then followed a beargrip of a fistclasp and a mighty handquake from the proud beaming father-in-law-to-be, to mark and handsel new hopeladen times. No sooner shaken up but hands were stocked with icy wineglasses for a toast. "Drink up, my men, drink up! Be not shy!"

How quickly the whole thing had been clapped up! And how quickly the rest was to be as well. The talkhub shifted straightway to setting a date. The sooner, the better, Cruikshank pushed, for why should the lovebirds be kept apart owing to any laggardliness on their elders' part? And then the door swung open, bringing to sight Machteld, who said that lunch was set forth and they were thus waited for in the eatingroom.

SHINDIGS AND SHINDIES

L IKE GREAT BACCHUSBELCHES, Aeolus' wayward playthings, the winds uppity and unfettered, blustered away this day, making willing or willynilly white sails as roundgutted as filled wineskins and frothy prows as dizzily yawful as any rollicking tipplers. This Bacchanalia in the rigging, tugged to-and-fro by wanton nereids unseen, had ripped Godwin away from Antwerp's walls and now ferried him downstream along the Scheldt to where the winedark sea lapped and licked long stretches of silvery sand, there where sand and wind were seemingly at the beck-and-call of the racekeen. Yes, it was off to the races today with Godwin and his Leeuwenhoks, or rather with the Leeuwenhoks and their Godwin, and with the unshakeable Cruikshank and brother in tow.

As above, so below it was to be—or the other way around—and thus the wine flowed freely down below upon the deck, staining lips and tongues a bloody hue, and all the while, the Leeuwenhok craft pushed its way boldly ahead, striving to overtop the surly waters. But this watery push came to a wishywashy standstill, at the sight of a warship prowling in the near offing. And so it was not long before the Leeuwenhok boat slowed to a full stop as the warship came along boardaboard.

What with all Henrietta's talk of bloodthirsty freebooters earlier, a somewhat worried Godwin wondered if Geert Laps, formerly no more than a tall tale's ghostly wisp, was now truly before him in flesh-and-blood, ready to make them all walk the plank! But no-one seemed greatly upset when a small band of beweaponed men from the warship boarded the Leeuwenhok boat. Indeed, the skipper of the latter greeted the band most slickly, brought forth some great roll of writing, showed it to the band's leader, who seemed happy with what he read therein. After a quick lookthrough of the boat and the handing-over of a baglet, this shortlived tryst of ships came to an end, and the men-of-war returned to their man-of-war and sailed off, leaving the Leeuwenhok bevy altogether unruffled. Kenkeen Godwin now asked after the meaning of all this.

"In truth, my young lord of Etenheighte," spoke Leeuwenhok, "they're sworn foes at war with us, Protestants against us Catholics, for as you see, she flies the flag of the Dutch freestate to the north. And they're the master of these waters, and they keep up a blockade of the Scheldt in their war against us. *Mare clausum* they call it. 'Cripple the Spanish king! Bring him to his knees by pinching shut his blowhole! Tighten a stranglehold to cut off his airway of ships, so that his coffers blanch for lack of ruddy gold!' Such is their stand. But there's always a backhole to crawl through, my young man of Etenheighte, always a *mare liberum* to sail through. And so we more farsighted traders buy warrants from our foes, who for a fee then allow us to sail these waters unhindered."

This was all news to Godwin, for he could not recall any such blocking, boarding, and bypassing in his earlier searfaring-hither. But then he had slept most of his way across the Channel and thus was not awake when a thwarting warship had likewise taken the wind out of *The Simia*'s sails before it too was allowed to pass, thanks to the showing-forth of a like warrant.

"But doesn't this lengthen out the war and make matters worse in the end? Wouldn't it be better to stand boldly, till the bitter end?"

"Now, my lad, we'd do well to leave such matters to statesmen and mind what's on our own plate. A good strong wind today! A handsome day for the races!"

At length, these boaters came aground, faddishly late, even last, it turned out, but hopefully not least. And what a great throng of folk upon this stretch of windy beach! Ay, here in all its blazery razzledazzled a great forgathering of Antwerp's smartset somebodies, gamesome *bon-viveur*-bevies of toffs and swells, staid clusters of bigwigs and bigshots, painterly *tableaux* of unwavering heavyweights, with all their swarmy flunkeying hangers-on, all in some way gogetters and getaheads, keen wouldbes or keening hasbeens, soaring bigplayers or sorry bitplayers. Here stood, stalked, strolled, strutted, or stumbled the crack gimcrackery of swell- and sidekick-dom, everyone and their everything eyecatchingly unshabby—such that outwardly there was no easy telling the up-markety from the down-, all, one, and any hankering, openly or unopenly, after the sweetmeats, or better said, the *bonbons* of highlife.

And into this glister of snooty glitz, far from Jack Rag, Tom Straw, and other homespun byreboobies, amongst all these offish-uppish sticklers for seemingly the uneverydayest things of life, or leastwise for what was every day deemed to be fittingly uneveryday, the Leeuwenhok bevy now peacocked forth, with enough footmen to staff a kingly abode, and strutted towards the tables upstacked with high-off-the-hog tidbits, sweetmeats, and fizzy booze.

This *grande arrivée* turned heads and raised eyebrows, and much of the talk, hitherto of musthaves and mustdos, now yawed otherwards. The Leeuwenhoks would have gladly fallen to flibbertigibbeting-about, before all these peepers and flaunters, and to rubbing shoulders—if not outrightly hobnobbing—with the highstepping oldline, those families of longstanding lofty standing, the toptip of Antwerp. For did not Faret write, in his *L'honnête homme*—and Leeuwenhok knew this gobbet by heart—that

> *tous nos soins doivent être employés à gagner de bonne heure, et par de bonnes voies, l'opinion des honnêtes gens, puisque tout le monde sait combien elle est importante à nous accourcir le chemin qui nous peut conduire à la haute réputation?**

But alack, the Leeuwenhoks did not bear that lofty tiptopsome stamp sported by kingly coinage long in freeflow, and lest they should somehow strike anyone as thickbooted dirtynailed moochers, they hung back a little, loafardwise, striving to feel around them the over- and under-tows.

But birthline, that leash to pull along the pack, was in their hand today, for the son-in-law-to-be stemmed from the topdrawer of life, that strongbox of sweetsmelling lawn, lace, and frill, and there was little worry that this blueblood would meet with any snubbing by even the highborn oldline. Indeed, there was more blue in one tumbler of Godwin's blood than in all the tubs and vats ruddily upfilled by Antwerp's bled best. And such blood

---

* 'We must take every care to win in good time and by good means the good word of upright folk, since everyone knows how weighty it is to shorten the path leading to a good name.'

was as much a costly seldomhood here as painter's bluestone. Unflabbergastingly, the wowkeen Leeuwenhoks had looked forward mightily to this
showful day.

As they sipped their *champagne*, Leeuwenhok seemed to scan the throng
for someone or something, his keeneyeing broken only by Henrietta's icy
under-the-breath "The wineglass is to be held by the stem, not by the bowl."
And hard upon, there followed a hasty blushful sleight-of-hand.

At last, someone was emboldened to come up and chat up Leeuwenhok. In no time, Godwin and Charles were foreworded to the newcomer,
seemingly a duniwassal by the name of MacGregor, although Godwin
thought he had seen the man only the day before lugging heavy bundles
up to the loft of the Leeuwenhok house. In all the asking and answering,
"my son-in-law, the elder son of Lord Charles Drighten, the fifteenth Earl
of Etenheighte," had been by no means whispered, and eavesdroppers, all
prickeared and keeneyed, goggling and gaping, began to draw nearer until
the Leeuwenhok and Drighten bevy, eked out even with Zwartenbok and
Montauciel, soon found themselves ringed round by a crowd.

And now, for the first time in his life, Godwin found that he could say
or do no wrong. He was a something after all, it seemed! And so he held
forth, giddyheaded. And no matter his words, to all those listening at least,
he seemed to speak stately homes and walk glittery balls and stand kingly
likenesses. And amidst all the oohing and ahing and giggly skylarking,
Charles too did his best to flaunt his own Albion stuff.

It was not long until all these flashes and flickerings of blueblooded
highlife lured in bigger game, and all fell speechless when there trod before
them no less than the sister to Antwerp's own boroughmaster, none other
than *mevrouw** Spotter, who, now in the afterglow of youth, was known,
or rather wished to be known, as *Lajeunesse*-Spotter. And this lady was
grandmother to the everfaddish young Jacoba Spotter, the nonesuch of all
unraffishness. Indeed, with her ruby lips, and diamond eyes, and golden
hair, and silver brow, she was reckoned by Antwerp to be a hoard of a
catch, as Jacoba herself well knew. And this twosome of granddaughter
and grandmother were the heart and soul of Antwerp's highlife, as anybody
who was anything knew.

---

* 'Misses.'

"Is it true what I have only now heard say, that we have among us some of England's best?" asked *Lajeunesse*-Spotter.

A jittery Leeuwenhok hastened to speak again of his newly gotten son-in-law-to-be, the next Earl of Etenheighte.

"So it is true indeed! Sir, you are right welcome to our little gathering here!" she said to Godwin. "It is not everyday that we meet men of your mark upon these sands," with a quick glance at Leeuwenhok.

"I fear that you flatter us greatly, not knowing us more narrowly," said Godwin, who was amazed at what a mistress of flawless English this woman was. Little did he know that *Lajeunesse*-Spotter had pretty much forsaken her mothertongue of Flemish, which she deemed so much outlandish chipchop gibberish, and had taken to speaking only French, Spanish, and English, at least most of the time.

"Know you," the woman went on, "that I was once to Whitehall and even saw the king eat with the queen! But that was in happier days! What *bêtise* now holds sway, when kings with their Godgiven right-to-rule are driven from their highseats by upstarts! Beware the *arrière-pensées* of *arrivistes!* Sheer blockheads and puzzlepates and fopdoodles run the world now!" And at each bout of yeaing niddlenoddle, the old wizened frow's dangling dewlap shook livelily, while she dandled her tightclutched little pugdog Ukki, whose snubnose and gaping jaws struggled for breath.

"Why, it was just such draff that has driven my brother from our homeland," said Charles, leaving Cruikshank to wince.

"There is far too much niminypiminy and nambypamby in the world nowadays! What could be more foolish than freestatehood! Damn the Parliament!"

"Oh, granny, let us hear no more about crowned heads tumbling! I am keen to hear if our handsome English guest loves racing as much as we do," interloped the young Spotter, no less a mistress of the king's English.

"I'm most fond of horses, indeed."

"Oh, we do not race horses here!" said *Lajeunesse*-Spotter, nearly smirking. "Let us leave beasts to the field! No, we race most handsomely here. We race in sandyachts." This was news to Godwin, for no-one had bothered to tell him about Simon Stevin's brainchild the *zeilwagen*, a fourwheeled cart fitted out with sails shipwise, which was not uncommonly raced along the

windy strands hereabouts. Indeed, no less than Prince Maurits van Nas-
souwen, in the spring of 1602, had landsailed from Scheveningen to Petten
within two hours, at horseoutstripping speeds.

"My betrothed and I will be flying over the sands in *The Argo,*" interloped
Henrietta.

"Indeed!" said Jacoba. "I hope, Sir, that you have been well taught the ins-
and-outs of sandyachting. I'm known to be one of the fastest yachters here.
My *Scylla* has been beaten only once, and that was only through a mishap."

"Oh, but my betrothed is outstanding in all things," boasted Henrietta,
before Godwin could speak.

"In all things! Well then, I will be watching him so that I might wonder
at his handling of all things," said Jacoba.

"How could anyone do otherwise?" countered Henrietta, as she clutched
Godwin tightly by the arm. But before another word could be uttered, a
great hornblast sounded, calling all landsailors to ready themselves for the
race. "Well, let the best man win then," said Henrietta.

"Or the best woman, as it may be," answered Jacoba.

"Indeed!" answered Henrietta, who trod off to where beckoning windcart-
sails wigwagged in the wind, she all the while clutching Godwin by the arm
in order to keep herself from stumbling, for she sported awkward pattens.

Standing at the ready, all abreast next to *The Argo,* which flew the Cross
of St. George, were the other yachts, yachts that had never felt the swirl of
sea, to wit, *The Pristis, The Centaurus, The Chimaera,* and of course Jacoba
Spotter's *Scylla,* gleaming in purple and gold. And before these carts, there
stretched their *hippodromos*—lengthy enough to hearten a half-Augustus
leastwise—and the midpoint was marked by a great *Colossus* of a stonepile
towering up out of the sands, its lofty head greyhaired from gulldroppings
and downweighted with cackling mews.

The Argo was boarded forthwith by Henrietta and Godwin, and then the
everspeechless Zwartenbok and the chatterful Montauciel, even if the latter
two brought nothing but needless deadweight. But the-more-the-merrier
it was to be. And a tight squeeze it was too, worsened by jittery Montauciel's endless clambering-about. And as Jacoba leered Godwinwards from
her *Scylla,* Henrietta had no choice but to hand over the steeringropes to
her betrothed, who had not the slightest inkling of what to do with them.
Indeed, no-one had even told him the gamerules. But any uttering of

knowledgelessness on his part was forestalled by Henrietta's blunt under-the-breath "Just do as I say," followed by a curt smile Jacobawards.

Once the watchership had taken up its stand on a hillock near the farend, another great hornblast rang out. Henrietta shrieked "Pull!" and *The Argo*, freed from its grounding, lurched forwards, as the wind took over the cart. The other yachts darted forth as well, with *The Chimaera* in the lead. From the outset, *The Argo* began to limp behind, yawing and veering, darting and doddling, which raised not a few snickers and giggles amongst the throng of onlookers.

Henrietta grew most upset and roughly upbraided Godwin, who could do no good now. The onlookers' laughter grew ever louder at the sight of *The Argo*'s paltry showing. At length, Henrietta threw Godwin's cloak over his arms, took a hold of his hands from beneath, and thus in huggermugger began to steer the yacht with great deftness. And so *The Argo* sped forth now, little-by-little gaining on the others.

The Chimaera was still in the lead, followed by *The Scylla*, with *The Pristis* and *The Centaurus* struggling for third place. And as this tight pack neared the *Colossus*, *The Chimaera* began to veer away a little towards to the shoreline, as if readying to give a wide berth to the stonepile, for winnership upon these grounds greatly hinged upon how skillfully one watched one's place and heeded the wind's mastership. But then *The Chimaera* began to falter, as its crew—Lodewyck Bontemantel and Jan de Boer—could not eye-to-eye about how near the *Colossus* they should steer their yacht.

This dithering, which slowed the cart down and brought it unsettlingly near the water, opened up a way for *The Scylla* to slip past, to the wild hand-clapping of onlookers and the wild wingclapping of upping gulls. She sped off down the homestretch, well in the lead.

In seeing how his cartmate had allowed Jacoba to gain the upperhand, Bontemantel grew most wrathful and began to scuffle with his steersman, who ended up tumbling out of the yacht and was left behind lying upon the strand as *The Chimaera* pushed on in Bontemantel's far less skillful hands.

This scuffle set *The Chimaera* behind, allowing *The Pristis* and *The Centaurus* to slip past her. The former of the two whizzed past the pile, even more nimbly than Jacoba, but then this cartlet was in the hands of the everfaddish Wouter de Hooghe and his betrothed Stephanie de Graaf. Jan Leeghwater, the master of *The Centaurus*, was not keen upon being outdone here and so crowded the stonepile daredevilishly but then lost wieldership and smashed into it.

In no time, *The Argo* cleared Leeghwater's wreckage. Then suddenly helpless before a gust, *The Argo* shot ahead, as if a plaything at Aeolus' beck-and-call, and quickly overtook *The Pristis,* and then came along boardaboard with the leading *Scylla.* Now it was neck-and-neck for firstlinghood, along this very narrow and unforgiving stretch of sand.

But this cheek-to-jowling sat well with neither Jacoba nor Henrietta. Nor did the thought of ending merely nextbest. And so it fell out that the one now strove to sideline the other, for this strandnarrow was bounded by the sea to one hand and rough stony turf to the other, and too great a nearness to either would upshoot in a falling-behind, if not in an outright mishap. And so the two cleave-sundered and cleave-sundered as they whizzed along. And with each jolt, when these *zeilwagens* rammed together, a frightened chattering Montauciel took his clambering-about to ever more crazed heights of jitteriness.

These rammings grew ever rougher and rougher, with spinning wheels grating and grinding against spinning wheels, so much so that Jacoba now feared that her *Scylla* might come undone and so shouted, "Keep clear! You drive too waywardly!"

"*The Argo* is manned well enough to keep all under good stewardship!" shouted back Henrietta.

But Jacoba's fear of yachtwreck would not get the better of her. And so again she shouldered *The Argo,* so bruntfully, however, that her axle broke, sending one of its wheels off into the sea. *The Scylla* ground to a wretched standstill, while *The Argo* sped off lightly before her, like a feather on a racegod's breath.

But the roughness of Jacoba's last ramming had sent Montauciel into a fit of madness, and the monkey ended up scrambling onto Godwin's face and digging its nails into his nape. As he struggled to get it out of his hair, he pulled wildly and blindly on the ropes, which sent *The Argo* into an unbridled gallop towards the tide. The cart struck a chunk of wormeaten washup, almost fully overlaid with sand, and then overturned, hurling man, woman, and monkey into the briny.

All eyes had been on the Englishman throughout much of this race, and now all rushed forward, fearing that harm might have befallen the Earl of

Etenheighte. Even *Lajeunesse*-Spotter, who in seeing the mishap had dropped her Ukki, hobbled breathlessly along behind.

As Henrietta rose from the sea, spitting out saltwater, she could see, narrowly beyond the nearing crowd, de Hoogh and de Graaf's *Pristis* sweep past as firstling of the race. Oh, what heartbreak! To be so near and yet so far away! With only a short stretch of race left, sure win had become sure loss, or so it seemed. And as the many began to throng in, the poutling stood there waiting for a hand to help her out of the water, or at least to offer her a dry hanky.

But the helpful busied themselves rather with kidgloving Godwin back to the tilts and tables. *Lajeunesse*-Spotter had by this time caught up, and rushing right up to him, she burst out, "I was all frights that you were killed! Praise the Lord that you are still in one piece!" And swept away by time and place, she reached out and squeezed his hand. "You must call upon us as soon as your racewounds have healed! No, no! I will brook no naysaying! I will not rest until you have brightened our home!" And on she nattered, barking orders to footmen, hers and others', to ready seats and what-not-else back at her great tent, whither the English lord was now led. And once again, the Earl of Etenheighte's son could do no wrong. And therein Godwin basked.

When the heap had begun to withdraw, Henrietta lastly bestirred herself, forsaking her soggy stand at the foreshore. In the end, a dry hanky was offered, even if only from Zwartenbok, who had stuck fast to the landyacht's innards. Henrietta may well have pouted a little longer in the water, were it not for the sight of Jacoba traipsing back. If she could not beat Jacoba acart, then let it leastwise be afoot.

It was with no great blitheness that Jacoba footed it back. She too had been forgotten. And she was not the cockahoop moppetkin that she had hoped to be that day. And the wound deepened when upon her return granny said to her, "Jacoba, I have mislaid Ukki. Go find the rascal!" But any unwholesome words wantoning on the granddaughter's tongue were swallowed down, leastwise for now.

But there were things that needed to be kept up with. And at length, the race having been won and lost, and racing Phoebus having long cleared the heaven's midpoint, the time had come for racers likewise to follow the god's lead and wend homewards. And while saltstained Henrietta lingered in her dumps, the father, however, was all merriness, for Godwin had made a splash, as it were. So it seemed even to the youth himself, and Cruikshank too was keen to underscore that his earlier spaewords—that everything was sure to turn out tiptoppishly for his ward, as long as he went along with the Drighten plan—now seemed well on their way to becoming truth. And this was not altogether irksome to Godwin now.

How snagless his life became in the following weeks, in the leadup to the wedding. To all outward seeming, his life had truly othered itself. Gone were all those lattertime binds and unsettlings of the soul that had hounded him at home, and gone was his father, with his cheerless swineflesh-Sundays, and gone would be Cruikshank right after the wedding, and hopefully also the brother. Yes, *glücklich ist, wer vergißt, was doch nicht zu ändern ist,* or so the saying goes.*

In these foreweddingdays, his time seemed to be taken up with the bustle of unbusyness, with all its housely havetos readying him for the coming husbandly mustdos. In the morning there were bloodless bouts of swordplay with Charles, who always won, but Godwin was not so greatly keen upon fighting—but then who would be, if always dogged with a losingstreak? In the afternoon, there were dancelessons under Henrietta's dancingmaster, wherein barrebound Godwin warred in fumbling French against feet that would not turn out enough to the master's liking, but before such high callings, he—or anyone else—could little hope to win. Yet he did his best nonetheless, so as to glimmer at least, if not sparkle, at all the balls in the wake of the betrothal.

Then there were those stints of fittings with Henrietta's seamsters, who turned out an endless spate of frippery for him, filling cupboard and trunk after cupboard and trunk, so much so that all these handsome weeds would be outfashioned long before outworn, if ever worn. And what a great wearisome deal of time it took, all that standing-about amidst the fiddling-about, and the more the seamsters' fingers struggled to find the flawless faddishmost fit, the more illfitting his duds somehow felt, what with now a chafing collar, now a binding armscye, now a jabbing busk, now an upriding crotchseam.

And when not standing for seamstrywork, Godwin would often see his afternoons wisp away with stints of sleepy stillstanding before a bevy of sketchers and painters hired by Henrietta to churn out scads of paintings sporting the betrothed. And if that was not enough, Cruikshank, upon his

---

* 'Happy is he who puts out of mind what cannot be otherwise.'

return to England, was to have drawings done up of all the Drighten forebears that coated the walls of the Drighten greathouse and was to send these back to Antwerp so that they too might be dolled up in paint and might likewise bedeck the Leeuwenhok walls. In life's aping of stilllife, with a body aching from stillstanding like a marble carving, Godwin nonetheless showed a stiff upper lip and said nothing of his soreness, all in the name of higher art.

But such strife, such strife between the laws of art and the laws of nature, had also stiffened the necks of Henrietta's hirelings—here a learnling of the great master Rubens himself, here one of van Dyck, here of Jordaens, here of Snyders—and none of these could eye-to-eye about how best to bring the groom to canvas. A *sine qua non* for one was that the youth must have Cupid's ruby lips; yet for another the youth must have the stern gob of a Charles V, no less the head of the *Sacrum Imperium Romanum Nationis Germanicae*, or leastwise, if it must be, that of a Philip II. And so on the bickering went, with one school's *modus operandi* warring against another's, which in the end led *de facto* only to a weltering illwilled *modus vivendi*, for *quot capita, tot sententiae*,* however mindslippingly at odds this may have been with the true Leeuwenhok householdly style, indeed, with that of most fadfollowing homes.

Seldom could Godwin make himself out in all the brushstrokes, so skilled was the painter's hand. Or rather the painters' hands, for there were many fingers in these pies. If Godwin's outline had been drawn by one master, his face was painted by another, his feet and hands by yet another, the draperyfolds by still another, and the groom-to-be did not shape up until he had passed through the hands of six or more wellschooled craftsmen. Yet in the end, only one name was underwritten. And nearly every day, at least one further Godwin was proudly hung upon one of the Leeuwenhok walls.

In the offtimes and betweentimes, there was still all that thriftless gadding-about, shopping and streeting. And happily that rough wooing which Henrietta had meted out to him, the morning after his coming to Antwerp, did not once-again itself, for he saw to it most carefully that the twain would find neither time nor place.

All this bustle, however, had to give way before the manifold calls to the drawingrooms and ballrooms of Antwerp's better and best, who never tired

---

* 'As many thoughts as heads.'

of seeing the English blueblood, even if the latter was fellowed unfailingly by the Leeuwenhok daughter and father. But why throw the baby out with the bathwater? Yes, there was no naysaying *Lajeunesse*-Spotter, whose boldness in opening up her doors to the tagging Leeuwenhoks had in turn been aped—willynilly albeit—by nearly everybody who was a somebody.

And herein sturdy little Henrietta kept her head above water most skillfully, for she knew the ins-and-outs of all the unspoken unwritten oughttos and oughtnots, gamerules brainfaggingly endless, yet stealthily breached here and there with the slittiest of loopholes. The father, however, proved to be less deftfooted upon the slippery drawingroomfloors, but his many *faux pas* were seemingly overlooked at their doing, only to be laughed at in aftergatherings, when the pitapatting of embroidered mules and the scroop and choice tittletattle of silkclad frows and frippets were Leeuwenhokfree, *en secret, bien sûr.**

But in one bycorner to this Etenheighte-Leeuwenhok bustle, there arose an angry little whirlpuff that went unmarked. This followed hard upon a tulipbulbsale, one of the many drawing hordes of bloomfanciers, like Henrietta herself, who, together with her father and betrothed, had done the unforgiveworthy of outbidding Jacoba over a *Semper-Augustus*-bulb. This was too much! Who did those bloody upstarts think they were? What! A bit of money—well, more than a bit—and some overbred hobbledehoy from abroad were to make silken purses out of sows' ears! Sow the wind and reap the whirlwind! That's what Jacoba thought, ready for a row.

So it befell that one rainy afternoon not long thereafter, Jacoba sent word that one Diederick Spieghel, an unknowner to the better part of the world, should call upon her that same afternoon. Such calls were far from everyday; only in the oddishmost setups, of a mainly hushhush kind, was his fellowship ever brooked.

Spieghel was enlightened about the newcome English lordling, and his forthcoming bridals with one Leeuwenhok wench, and—why!—the uppityness of it all. To Spieghel it was likewise unshrouded how some bodies here in Antwerp—she could not say which—would be most freehanded to any him so knowledgeful that he might better enlighten these same bodies about how best to grasp the aforesaid matter, for it would be a beweepworthy shame indeed if those with shame to hide were somehow

---

* 'In huggermugger, needless-to-say.'

to get away with befooling their betters, not that Jacoba herself would wish to see anyone's illfare.

And given that she had kindly freewilled to work on behalf of the aforesaid unnamed bodies, she had been entrusted with an unlittle heap of guilders to do with as she deemed fit, all in the furthering of this undertaking. And since she weened that—what with war and pricehikes and the like—the sorry Diederick Spieghel must be cashstrapped, she most givingly handed a tidy sum over to the man, lest he overlook some meaningful snicksnarl for want of ready money to tide him over, above all since he most likely would need to ship himself off to England. Who knows what unbecomingness the great briny wash might be keeping from upright folk here? Thereupon Spieghel was sent packing.

The would-be mudraker hastened down to the wharf to find outfare upon the first Britbound ship he stumbled across, as it were. And stumble he nearly did, when some stripling, having newly unshipped himself and now shoving himself hurriedly through the narrow openings of the throng, when this stripling, I say, banged into Spieghel. The hothead did not even stop to say his sorries but madcapped on, and unluckily so for Spieghel, since this throughhustler could have spared the spy his trip to England, had the tongue in that head been loosened. The newcomer was Godwin's lost friend, Oswin himself.

Oswin in Antwerp! Did we not leave him in Ireland? Yes, in Ireland, which he left, set as he was upon a homecoming, even if he would be wanted—or rather unwanted—dead or alive in England. Indeed, it was death for any shipped-away lawbreaker to back before the end of his outcastship. Yet the youth deemed it all somehow well worth the giving of one's all, so great was the dread of an underlived life.

And so Oswin had come to stand once again upon his old stomping-grounds, having reached, narrowly after nightfall, the threshold of his one-time tumbledown cottage in the nearness of Kingswood. He hoped to find his sister well within, for the thought of her plight and his hand therein had been a great mindsore to him. But in bursting in, he was flabbergasted to find a gathering of unknowners, who were straightway robbed of their merry looks.

"Where's Maddy?" asked Oswin halfthreateningly.

"No Maddy here."

"Who are you, and why are you here?"

"We've newly taken over this croft. Who are you?"

"What became of the folk who were here before?"

"I know not. What's your business here?"

Oswin left the cottage and set off into the darkness, greatly worried that some ill had befallen his sister. At length he came to the toft of Goodwife Hardy, his former nearby neighbour.

"God spare us, a ghost from the past!" gasped the woman, when Oswin came to stand in her doorway. "What do you want here?"

"I'm looking for my sister."

"You'll not find her here," said the woman, who did not keep herself from her work, clearing off the table and setting about the washup after the eveningmeal.

"Where's she gone?"

"Hardset you'll be to find anyone who knows that. Wisped away into the night, as if taken by fairyfolk."

"You've no inkling then of where she went? And why?"

"Gone to hide her shame, I should think, as far away as she might. Not that the wretched lamb had much of a choice, for that stoat of a man Drighten ran her off and let the land to some newcomers."

"And he shall bloody well answer for that, and for other things!"

"'Answer for that'?! Who are you that he must answer to you? He and his brood do as they wish! Even if some are too thickheaded to see it! Why, those rogues he has for sons, they murdered a turnkey of late, and now, it's said, they live high-and-mightily, after all their raping and killing and dallying, and the elder one's to wed some richman's daughter on the mainland. But some are born to happiness and others to hardship."

"The elder son is still alive?"

"He called upon your sister after you sailed. So she told me herself. Said that he was running away, of all things!"

"Running away, where?"

"Some hole called Aunt Twerp, or so the whisper goes."

"'Aunt Twerp' you say?"

"So I've heard. And you'd do well to stay away from where you don't belong! See what sorrow's come of your foolishness already! And did I not forewarn you? But no, no, you would not leave well enough alone. And now you've got a fine kettle of fish to feed upon! If you're wise, which I fear you are not, you'll find some out-of-the-way hideaway God-knows-where, before you yet lose your head for good. Off with you now, before your illluck rubs off on others and you bring further harm. I've no wish to be seen abetting the likes of you." Thereupon she turned her back and washed on.

What should he do now? Where to go? He could not leave his wronged sister in the lurch, could he? No, he would stomp over the whole of England if he must. But where would he even begin such a search? Damn that bloody Drighten for this mess!

He trudged off—one bearing was as good as any other. But before long he downslumped upon soft dewy sod, with his back against a low stonen hurdle. Something within him had rather suddenly brittled away, and he wondered now if he could truly ever find his sister. "Better a dead brother than half a one!" Yes, those were her last words to him. It was not the first time that anyone had turned a back on him. He knew how to live with it. Old bloody hat. Was there a point in pushing on?

The seat of his breeches had by now dankened. He looked down to see that his weary legs were carrying him off along a counterset line of bearing, undoing his earlier footslogging. Shorebound. And he went along becomingly, without any armtwisting, with a heartful of some unwordable hope.

Thanks to those crowns that he had grubbed up amongst *The Coinon*'s wreakage, Oswin had enough wherewithal, and more, for a fare to the Spanish Netherlands, and even for a new set of duds. Why, even from only a little away, he might pass now as a lad of some upright unbumpkinish clan. And so it happened that with a little careful stealth on his part, Oswin now found himself at wharfside in Antwerp this drizzly late afternoon, having newly brushed up against Jacoba Spotter's downcome Dutchman. And after much searching, Oswin came to stand before the Leeuwenhok townhouse by nightfall.

The wrong evening, the wrong hour, the wrong minute, it was for a call upon Godwin, who was wholly wrapped up in shindigbustle, part of all the to-dos leading up to the wedding, now only days away. And merry was the word with this wowfulmost of shindigs masterminded by the Leeuwenhoks, a boot for every bane, wherein it seemed as if fistfuls of guilders had been tossed to the winds, in madcap outlay to enlife Fairyland.

The evening had opened with the most faddish English countrydances.

Leeuwenhok went so far as to have an English dancingmaster, by the name of Monsieur Malpied, brought over to teach the latest: *Upon a Summer's Day; Touch and Take; Woodycock; Hit and Miss; Boatman; Irish Trot; I Love Thee Once, I Love No More; Step Stately; Rose is White and Rose is Red; Fain I Would if I Could; The Slip; The Shaking of the Sheets; The Wish; A Soldier's Life; Prince Rupert's March; Cast a Bell; The Spanish Gypsy; Up Tails All;* and *Heart's Ease.* Notwithstanding the names, which seemed to bode something new, one dance turned out to be pretty much the same pretty thing as the next, yet Godwin forgot his place more than once, making others lose theirs.

There was no dearth of markworthy folk to talk to or of. Among the bidden guests were most noteworthily *Lajeunesse*-Spotter and her granddaughter Jacoba Spotter, in waterbloomish green, and even *Lajeunesse*-Spotter's stay-at-home brother the boroughmaster Joost van Tromp, who had stayed at home in heart and soul.

Then came the highlight of the evening's merrymaking. Instead of some wearisome burbling play, Leeuwenhok had wanted a danced dumbshow blended with song, that is, a *masque,* as such a work was called in England. Many markworthy masques had been given earlier by His Highness King Charles of England together with his French queen, in happier strifeless times.

To this masque in the gamesroom then, Leeuwenhok led his guests. Wishful to play the *galant,* and mindful of a gobbet from his trusty Faret, who said, *"ceux qui sont officieux ne sauraient manquer d'amis, et ceux qui ne manquent point d'amis ne sauraient manquer de fortune,"** Leeuwenhok pulled out his lacy hanky and therewith seemed to dust the seat offered to *Lajeunesse*-Spotter, at the head of the incoming throng.

"If you have misgivings about the cleanliness of this seat, I will not sit here!" boomed the great lady aghast, and then fingering to another nearby, barked, "There! I will take that one!" Before a blushing Leeuwenhok could straighten himself up and stuff away his shameful hanky, *Lajeunesse*-Spotter had seated herself as she deemed fit. Leeuwenhok's heart fell when he saw that she had taken his own seat, for he had meant to keep the handsomest for himself. What could he say now? He could not order such a woman to up and sit elsewhere.

As he stood there somewhat at a loss, all the other seats were quickly

---

* 'The keenly helpful will not want for friends, and the befriended will not want for wealth.'

taken, outtaking the one which the great lady had damned. And given that no less than *Lajeunesse*-Spotter had turned up her nose at that foul seat, no-one else could downcome to sit there either, not even Leeuwenhok, who found himself seatless, like other untimely stragglers to the gamesroom. His great wealth notwithstanding, there were only a bounded number of seats in the house for a greater number of bums, and so he lumbered to the back of the room to find standingroom. There he wondered to himself if he had indeed understood Faret right. His French was not that bad. No, he was not one to be mistaken. Should've let the old bag's ass plop down on it undusted. But shush! It's beginning!

Now opened the evening's enlivener, which was a most cunningly wrought ballet for dwarves, benamed *Zorghvliet*. Here, a bevy of landlubberish lowland dwarves, upstanding in their hard work and godfearing thrift, struggled against a swarm of evil mermannish dwarves, who strove to strip the former of their dry land. But thanks to an unsodden *coup de maître*, a bold and timely *coup de main* led, by way of a bloody *coup de grâce*, to an uneschewable *coup d'état*, all to the handicap of the woeful watery dwarves, in this midgity turfwar.

One of the work's most striking *coups d'éclat*, amidst the unabated *coup-upon-coup*-ing, was the sight of some of the dancing dwarves footing it on stilts, a few of whom took a nasty tumble to the floor, much to the merriness of the forgathered, wherein Leeuwenhok's great barrellaughs could be heard markedly above all others. Such mishaps were surely owing to the heeded new dancefad of greatly turning out the feet, so that one toe looked unsteadily to the left and the other unsteadily to the right, like a husband and his yearling bride newly wedlockweary, but then, *naturam expellas furca, tamen usque recurret.* *

As with the other showful things belonging to this evening's merrymaking, Leeuwenhok had spared himself no cost and had hired the most sought-after wonderworking wrights of playhouse makebelieve and mocklife. And thus, this *Zorghvliet* had been, in the main, the brainchild of the rising star amongst dancingmasters Monsieur Guillaume du Bosquet—better known to his mother as Willem van den Bosch—a master of the *pas grave, glissade relevée,* and *feinte,* who had been helpmated herein by a handful of other French song- and dance-wrights of less lofty name and standing.

---

* 'You can drive Nature off with a pitchfork, but she always keeps coming back.'

While the dwarves of Guillaume du Bosquet's *Zorghvliet* twirled about clockwise upon one toe, as if Dervishes short of a leg, Oswin came to stand outside the Leeuwenhok house. It was dark and rainy. He was tired and hungry. There the sodden youth stood, on two sturdy legs. Somewhere in this great hulking house must be Godwin. How the devil was he to find him in all that? And how to talk to him?

Maybe he could wait in the street until Godwin came forth in his own time. But that might take days of standing and sleeping in the street. Maybe he could throw a pebble at Godwin's bedroomwindow in the night, while all slept. He had heard of suchlike in a story once. But which window was Godwin's? And there were no pebbles underfoot, only great chucky cobblestones, which would surely take out the whole window and raise the house in anger. Oswin was not even sure that Godwin was within. He stood there awhile longer, weighing and mulling.

The sound of the merrymaking within could be heard, albeit barely. The thought weakly padded through Oswin's head that perhaps this was an untoward time to call. Maybe it were best for him to call it an evening—haggard and hagridden as he was—and go now to find a lodging somewhere, and come back in the morning with a rested head and a full belly, when there were fewer goings-on.

But maybe by morning, he would be somehow too late. Maybe some golden opening would be wrenched from his fingers in the betweentime—he knew how that felt!—by a trollish nightthief, while he himself slumbered away like some whelp by a bitch's teat. No, he had come all this way and—blast it!—bootful or bootless, he would not wait for any man's time or tide. To Hell! He was no lesser a being than anyone else, and he, like any other upstanding folk, had no less a right to come calling if it tickled him. What did he have to be ashamed of, such that he might not knock at a bloody door? His duds were not so shabby now as before, and too bloody bad if they weren't!

He stomped up the steps and banged away with the great knocker. And when no answer came, he banged again, and longer, and yet again, until the shaking door seemingly threatened to come loose and fall upon him. At length, a flunkey showed up, a gilded gangly thing, to Oswin's thinking, who unlocked and then asked, *"Wat moet u?"**

---

* 'What do you want?'

Mere gabble to him, that. "I'm looking for a Godwin Drighten. I believe he's staying here. I would like to speak to him now. Do you understand? Godwin Drighten, an Englishman."

The gilded thing eyed Oswin from head to toe and then said in the king's English, "He is not free now," whereupon he meant to shut the door in Oswin's face but was forestalled by Oswin's timely footthrust into the doorframe.

"It's of great weight that I speak to him. You must tell him I'm here. I will not go away until I see him!"

Seeing that the youth would not be downfaced, the footman opened up and let him into the forehall. With a rough order to "Wait here," the gilded thing then went off in search of Godwin. When the flunkey reached the crowded gamesroom, where *Zorghvliet* was in midflow, he saw from the door that Godwin had been seated at the very forefront, beside *Lajeunesse*-Spotter, and nowise could be reached now for the tight pack of bodies.

Charles, who had taken up a stand at the very back, and who had been hardset to mask his scorn for Leeuwenhok's capered "freakshow," as he dimly deemed it, now settled upon leaving before the end. And as he left the room, the footman came up to him and enlightened him about a newly come Englishman most keen to see his brother. Charles would see the man in the bookroom.

"Well, well! The ghost of the shipped-off swain! What, have even the clodhoppers in Virginia spit you back across the sea, having as little use for you? What do you want here?"

"Not to see you, unless skewered alive."

"No less cheeky before his betters, I see. But, alack, some things do not better themselves. If you have come about some new fondling of a sister's wellhandled goods, I swear that I'm altogether guiltless, as I happen to have been here for some weeks now and could in no wise have had any business with the wench, unless she peddles her tarnished wares here now as well."

"It's the touch of some that tarnishes."

"What's your business here?"

"I've come to see Godwin."

"My brother's not in."

"When will he be back?"

"Not for a very long time."

"Then I'll wait till he's back."

"You're not welcome to stay."

"I care not."

"Let me be frank. I'm my brother's keeper here, and I mean to keep him on the straight and narrow."

"Did he ask to be kept?"

"Were you asked to come?"

"No more than my sister was asked to be raped!"

"'Raped'?! I would put it no higher than taken unawares."

By God, this was too much! How dare the bastardly lout! And with a scream "You dog!" Oswin hurled himself at Charles, knocking him to the floor, and bestriding him, began to throttle the life out of him.

The high words and sounds of struggle within drew the footman, who had been standing outside the room. How hardset the man was to pull Oswin off the nearly plumblue Charles, and not before Oswin had nearly bitten off the man's finger. The threesome tussled and scuffled fiendishly, out into the forehall, out through the maindoor, and out into the rainy street, where Charles and the flunkey got the better of Oswin. As blow fell upon blow, and as rain beat upon his back, until he could no more, all went still and blank and hushed.

Bittersweet sleep had come and now stayed and now stayed. And it was nearly two days before that likeness of true death died away, allowing Oswin's blackened eyes to halfopen and strive to unblur themselves. The world began to show itself in splotchy black and white, until the outlines of a man and woman could be made out.

*"Hoe gaat het met u?"** asked the woman, who had become aware of Oswin's waking and rose from her desk cluttered with old papers and trod near.

Oswin was suddenly feargripped and tried to get to his feet, but his battered trunk could rise no more than a hand's breadth. Looking around him, seeing that he lay on a cot in some dodgy backroom, seemingly both a kitchen and a workroom, he asked worriedly, "Where am I?"

"You're at the *Duivel aan de Ketting,* an inn near the dockyard. I'm Percy Dighel, and this is Wilhelmina Brinkman, the innowner," said the man.

"You're English?" asked Oswin.

"Yes, albeit an outcast one. And you, my good man, were nearly a dead

---

* 'How are you?'

one. We had almost given up that you would outlive the nasty thrashing that someone dealt out to you."

"Water off a duck's back," said Oswin, easing himself back down onto the cot, between sudden stitches and stabs of pain.

"So the young Englishman has a taste for fighting! A man after my own heart!" cackled the woman.

"How came I to lie here?"

"By happenstance I found you headfirst in a tangle of ropen net hanging off the edge of the wharf and brought you here. It would seem that someone had taken a great misliking towards you and meant to throw you into the water, after your thrashing."

"Damn the bastards! They shall answer for this! As soon as I'm up and about."

"Well that won't be for a while! Oh, they've made a fine mash of you! You're bluer than a ripe plum!" cackled the woman.

There was little that Oswin could do about anything, in this his lowly fettle, as a further bootless trial to stand proved. He had been brought low, and here he would have to bide, leastwise for a few days, however much he might kick. And thus began a groggy stint of bedriddenness, with bouts of wakefulness ever coming and going, over the following days. But youth, for once, was on the youth's side.

How lucky for Oswin that his would-be tumble into the Scheldt had been thwarted by entangling rope, a net like some great devilish nest of snakes. And how lucky that Dighel had happened upon him that night and was kindhearted enough to bring him back and care for him. Indeed, over the following days, Dighel fussed over Oswin like a mother about a sickly child. It did his heart good to have the fellowship of a countryman. It was a while now since the man had seen England, whence he had fled choicelessly. He had written too many chapbooks bashing first King Charles' rule and then Parliament's heavyhanded taxing. And there lurked within him the belief that henchmen of king and Parliament were shadowily afoot after his head, and in such a bind, he needed to watch his back and befriend whomever he could.

Within days, Oswin was well enough to sit up and even stir about a little. He was soon set to chopping onions, for he had to do something to earn his keep; so he was told. The task of taking a heavy knife to those bloated bulbs was not, however, altogether irksome, and so heated he would become that he more than once cut his finger, or his eyes fell to tearing, such that he could no more.

And thuswise, things plodded along for Oswin until one midmorning, by the end of the week, Dighel, the evernewskeen Dighel, burst into the kitchen with tidings. "What a heap of talk there is in the streets! There's some bigwigwedding today. Anybody who's a somebody will be there. Folk have already begun crowding about the *Vrouwekerk* to gawk and gape. I've never seen the streets so alive."

"And who's to be wedded?" asked Brinkman halflistlessly, busy with her reckonings.

"A dandy English lord and the daughter of some Croesus of a business-man here in town."

"What family does the girl belong to?" asked Brinkman, now kenkeen.

"I heard the name Leeuwenhok."

"Leeuwenhok!" she rasped. "I'd sooner see that bitch of a brat on a spit! And the father as the burning coals beneath it!"

"Who's the English lord?" asked Oswin.

"A Drighten, I think they said. What? Have I said something wrong?" asked Dighel, as Oswin hastened out.

Where had his head been these past days? Playing the lieabout and kitchenmaid! And now it seemed that a golden opening was ready to shut itself up on him. He began to halfrun, wincing at each painful stride. He did not need to stop and ask anyone where the church stood, for its towers lorded it over the town's skyline, for all to see.

This was indeed the day of bridals for the Leeuwenhoks and Drightens. And what a fuss the wedding had already spawned in the streets, bloated with hundreds of carriages parked everywhere, with crowds of folk stopping and talking and wayblocking, not to speak of the workadaybustle at its busiest. What a to-do to push through! It seemed that a camel could more easily pass through the eye of a needle than Oswin through the streets of Antwerp!

However eyepopping all the needlework and silks, and ogleworthy the costly stones, and fairytalelike the lordly bearings, the day had begun not so handsomely for one of the keyplayers. With guts gurgling, that's how it started for Godwin, all gurgling and rumbling early that morning, until it seethed outright uproarishly. Why, it seemed that illness after all would strongarm him into taking a raincheck on his wedding.

When news of this upheaval reached Cruikshank, the halfclad warder madcapped into Godwin's room, where he found the groom heartily upspewing nearly everything that had been stuffed into him.

"Oh, I'm unwell! I can't go to the wedding today!"

"But everything's set! You must, Mr. Godwin, you must! Think of what your father would say if you didn't! You must bear up and ready yourself lest we be late!"

"Oh, I cannot!" Fresh upchuck.

Tizzystricken, Cruikshank dashed off to Charles' room.

"What a load of rubbish this is! He never makes things easy!" grumbled Charles, upon coming and seeing his brother retching into a bedpan.

Inbetween the fetchupfits, Charles and Cruikshank saw to the cladding of the groom, who at length, mug- and gob-cleansed with a wet hanky, thought that he might be up to bearing with it after all, even if he felt weakly empty. And by-and-by he found himself at the foot of the *Vrouwekerk,* or the Church of Our Lady. In a fleeting stop at the threshold, he gazed up, his eyes tugged up by the overhead churchclockclang, and he saw the stiff hand heed the bidding of the oily gearworks. Noon, right on the nose, and the curling lips of Father Time.

The groom having found his allotted place, the Flemish wedding began in earnest, and—of all things—in English, for Leeuwenhok had done the unheard-of of having a priest shipped over from greenergrassed England to do the knotting, in one further wowful *coup de théâtre.*

On pattered the man-of-the-cloth, and on ticked the clock, until that time of asking came which a man with a past dreads to hear, and Leeuwenhok began to fidget on his hard bench. Yet who had ever lived to see Hymen's rites undertrodden by an inrunning bearer of illtidings, loosed at the last? Such things belonged to the twistywisty plots of badly cobbled tales, did they not?

"If any man hath grounds why these two may not be brought together in holy wedlock, let him speak now." Both Leeuwenhok and Cruikshank grew dizzy from bated breath in the pindropstillness following. It came, it went. The worst was behind. Or was it?

"Will you Godwin Drighten, take this woman, Henrietta Leeuwenhok, to be your lawfully wedded wife, to have and to hold from this day forward, for better or for worse, in sickness and in health, until death do you part?" Having spoken these words so umpteenfully often, Rev. Dudley did not even need to peer into his prayerbook to find the fitting words and shut his eyes in not doing so. Again a pindropstillness, again bated breaths. At length a hem and a cough, which brought forth "I, I do." It came, it went. The worst was now behind.

A hasty yeaing answer from the bride led to the allowed bridal kiss. But a backfling of the veil was followed by a backjerk of the head, as bride's lips met groom's lips, and as the bride's nostrils whiffed the groom's foul breath, a leftover from the morning's fetchup.

It was all over now. The witnesses to this holy bonding fell to tittletattling amongst themselves as they upped and began to flock forth from their benches, drawn in tow by the leading bride and groom. And all had something to say or leastwise to think hereupon. One guest fancied in his unspoken thoughts how happy the lusty youth, to lead a callow young maiden like that to the bridal bed, to pluck there the untouched ruby bud from such a tender green shoot of a girl. Elsewhere, *Lajeunesse*-Spotter bemoaned to her granddaughter, in English, "What a handsome youth he is! If only he had been more handsomely bestowed!"

"Handsome is that handsome does," muttered back Jacoba, with a wry smile.

Further ahead of them, Charles spoke softly to his warder, "Well, it's all clapped up now, Cruikshank, with tubs of guilders to show for it. What a smile that'll put on the old man's face! And you, you lucky dog, will be back in England by Sunday, while I'm stuck here. How I loathe this land of dikes and drains, and these boggy upstarts, these the crablice and cheeseworms of Europe, who speak English too well!"

"My dear Mr. Charles, you must bide your time. Your brother will keep you in fair fettle here, until your father may find a place for you."

Coming to a stop on the steps, the bridegroom breathed a sigh that, yes, he had risen to the task after all. He had been ordered to wed and bed the wench. His job was over. It was all out of his hands now. And Henrietta, oh, she had gotten her man at last, and the grinning bride gazed out at the onlooking throng that filled much of the square, prating and taking in the showfulness of it all.

Oswin only now reached the square. Fearless of afterclap, he thrust his way through and rushed up the steps, coming up against the bridal pair. Who here would have looked for such a heftless guest, still thought dead, if thought of at all? Godwin had never learnt of Oswin's calling the night of *Zorghvliet*, for Charles had ordered the footmen most threateningly neither to speak of that happening nor to open the door to the swain nor to take any word or letter from the same, should he somehow rise from his watery grave, into which he was thought to have been dumped.

And now the unlooked-for came to be looked upon.

"Oswin! You're alive!" Godwin nearly shouted.

"You've wedded."

"It seems so," said Godwin, leaving his bride and coming down a few steps to Oswin.

"Why?"

How this word topsyturved Godwin! "It, uh, it came my way, I guess."

"Come away with me."

"What, now?"

"When else?"

"But—"

"A 'no,' and we'll be gone."

Godwin stood there, his head all awhirl as if in eddying water, for oh, how the nearness of the swain thrilled through his being, and he found himself helpless now before this ghost from the past, who seemed to warlock up before Godwin's eyes sights of forgotten meadows and leafy groves. Overwhelmed, he turned to his bride, standing only yards away, and said, "I don't think I can wed you now."

"What do you mean?! You're already wedded to me!"

"I don't think that I can be your husband now."

"But you've already sworn before God to be my lawful husband forever! You've sworn it in a holy oath! You've given your word! You cannot take it back now! Who is this unknowner, that he should make you waver now? Send him away, or I shall!" A blank look from Godwin. She trod forth, and with a rough thrust to Oswin's sore shoulder, she ordered, *"Maak dat je wegkomt!"** (So shaken was she that she lost her English altogether and had backslipped into her mothertongue.) But how much more shocked and

---

* 'Get out of here!'

shaken she was when Oswin angrily shoved back, such that she staggered back and fell.

No-one had ever made so bold with her before. No-one should get away with it now, least of all some upstart from God-knows-where, above all on this her longawaited day. A sudden onrush of fear, fear of loss, clouded her eyes, as they saw happiness about to slip away somehow. She could not bear it, and overcome, she got up and began to whip Oswin with her nosegay, bidding him in Flemish to be off, as much as her tears would allow.

Like nearly everyone else, Godwin stood by and gawked on dumbly, until Charles ordered footmen to drive off the weddingcrasher and stay the bride. And as the latter squirmed against her holders and blubbered unwieldily, and as footmen hastened forward, Godwin grasped Oswin's hand and, trusting to his footmanship, drew Oswin along behind himself, down the steps and into the milling crowd, which either twitted and taunted or smirked and laughed.

The footmen stopped at the foot of the steps, where the unruly mob began. Shrieks from Charles to follow after were not enough to make them overtake the flightlings now lost in the crowd, and so the manhunt was given over.

In the madcap dashaway, Godwin thought to himself, what a breeze this had turned out to be, this barefacing of Hymen and offing of wedlock! Why, no more than a walkaway! But he was at length strained to stop, having run out of breath and having outrun Oswin, who could not keep up.

In the end, without any further sightings of their followers, they reached the *Duivel aan de Ketting*, where Oswin the bigspender had himself and Godwin lodged in the roomiest room. To all seeming, they had come off losslessly, nay, gainfully, and to Oswin's thinking, this called for the merriest of evenings. And that meant the broaching of casks to ease all the catching-up.

"But is it wise to linger here? Should we not find outfare on the next boat this very evening and be gone for good?" asked Godwin thoughtfully, even a little worriedly.

"I've footed enough for one day. Besides, we've done nothing wrong. What can they do to us now?"

He was likely right. Surely it was all dead-and-done-with now. Why rush? It was all out of his hands now, in any wise.

And so thinking the Flemish fling to be over, the two sozzled away until they were besotted, which did not take long, for little did they know that the brewers here strengthened their brews with belladonna, or other such drugs as thornapple, which sent the too eager quaffer into the heights and depths of drunkenness unbeknown to these two. But this day, Oswin and Godwin cared not: the world could slide, and the Weirdsisters could go abegging. Such at least were their last thoughts before downslumping into the clutches of a snory drunkenness.

BACKWASH

OEOS, GODDESS OF THE DAWN, thou comst too soon, drawing behind thee the harshest light! Oh, wherefore the rush, the heartless shove to night? Canst thou not slumber a little longer?

No, she could not. No, she would not. Why, she had already come and gone by the time hungover Oswin rose, the late, late foggygroggy morning after, on this first day of a brideless honeymoon. Indeed, by the time Dighel and he had set out for the wharves to find fare upon any outbound ship—Dighel's knowledge of Flemish far outstripping Oswin's—the stiff hand of the clock was already fingering high-and-mightily.

However unwell Oswin may have felt, he at least was fit enough to rise and walk, unlike Godwin, who still lay hopelessly lost to the world and was thus left behind. Thank God for dear ol' Dighel, who seemed to know all the ropes here and so led on, all eyes-and-ears. But it was not long before those eyes, ever watchful for any lurking could-be headhunters after his noggin, caught sight of something seemingly unwholesome looming ahead. While everything was a kind of blur to Oswin, Dighel, however, keeneyed five thuggishlooking men, one of whom fingered at the two, and now all of them began to hasten towards the two meaningfully.

Down a narrow bylane Dighel and Oswin rushed to get out of sight, and into a tumbledown storeshed filled with shippingboxes they whisked themselves. And there in the darkness, they stood still and breathless, until they saw, through the wallcracks, their afterfollowers hurtle past.

After a bit, Dighel said, "I think we've given them the slip. We'd best

get back to the inn and keep low awhile. The boat'll have to wait for now."
And back they slunk, to unsettling tidings.

"So the man-of-the-hour is back!" hooted Goodwife Brinkman, big
with knowing. "Folk are looking high-and-low for you, folk of a none too
sweet kind. Like a bruised plum, they said. That's how he looks," and she
cackled. "And like a crushed plum, that's how you'll look once they get a
hold of you!"

Dighel began to fidget frightfully, for he mindspun that this talk was
somehow meant for him, until the woman went on. "And your mate, they're
looking for him too. And they even had his face painted on a bit of sailcloth,
showing it in the street to passers-by. And they were here, the great lum-
moxes, asking if I had seen two Englishmen, one thrashed and the other as
painted on the sailcloth. And they're ready to yield a handsome penny to
anyone with knowledge of your whereabouts."

"They're after you and your friend!" sighed Dighel, who seeing himself
in the free, straightway left the room.

Oswin found Godwin idling in their lodging and told him of the latest.
The two went back down.

"What did you say to the men who were asking about us?" asked Oswin,
almost threateningly.

"First, you'll tell me what you're wrapped up in," she said cagily.

Fearing that Oswin might worsen things, Godwin spoke up at once,
telling the woman of his part in the botched Leeuwenhok wedding.

"Leeuwenhok!" growled the woman. "Oh, that shifts everything!" She
sat on stilly, lost in seething thoughts. Both Oswin and Godwin were at a
loss to know whether he had worsened their lot by namedropping.

At length Oswin asked again, "What did you say about us?"

"I told them that, if their gold was good, I would keep a sharp eye out
for those they were seeking."

"So you mean to betray us?"

The word *betray* nettled her. "I would dig out my right eye if it would
shorten his life! I curse the man and his kind, and this dunghill of a world
for having spawned him! And I see from your blank mugs that you know
nothing about him. Oh, you are babes that have blundered into a lion's den,
like forgotten others before you! Bitter will be the grudge he bears you now.
And he will not rest until you are grub for his hounds! Few here know what

lies behind Leeuwenhok. Deadmen tell no tales, as surely as pain is the last gasp of mirth. But I will say no more about bygones."

What to make of this tearless sadsack halfstory? It did come to Godwin's mind that in all his time as Leeuwenhok's guest, nothing had ever been said about Leeuwenhok's background, nor had anyone ever asked about it, and so maybe there was some truth here. And the whole truth here was that the two knew not the half of it, not even half of what had befallen the day before, in upshot of their scotching the wedding. But then, they had not bothered to ask.

And what did happen the day before? Why—let us be no mincespeech— nothing short of a clusterfuck. The cut-and-run twain had left behind a more-than-overwrought Henrietta wailing in the arms of footmen, until overcome, she stooped low in a painful cringe. And when one fishwife at the foot of the churchsteps bellowed out, "Looks like the heifer will drop her calf aforetime!" many of the more scathehappy in the mob broke out into wild cackling. The bride, nearly jackknifed, was swiftly straitjacketed out of all sight, into a soon-homebound carriage. This showfulness illwowed the more dyed-in-the-silk lofty weddingguests, such as *Lajeunnesse*-Spotter, who asked in unbelief, "Was wedlock ever wound up and dragged down so quickly?"

"Have you seen enough, Granny?" asked Jacoba.

"More than enough! Let us go!" And this withdrawal of Antwerp's best led in turn to a quick melting-away of Antwerp's better.

But Leeuwenhok had too much on his plate to cater to weddingguests. As Henrietta writhed on in pain, one soon marked that her skirt was stained. Blood! Alack! The girl was truly unwell! Home at once! Fetch Dr. Pot! Make haste, blast you! But how was one to hasten when the streets were swollen with bodies keen to see those who now did not want to be seen?

Home at last, and bride to bedroom, hithering and dithering house-maids, skirt dappled red and white, clean towels! Hustle! At last Dr. Pot! Out everyone! No, two maids stay! A glass of strongwater for the father. A hard seat in the hallway outside the room. He could not afford to lose her. Shush! A long wait. An *Ave Maria* or two, God spare his lamb! Tears. At length, an opened door and Dr. Pot. What blasted illness? Will she live?

"My dear Mr. Leeuwenhok, do put yourself at ease. Your daughter is out of harm's way now. She has undergone a great shock and needs rest."

"Speak, man! What ails her?"

"Love's dart, untimely shot, if I may word it thus."

"'Love's dart'?! What twaddle is that? Speak Flemish, man!"

"To be blunt, sir, your daughter has miscarried."

"'Miscarried'? How can that be?"

"As I said, sir, love's dart untimely shot."

Leeuwenhok first blanched and then blackened. "Why, the strumpet!"

"Sir! Your daughter needs rest. You'd do well to leave her alone for a while."

"And you can kiss my ass! Where is the slut? Out of my way, or you'll be the one needing a doctor!" Leeuwenhok burst into the room.

Dr. Pot was not wrong. Yes, there had been more to that little roundness of her belly than a woman's hummock of Venus, for in that onetime lovemaking with Godwin, the greenhorn heartgushy girl had given no thought to the needfulness of some kind of birthblock, but then why should she have, given that he would be bound to her soon enough?

And there was to be no burking of this sooterkin now, even if she had hitherto blindsided her father, and the whole world, to the little stowaway that had lurked in her womb. And no great task that had been, leastwise in the beginning, for it was only latterly that the wombling began to bring Henrietta queasiness amorning, robbing her of her landlegs. But even that had been fullhidden by her cleverly shamming, nearly every morning, bouts of womanly peakiness, wherein it behooved her to lie late abed, like any other faddish young lady. Yet now in hindsight, it was sure to seem to any old seadog almost as if the little stowaway had known that he was some kind of contraband and therefore cagily jumped ship when scarcely out of harbour, to the end of sparing himself some dicey or gainless landfall following a shaky seacrossing, the wretchkin's wee heart having perhaps misgiven about even the seaworthiness of his stormtossed stealthcraft.

And the telltale little hatchling of a rascal, scarcely enwombed and now cheekily unwombed, would surely not have rued missing out on the outburst at hand, wherein the father came boardaboard, laid to and laid on, letting into his own flesh-and-blood, with "Loose Slut!" and "Whoring Hussy!" and "Tuppencetootsie," and "As untrustworthy as a leaky freighter!" What brashery, to have thrown away everything on soft nothings! And to have his house made into a playhouse of besmirching play!

Yet it was well known to the father, even if not to the daughter, that—as far as the roughhewn would deem—Henrietta herself rightly belonged to bastarddom, or better said, had been born out of wedlock, in huggermugger albeit, or at least in unknownness, for in that rank into which she had been born, lawfulness of birth weighed little. But the father had since taken steps that no-one would ever find out, and things were otherwise now. And at the back of his mind, Leeuwenhok wondered if the wench had somehow turned out addlebrained after all, perhaps owing to some kind of botched bedding of the mother, or owing to her having sucked shrewishness from the teat of her bearer.

To the daughter, how greatly flabbergasting this all was, such hitherto-unknown unkindliness from one's own kindred. But not to be gainsaid or downfaced anymore than the father—for as the old sing, so the young pipe—Henrietta backlashed, "What would a great luggard like you know about anything that does not stink of dirty seachests and smudgy ledgers?"

How dare the waspish little floosie speak to her father thus! Who was the dirty one here? By God! He would wash her mouth out! Treading to her bedside, he yanked away the bedding, ripping lace loose, and took rough hold of the bedling, drew her from her hideaway between the sheets, and dragged her by the hair to the washbasin. And taking up a brush and splashing it in, and nearly thrusting her head into the water, he began to scrub her mouth with the greatest of roughness. He would teach her cleanliness and daughterly beholdenness. Did she not know that the law did not stand up for bastards nor bringers-forth of bastards? Did she not know that the lofty would not stand for bastards nor bringers-forth of bastards? And did she not know that Leeuwenhok would not stand by bastards nor bringers-forth of bastards?

She had thought it was going to be all cakes-and-ale. And now she was overwhelmed by the saddening truth that her own family had snipped her heartstrings unfeelingly. And like an unstrung puppet, she fell into a heavy sobbing heap afloor, outhowling any banshee, with all the heartache of being thrice jilted on the same day, by her would-not-be husband, her would-not-be son, and now even her own would-not-be father. And there she lay, unstoppably blubbering, earless and eyeless to Leeuwenhok's further shrieks and twits. Seeing that bootless was all further rant, and having had his fill of her by now at any rate, Leeuwenhok turned his back on his daughter, boonless thus upon wedlock's barrow, and lumbered down to the readingroom.

My God! He had misreckoned. The unhappenable had happened. Lurking underbeliefs had cozened him into fancying that wedlock could be as binding as any businesslike wordbond underwritten on the wharf. Oddish thoughts indeed, for one who had rid himself of a wife early on!

There he sat and brooded, adrift in mindhaze, for the rest of the day. Yet under the sway of hardy ingrained seamanship, his mind with time selfsharpened, busily taking bearings. Although it had borne in upon him overwhelmingly that his highclimbing was not the laze-about picnic he thought it would be, he nonetheless heartsoothed himself with the afterthought that all was not yet lost. Where there's a will, there's a way. He had overlived greater setbacks than this. As his head, all awash with brainwaves for the morrow, began to sink into dimmed wakefulness, heartened Leeuwenhok turned in.

Yet for all the man's dusky hopefulness, the following morning would find the Leeuwenhok household in even greater uproar and kerfuffle, with daughter and father once again at loggerheads. It had been clear the evening before that he first needed to weigh up the full breadth of the harm done about town. To this end, Leeuwenhok rose early, primped himself out most handsomely, and set out breakfastless into the hopeladen forenoon.

As his spotless coach made its way swimmingly through the streets, he seemed the very pink of a *Laughing Cavalier*, for he had sworn to himself the night before that he would not stoop to unwarranted hopelessness. Neither lackguts nor pussyfooter was he! No, he would live to see any scouting sleevelaughers heartily choke on their chortles! He would out-sticks-and-stones them, by God! If Fortuna be rough, be rough with Fortuna, for there was nothing that a good clout could not mend.

The coach stopped before the boroughmaster's house. Leeuwenhok had never called alone there before without Godwin in fellowship, but there was a first for everything. Knock, knock, who's there? The boroughmaster not at home. Very well, next on the list, the boroughmaster's sister, *Lajeunesse-*Spotter. Knock, knock again, curt footman, the lady not in. Well enough, off to the next. By the thirteenth and last call, it was clear that no-one was at home to Leeuwenhok today. What letdown. This did not bode well. There was nothing else for it but to home. Try again tomorrow. *Uitstel is geen afstel.**

The coachman meant to back by way of the *Vrouwekerk*-square. What

---

* 'Put off is not put away.'

a booboo this turned out to be. The coach soon found itself stymied in a bottleneck, as the roomth all around was suddenly filled by throngs of folk, coming out of the woodwork, as it were, and there was no going-back either, for the way-behind was no less plugged up. Peering out of his coachwindow, Leeuwenhok saw that a makeshift platform had been set up, and some skit had begun, the handiwork of a wayfaring band of Italian players.

A cowed and rueful Scaramuccia (played by the great Sebastiano) is led to an altar at gunpoint by an angry doddering old Pantalone (the everfunny Venetian Tagliavene), the latter weakly shambling along behind in illfitting houseslippers, while yet struggling to hold up in his jittery arms a far too heavy musket. Waiting at the altar is Pantalone's daughter, the ugly Isabella (played by Bastardi), who is big beyond belief with child. This shotgunwedding is stalled time and time again, through all manner of slapstick, with Scaramuccia at one point unrulily drinking the holy wine, only to pass out, and then be brought to by smellingsalts, which leads in turn to a sneezingfit, wherein a buffeting "Achoo!" floors the priest and fouls Pantalone's face.

The whole wacky rigmarole is cut short by a weddingcrashing Arlequino (the tumbler Urano), who flipflops into sight, like a drunken whirlwind twisting head over heels. He takes rough hold of Isabella, whom he kisses with such brunt that their lips become stuck together, and only after much hard pushing-apart do their lips pop apart. In a great fit of anger now, Isabella backlashes at this cheeky interloper with an illswung fist, which in missing its target strikes the priest by mishap, laying him out cold. Scaramuccia then jumps into Arlequino's arms, quaking and biting his fingernails. Arlequino's knees begin to knock together as well, and the rogue takes to his heels, carrying off Scaramuccia still in his arms.

Isabella orders her father to fire at them. The old man struggles to hold up his heavy musket, which misfires. He bangs the musketbutt down in anger, blunderingly hitting his own toe, and the gun goes off, blackening his face and bringing down a stork, which falls on the graybeard's head, as he hops about dizzily on one foot, with the banged toe held in his hands.

Isabella, utterly overwrought, now stoops low in a painful cringe, in the sudden throes of birthing. A string of worried housemaids and footmen rush forth and, lined up tug-of-war-wise, heave and draw, towing the family line, as it were, and lastly, to the pop of a stopple, pull forth a piglet out from under their mistress' skirts, one tugging footman falling back upon the other in a pratfall. The newborn is shown to Pantalone, who swoons for shame.

Unlike most of those forgathered there, Leeuwenhok failed to find any funniness herein, in all his now sourish upset. And, what is more, he would fail to understand the deeper meaning of the whole until some time later.

Painfully keen to be on his way, he thrust his head out and bellowed to his driver to go on—bodies blocking be damned!—and began to shout, evermore churlishly, at those in his nearness to make way. The crowd roundabout began to finger and laugh at him and began to throng about his fastness even more tightly. Some pushed themselves up against the sides of the coach and stormily rocked it from side to side, tossling Leeuwenhok within.

The coachman brought curse and whip, jackboot and horsepower to bear, and the mob gave way. Yet not to be outdone by such pushiness, some, having stripped a few hawkers in their midst of their goods, pelted the coach with eggs as it drove off.

It seemed an endlessness before Leeuwenhok reached home, where a deeply furrowed brow towed him out of the dirty skin of his coach, over his brightly scrubbed threshold, and into the welcome enwalling of his eyecandied house. The sweating slamming puffer was barely behind the door to the sittingroom when there suddenly upspoke a hoarseness from one corner, "Good morning, Skipper!" The bobbing buoy of a body belonging thereto rose swiftly. A quick glance brought to sight a brawny roughhewn man wellknown to this "Skipper," to wit, one Hendrik de Keyser, Leeuwenhok's longtrusted righthand in murkier hushhush businessdealings.

"'Good'?! Good for what?" snapped Leeuwenhok. He sank down in his seat, slightly irked, above and beyond the great upheaval within his heart, by this lowly tag "Skipper." He nonetheless let it pass, as always, in the knowledge that the word cropped up not by choice but through old ingrain.

De Keyser, whose rugged outwardness belied an even rougher inwardness, was not a man to flinch from grasping the nettle, and so most businessmanlike, he cut to the chase. "Home ashore early this morning, I catch wind, on the wharf, of great mistalk touching yourself, Skipper. It is the talk that the English lord newly wedded to your daughter is a wanted outlaw in England, who latterly was found guilty of sodomy but murdered a turnkey in breaking jail. The brother is wanted no less in the slaying, and the third man, he that made off with your son-in-law, is the fellow sodomite, a lowly jailbird from Virginia. I heard all this from Spieghel himself, who was back yesterday from England."

These newcome tidings, which like newly turned turf bewrayed more unwanted wormy underside, cut Leeuwenhok to the quick unsparingly. The meaning of all the forenoon's cold shoulder and hot jeering tongue now blazed forth. His daughter, formerly loose wench, now forsaken wife of a sodomizing bloodyhanded fly-by-night jailbird; his stunted bastardly grandson and bequestling, newly borne out to the middenheap in a bedpan; and his name, not even his own by birthright, now a hook to hang up a fool's cap; all this was little better than ball-and-chain.

Such a chuckling likeness of the man and his family—while not a spot-on *gezelschapje*,* yet to some Antwerpers a spitting likeness nonetheless, one seemingly from the workshop of the budding Jan Steen rather than the setup van Dyck—had been hurriedly sketched in smudgy charcoal before the Leeuwenhoks even sat for it. But these blackening tidings had reached Antwerp only yesterday (along with other smuggled lading), roundaboutly from England.

Indeed, by the afternoon following the Leeuwenhok wedding, Antwerp had been rife already with hearsay, thanks in no small wise to Jacoba Spotter, who had flittered about town tirelessly gossipmongering, seeing to it that all the fanhidden snickering tittletattle of yesterday was the open hawhaws, hoots, and tehees of today. In few, Leeuwenhok's name now lay hopelessly blackwashed upon the curling lips of Antwerp, and soon every other snig-gering town within earshot of the likes of hooting cockahoop Jacoba Spotter. Yes, *Lajeunesse*-Spotter's granddaughter had sown and reaped, for Spieghel had done his work well and had unloaded baggage to unlord.

As all perhapshood for his pipedream wisped away, sickblanched Leeu-wenhok wordlessly, shakenly, fumblingly, withdrew to his readingroom. There, downflumped at his desk, seated beneath his hueshot maps of the world's great begirding seas, Leeuwenhok strove manfully, strove manfully to find his bearings above the unseen understir of heartflushes powerfully eddying. As he had well known, it was only the outward seeming of high seemliness rather than the thing itself that carried weight at the lofty pitch whither he had longed to rise. And yet for all his fulsome toadying and lickspittlery, he was now, in the eyes of the uppermost above all, little better

---

* 'Little gathering.'

than a great slimy toad, warts and all, as unwishworthy as his daughter was unwedworthy, a great bloated frogprince unkissed, who, floundering upon the slippery slope, had fallen short of shapeshifting. Willynilly, the sad truth homethrust itself upon Leeuwenhok that he, like many of his ilk before and after, had stumbled into a foul pitfall, had traded too much in the wind, and a wind blustery at that, one to trouble the wrong shoulder of the sail. There would be no patcome opening now for offloading his worthless stock. As his trusty Faret put it, *"aussi aux occasions d'honneur, comme aux grandes conduites de la guerre, il n'est pas permis de faillir deux fois."*

Feeling to the utmost his shaming before all, and perhaps worse, feeling the dreadful fleetingness of all things worldly to his great teen and cost, Leeuwenhok battered his breast and beat his brow. Had ever a man been so bedaughtered? Had ever a man been so beknaved? Leeuwenhok wailed and gnashed his teeth. Thus he sat, while he watched his carefully shored-up world fall apart all around him, like a mighty dike breaking up under the hammering blows of plundering seawaves eager to overflood his costly polder and carry off years of hard work and money, eager to wash away sheddings of much blood, sweat, and tears. And he could see that this heady thieving strongwater of the sea flowed forth as hurlingly as contraband rotgut upspewed by a poxy drunkard, some bastardly briny draught best spat out no sooner sipped! But how could wretched Leeuwenhok have seen the buried weaknesses within, those wooden holdingbeams honeycombed by boring worms, worms that would not rest until they had gnawed through the innards of his great dike, weakening the hidden framework of all those strengthening oaken ties?

With his head blubbering into his brawny hands, he blackguarded that fickle whore Fortuna, with all her crinkumcrankum ways. Oh, what hardhearted curmudgeonliness, to show breasts but give no suck! Oh, to have laden him with a selfwilled hussy of a daughter tied to a nothinghusband! Such roughness now cried out for roughness, and he pledged in all his bitterness that those dry wormwoody dugs would feel his bite to the pain of all.

Leeuwenhok was startled by the sight of Zwartenbok standing before him at desk's edge, sent to sound out roundaboutly the waters of peacebrokering. But alack! This wretched middleman, altogether untaskworthy,

---

* 'When it comes to that which touches one's upstandingness, just as when it comes to broad warfare, one is not allowed to fail twice.'

found himself very much in the wrong place at the wrong time. Bolting to his feet and snatching his ebony cane, seething Leeuwenhok made at the boy before the latter could say so much as a word and began to bludgeon him black-and-blue and bloody. The hapless boy, giving way under this fiendish onslaught, strove to flee, but the more he shifted ground, the more wrathful his master grew, and the more the two thrashed about, the more they trashed Leeuwenhok's prized havings outlaid atable. The cringing boy burst into the forehall only to run up against a wall, where he was brought from toes and heels to knees and hands, never to rise again.

In all the hubbub, Zwartenbok had knocked to the floor a brace of great priceless eastern vases, which in shattering dinned and aftersounded throughout the house, together with his panged yells and calls for help. This racket drew forth a throng of householdstaff, even the withdrawn Henrietta. Now to a mistress' shrieked behests to step in, now to a master's angry threats to stand back, a thick huddle of wary footmen strove fitfully, all helterskelter, to come between striker and stricken, but it was only De Keyser's masterful interloping and soothing words to his "Skipper" that in the end avasted the tussle, by which time the houseboy lay at death's threshold.

As Zwartenbok was whisked out of sight and into care, De Keyser helped the bedeviled man back into the stillness of the readingroom. After downswigging, between sweated pants and gasps, a goodly bit of strongdrink spiked with a smidgen of thornapple, the heavyweight, by little-and-little, regained his selfhold. He sat awhile and blankly gazed at the welter of shouldbes and shouldhavebeens that streamed past his eyes. Having missed his tide, he meant to see the faithless blueblood and his sidekick feel a harsh backwash and battering of tiderips.

And rough means to Leeuwenhok's rough ends were pat to hand in the shape of De Keyser, who, foreguessing his master's mindedness, at length broke the stillness and asked, "What do you want done about this, Skipper?"

"I want the blueblood hunted down," answered Leeuwenhok in a grim undervoice, still somewhat lost in his mullings.

"Only the one, Skipper?"

"Catch the hart and you catch the hind."

"What do you want us to do with them, Skipper?"

"I will feed their privyparts to my dogs. Where you dump the other parts is up to you." The last gulp. "Fetch the men." De Keyser left straightway to

gather together in all haste the blistered thumbs and fingers of Leeuwenhok's long grasp.

Like most of the household, Cruikshank and Charles had also been
drawn by the ruckus and, flabbergasted, had witnessed Leeuwenhok at his
grimmest and wildest. With the bridegroom hopelessly missing and havoc
and hazard rife in their midst, the two had eye-to-eyed that they would do
well to leave forthwith, lest they too find themselves whippingboys, and had
hastened to their rooms in order to pack.

Before even halfpacked, however, both men were startled to find at their
doors newly returned De Keyser, together with a handful of burly heavies,
who enlightened them that "Skipper wants to see you below." And down,
willynilly, the two went as one, through a flurry of uncouth manpower bus-
tling about the household, of a kind unseen heretofore, until they came to
stand before Leeuwenhok in the readingroom, which yet lay all in shambles.

"Your family has done me great wrong, and now you will help make
amends for it. Mr. De Keyser here is heading a manhunt for your turncoat
brother, and you, Charles, will be part of it. Indeed, I make you answerable
for any fallthrough. Mr. Cruikshank will stay here until the flightling is
found and brought back. He will be kept under lock and key until such time.
Nor will any dowry be paid, since my daughter, only newly wedded, finds
herself now queerly out of wedlock, through no shortcoming of her own."

"My brother is wedded to this family, not I, and I will not be lorded over
by you or anyone else in this sooterkinbog! We leave as we will!"

"You will do as you are told, or you will end up not a little worse than
your warder." At this, Leeuwenhok's darkling hint and knowing nod, a few
henchmen rushed forwards, took rough hold of Cruikshank, and held his
arms out to the fore, while De Keyser broke the helpless man's thumbs, as
if wishbones.

"I've seen youths less overbold than you end up at the bottom of the
Scheldt for much less. You would do well not to cross me. You know the
man best, if one he be. You he trusts. And him you will find, for your own
good. God help you if you don't."

Charles and Cruikshank were led back up to their rooms, where the
ward took leave of his handicapped warder, whom he would never see again.
Wardship of Charles now passed to Diederick Spieghel, who henceforth
would shadow Charles tirelessly, like a brother's keeper.

Spieghel began to rifle through Charles' things. The Drighten was to be stripped of all wherewithal and weapons, nay, bestripped of all his ownings brought along from England, outtaking only those things utterly needful for the undertaking at hand, to wit, a few shifts of clothes.

Charles began to feel the earth beneath his feet shift, like a quivery scaledish beneath a lowering downweight, yet stilly he stood there nonetheless, taking all this in his stride. But then, what else could he do? Was not the heavyweight's law now the law?

It bore in upon Charles, how by an oddish runaway twist of weird, he found himself now the willynilly henchman of his own brother's foeman. Yet upon further thought, it began to seem to him that his lot was maybe not so odd at all. Here in the Netherlands, northern Lowlanders fought against southern Lowlanders, with the land sundercloven through seemingly unending warfare, and Lowlander's hands ruddied with fellow Lowlander's blood. And everyday there came tidings from abroad of begetter slaying begotten, of kin skewering kin, of brother slaughtering brother, in the great war that tore apart Germany, in the great inland war that tore apart England, his homeland whither he could not return, for he had damned himself there in unwillingly helping a wilful black sheep of a brother, who in turn had wilily betrayed family both lawful and inlaw.

Alack! Where be those who do not in one way or another raise Cain for some kin of their own? Yet where does it say that a man must love kin more than unkin, and by what right? And are not kinshipbonds but kinds of bondage? Is not bloodbetrayal and infighting the way of the world and the way of all flesh? Indeed, does not one flesh-and-blood hide beneath its one hide and skin sundry over-, under,- and athwart-lying brawn- and sinew-bands and manifold crisscrossing bloodstreams, like so many twisting roadways and waterways cutting up a riftless land, each fraught with its own cart- or ship-borne lading meant for counterset markets? And is not one man's leaden burden another man's light bundle? One man's fancy another's fright? One man's food but foul poison to another? Brother be damned for this bloody mess!

Yet the more he mulled, the more his new lot irked him less and less, for how like a tightfitting glove of stretching sheepskin, our lots in life grow easy with wear, how fear of the thumbscrew makes flockards of us all, or nearly so. And thus it was that this younger sibling of the Drighten clan warmed evermore quickly to the thought of lipbrotherhood, although he had never cared much for his now wayward brother. Besides, there was sure to come some opening hereafter wherein he might break free from the fat Fleming's grip. Let the fatling do his own dirty work! Fat Leeuwenhok be damned as well! Well, at least not for now.

Worsted Cruikshank left little if any wake amidst these brainwaves. Papa's brokenthumbed do-all would have to find his own way out of this mess. If the busybody found himself short of straws, well, he had only himself to blame for making a broom of himself!

The direness of Charles and Cruikshank's lot as yet fell short of Zwartenbok's, and the latter was, at his very last, to offer his master, willynilly, one last helping hand. What had begun as thoughtless whim now became careful forelay, wherein two birds were to be hopefully downed with one bigger stone. That is to say, the unaforethought bethrashing of Zwartenbok was to be shapeshifted into damning lawful proof against Oswin, and thus against Godwin as well, proof that would greatly help lengthen the Fleming's long grasp, for shrewd De Keyser had been quick to unfold how the battery might be turned to his Skipper's boon.

Of little avail would be the care given Zwartenbok, wherein Henrietta had seen to it that a bevy of housemaids tended him, while a footman was sent to fetch Dr. Pot. In the betweentime, however, De Keyser turned up at the sickbed in order to take over caregivership, for the housemaids, he said, were needed elsewhere. And once alone, he snapped the boy's neck—a last twist home to a stubborn corken stopple—thereby ending his life, even though it now put Leeuwenhok out of fifty guilders, the price he had payed for him a few years earlier.

But why such haste? Why not let nature run its own wendway, given that the busted body was already in its deaththroes? It all came down to a matter of time. Leeuwenhok could not afford to wait for a leadenfooted Grim Reaper to mow down what had already been brought down, since too great a tarrying would surely let Oswin and Godwin slip through his fingers. Once these rogues boarded God-knows-what seacraft, with all manner of ships and boats coming and going from the wharves hourly, they would be nearly as good as gone. No, now, with the iron hot, was the time to strike, to hasten nature along to her uneschewable end.

Besides, a body need not stink before it is ravenready, whatever quibbling pettifoggers might say about where life ends and death begins, or where death ends and life begins. Indeed, as Leeuwenhok himself and many others could well witness, Antwerp, like many other burgs, was everywhere haunted by breathing bodies that long ago had sighed their last and given up the ghost. Were they—having melted so mildly away in all their tarrying here, now utterly bloodless and heartless—any less dead than the indwellership of a graveyard? No need to split splitends here.

By the time Dr. Pot reached the Leeuwenhok household, the boy was already dead, and the leech thus needed merely to warrant that it was so. And who was to answer for it? Tokens of foul play were readily to be seen upon the body, enough to warrant the bringing-in of a lawman. And Dr. Pot found himself swept aside at the doorway by Cloppenburgh and his underlings, who burst into the Leeuwenhok home and bestrode the forehall, with the sniff of murder in their noses.

Forthwith, the lawmen were led to Zwartenbok's cotside. Cloppenburgh poked the body once or twice with his cane. Yup, it seemed pretty dead. Dr. Pot's warrant was brought, whereat Cloppenburgh cast a listless glance, but then bellowed, "Witnesses?" Two shaken but pretty housemaids were called forth to bear the heavy *onus probandi* and, with hands upon the Holy Writ, swore to tell the truth, the whole truth, and nothing but the truth.

And the truth went something like this. "A young Englishman it was, with a scarred and bruised mug. Ay, he looked like a true rogue. We all heard uproar in the forehall, and from the upper stairs we saw the foul cutthroat beating the little tyke so. The madman must have broken in, and Zwartenbok must have come across him. And sorely the wee thing was paid for guarding our master's home, for there he lies all beaten to death. Oh, that this drossy age should bring forth such wicked men who illhandle helpless children! May the law not grow soft on those fit for the hangman's noose!"

With a handflick, Cloppenburgh sent these witnesses away and was about to go himself, for he had all that he needed, or nearly so. De Keyser was quick to enlighten further that the murderer, a sodomite benamed Oswin Underhill, had showed up here a week or so ago and had picked a fight with one of the footmen and was likely to be found now in the fellowship of Godwin Drighten. And the latter was wanted in England for murder as well. De Keyser was happy to add that his master, Mr. Leeuwenhok, was greatly saddened by the loss of his houseboy and would kindly, out of his own pocket, help the powers-that-be hunt down the murdering lowlives.

This seemed fair enough to Cloppenburgh, who was shortstaffed thanks to the war, and so he nidnodded and left. And so it was that Antwerp's law and Leeuwenhok's law—the latter never set down in any lawbook—were now fastwedded together, more tightly than his daughter and that short-comer of a groom had been.

De Keyser and his underthugs set about readying themselves for the manhunt. The walls were first to be flayed of their many likenesses of Godwin that Henrietta, in all her lovebesottedness, had had limned, at Leeuwenhok's great cost. And once these canvases were taken down, Godwin's mug was taken out, like some misreckoning in life's ledgerbook, that is, very much cut out, until all begirding time and place fell away, leaving the head alone in the hand, and the leftovers, ripped from their frames, were tossed down upon the floor, to be gathered up later and burnt. But why? Well, a painted face is worth a thousand hazy words, and this was to be the face that would float the Leeuwenhok manhunt, a face to be shown in the streets to passers-by until someone, having seen the face in the flesh, might finger out where the rogue was lurking.

It was not long before this ruckus drew forth Henrietta from her bower. She was in no little wise aghast to find rough boots traipsing underfoot the mugless likenesses of her blueblood. Ah, love! At its very strongest, is it not only blind but also deaf and dumb? Yes, she could neither utter a gasp at such unheard-of handling of her groom nor brook the sight of it. Down she trod to face her father yet again and cry blue murder.

And this upshot in an even harsher bout of wrangling between father and daughter than earlier. But she was no match for the master-of-the-household, who had turned out to be not the softfisted father she once thought him to be. In no time, she was dragged back up to her room and locked up there. And there she could bloody well rot, for all he cared! By God, she would learn to put up and shut up, or he would find a lodging for her in the *Maagdenhuis* or in a nunnery, whichever was the more grueling!

Oh, his mind was set. He would go the whole hog now. Let everyman be his own Judas and hang himself for no more than a handful of silver, in the fallout of stillborn dreams! Did it not stand written in that bedside Bible, Faret's *L'honnête homme,* that

*tout en un temps il faut songer aux moyens de conserver de que nous pos-
sédons, d'acquérir ce qui nous manque, de rendre vains les efforts de ceux
qui nous contrarient, de surmonter la haine, et l'envie, de reculer ceux qui
vont devant nous, d'arrêter ceux qui nous suivent; et le salut d'un chacun
ne consiste pas tant, ce semble, à se garder soi-même, qu'à ruiner les autres.**

And so under De Keyser's mastermindship, a townwide manhunt was
launched for Oswin and Godwin, who were as good as marked men now,
having been written into the blackbooks of Antwerp. And what an able-
hand De Keyser had shown himself to be, who had spinmastered it all, in
the hope of turning a nasty aboutturn altogether about. And so it was that
Cloppenburgh's underlings and De Keyser's underrogues came to comb
through the streets of Antwerp, in search of flotsam from the Leeuwenhok
wedding, and nearly nabbed Oswin on his way to the wharves. And even
now, the two youths kenned not even the half of it, as they sat dumbly in a
backroom of the *Duivel aan de Ketting,* mulling over the innkeeper's dark
words touching upon Leeuwenhok.

"Speak of the devil! They're back again!" said Goodwife Brinkman, in
glancing, as was her wont, through the spyhole, which looked out into the
drinkingroom on the other side of the wall. She rose and left the room. The
two youths rushed to the hole to gawk out and saw five burly thugs eyeing
the few innguests, as they spoke and showed something to Brinkman, seemingly the aforesaid bit of sailcloth bearing a likeness of Godwin.

Their hearts began to knock up against their ribs, as they waited to see
whether the innkeeper would betray their whereabouts to these heavies,
among whom Godwin was sure that he spotted a Leeuwenhok footman.
So the woman was right after all. Leeuwenhok was indeed behind all this.
Words passed between the innkeeper and the band, until the latter turned
and left. Brinkman came back, with hardhitting news.

"So, you're murderers as well as turncoats! Oh, you need not stand there
gaping and gawking! And you need not fear that I've said a word about you.
Oh, what a handsome day this has turned out to be! The day of Leeuwenhok's

---

* 'At the same time, we must think of ways to keep what we have and get what we lack,
to baffle those who would thwart us, to overcome hate and greeneye, to thrust back those
who go ahead of us, to stop those who come after us; and our freedom from harm, it seems,
is found not so much in guarding ourselves but in undoing others.'

fall! Oh, I could kiss the pair of you! And there'll be time enough for that, since there'll be no getting out of town now for either of you. They're minding the towngates and wharves, and there's no getting beyond the townwalls. Oh, you've made a hard bed to lie in, you have!"

Within less than a day then, their hopes of first an unrushed leavetaking, and now a leavetaking of any kind, had miscarried. It seemed that the tie to the Leeuwenhoks would prove to be of much sterner stuff, for better or for worse, through up-times and through down-, in weal and in woe.

IN FOR A PENNY, IN FOR A POUND

CATCHPENNY UNDERTAKINGS, how often do they not get caught up in Lady Luck's curling dimples, those kinklekins in a mug at once so fair and so foul—nay, a face without a heart, the heartbroken might twit, or leastwise a taking face with a heart unfickle in its fickleness? But why only "catchpenny"? For are not Fortuna's skirts but broadsweeping dragnets, catchalls for all manner of births and misbirths? Do those wanton skirts not flap and flout the cheeks of all, giving flirty glimpses of the underhidden, within or beyond grasp? Does she not, in all her playfulness, fall behind at times, only to rush forwards to catch up, clad now as Handiness, now as Happenstance, now as Plight, now as Fluke?

And now as Fluke—the kind often shrugged off as unlikely and blithely left to the world of story—Fortuna interlopes boldly into life, and into our story, and would have it that Oswin and Godwin find themselves not altogether trussless. Help for the twain was to come from unlikely quarters, to wit, from the backroom of the shabby *Duivel aan de Ketting* itself. Not from Dighel, who had whisked himself out of all sight upon his learning that Oswin and Godwin were wanted men and who had not been seen since. No, it was Wilhelmina Brinkman herself that would lend a helping hand.

And yet no highmindedness underlay her forthcoming deeds, although she thought otherwise. True, the woman earlier had allowed Oswin to lie low in her workroom, following his battery the evening of *Zorghvliet*. But then the youth had worked somewhat towards earning his keep, as did homesick Dighel, and so therein she had found herself not out of pocket.

But things were to be otherwise now. The innkeeper's illwill to one man was as good here as goodwill to another, and so luckily for the two youths, bad in Leeuwenhok's eyes meant good in hers. By God! She could not pass up thwarting the hated man, law or no law!

But this would not come without a gowithout. She well knew that knowledge of their whereabouts was a gainful springhead, but out of all keeping, she was ready to forgo this golden opening to squeeze hushmoney out of the two, or to pocket a handsome pawful of snitchmoney, or both, for there was Jan to think about, her longlost Jan. O Jan! There's not a man alive who can hold a candle to you! Even if you had been no upright man, deep as we were in unlawry. He had been her heart of hearts, through all those dark fistuppy times, until De Loo—as the dirty bograt was then called—took away from her her Jan, and her Jan's money. And the rat had bloated himself since and was ready now for bursting. Oh, there's nothing prouder than what grows in shyte! O Leeuwenhok, I have not forgotten!

But it would take more than illgoodwill to unglitch things, as the woman well knew. And she would need to tread carefully, for if word were to get out that she somehow had a hand in abetting these two, she herself would not outlive the helping. But Jan's commonlawwidow was not trussless herself, for she too had friends in low places.

Up she trod to Oswin and Godwin's room. With no answer to her knocking, she nonetheless trod in, finding the two still there, for they had meant to wait for nightfall to dare steal forth.

"No need to fear. It's only me. You've done well not to leave. You'd have been taken before ever reaching the wharves."

"What catch is there now with you?" asked Oswin.

"'Catch'? I would not be so roughtongued to anyone willing to help in a bind. And you've few friends knocking at your door these days, or haven't you heard?"

"'Help'? What can *you* do?"

"Much more than the pair of you ever will on your own. If you had walked twoscore years in my shoes, you'd know a thing or two about how the world works."

"Hear her out," begged Godwin.

"I can get you aboard a ship and out of town before nightfall."

"And why should you?"

"Why should I? Why shouldn't I? I've got my own grounds." Here she faltered, and a grudging tear streamed down her cheek, which she quickly brushed away, and then stiffening, she said, "There are things that need to be set aright."

Oswin found himself somehow stirred by this unguarded but fleeting hint of bygone sorrow. A lump rose in his throat.

"I think we've little choice but to go along," said Godwin. Oswin grudgingly nodded.

"You sit tight until I get back," said the woman, who left straightaway. And within the hour she was back and brought the two down to her backroom. There they found two great winebarrels, drained to the dregs, and a few tools beside.

"These will get you to the wharf and onto a ship bound for Amsterdam. Well, don't stand there gawking! These tops need to be hinged on and fitted out with a bolt on the inside. And airholes need to drilled through all along the hoops."

The two fell to their work straightaway, at the same time trying to mindspin how all this was to work out. Oswin strove hard to see how they would get aboard without being stuffed into the frowzy innards of these barrels.

When their work was done, and Vos showed up to cart the barrels to the wharf, Oswin, however, would have none of it. He knew all too well how it felt to be crushed into an airless hovel. What, they were to lock themselves inside and sit there as in a pillory, while whoever wished could knock them about! No bloody way! By God, he would sooner walk out into the open streets right now with guns blazing!

Time ticked on, and Godwin tried to talk him into this, and into the barrel. Either into the barrel or into the hangman's noose. Hadn't he already had a foretaste of Leeuwenhok-Drighten guestfriendliness the night of *Zorghvliet?* He needed only to look at himself, still all black-and-blue and scarred. If Oswin wanted to stay behind, so be it, but Godwin was not minded to hang around to be hanged. And so Godwin climbed into his barrel, locked himself in, and Vos rolled it out to the cart. It was now or never. Unwillingly, most unwillingly, Oswin climbed down into his barrel and bolted himself in. He was sure he would go mad.

The cart trundled past dozens of Cloppenburgh's and De Keyser's men swarming through the streets. Once at wharfside, the two barrels were again rolled off, and the two youths thought that they would fetch up from dizziness. Down into the maw of *De Gouden Kruistocht* they were lowered in a ropen net, there where life had been broken down into orderly stacks and rows of pints, stoops, kemps, kegs, kilderkins, aams, boxes and other barrels, filled with Malaccapepper, saltpetre, cloves, blue Ming ware, Persian silks, Kandysugar, gunpowder, and suchlike goods, all worth bagfuls of stooters, stuivers, and guilders.

There the stowaways were to stay hushhush until the time was right to come forth. And in the clammy stifling guts of the barrels, the two waited away—it seemed an endlessness—until lastly *De Gouden Kruistocht* set forth down the foggy Scheldt. An unspoken tearless farewell to Antwerp, to the Leeuwenhoks, and all that they dragged in their wake.

Dighel had never showed up to bid farewell to his countrymen, not that he had known they were outbound. No, he had grounds for being away, and not wholly of his own making. In carefully sidestepping the fellowship of the wanted, to keep his own neck out of harm's way, he had loitered long in the street, where the fivesome who had spotted him earlier with Oswin came across the shirker again and nabbed him unawares. In a dingy shed, he was roughly sifted about Oswin and Godwin's whereabouts. No great pilliwinksing it took to loosen his tongue. Indeed, never had a fearful man more easily given in and betrayed a countryman.

When the news was handed on to De Keyser, a fearsome band of heavies led by De Keyser himself fell upon *De Duivel aan de Ketting*. Behind the shut doors of its backroom, Wilhelmina Brinkman was throttled into yielding up knowledge of her part in helping the youths, although she would gasp her last before ever making known the ship's name or landingplace. To the crows with the dirty bastards! Even at her last, she outfaced her harriers, leastwise in part.

With the woman dead, a great swarm of manhunters then fell upon the wharves, and thanks to Cloppenburgh's backing, ships were lawfully held up and searched through, but bootlessly so, for *De Gouden Kruistocht* had already left. Either the bitch had lied, or the hunted had jinked their hounds. And so bidding his men keep up their watchfulness, De Keyser backed to his master.

The once merry Leeuwenhok home was now grimly overcast, still in a shambles after the thrashing of Zwartenbok and the unfacing of Godwin, with the table still set for the weddingfeast and the room behung with now drooping sprigs of greenery. But Leeuwenhok would have nothing touched: it could stay thus until the crack of doom, for all he cared. Amidst this *itus interruptus,* the newskeen man was darksomely enlightened about the morning's little headway.

"What now, Skipper?"

"I told you! I want the rogues hunted down!"

"Where would you have us go now?"

"To Spitsbergen, if need be!"

"I think it best we sift the brother. The pair may well think along the same line."

Charles was brought forth, shadowed by Spieghel, and asked about a likely endpoint to his brother's flight. But, truly, how was he to know? Yet he had to say something now, and it quickly bore in upon him that here lay a handsome opening for him to get back onto hometurf, where he would have more of an upperhand, and thus a greater hope of freeing himself. And so he said, "Behind your back, my thankless brother griped endlessly, whining about how much he loathed this town and how much he missed England. I think it most likely indeed that the turncoat has headed home. Even for a wanted man, there is no shortness of places there to hide and still go about one's business."

This seemed likely enough, and Leeuwenhok blurted out, "To England then, and speedily!"

"This'll be a costly undertaking, and not much gain to be had from it. Pretty much throwing good money after bad. Is it worth it, Skipper?"

The wan man reddened and then growled back, "Worth every penny!" And unheard by De Keyser, a scornful voice within muttered to itself, "What niggling moneymindedness!" Yes, oddly enough, this asking irked Leeuwenhok greatly, for so it was that he who had formerly made a killing on tulipbulbs, and merrily so, now somehow found all his great deadstock a meaningless heap, no better than a stale chubby mistress. He could think of nothing but the killjoys answerable for it. After all, rightness and uprightness had been downtrodden, and he had his *principes, bien sûr.* Besides, what else should he do with his money? God, there was more to life than bleeding money!

"As you wish, Skipper."

Since time and money are the sinews of war, no less than of business, and since the great man was ready to put his money where his mouth was, whatever the cost, the manhunt was now heightened and broadened. Men were called in by the drove. Money was handed out by the bagful. Places aboard Britbound ships were booked by the score. Not one to put all his manpower in one boat, as it were, De Keyser thought it wise to send at least a few bands to France and Spain as well, since it was not at all sure where the flightlings might be heading. To this Leeuwenhok nidnodded. The more the merrier.

As De Keyser and his men began to ship themselves for England, France, and Spain, and as *De Gouden Kruistocht* sailed on Amsterdambound, there arose a kinkle in it all, and things were to go awry unforeseenly. But then the laws of likelihood, no less than Leeuwenhok's own shadowy laws, had not been set up goodwillfully.

It had been settled upon beforehand, by the outlaws and their smuggler Vos, that once stowed away in the ship, the two were to stay hidden inside their barrels until the ship had left Antwerp well behind. Vos would come and knock three times on each, and only then were they to out themselves.

A deal of fuss it surely was, but stealing-aboard was as good as stealing, and if they were not to find themselves wrongways to the skipper, things would need to seem aboveboard outwardly, right from the outset. Thus, the two could not have straightforwardly moseyed aboard at wharfside, slapped coin down before the skipper, and said, "Take me with!" what with the streets and bylanes of Antwerp then crawling with manhunters, who would have nabbed the two before ever betreading the gangway. Even once smuggled aboard, with ship still at wharfside, the two could not have straightforwardly unbarreled themselves, slapped coin down before the skipper, and said, "Take me with!" for shipmaster Van Heemskerck, being an upstanding Godfearing man—no less than his sister Machteld van Reuzendyk, who magistratically oversaw a number of Amsterdam's almshouses and workhouses—would never have been party to outsmuggling wanted outlaws and would have unshipped them on the spot.

All this, Vos well knew. A roundabout way needed to be blazed out, and Vos settled upon the following. Given that the ship was undermanned, the sailor would wait until the boat was beyond any turnback, would then stealthily unbarrel the stowaways, and set them about some easy out-of-the-way work, as if newly hired shipmates. When the skipper would eyemark their thereness and ask for a wherefore, Vos would step forward and say his sorries. Yes, it had utterly slipped his mind in all their busyness to let Van Heemskerck know that he, on the skipper's behalf, had somewhat highhandedly taken on these badly needed hands, even if landlubberishly green, and would hope the skipper would not mind his choice of manpower. As Vos well knew, no winterer turns up his nose at firefeeding driftwood handily underfoot, even if he must stoop down to gather it up. And so the two outlaws then were to be stopgap seamen until Amsterdam, uprightly swinking and sweating to earn their keep. Not a flawless plan, but the bettermost that Vos could hatch up offhand.

De Gouden Kruistocht sailed on, and the two bided their time embarreled, but busy Vos, who had long since been feed by Brinkman and whose mind now was elsewhere, forgot about his stowaways. And while Godwin had made his peace with the hemming-in—why, he had nearly dozed off in the encradling ship's sway!—Oswin, however, had grown restless and squirmed until he could underbear it no more. Oh, abide coopy places he could not! And with a no-show from Vos, Oswin began to think that something had indeed misfared. He could hold himself in no longer. He would out and peek about.

Vos had seen to it that the barrels were not stowed away deeply in the other upstacked freight but left freestanding as borderers thereto, so as to allow for speedy and snagless outletting later. With no hurdle to opening-up, Oswin unbolted and popped his head out to peer about. But this popup proved to be mistimed, for no sooner was he headfree but shipman Potgieter showed up belowdeck to fetch gear needed above. Catching sight of him, Oswin ducked back down into his barrel and bolted up, as Potgieter's eyes righted themselves in the netherworldish gloom. What was that over there? Potgieter was sure he had glimpsed something. Was it not a head? It truly looked like one. Nah, it couldn't have been. The sailor went about his business.

But in his passing again, his legs stopped under him, and he found himself warily gawking again at the lonestanding barrel. By God, he could have sworn that he had spotted a head on top. What kind of lading sprouts a head and then loses it? Surely none that he had ever seen. And the more he bethought himself, the more eerily unsettling he found it all. With a fretful heart, he nighed the barrel. He put hand to barreltop and guardedly pushed down. Nope, nuthin. He put ear to top and carefully listened. Nope, nuthin.

Then crouching down, he narrowly eyed the outside and, the dimness notwithstanding, could see that a row of holes had been drilled through along the hoops. Odd. And peering in through one of these holes, the sailor felt his heart nearly stop when he made out an outpeeping eye within. Under the weight of a seaman's ingrained bogybelief, he started back slapbang and, loosing his footing, tripped over his gear. What kind of goblinry was this? Had some fiend taken root here, in the darksome guts of this ship? Potgieter scrambled to his feet, and before hastening off, he hurriedly piled a few nearlying heavy boxes on top of the barrel, to hold in whatever was within. Better safe than sorry! In a flash, he was gone.

Yes, Potgieter had glimpsed Oswin within. And Oswin had glimpsed Potgieter without and, worse, had felt the downflump of boxes. He tried the hinged top, but it would not open out. Alack, he was trapped inside! Drat himself for having yielded to all the encasking coaxing! Where had his head been? Never, never trust an axegrinding innkeeper! The staves seemed to squeeze in upon him, and he fell into a flap, and like an ensnared beast, he pawed and jogged away, and then began to bellow, bawl, yell, call, shout, shriek to Godwin to come and help him out before he went mad. But dozy Godwin heard nothing.

How heartlightened Potgieter was to be back up adeck. And once back in the light of day, however foggy and overcast the day, the whole thing seemed to him a little silly now, even a little shaming. All tricksy mindplay surely. It does happen, you know. Yes, thinking makes it so. And yes, he'd do well to shun the bottle for a while, again.

As *De Gouden Kruistocht* slipped along the bights and bends of the Scheldt, the fog began to thicken, until one could barely make out the stem from the stern, or the stern from the stem. Potgieter was ordered to stand lookout at the prow, for the craft had by now nearly reached the sea, there where the *mare clausum* began, there where the mouth of the Scheldt had been muzzled by a would-be stranglehold of blockading ships from the northern freestate, prowling for blockaderunners. With a smidgen of upluck, the skipper thought that, under this blanket of fog, he might sideslip any runins with the foeful and get by unscathed and scotfree, that is, might push through without the crossing of swords or, worse, the handing-over of dirty bribes.

In the eerie stillness and sightlessness, in this inbetweenworld, with cutthroat Seabeggars lurking somewhere out yonder, and cosy Antwerp lying somewhere back yonder, Potgieter's stalwartness dampened, and his mind backslipped again and again to that queersomeness below, where insight had met outsight through the eyey barrel, until his forewardcast squint saw naught but behind. He could bear it no longer. He would scrimshank off, as soon as any eye was off him, sneakily untread his path back down to that something, and settle his mind, one way or the other. Surely it would last no more than an eyetwink.

By the time Potgieter found himself back belowdeck, Oswin was truly fit to tied, and even from a ways-off, the seaman could hear muffled beastlike howlings and growlings from inside the jolty barrel. Something cudgellike the seaman snatched up and then drew near, ready for God-knows-what, as the ship blinded onwards through the fog without its foremost lookout. Yet the sailor's manful show notwithstanding, smirking Fortuna would hinder him from any cudgelplay, for no sooner had he overshouldered his stick but suddenly the hull hardlurched, shivered, and groaned, toppling Potgieter and oversetting the barrels.

As heavy swirls of seawater began to overflood the underdeck, Oswin freed himself at last, and greatly amazed to meet with water, he rushed to Godwin's barrel and pulled out its dazed indweller. Everywhere water, everywhere shouts, everywhere stirup. What had happened? What was to be done?

There was nothing for it but to betake oneself to topdeck—no need to be squeamish about stowawayhood now—where Oswin and Godwin saw that in the thickest of fogs *De Gouden Kruistocht* had been blindly rammed at the fore-end by another ship, which yet lay alongside, the stronger latter having worsted the weaker more rotten former, with a nasty gash to the hull running down below the waterline. In all the huddlemuddle, skipper Van Heemskerck made shift to send sailors down to the hopeful end of stemming the ingush, while lowermost stowed-away bales and boxes nighed bursting as their sodden inholdings swelled.

Had it been only this! Yet it never rains but it drenches. The crew of the undermanned *Gouden Kruistocht* was hardset enough in dealing with the hull but was altogether overwhelmed now as warmanlike sailors from *De Fortuin*—so the other ship was called—fell up them in their sorry weakness, like the overmany grippers of a great seaspider ready to take what had fallen in its way.

Little egging-on *De Fortuin*'s shipmen needed from Graegryck, the ship-master of this freestatecraft, and little goading-on the holdfast Graegryck himself needed, fired as he was with great warlikeness against the Spanish Netherlands. Well, weren't the two lands at war? And didn't war mean plundering? And didn't plundering mean killing? To Hell with sneakaround warrants and piddling buyoffs, when a whole bloody ship with lading to boot could be gotten at the cheap price of a bit of blood! Besides, hadn't the bloated King of Spain bloodsucked enough already, at the great cost of the Freestate? So it was to be, with Graegryck, "Suck or be sucked!"

And now amidst flurries, hurries, and frights, those hapless seamen from *De Gouden Kruistocht* who found themselves afore were cut down ruthlessly. This was indeed the wrong time for any bystanding gawkers to be adeck wondering why water flowed below. And as *De Fortuin*'s men from afore began to push along to meet *De Gouden Kruistocht*'s men coming up from aft, Oswin and Godwin, being unknowners to both these heaps, found themselves caught inbetween, as good as foes to either crew.

As good as goners, it seemed to Godwin, who could think of nothing but flight. And when he saw that Oswin had snatched up something cudgellike and now stood fast to take on all, Godwin grabbed him by the arm and pulled him after himself as he jumped through the open hatchway midship down into the swirling seawater belowdeck. And as the two splashed down as one, Oswin's leg was hurt, but at least, it seemed to Godwin, they were out of harm's way for now.

In no time, *De Gouden Kruistocht* was taken, hardly flabbergasting given the unevenmatchedness of the fight. And so it was that the gateway to the sea had proven to be too narrow for Van Heemskerck to squeeze through without roughly brushing up against foe. And that gateway now shut in upon the man, as he ordered those of his shipmen still standing to whiteflag and down their weapons.

De Fortuin's crew swarmed throughout *De Gouden Kruistocht*, stocktaking. Oswin and Godwin were found and dragged to topdeck to make one with the others taken. In limping along, Oswin came to tread over Potgieter's lifeless body, that cat of byword killed in the end by his own kenkeenness. But surely no-one aboard was aware that this whole bloody business might have been sidestepped if Potgieter had not forsaken his lookout, drawn below as he was by Oswin.

What a hodgepodge of tongues filled the aboutair—now German, now Dutch, now Swedish, now Danish, now some kind of Norse, now even Spanish and French—as *De Fortuin*'s piebald crew fell to chattering about their gets illgotten. Let it be known that this crossborder undertaking, like so many other seagoing partnerships hereabouts, was Dutch mainly in name and flag, and any narrow underseeking would have been hardset to untangle the twisting roots of folkdoms that made up this *rederij.**

Even the ship herself had been Spanish at the outset—the *Santa María* she once was hight—but her winsomeness had proven to be all too bewitching, such that in time she was roughly mauled and taken by the Dutch and then, as warbooty, sold for a tidy gain, for let no man hold cheap what is gotten dirtcheap. Dolled up again with a coat of paint—a bit of blush will turn even a landbred wench into a streetstrutting lady—the ship was newnamed *De Fortuin*, and she sailed forth as a plucky Pallas Athene against Spain and the Spanish Netherlands.

The backing for this warlike undertaking was seemingly placebound, yet most of the backers were Amsterdam brokers working on behalf of a patchwork of nameless moneymen: Portuguese Jews, French Huguenots now holding out in London, Spanish Dons bored with the war, English shippers, the odd hedging Antwerper, besides a token number of wealthy Dutch burghers mainly from Middelburg. And this looselimbed partnership had been paperworked and rubberstamped by the Dutch into a fullblooded freestate-*rederij*, empowered to batten on any searfarers bearing the slightest Spanish hue, such as Van Heemskerck and his *Gouden Kruistocht.*

Such minduntidying inlines were beyond the sight of Oswin and Godwin, who found themselves thrust to the deckboards beside Vos and the few others who had overlived the onslaught, now all sitting in a huddle overwatched by a few sword- and gun-toting heavies from *De Fortuin*. They were as good as foe now. Nearby stood overtowering Graegryck smuglordily.

One of Graegryck's shipmen came up to him and spoke away. To Vos sitting leftwards, who spoke a fair English, Dutchless Oswin whispered, "What are they saying?"

"The runt seems to be the master's mate," whispered back Vos. "He said that he's looked through the ship and is happy to tell the master that they've won much booty, but he thinks the ship's too badly smashed, and they cannot

---

* 'Shippingpartnership.'

save her. The skipper's angry, for that'll be a great loss of money. He's cursing the crew now. He wants them to go back down and patch it up, or he will make boards out of them and nail them over the hole."

Waermondt, as the master's mate was called, went back down to try and work wonders with the crew's handiest, to undo Potgieter's handiwork. Oswin whispered again, "What do you think they'll do now?"

"The ship's lost and will sink within the hour. When the skipper sees that, he'll likely want to shift as much of the lading onto his own ship as he can."

"What do you think they'll do with us?"asked Godwin.

"Kill us if they can't get any ransom, or sell us to the Turk as slave oarsmen."

"Hold your gob, dogmug!" barked one of their watchmen.

As Vos had foreguessed, a sheepishlooking Waermondt backed in no time with tidings of hopelessness, whereupon Graegryck blackguarded and then struck him a few times with his ebony cane. He then ordered all hands to shift as much of the unsodden lading as could be done. And to this end, even the leftovers of De Gouden Kruistocht's crew were pressganged into helping out these their foes, all outtaking Van Heemskerck. A far grislier lending-of-hand awaited him.

Nearly all felt the downflump of a heavy box or bundle upon their backs in the crossshifting of freight. In limping onto De Fortuin, Oswin looked up when Godwin, only a little ahead of him, fingered up to a yardarm. There Van Heemskerck could be seen in the rigging, held by two of Graegryck's understrappers. The onetime skipper stood stiffnecked, with his hands bound behind his back, and these in turn tied to a length of rope knotted to a yardarm.

The whole crew fell breathlessly still, upgazing. Following a proud bearding headshake from Van Heemskerck, the two men thrust him away, and he then fell to the length of his rope, such that his bound hands were snapped high up behind his back, hardwrenching his arms at the shoulders, in a ghastly and painful ripping of brawn and sinew. The wretch gave forth a frightful shriek and then dangled limply above the deck from his sorry limbs at rope's end, as if he somehow wished to hang upsidedown but could not bring himself thereto.

In beholding this, Oswin nearly dropped his load, for he somehow felt a sudden knifing twinge in his own upper arms, as if he himself had been yardarmed. "My God, the sorry wretch!" he muttered. The youth had fancied that he had hitherto witnessed his fair share of knavery in this world, but this gruesome show of heartlessness was to him utterly mindboggling. "We've fallen in among the worst of cutthroats!" he said to Godwin, who had turned away.

"Your first yardarming is it, boy?" said Waermondt, who had overheard, and guffawed. "They call it *estrapade* in French. Has a pretty ring in the ear, don't you think? But then everything sounds better in French, even when you can't understand a word of it."

"What did the man do to earn such handling?" snapped Oswin.

"Oh, gutsy, ain't ye?" Waermondt chortled. "It does my heart good to see it. Always liked the Brits, you know. What did he do? Why, he wouldn't play by the skipper's rules, and so he's got his hands full now, so to speak." He cackled. "You know, by the third or fourth drop, the arms come clean off."

"But why?"

"Oh, I don't know rightly. I guess he was unwilling to steal from Peter to pay Paul, which means in the end that he stole from Paul. Oh, somebody ought to write a story about him, the high-and-mighty skipper who went down with his ship but without his arms." And he fell acackling again.

As Van Heemskerck was hauled back up for a further drop, Graegryck caught sight of the crew's unbustle and shrieked that it would be fifty lashes for the next worthless dog caught loafing. In seeing his cane fall upon a nearby backside with a mighty thwack, the meekened crew hopped to it again. No-one was bold enough to stop and watch the two further droppings, after which Van Heemskerck's lifeless body was cast overboard and sank into sea without his ship. And Graegryck had to like it or lump it, in not getting what he wanted from Van Heemskerck, for the latter would not lift a finger to help out the skipper.

For its own part, *De Gouden Kruistocht* had long since given up, keen now to follow after its onetime shipmaster, for no patching-away at its rotting hull could stop the leaking, and so the ship sat heavier and heavier in the briny as water kept seeping in. Much of the lading was now worthless, hopelessly waterwrecked. The little that was otherwise found its way onto *De Fortuin*, and Waermondt was most finicking about where all this freight was to be stowed. More than once, Oswin and Godwin downed their load in the wrong place, only to be upbraided by Waermondt, "Not there, you sleepy sot! Here!"

Once, Oswin was emboldened to ask, "How am I to know?"

"There's a right side and wrong side for all these goods. Mind it!"

"But which is the right side for this?"

"Goods for upfrontsale along here, goods for smuggling along there."

This tweedledum-here-tweedledee-there was not greatly helpful, but Oswin's thoughts now yawed otherwards. "You're freebooters and smugglers to boot?"

"Fighters! In a holy war against the bloody Spanish, the bloody bastards! Fighters in the name of freedom! Free goods and free ships. Intrade, out-trade, fartrade—call it what you like—it's all freetrade. And if we stick up the stuckup and swag swaggerers in doing so, who's any right to whine about it? As my dear ol' father would always say, 'We moneystarved folk are flies to hawks, yet however small, we might be a sting in the throat.'"

De Gouden Kruistocht yielded up all that she could, and Graegryck and his crew turned their backs on the hulk lying helpless in the fog. And as the *De Fortuin* sailed off, Van Heemskerck's ship gave forth one last bub-bly gurgling gasp and then sank, as if long worldweary. On towards Deal, Graegryck and his craft sailed now, to the southern shore of England, for they had dealings there.

The leftovers of Van Heemskerck's crew had not been prodded into loftily walking the plank or going down with their ship but rather had also been loaded onto *De Fortuin*. Once fleeced of whatever worthful hav-ings they had upon themselves—here both Oswin and Godwin lost their coinpouches—this flesh-and-blood freight was stowed away below, locked up behind a stout bulkhead, in the frowzy innards of a hold, there to mull upon their bleak lot-to-come. Farewell ship! Hail hardship!

Oswin had hung back somewhat and sat apart, little caring for fellowship. His leg was sore. His heart was weary. In the darkness, his mind backslipped again and again to the sight of Van Heemskerck's fall from the yardarm and the ghastly sound of his shrieks—softgirly shrieks—as limbs were ripped from body. Again and again, the youth wondered what it was that Graeg-ryck had wanted of him, and why it was that Van Heemskerck would not yield. What could have been worth so much to suffer so much? How could a heart be so hard as to make a man thus dree? To make oneself thus dree?

And then the sad truth homethrust itself upon him that for all his struggling to free himself fair-and-square-like, he had in the end some-how tumbled into the shades of an underlife befolked by the riffraffiest of cutthroats. Why should this be so? Where were all the good folk in this world? And why did they not cross his path? His restless mind came lastly to brood upon earlier times, hard times that had seen the bitter loss of a sister, a mother, a stepfather, a father. It heartsickened him.

It was not long before Godwin gropped his way through the darkness to Oswin's side.

"Why did you pull me down?"

"I saw no other way-out."

"My leg was hurt."

"I, I thought all for the best. I thought, I—"

Godwin was unsure whether he ought to slink off, even though he had indeed thought all for the best. He was sorry now he had meddled. He should have stood there and let himself be cut down like a man. If only he had the Midasfinger! Dream on. Who did he think he was? At best a feckless bungler. Godiva indeed! Ought to leave well enough alone lest his touch tarnish. He blundered back to his former sittingplace, where he tried to think of gladdening things, however farfetched.

It had been a long day. Both had begun the day with a hangover. Neither had eaten. Both had fretted most of the day through. Neither could sleep. And more care was bound their way, before they would see the light of day.

De Fortuin reached a deep narrow inlet along the English shoreline, a cove carefully chosen to allow for all manner of in- and out-sneaking. Here the smugglerwares were to be offloaded, into the hands of English underdealers. And here again, the leftovers of Van Heemskerck's crew were pressganged into helping-out. A fleetlet of small rowboats had oared up to the ship and were then laden with goods to be ferried ashore.

Lying penned up in a such an inlet, even under the helm of darkness, was hardly riskless, for the English Parliament—the wardrain notwithstanding—had striven to keep up a hardnosed struggle against smuggling, to the end of keeping would-be warfodder, above all, out of the king's hands. And so Graegryck had all hands fall to, loading and unloading, to allow a speedymost dropoff-and-run.

This meant that Oswin and Godwin were also unshipped, down into the rowboats, to help out ashore. As they neared the strand, Godwin could not help but think that here now was a golden opening. Once ashore, while all were busy, they could surely sneak off in the darkness and trust to their footmanship again, that is, if Oswin would want to go along with him. It would all be a matter of timing. And such an opening would indeed arise.

When the rowboats were nearly emptied, there suddenly befell a mighty bang-and-blaze, followed by the groan and fall of men, then another, and then another. Muddlehuddle followed, more helterskelter, a welter of shouts and dithering dodging. Graegryck's worst nightmare had come to pass: they had been waylaid and fired upon by English lawmen, while out in the open upon the shore.

Graegryck's English sidekicks, being somewhat further upshore, were the bruntbearers in this, standing between the gunning lawmen and Graegryck's shipmen, and Oswin and Godwin in turn found themselves sandwiched inbetween the bruntbearers and the seafarers. Muzzleflashes and burning match betrayed the gunmen's whereabouts in the darkness, and in no time the smugglers, having taken up squats and crouches behind freight, made jumbled shift to fire back. Amidst all this stirup, the thought of flight returned to Godwin, if it had ever fully left him, and turning to Oswin he cried, "Come! We must fly! Into the bushes!"

There was little ground for staying-put in the crossfire, and so with little misgiving, Oswin limped after. But the hurt he had gotten, worsened by all the lugging, held him back, and fleetfooted Godwin, who had far outstripped him, had to back to his plodding mate in order to help him along. But as one, the two did not get far, for Waermondt had spotted the flighty sideshow and stopped them at gunpoint. "We've lost enough freight today! Back to the rowboats!" With a sunken heart, Godwin saw their golden opening shut itself on them, and they were driven back to their masters.

The lawmen began to be worsted in the fireback, and there arose a short-lived lull in the fighting, enough for Graegryck to have his men fall back, board the rowboats, and oar to the ship, turning their backs on their badly mauled English partners and forsaking all the barrels, boxes, and bales lying ashore, like so much strandstrewn washup.

This runin had been costly. For all their pains, they were richer by not even a crown. With Graegryck, it had always been "Suck or be sucked!" and now the holdfast skipper found himself sucked dry. Wrathful beyond belief, he blackguarded and caned his crew for this foulup, even though blame for the fallthrough rightly rested elsewhere. Far more upsetting was the illfettle of the crew. A number of his men had been shot dead ashore, others had been wounded and left behind, and still others, who had straggled back with their skipper, were unablehanded now, some of whom would die before landfall. Of Van Heemskerck's crew, only Oswin and Godwin were left. With such shortness of manpower, who was to man the ship?

To scratch together a barebonescrew, barely enough to run the ship, Oswin and Godwin were pressganged into sailorhood. No bloody way would Graegryck float helplessly there like filth upon the water's face! These worthless rotting knaves would man his ship dead or alive, and even paddle it with teaspoons if need be!

Graegryck's best bet was to limp to nearby London, where he could hunt up a new crew, sell off the leftovers of his lading, and then as quickly be gone again. To London then *De Fortuin* bungled its way. And so it was that yet again Oswin and Godwin found themselves hijacked, bound, for the nonce, to their Jolly-Roger masters, bound for the wrong place, and bound to be sold at wharfside upon landfall.

Seamanship did not come easily to either, and they blundered through their tasks. But how could they do otherwise? Were they not green? Were they not weary from want of food and want of shuteye? From want of freedom? From want?

Oswin could think of nothing but his pain, wincing at each shift of his hurt leg and glowering at all around. And Godwin grew queasy with seasickness, once hoisted aloft into the rigging, where, dizzy from the height, he felt like a measly wingclipped gallowsbird up in a tree. How cheap was life. How much cheaper would it get? Didn't Vos say that they were likely to be sold "to the Turk as slave oarsmen," or worse?

Shutting his eyes, Godwin could see it all now. He would be sold at dockside to some sweaty beturbaned fatling in some Ottoman shithole unknown to any map, where he would drudge away for the rest of his wretched life. His days would be spent minding swine in a sunken sty under a scorching sky, and when his hunger and thirst would grow unbearable, he would stoop down to the trough and share the foul nasty fare. And whenever he bungled—a few times a day at the least—he would be blackguarded in some raspy outlandish tongue, stripped, and beaten black-and-blue by an overtowering one-eyed taskmaster by the name of Muhtmet. And when his wearisome day ended, he would be housed in some hutchlike hovel, ratbitten as he shivered through the night. And when he was old, toothless, blind, and utterly wornout from drudgery, beyond the earning of his keep, Muhtmet would lead him out to some overhanging cliff and shove him off with a kick, and down into the swirling seawater he would headlong to meet a longwished-for death, as rotting food for fish. And nobody would be the wiser for any of it.

Maybe he should jump from the yardarm now, down into the sea, and spare himself a good deal of hardship-to-come. Even now he could feel the sweetly toying airrush along his cheeks and through his hair, as he mind-played yielding to the earth's downpull and falling from this height, down, down, like a buckling silver swan slipping through a chink in the water's winedark satiny wall, down into an enfathoming world, heightened and timeless, bypassed by all manner of waywending fishes.

Startled, he opened his eyes and looked down again, to the beckoning sea below, swishing and swaying, whispering and rounding Loreleilike. And in the bewitching cradlerock of ship and sea, Godwin's grip loosened until lastly his hold was no more, and he bade farewell. But unforeseenly, a nearby hand, out-of-the-blue, grabbed him as he began his fall, and with the knack of a wrestler, the seadog's paw pulled him roughly back into the ropes, where Godwin mustered himself to hold fast like an acornshell.

In time, *De Fortuin* somehow found itself in the Thames and then at wharfside in London. How heartlightened Graegryck was to be dryshod. And how odd for such a hardened seaman like him to be happily ashore landlubberlike! Straightway, he put the ship under the care of Waermondt, who was to see to it that all the lading was offloaded and the tidewaiter bought off. Had he not paid dearly enough already for this blasted paltry load?

The more badly wounded were also to be unshipped and stretchered to backstreet bonesetters, under whose care they would die when quackish leechdoms misfared. But then, they were pretty much useless to any ship-master as it was. Be that as it may, they were out of Graegryck's hair now.

Graegryck himself headed for the many wharfside wateringholes to drum up a new crew. And to this end, he took along wheellockpacking Kobenhafen, a great burly blue-eyed blondelocked Teuton, who seemingly could crush a man's headpan barehanded, even if pretty much feckless when it came to speaking English, or any other tongue. So the skipper took along as well the gabgifted Italian Cappella, for this swarthy hawknosed runt of a seadog could, in a halfdozen tongues, find money for old rope. Thus, strengthened with brawn and brain—well, brawn and tongue at least—the skipper could safely wow up would-be sailors and still ward off any unforeseen onfalls in the roughtumble world of seamandom.

With so many men off *De Fortuin*, the task of offloading fell to Oswin and Godwin, who alone were kept belowdeck to load the ropen net of the wharfside crane, each time that it was lowered down through the hatchway. And when the net was filled, they were to yell out "Hoist!" in order to raise the netting, which always came back emptyhanded and hungry for more. Backbreaking work it was, given that the little lading left aboard was mainly bulky warfodder, amongst which there lurked a heaplet of heavy powderkegs.

Godwin would now and then eye his friend but warily held his tongue, for oh, Oswin, he was a stinker now! His pain had gotten the better of him. He had had enough! Enough of being boxed in and boxed around! And it could not but happen that overweary Oswin came to lose his grip, as the two of them struggled to hoist a heavy box onto the open netting, and the box then fell against his sore leg. That was the last straw.

He well knew what lay behind the staves of some of those kegs, for Vos had told him—gunpowder. He well knew what it could do. No more of this! He was getting off this bloody boat now, if it was the last thing he did, even if he had to take out the whole bloody crew, and the ship and himself along with it! To Hell with all and everything!

Like a madman, he fell to banging away at one of these powderkegs with whatever was to hand. A halfriddled and worried Godwin asked, "What are you doing?" but Oswin only grunted and snarled on in his wildness. Before long he had smashed open a keg, and then another, and then another, and clawing into the blackness with his hands, he began to make a thick back-wending trail along the deckfloor to the upstacked powderkegs, the latter further enriched with chunks of pitch from a pitchpot. A lone hanging oillamp still flickered a ways-off belowdeck, a laststander from *De Fortuin*'s busy nightlife, and Oswin at last snapped at Godwin, "Fetch the lamp! I'm blowing this ship skyhigh!"

"Are you out of your mind? You'll kill us all!"

"Get the bloody lamp!"

Godwin fetched, willynilly. Then handing over the lamp, he begged, "For God sake, let it be!"

But Oswin unheard and yelled "Hoist!" And as the ladened netting shaped itself into a giant's fist and began to rise through the hatchway, Oswin smashed the lamp to the floor, and flickering oil flooded forth until it trysted with strewn gunpowder, and that blackness turned red with anger and sparked and flared and smoked its way in a wild gallop back to that orderly stout pile waiting to burst and belch forth fire.

Godwin saw his life pass before his eyes, until, the net being headhigh above the deckfloor, Oswin raised his arms and clung fast to the bottom of the netting and shouted to Godwin, "Grab a hold!" And up they were pulled, like holdfast roots of lifted sod. "What a clystercleansing this'll be!" smirked Oswin.

Once they had cleared the hatchway, Oswin, crying "Follow me!" swung himself onto the deck under Waermondt's dumb gaze and then dashed to the gunnel and hurled himself over into the Thames. Godwin followed until he reached the gunnel, where he stopped and looked back, only to see Waermondt coming up behind, shouting, "Stop, you worm!" It was now or never. Now or never. Shutting his eyes, Godwin headlonged into the water, and not an eyetwink too soon, for belowdeck, fire kissed gunpowder, and all Hell broke loose. Oswin got his way.

IN A STEW

EVERYONE THERE HAD HEARD IT. Even the Gods up on Olympus had heard it. And those who had not heard it would soon hear of it. Nearly everyone in the nearness of Southwark's wharf had heard Oswin's bigbang, had heard or seen *De Fortuin* go out in a great wavemaking bang-and-blaze. Oh yes, the blast had turned heads at wharfside—that is, heads that had not been blown off, unlike those belonging to the sorry leftovers of *De Fortuin's* crew then aboard, Waermondt and the few other wretches, who had gone up with the ship. Why, the blast had done more than turn heads awharf: many bypassers and bystanders in the nearness of the ship were hurt, and untold windows smashed, and much gear and goods toppled and strewn about. To the newcome onlooker, it might have seemed as if billowborne loads of shipwreckage had somehow washed up onto the wharf.

But Oswin, who had come up further away, saw nothing of this byhavoc, only the upbillowy smoke and proud blaze spewing forth from the gutted ship, which gave up the ghost and began to sink. What goes around comes around, he thought. And most happy with his handiwork, he began to laugh out loud, and with a mighty smack, he thwacked his hands down against his buttocks. Why, he could have danced atable for glee, if, that is, he had not been lame.

Once Godwin had struggled up out of the Thames, he made one with his friend and onlooked as well. Wow! It had worked! Hell, there was surely something to be learned from all this. The whole caboodle, they had indeed smithereened—well, Oswin had, not him. Yet Godwin felt that he could now, even on his own, downswoop thither and with one mighty Herculean netherthrust sink the ship's wretched leavings still afloat. And he likewise broke out into gleeful laughter.

All until in a clap he glanced something unsettling further upwharf to Oswin's rear, and his face blanched and his heart sank. There was no mistaking: he could make out Charles together with a bandlet of seeming toughies, of a markedly Netherlandish cut and cast. And worse, they had sighted him and began to hasten towards him. It did not look as if they bore a heartfelt welcome.

Anyone in the know would not have been taken aback at all to meet with such folk upon London's wharves, for De Keyser's Britbound gang had, as forelaid, landed here somewhat earlier than *De Fortuin* and now was spending its time stalking up-and-down the wharves, traipsing through the streets, and passing through wateringholes and the like, all in the hope of coming upon the hunted or at least word of the hunted. And like nearly everyone else awharf that day, the band too had been drawn by the hurlyburly born of Oswin's will-to-powder.

Godwin's wan stare soon dampened his mate's merriness, bringing Oswin to overshoulder a glance, wherein he likewise sighted the oncoming gang. "We must bustle on!" said Godwin, who took to his heels, with Oswin limping behind.

The throng of onlookers had greatly thickened along the wharf, and the twain's only hope was seemingly to lose themselves in this crowd. What with all the goings-on, none of the bystanders much heeded those through-hustling or those afterfooting. Godwin was all too well aware that given Oswin's lameness they would not outrun their afterfollowers and so slipped behind a great jumble of goods, which seemed to make a kind of hideaway up against one of the walls. Here they tarried, looking out through the crannies, hoping that they had somehow given their manhunters the slip. In no time, they saw the gang whisk by and away.

But any heartlightening soon yielded to newborn worry when they heard great shouts nearby. They made out Graegryck's raspy voice, cursing and cussing. *"Ik knoop de klootzakken op die mijn schip hebben vernield!"** And the skipper turned his cane on Cappella. The youths then overheard a bystander

---

* 'I'll string up the bastards that wrecked my ship!'

say, "Look! They've called in the law! By God, I hope they find the rogue
who did this and string him up!"

Indeed, unseen by the two, a lawman, fellowed by a handful of underlings, had also been drawn at once by the stirup and began his underseeking, with his henchmen sifting witnesses and searching the wharf. And so
Graegryck found himself not altogether friendless, as English law offered
its helping hand in the hunt for the undoers of his ship, a hand that the
skipper readily took.

"This is not good, not good at all!" whispered or rather whimpered
Godwin. And a sheepishlooking Oswin brought himself to nidnod a little.
Yes, there was little to laugh at now, and a weakling of a thought padded
through his noggin that a less bigbangful way of jumping ship might have
been better.

Again they overheard their bystander, "Did you hear? A pair of lads
saw two sailors jump off the ship right before it blew up. Likely they be
the ones who did it. And someone else saw two rogues come up out of the
water over there."

"Worse and worse," whimpered Godwin, who was near losing his head
now and began to fidget frightfully. And what was worse? To be taken back
as grub for Leeuwenhok's hounds? To be caned to a mash by a wrathful
Graegryck and then, if still alive, maybe sold to the Turk? To be hanged by
English lawmen as a wanted outlaw? Oh, God help me now! There must be
a way out of this bind! He fell to eyeing about him until he caught sight of
a wellworn illhung door nearly behind them. And pulling it ajar, he found
it gave way to a walkway cut through this row of wharfside buildings, no
broader than a man's breadth and no higher than a man's height. "Look!
Let's go!" he whispered to Oswin and dashed off.

"But where does it lead?" asked a wary Oswin, limping well behind.

"Away!"

This walkway opened up onto a dingydirtymuggy maze of backstreets and
offstreets, befolked by the grittiest and seediest that London had to offer:
swindlers, bilkers, footpads, highwaymen, pickpockets, blackmailers, thieves,
whores, bawds, pimps, in short, the indwellership of a rookery going about its
winding business. Along these backlanes the twosome crinkumcrankumed,
past warehouses, slophouses, whorehouses, flophouses, lodginghouses, hang-
outs, hideaways, gamingdens, cockpits, thick with the smell of fresh blood,

until they found themselves deadended in one snaking bylane so narrow that it could not have been more than eight or nine feet wide.

"Now what?" asked Oswin, who would have gladly pointed out the foolishness of blindly following these God-only-knows-whither-leading lanes and the unwisdom of bottling themselves up like this, but still smarting under the shame of his own bigbangful blunder, he bit his tongue and said nothing.

"We must backtrack a little."

They strove to untread their path, until hardly around one corner, Godwin sighted his brother with a band of toughies prowling along. Their opening had come and gone.

"What now?" asked Oswin sharply, without looking for an answer, for his mind was taken up with thoughts of somehow readying himself for the upcoming showdown. There must be something weaponlike lying hereabouts!

Godwin then eyemarked a small bevy finding inlet into a building. Some kind of business it seemed to be, for above the door there hung a welcoming signboard, *Dove's Nest*. To Godwin's mind, the name seemed to hint at something sweetly cosy, as did the freshly painted buildingface, in sharp unalikeness to its drab fellows roundabout. He hastened thither, followed by Oswin. The door was seemingly locked.

He knocked at the stout door, which was strengthened with heavy iron bands. No answer. He knocked again. Again no answer. What now? But then a small grilled wicket suddenly opened, and a cutthroatlooking rascal peered out. "What do you milksops want here?"

"What the milksops already inside want," answered Godwin, not rightly knowing what one would seek in a *Dove's Nest*. The doorman glowered and then slamshut the wicket. Now what? But then there came a banging and clanging, and the door was opened grudgingly. Oswin and Godwin were let in, one at a time, through the narrow opening. No sooner were they both inside but the door was shut forthwith and locked with a mighty iron bolt by the doorman, known to those hereabout as Lethercote, an overtowering burly man of such great strength that for the price of a mere drink he would willingly lie down in the street and allow a carriage to drive over his chest.

Not altogether sure about what they had gotten themselves into, Oswin and Godwin hung about the door, overawed by the sheer size of Lethercote, all clad in ironsided black, and somewhat worried how they would get beyond the heavily bolted door again without Lethercote's good will, which boded well to be something of a seldomhood. Irked by their lingering underfoot, the doorman snapped, "What are you two drowned rats standing in the way for? If you be not man enough for this stew, then off with you!"

As they peered around, beholding the great topsyturvydom before them, it was clear to any eye that they found themselves in one of London's seediest brothels, where the boozeswigging and knifetoting of boordom came to drink and drab in frothy wantonness, a haven away from the humdrum where all manner of thrillseeking bucks, bloods, and lewd blades came to rowdy away in life's nethermost grit and grime.

A knocking from without at Lethercote's door suddenly brought the two back to themselves, and mindful once again of what hounded them, they were emboldened to tread forth into the wildness holding sway. Indeed, they had little choice but to shift ground given that there pushed past them one skirmisher unhappily scarred in the latest wars of Venus. In pushing and passing, the selfsorry man, bescratched and benogginlumped, stopped short and said, "Beware these linenlifters! They are freshfaced to all who have a crown, but foultongued to all who have none!"

Oswin and Godwin hastened forth through the dinning welter of merrymaking, hoping to be lost in the crowd. In this, the first in a string of commonrooms, they beheld a great bedlam of whoremongers tightly clustered around tables: some thimblerigging or gambling with marked cards and weighted dice, to the loss of the unwary; others carousing to a Babellike clatter of cackling and curses, now in thief's cant, now in some outlandish otherlandish tongue; some wallowing helplessly on the floor in their upspewings of mawgnawing rotgut, the latter too unsettling to stay down all hidden away; others hopelessly drifting out of wakefulness's reach with each ebb of the tankard to the table. And amidst all this to-do, there held sway an unbridled groping and fondling of bodyparts, a teasing foreplay that was but the unhidden tip to the bustle and busyness of harlotry making unlawry pay, for *Dove's Nest* was a true highschool for the lowest kind of whorecraft, wherein its learned knew more than one way to get marrow out of a bone.

They again grew mindful of their need for haven and hastened on into the next commonroom, where their ears were beset by a most painful caterwauling, a shrill soundsmudge coming from a handful of fiddles, so illtuned and illplayed that it was hard to make out where one note began and the other ended. And to this mishmash of music, twenty or more pairs of leaden feet struggled hopelessly to keep time in jigging through a countrydance, such that twenty or more jockeying downbeats could be heard in any given bar. And upon a table, a lone dwarf jigged away on his own, as if too good to mix with the mob.

In one corner of the gamingroom, the next in the string on their way deeper and deeper into the bowels of this leapinghouse, the two beheld a brace of topless whores wrestling tooth-and-claw, their tresses bepawed and their flabbing breasts bloody from scratching and tearing. Grimly squealing and shrieking, they scrapped and scuffled away with a doggedness worthy of any doughty Roundhead or Cavalier, one that would have shamed no warring Protestant or Catholic warband. Then at the knelling of a timekeeper's bell, they suddenly ended their grappling and stood down with great offhandedness, as if a paymaster had shown up emptyhanded.

In another corner, whoremasters were treated to an even more outlandish trick, one known as the "chuckgame." Here Fanny Heath, one of the brothel's most skilled workers, stood waveringly on her head—on an oversize silvern platter set upon the floor—with breech and belly starknaked and legs splayed, while sundry "marksmen-of-the-brothel," standing at some breadth, sought to chuck halfcrowns into her netherpart. Seemingly, it was greatly fulfilling for Fanny, with her hardheaded knack for gain, to watch the upsidedown world toss coin into her "coffer," as she and others of her ilk were wont to call that bodypart.

Feeling not a little naked to marksmen of their own, Oswin and Godwin were loath to loiter any further, fishbowled thus in these commonrooms. Yet they knew that backing to the street through Lethercote's door would be unwise until some of the manhuntflurry outside had settled down. Indeed, their wet duds and goggling eyes made them all too kenspeckle in this lair of twisty cunning and trustless greed, and something needed to be done straightaway.

Catching sight of the great comings and goings up and down the stairs, which clearly led wenches and wenchers to sundry sunderly rooms above, Godwin, yielding to a brainflash, said, "When in London, do as Londoners. We must hire ourselves a whore so that we may take a room above to keep out of sight." He trod forth on the prowl, leaving Oswin behind somewhat stunned. Benighted about the laws underlying the running of such a lawless dive, Godwin fancied that, as in any everyday inn, the guest settled his bill only after partaking of the fare, and without any ado, he helped himself overboldly to one scantily clad wench on the loose, taking her by the hand and pulling her along in his haste to reach the stairs.

"Not so fast!" bellowed the girl, withstanding the pull.

And then there came hurdlewise before them one of the most forbidding beings that Oswin and Godwin had ever beheld, a great man of a woman, or woman of a man, known as Mistress Charlotte Straddle, who was the keeper of this lewd den, and who now threatened, "No money, no cunny!"

"How much then, for this one, *ma dame?*" asked Godwin, sheepishly aware now of his unguestly behaviour.

"Halfcrown an hour."

"Half a crown? What, is she made of gold?" cried Oswin, overtaking them.

"Either put out your mint or put away your pricks!"

Godwin groped himself for a coinpouch, only to recall that he had been fleeced aboard *De Fortuin*. He looked helplessly at Oswin and asked, "Do you have any money?"

"Yes," he said grudgingly.

"Can you fee the woman?"

"This is madness!"

"What other choice do we have?"

With no better plan of his own, Oswin lastly turned somewhat away, thrust his hand inside his doublet, ripped open the lining a little, and pulled forth coin, which Mistress Charlotte snatched up.

Even though he too had been bereft of his coinpouch aboard *De Fortuin*, he had earlier sewn a good deal of his money into his doublet beneath the lining, in the time that he had spent bedridden in the backroom of *De Duivel aan de Ketting*. It was Dighel who had told Oswin to take such forecare, so that he would not be penniless if robbed. And at the time, Oswin had thought it was a kind of sneaking cravenly thing to do, but now he was a little glad that he had followed Dighel's rede.

It seemed then that, with the reckoning settled, Oswin and Godwin had farthinged and groated their way over some threshold into a nameless unthreatened hiddenness. The stowaways were now hideaways. They hastened

towards the stairs, Godwin tugging behind himself their golden girl. Moll
was her name, or so she would say.

Once up the stairs, they hastened down snaking hallways in search of an
empty room to get themselves out of sight. And snaking these ways were,
for not a beam nor floorboard, not a wall nor hallway within this great
rambling building ran straight and even, but rather twisted and heaved and
troughed and swelled no less than billowing sea. And rambling the brothel
was, for *Dove's Nest* was not one building but rather a whole streetlong row
of buildings, one mated to the next like a string of cheating lovers, although
the streetface belied what lay behind, for to the eye of the unknowing
bypasser without, here was seemingly a row of sundry unlinked shops, each
smartened up to have, it seemed, its own working door topped by a fitting
signboard blazing forth the businessname—*Miss Nancy's School of Manners,
Mr. Prymme's Finely Seamstered Churchgarb,* and so forth—names that, in
this neighbourhood leastwise, were most unlikely to draw any callers to
their deadend doors.

This warren was the upshot of the unplanned growth and boom that
came Mistress Charlotte's way as she begged, borrowed, blackmailed, and
burglared her way to the top of Southwark's netherworld, buying up one
neighbouring building after another, breaching one blocking wall after
another, binding one taken framework to another, all with the knack of
those dwarfminers from sagas of eld, in their burrowing and deep delving
in search of gold.

Such a building, with a false face and farreaching innards, was no handicap to the likes of Mistress Charlotte, above all on Shrove-Tuesday, when
young godcrazed Puritans, in a pitch of sweaty faithheat, would fall upon
the stews and endeavour wholly to unbuild these bawdyhouses, or leastwise
upset their working. Misled by the streetfront, such vandals would leave
most of Mistress Charlotte's cattery untouched, narrowing their onslaught
to the door beneath the signboard *Dove's Nest.* Those would-be vandals who
knew better would always keep their better knowledge to themselves, not
wishing to let on that they had been within.

If the narrow shopfront befooled those without, the inner maze of rooms
and hallways befuddled those within, making it hard for its foundins to find
their way-out once inside. And Oswin and Godwin found themselves no
less at a loss in trying to maze through illlit hallways in search of an empty

room. Little help they had from Moll, who, in being jerked and pulled about, kept up an unbroken spate of "Where's the fire, anyways? I'm no draycart, mind you! Is this how you treat a lady? You've got a full hour!"

Not knowing which room might be yet untaken in this, one of Southwark's busiest brothels, Oswin needed to open door upon door, none being locked or lockable without Mistress Charlotte's keys and leave, her will being law here. And with each door opened, it seemed to the two as if they had lifted some bright rainwashed treadstone, wellsquared and straightlaid, only to find beneath it all manner of foul wantonly mazing bugs and crawlers, with the dank dungy earth still clinging to the underside, the dead and rotting all higgledypiggledy with the living and thriving.

In one room, they saw a naked whore blindfolded and outstretched upon a bed, with her four limbs tied to the four bedposts, as if she were some newtaken quisling ready to be quartered. And upon this wench, one furloughed soldier, having overslaughed battle for bed, worked his rough warlike will, while his fellowfighters for the fatherland, in sundry states of strippedness and arousal, stood by on watchful guard.

In another room, they saw an elderly man lying abed, with a straddling whore busily licking his shut eyelids, while another sucked the toes of his gnarly feet, and the last harlot to make up this drooly foursome tongued the lesser limb of his body, which somehow seemed to need this baptismal spitbath, a dipping that would hopefully bring taut youth back to drooping lifeless flesh Lazaruswise, as surely as the water from any fabled wellspring of youth. And when the birthcord to these wanton midwives of youthfulness would be later cut, the greybeard—so he hoped—would be enlivened enough to outlive another week of shrewish housewife at home.

A further door set ajar by Oswin brought to sight a very fleshy man down on all fours, naked but for a reined bit in his mouth and a roughing whore upon his back, this wench clad in nothing but spurred ridingboots, with crop in one hand and reins in the other. And with a mighty smack, she brought the end of her crop smartly down against her steed's rump, at the same time bellowing, "Come on, you jade! Prance for Princess Rupert!" This was clearly not the first time that such righting had been given, for the once milkwhite flab of his sagging buttocks was redder now than the cheeks of churchbound spinsters aghast at hearing bawdry on Sundays. Not in the least unheartened, he slogged on manfully with his lesson, knowing full well that his stickler of a taskmistress would never be happy with his *pesade, courbette,* or *cabriole.* He nonetheless showed great eagerness to better himself in his learning by whinnying and neighing with headbobs, as lustily as his beweighted trunk would allow.

Catching sight of two dropchinned mugs peering through the halfopen door, Princess Rupert shouted, "Out! Get out! You must wait your turn!"

"Is this run-of-the-mill?" asked Oswin, wholly awestruck.

No less amazed, but then suddenly mindful of the bites and scratches that his onetime betrothed had given him in the roughness of her lovemaking, Godwin answered, "I fear so." Turning to Moll, who was clearly more steeped in brothellore, Godwin asked, as the three bustled on again down the hallway, "Is this all lawful?"

"'Lawful'?!" she snorted. "Princess Rupert's steed is a magistrate. Where are you two from, anyways?"

"We're not from these parts," said Godwin.

"Ay, fish out of water, as wet behind the ears as your duds! And why are you two so wet? All slimy like frogs! If you were to croak and speak all throaty, I'd swear you were Lowlanders!"

"A bit of a boatingmishap," said Godwin.

"In the Thames?! Do you know how dirty the water is? And you mean to befoul me and the sheets with your dirty duds?"

"We will take them off," answered Godwin.

"Well, you still get only an hour! If you want to waste your time taking off and putting on and drying off and wandering the hallways and God-knows-what-else, that's your business! Trust my luck to have to lie with blokes all wet and dirty, who can't even get into a boat without falling in the water."

At length, the threesome came to a door, seemingly one which might have been ripped off some great black forsaken cupboard. Finding the little hovel of a room bodiless, the squatters took it over. No sooner behind the door but Godwin strove to make it fast but could not and so asked, "How do I lock it?"

"What, afraid of the bogyman?" guffawed Moll. "Mistress Charlotte lays down the law here, and the law says that only she locks and unlocks doors."

As a kind of forlorn hope, Godwin nonetheless jammed a backstool under the latch, while Oswin limped to the lone windowlet which overlooked the street below and peered out, followed by Godwin.

Unwonted to being unwanted, and not a little put out by being passed over for a window, Moll whined, "You're a queer pair, the two of you! You come to a leapinghouse only to leap to a window? If you were gentlemen, you'd buy the lady a drink."

"As the lady wishes," said Godwin, whereupon Moll hastened out of the room to fetch a bottle of what the house boasted to be its best.

"How much do you think it'll cost us to keep that shrew away?" asked Oswin, in the welcome hush.

"It would be best for us not to rock the boat now. We must blend in until nightfall, when we can slip out and make our way in the dark."

"And what do we do in the betweentime? She'll be looking to go to bed with us."

Godwin had not thought that far ahead, or perhaps had not wanted to do so. "Well, we can sideslip by way of other things: food and drink and games."

"Like sitting ducks, while this whorehouse bleeds us of wherewithal. We must pay by the hour."

"It's only money."

"Something not so bloody easy to live without! But then you wouldn't know anything of that."

These words went to Godwin's heart, even if, as he knew, they were true. He said nothing further, and they stood and gawked out the window, at a loss.

And then Oswin wished his biting words unsaid, but he had had his grounds. He had never forgotten it, years ago, the sight of hunger born of dearth, and the sight of death born of hunger, while the fat rich stayed fat and rich.

And now Moll was back, with bottle and tankards. It had been more than a day since either youth had eaten, drunk, or slept, and so something to drink was most welcome indeed. As Godwin reached for the bottle, Moll pulled it away, "You must pay up first. Half a crown."

"'Half a crown'?! For a bloody bottle of wine?!" blurted out Oswin.

"This ain't some fleabitten flophouse! If you don't like the prices here, then find somewhere else to slake your nasty thirst!"

Oswin was ready to take up her offer, but a fleeting glance through the window brought to sight Charles and his heavies right below. This was hardly the time for a row. And so grudgingly, he turned aside, thrust his hand into his lining, and tugged out enough coin to soothe the put-out *bacchante*.

Moll then handed over the bottle, which Godwin snatched and in his haste spilled some of its inholding, nettling Moll. "Have a care! Who's going to clean that up?" Godwin handed the bottle on to Oswin. "I thought you bought the lady a drink?" squawked Moll.

"Then ladies first," said Oswin, not without something of a sneer. Besides, for all he knew, the bottle could have boasted more ratsbane than wine, and so it might be best to see if she would drink some herself, which she did. And then filling his own tankard, Oswin downed the wine, or rather the spiked water shabbily dolled up to be wine. And at what cost. "Where the swine be many, the swill runs thin!"

"Are you calling me a swine?" asked Moll in high dudgeon.

"Ah, my friend means merely that our hard morning has left a bitter aftertaste that has soured the wine for him."

"An odd way of putting it, he has."

"A bard by blood, with a weakness for the hidden and unstraightforward."

"And he's awfully keen on windows too. And what's outside that's worth so much looking?" She trod over and likewise gawked out.

This busyness, of three shifting heads struggling to peer, drew the eye of Charles down below in the street, and he looked up and made out the faces of his brother and the sidekick behind the leaded glass. Seeing themselves seen, Oswin and Godwin swiftly withdrew from the window.

Yes, down below stood Godwin's brother, shadowed by Spieghel, and sided by De Keyser, and tailed by a handful of cutthroat Antwerpers and even some London riffraff newly hired for the hunt. And yes, Charles knew again his brother. But did the others also catch sight of Godwin, or of Charles catching sight of something? An offhanded aboutglance by Charles fell upon blank mugs. Seemingly none of them had marked him look up.

And what should he do now? Burst out with an Archimedean *heureka?* Huddle with his mates and whisper about what's up? Or how about a harmless dropin on the whorehouse and a happenstancy stumble upon the hunted? What was best for him?

He would put a lid on it and hoard up this business until a time more fitting for himself. If they were going to find his brother, it would be to his own boon, when an opening for his own flight was surefast and De Keyser's tailing henchmen were more scatteredly out-of-the-way.

"This street seems to be mainly whorehouses, an unlikely place for my brother to hide. Let's push on. Leave a few men here to keep watch over the comings and goings until we're back. Be sure they have one of the likenesses and stand there."

"Why unlikely?" asked De Keyser.

"My brother loathes women, good grounds to skirt a whorehouse, to my thinking."

"You seem oversure," said De Keyser, looking about warily.

"Well, if you wish to waste time rifling through spunky beds filled with flabby drabs and humping whoremasters while my brother slinks off somewhere else, then go ahead. You've been forewarned, and you, not I, will have to answer to Leeuwenhok for it."

De Keyser eyed Charles sharply. Cocky English smartass! Never liked the breed. Then he scanned the buildings and streetfolk roundabout again, as if he were still missing something. Grudgingly he said, "We will do as the Englishman says."

Still peering out, Moll said, "Him! I know him, the great oaf. I gave him the pox not but six months ago."

"Who?" asked Oswin worriedly, shunning the window carefully.

"Well, you needn't be so scared of him. He's not going to mess you up from down there!" smirked Moll.

"We'd rather not be seen by him, all the same," said Godwin. "Are the others still down there?"

"Nah, they've pushed on. There's only Clinch there now, and some other illlooked fellow. But who else would flock with such a nasty piece-of-work? Unhandsome is that unhandsome does."

"Are you sure that the others have gone?" asked Godwin.

"Why are you so keen on knowing? Is he why you're all wet?" asked Moll mistrustfully.

"You'd do well to mind your own business," snapped Oswin.

"You'd do well to mind your step, for I'll not be pushed around by some lowlife bumpkin that's slithered out of the Thames! If you lay one finger on me, by God, I'll bring in the law!"

"Why, there's no need for the law! Come, let's be merry! More wine!" interloped Godwin.

"There's something fishy here, and I'll not stand down until you tell me what!"

Oswin had not shown the best bedsidemanner, even in this brothel, and

Godwin felt now that something lastditched needed to be done. "We've sworn a most holy oath on a stack of Bibles to keep hidden our weighty business, but seeing that you seem to be a goodhearted and trustworthy girl, one surely keen to help out the fatherland, we'll tell you, but you must swear not to tell a soul. Do you swear?"

"On my soul and my pet parrot's grave, I swear!"

"We are—swear again, not to tell a soul!"

"I swear, I swear, for Christ sake!"

"We are—spies."

"'Spies'?!"

"Spies, working for none other than Sir Thomas Fairfax."

"Nah!"

"Yes."

"Spies, with hidden writing and daggerblades in canes and all that?"

"The very kind. But you mustn't tell anyone."

"I've met all kinds of knaves here but never spies."

"Will you help dear ol' England in her fight for freedom against kingly highhand?"

"Does that make me a spy too?"

"If you wish."

"Wait till granny hears about this!"

"But you mustn't tell anyone! Not yet, at least. Wait till after the war to tell granny."

This cloak-and-dagger dodge was too much for Oswin, who fearful of being caught in liewebbery, pulled Godwin somewhat away and, under-four-eyes, whispered, "Are you out of your mind? This cock-and-bull story'll only make her more mistrustful!"

"If you hadn't ruffled her feathers, this would hardly be needful!"

"It's not my fault that the wench is such a goose!"

"Well, it's too late now! I can't unsay what I've already told her! And if you mutter on so heatedly like this, she'll turn lacktrust for sure!"

Oswin had to yield that, yes, it seemed too late now. And worse, he could think of nothing better himself. And so he frowned and bit his lip.

"Do forgive my friend. He's most finicking about forswearing oaths. The long-and-short of it all now is that we need some kind of disguise to carry on our spywork."

"Who are you spying on?"

"The men that you saw in the street."

"Are they why you're so wet?"

"Partly."

"What are you spying on them for?"

"I cannot tell you all, but this I will say. Those men are believed to be working for the king, smuggling warfodder in from the mainland, and stock-piling it here and there outside London, all to allow the king's warband to fall upon this town and put it to fire and sword. Nothing'll be left standing, not a body left breathing."

"The bastards!"

"Yes. Now all we need from you is to get us two disguises."

"We've nothing here but women's clothes."

"The unlikelier the better."

Again this was too much for Oswin, who once again drew Godwin somewhat away and said, "This's gone too far! Stop while we're still ahead!"

"How else are we going to get out of here, if not by disguise? That's how my brother got me out of lockup. It worked then, why not again?"

"So we're to walk our way out of London as a limping Amazon and a courtlady? Maybe we should strip ourselves naked and ride out on painted donkeys in broad daylight! No, I will not be caught dead in a wench's clothes!"

"Trust me!"

Again, Oswin was weaponless before all this, although he swore to himself that in no wise would he don a woman's weeds. And Godwin said nothing about the need to kill a turnkey earlier when his brother's smokescreen had been blown off. The heated worried mutterings notwithstanding, Godwin's outward show of unflinching earnestness had taken in the girl. But hadn't his brother told him then to "watch and learn"?

"You're too big to fit into anything here, outtaking Mistress Charlotte's things, but she won't take kindly to me selling her stuff. I'll need to go out to the fleamarket. It'll cost you four crowns."

"Four—." What was the use? But wait, thought Oswin, at least they would be rid of her for a while, and then something levelheaded could be worked out in her missing. And so once again, he turned a little to the side, reached into his doublet, and pulled out coin. God! With all the money spent owing to this wench, they could have bought a horse by now and boldly galloped out of the town on it.

Gone was Moll, out into the streets, in search of skirts. With the pick of offbeatdom, why did they have to end up with her? Hush at last now!

"You know this is madness. We must work towards finding some better way out of this."

"You're mistaken. No-one will know us clad thus, above all after sundown."

"I'll have none of this! If you wish—"

"Enough, I beg you! I'm so tired, and I've a crushing headache." Godwin slumped down onto the bed. "We must rest as best we can. It'll be another long night, I fear." In no time he was fast asleep.

Oswin stood on. He could barely shift his leg. He helped himself to more wine—on an empty maw—and soon his head grew befuddled, and weariness downswept upon him, and before he knew it, he too was stretched out upon the bed. How sweet to lie there, while the room spun about like a millwheel. Only for a bit, to gather strength. Besides, one swallow does not a summer make, and Charles, Charles footloose in London, did not spell—. He too was fast asleep.

How much less slumberful their lieup, had they fullknown the lie-of-things! For it was only a matter of time now before the widespread net cast about them shut itself up. And still they slumbered on.

And onwards footed Moll fleamarketbound, happy with herself for all her earned crowns, gotten without even a spread of the thighs. Hee, hee! And of her spymoney, she would breathe naught to Mistress Charlotte. After all, this was not trickmoney, so the bawd had no right to it, or so it seemed to Moll.

But Mistress Charlotte was no booby, unflabbergastingly, since this flintyhearted cathousekeeper had not had the sweetest start to life: bedded, poxed, Newgated before fourteen—indeed, rotten before ever ripe—she had hoarded up great knowledge from the school-of-hard-knocks. Now overgrown with age and overworn from her former unwholesome claspings, now a sorry womb for Love's sad sickness, this toughminded and hardnosed she had never looked back, unless with bitterness, and "forever young" had been the keystone of her selfbuilding. And when holdfast "Charlotte the Young" could no longer find herself in the craggy mug that gawked back from the lookingglass, caked-on blush and the like notwithstanding, she became a masterhand in the trade of maidenhoods, handsomely selling off her fresh youthful stock, only to patch them up again in huggermugger for further handsome sale, for there was nothing that a good needle and thread could not mend.

When Lethercote came to tell Mistress Charlotte that Moll had slipped out on "some weighty business for the Mistress"—these wenches were kept pretty much on a tight rein—the bawd grew mistrustful. Was there something rotten in the beds of her whorehouse? She had a nose for suchlike, and by God she would nose it out.

Up she went, opening door upon door, in search of that sodden cheapskate twosome. At length she reached the door, and setting it slightly ajar, she peered in through the opening, and beheld the two sleeping. She popped her head in further, breaching the stillness, and rubbernecked around. No Moll. Queer this sight of slumbery overchumsiness, a little too hand-and-glove for whoremasters. What was afoot here? And why had they shown up so wet? And why so keen for a wench and then Moll gone? What, was she out gadding about as if Lady Chubsby, when there was work to be done here, with the house so busy this day?

Down she trod with roguish misgivings, but not before locking the slumberers inside their room. And making one of the tapsters stopgapdoorman, with orders to let no-one out until her return, she set forth into the streets after Moll, with Lethercote as bodyguard. The house was far too shortstaffed, and the staff far too dimwitted, for anyone else to be sent out on this errand.

By now Moll had reached the wharf, the latter still misordered from Oswin's earlier gunpowderplot. And standing-gawking there, she was buttonholed by a bruiserish twosome, who, showing forth a painted face, asked if she had seen such a man together with a limping rogue, both all wet.

"What have they done?" asked Moll, like a wide-eyed greenhorn.

"See this mess? Murdering outlaws, with a price on their heads."

"'With a price on their heads'?"

"A handsome price."

"'A handsome price'?"

"Fivehundred pound."

Moll nearly swooned. Flustered, she said, "I'll keep my eye out!" The men walked on. And there she stood stunned, staring at the shipwreckage. Had she been taken in? The liars!

And what's more, what were four crowns to fivehundred pounds? Five-hundred pounds! Could she even count that high? With fivehundred pounds she could tell Mistress Charlotte to hang herself and then go her own way. But alack! There was the rub, Mistress Charlotte! How to snitch, pocket the money, and yield up the goods under her nose without having to share earnings with the old bitch, or worse, without being browbeaten out of it all?

Moll's pretty little noggin, however, would be spared overmuch mulling, for she had stood there not five minutes when she felt a powerful grip upon her arm and heard behind her back Mistress Charlotte rasp out, "Come along, you sneaky slut! I've a bone to pick with you!" And along into a narrow nearby sidelane she was strongarmed by Lethercote.

"What's up with those two wet duds? Why did you leave them? And what are you doing here? Speak! Or Lethercote'll knock your brains out, if you've got any! Out with it, or from now on you'll lie with the Thames!"

Lief-or-loath, Moll had seemingly little choice now but to do the right thing, which would prove to be the wrong thing, and so she spilled the beans, and she did so becomingly, without any further armtwisting.

Fivehundred pounds! Oh, Mistress Charlotte knew a rat when she smelt one! And now where were those men with snitchmoney for the offering? Off the threesome whisked themselves, down the wharf, until at length Moll sighted them again. They hailed, they haggled, they handshook. And as one of the men hastened off to De Keyser with heartening tidings, Mistress Charlotte, Lethercote, Moll, and the other thug were to betake themselves back to *Dove's Nest* and keep the hunted pinned down there until De Keyser showed up with a band of heavies for the fetching.

Yet, amidst all these dealings and doubledealings, the fickle world shifted, and Fluke would have it now that the unlooked-for interlope. For as to looking or unlooking, skipper Graegryck, in a fit of selfsorriness, had withdrawn to *The Dog and Duck* to drown his sorrows, letting English law do the legwork of hunting down the blowers-up of his craft on his behalf. Having thus turned his back on seamanship for the sweets of the bottle, leastwise for the nonce, the sorry leftovers of his crew had to make shift for themselves as best they could, hardset as they were to find work on any outbound ships leaving that day or the next.

So it happened that Kobenhafen and Cappella were squeezed into finding other springheads of wherewithal to tide themselves over while shorebound. And they were not squeamish about squeezing back. Why, were not housebreaking and robbery but freebooting carried out ashore? And did God not help those who helped themselves?

Thus it came to pass that this twosome likewise found its way into Southwark's rookery and, as it happened, had broken into the endmost building on the block that had not been bought up by Mistress Charlotte and linked up to *Dove's Nest*. But what a letdown when they found their chosen-for-plundering pretty much empty of folk and havings, only an old fallen-upon-hard-times widow and her crippled mother, the latter brought down from legs to wheels.

Kobenhafen was ready to blow the women's brains out for having somehow thwarted his gaingetting. But the widow kept her head, and by the seat of her drawers, thus she spoke, as Kobenhafen held his great wheellock to her forehead, "You've missed by one the inlet to wealth! All that you could want lies hidden next door! There lives an old skinflint who has not outlaid a penny these past fifteen years. And these old houses are flimsywalled, nothing but a bit of wattle-and-dab between the beams. A great strong man like you could easily smash through the wall, crawl through, and take all that gold lying within, like a green maiden's rosebud ready for the plucking!"

As Kobenhafen's knowledge of English, among other things, was greatly bounded, Cappella nimbletongued her words into understandable German, as was needful. And oh, how the woman's heavenly words—or rather those of Cappella, who had heightened even further the dreaminess of the sweets waiting beyond—oh, how these words and afterwords stirred Kobenhafen's lust for gain!

The two women were straightway bound and gagged, in the upper bedroom where they found themselves. With a great sledgehammer fetched from the cellar, Kobenhafen fell to banging away at the thinnish wall, which yielded to his hard knocks and thrusts as if no more than soft flesh. In no time he opened up a hole big enough for him to squeeze into, while the women watched on achingly—and hopefully, for they well knew what would befall these heavyhands once they broke into Mistress Charlotte's *Nest*.

And it so happened that the room of the brothel into which Kobenhafen and Cappella had broken was the same room wherein Oswin and Godwin lay asleep, fast asleep, druggedly asleep, the same room whither Mistress Charlotte and her unfriendly fellowship now headed. Wakefulness lastly burst in upon these youths' slumbering, as chunks of flying clay hopped and tumbled upon the floor of their room. Cappella was already halfway through the hole by the time Godwin got to his feet—Oswin struggled bootlessly to rise, for his hurt leg was as stiff and useless as a heavy wormeaten log. Given that incrawling Cappella bore a dagger in hand, there were little grounds for believing this to be a friendly call.

Godwin, still lingering in an inbetweenworld, betwixt sleep and wakefulness, not yet feeling himself, and not knowing what he was doing, yielded to an oddish whim and fell upon the man warmanlike. It was the first time, yes, the first time, that he had ever fought with anyone, that is, fisticuffed in earnest, and he wondered now at his own strength and inborn skillfulness, as he easily got the better of little Cappella and roughed him up. Hell, he was not such a weakling after all!

But alack! Godwin knew not that more was acoming. With his back unwisely to the hole, Godwin did not see Kobenhafen struggling to get his great hulking body through, and before long the youth felt the muzzle of Kobenhafen's wheellock against his forehead.

"Let my Cappellakin to peace, pikdok!" And then to Cappella, *"Dem jag ich 'ne Kugel durch 'n Kopf!"*

"Nein, Gianni! Sonst finden wir nicht raus, wo er das Geld versteckt hat!"* These Cappella's words somewhat dampened Kobenhafen's bloodymindedness, and the bruiser now asked Godwin, "Vhere iss ze money?"

"What money?" asked Godwin dumbly, who had by now freed Cappella.

"You play viss me, pikdok?!"

Cappella had since looked about, and his heart sank in seeing that this room outstripped their former in shabbiness and dreariness. Skinflint or no skinflint, this abode did not bode well, and the seaman grew keen upon withdrawing. *"Los, hauen wir ab, Gianni, und suchen wir ein anderes Haus!"*†

"Vhere iss ze money??!"

"It's in the room at the farend of the hallway," came a voice from elsewhere in the room. Stunned Kobenhafen and Cappella looked about themselves, only to see that there was yet another youth in this room, one lying stilly abed, for Oswin was too lame to rise up.

---

* 'I'll put a ball through his head!' 'No, Johnny! Otherwise we won't find out where he hid the money!'

† 'Come on, Johnny. Let's go and find another house.'

With Godwin in one powerful grip and the wheellock in the other, Kobenhafen trod to bedside and squinted at Oswin for a little. Then struggling for words, he said, "I haff zeen you before, no?" And then to Cappella, *"Ich hab'n schon mal gesehn, glaub ich."*

*"Ach Gianni, die Briten, diese Inselaffen, sehen alle gleich aus!"**

"It's the last door on the right, at the end of the long hallway. The money's hidden under the bed. You'll need to break open the floorboards," said Oswin, like a wide-eyed green girl.

He did not know why he mouthed such foolishness, as if some backbone-less thing stymied in a mudpatch. It would have been far better, it seemed to him, if he had somehow upped when they had not been looking and, with a swing of the stool, knocked out the great oaf and then torn the runtling to shreds. But what choice did he have, being lame thus, and still so weary? And before such a bruiser? Perhaps too, the overkill from the morning, to wit, the blowing-up of *De Fortuin,* lingered unwelcomely in his thoughts. His hands, or rather legs, were seemingly tied, and he had wit enough to acknowledge it, however cowardly and newfangled it felt.

"Vhy are you in ze bett?"

"I was up all night counting money for my master. There was so much to count, and I'm greatly tired from it. And would you kindly let me go back to sleep now?" And with that, Oswin rolled over, turning his back on Kobenhafen, and seemingly went back to sleep.

Kobenhafen poked Oswin with his great wheellock, but the youth neither answered nor shifted. Kobenhafen stood there dumbly, until Cappella egged on, *"Komm, Gianni, das Geld!"*

"Fessel die beiden zusammen, am besten mit 'm Bettuch!"† barked Kobenhafen. These roomers could not be left behind footloose and free. And so Cappella cut and ripped a few lengths of bedsheet, and with Godwin pushed down beside Oswin, the seaman bound the two together with twisted lengths of bedding, which might have passed for birthcord. Whereupon the would-be looters broke open the locked door and hastened out into the long winding dark hallways of *Dove's Nest.*

Godwin straightway fell to squirming and pulling until the old threadbare

---

* 'I've seen him before, I think.' 'Oh, Johnny, these Islandmonkeys, the Brits, all look the same.'

† 'Come, Johnny, the money!' 'Tie the two of them together, with the bedsheet.'

sheeting, in stretching and ripping, yielded up their limbs, and thus freed, Godwin helped his hobbling mate to the hole in the wall, and, one by one, they crawled through. They were somewhat taken aback to find folk beyond, for there still sat the two women bound and gagged. But the youths had no time to help these ladies out and were about to pass through, when Godwin stopped short and gasped, "The chair!"

Yes, the elder of the two, with her hands and feet cold and feelingless from lack of bloodflow, squirmed helplessly in her wheelchair. She would gladly have bitten Godwin's wrists and scratched out his eyes, when the youth robbed her of her seat, leaving her souring on the floor and muttering muffled curses through her gag. He trundled the wheeler over to Oswin and told him to sit. A bit of a comedown, this, but beggars can't be choosers. And so lame Oswin, halfwillynilly, downflumped into the chair, and they were gone.

Out in the street, Godwin backglanced as he wheeled along, away from the brothel. He saw rowdy folk standing about the door to *Dove's Nest*, doing their darnedest to get in. He pushed on unmarked.

A little later, Godwin was emboldened to stop once in order to ask how to unmaze themselves from this rookery, and this late afternoon being hot and he overheated, the youth pulled off his doublet and shirt and spread them over Oswin's legs and lap. Off they trundled again, Godwin barechested and Oswin halfblanketed, both lost in the crowds thronging the streets. And they did not stop again until they found themselves on the outskirts, outside the heavy walls. Then forsaking footmanship and wheelchair for two nags—and half of all Oswin's coin to buy them—and outfitting themselves with other needfuls, they rode off into the countryside beyond, turning their backs on the great wen of London.

The twosome never saw the muzzleflash nor heard the gunshot nor witnessed all the hurlyburly in their wake, in the great maw of Mistress Charlotte's cattery. Kobenhafen and Cappella had soon found themselves lost in the seemingly endless hallways winding and dimlit, and what's more, found themselves utterly bewildered by all the scantily clad wenches, who fell to shrieks and flights at the sight of mighty sourfaced Kobenhafen wielding his wheellock and Cappella flashing his dagger, such that even Kobenhafen at length wondered what kind of bawdyhouse of gold this was! Yet unwilling to take gilt for gold, he pushed on, however willing his sidekick was to withdraw.

At the same time that these looters wormed their way through *Dove's Nest*'s innards, Mistress Charlotte and her fellowship backed. Lethercote straightway padlocked the door, lest anyone fly the place. Then Mistress Charlotte and Lethercote took up their trusty cudgels of eld—she had not gotten this far by softfisting—and headed for Oswin and Godwin's room to the end of making fast their goods, while they waited for De Keyser and his henchmen to show up.

And so it was that *Dove's Nest* now burnt its candle at both ends, as it were, such that counterset flickers would meet and snuff each other out midway. The ball from Kobenhafen's great wheellock burst through Mistress Charlotte's lowerparts as if they were no more than flimsy wattle-and-dab, and this wallbreaching hard knock of lead would not rest until it pushed onwards and embedded itself in the soft belly of Moll, who had cringed along behind her dreadnaughty bawd. Alack! No good needle and thread could mend these bloody holes! And what Lethercote did with the bodies of Kobenhafen and Cappella, one was hardset to know.

BEDEVILED

How quickly it burns, naked unclothèd flesh. And what soreness overwhelms when skin is scorched by the eye of heaven and left on its own. Do but ask Adam, if you can find him, that wretched firstling of mankind, who tilled a hard unyielding earth under a beating sun, and he will tell you, "Beware the wrath of God, for he will send you into a waste-land and make a drudge of you!" And yet ask him not, for you will not find him. And besides, what good would it do? For who needs the words of a Puritan windbag to regain Paradise? And unless the rain it raineth every day, what need the leadingmen of this tale, Oswin Underhill and Godwin Drighten, with inn or brothel, shack or townhouse, tick or featherbed, when Pan's fair world of meadow, grove, and greenery outspreads itself in spring's warm clasp?

To Hell with the world of mankind! That's what Oswin and Godwin thought, as they went their way through the gloaming, having put breadth between themselves and London, and with it, their manhunters. They rode as far as their weariness would allow, then stopped in an out-of-the-way grove, where they would hold out for the following six or seven days.

And why should they rush? Had they not outsmarted their foe and given them the slip? And did not Oswin's leg need healing? They seemingly had everything they needed—horses, food, weapons, money—and they were now on an even keel, free at last, lost to the world. Yes, they would take their time.

And even in the failing twilight, this their stumbled-upon grove—far, or leastwise far enough, from the madding crowd—seemed truly wizardwoven.

It was a dream come true. Lying cosily upon the green, where waterflow met land, beneath the heady craddling overhang of sweetly swaying boughs and leaves, before a fire flickering more boldly than it did, they had their fill of drink and meat. And they were giddy from the daring newness of it all, giddy from a wot-not something that had ensouled them in their great breakout. A kind of breakthrough it was.

And what odd dreams they dreamed that night, as never before. Oswin found himself to be a great lumbering shieldback, which crawled out of the sea, up onto a sunny strand, where, with paws and noggin hanging out of his shell, he sunbasked dreamily upon the hard burning sand, happy as could be. But then a storm blew up, with the wind whipping boughs and leaves wildly, and he grew afraid, afraid that it would all fall in upon him. And then with a heart knocking up against his ribs, he aboutfaced and began to crawl back to the sea. But his limbs were as if leaden, and he struggled and struggled, fearing he would never reach the water again, for trees were uprooted and fell in his path, narrowly missing him. Lastly, he reached the sea and sank into its cooling water, and in the easy sway of seaweeds, now this way, now that, he found his strength and swam away, while the storm roared above, unseen and unheard.

And in his dream, Godwin found himself in a great wasteland, under a sweltering sun that beat down on him. And his flesh seemed to melt away into sweat, until he could no more and sank down limply upon the hard scorched earth. But then he awoke in his dream and found himself in heavy head-to-toe warcladding, and he worried how he would ever get to his feet owing to the crushing weight. And he knew not the whence of this iron, nor the wherefore that it should be upon him, nor the who that had put it upon him. Then the trees about him burst asunder, showing forth a great hornyskinned firedrake that roared and snapped its jaws at him, ready to tooth-and-claw him. And he lay there feargripped, until finding a sword in the rank grass beside him, he rose up and with a mighty blow offstruck the worm's head, which tumbled away. And out of the wound flowed not scalding blood but streams of lightsome gold coin. Whereupon the dragon's body began to shrivel up, only to shapeshift itself into a mirthful but shy mermaid seated upon a bridge built of the hardest stone.

Oddish dreams indeed! But by morning Oswin and Godwin had forgotten them altogether. In the morning's cheery sunlight, they had thoughts only for things easeful, to wit, things easeful of old. And thus began their stint in the woods.

Even in this easefulness, there would still be much to do. The morning after their flight, Oswin pulled out one of the wheellocks that Godwin had bought and wondered at it in his hands and then asked childlike, "How does it work?"

"What!? You don't know how to handle one?"

"How could I?" said Oswin, a little bitter, and then a little sheepishly, "I've never even held a dagger."

The thought had never crossed Godwin's mind that Oswin was a babe to warcraft, that he had indeed never fired a weapon before, nor wielded a rapier, nor handled a dagger, nor thought of breastworks, ditches, moats, waylayings, onslaughts, fallbacks, and what-not-else. And what is more, he had never even learnt to ride a horse, as his falls and nearfalls since London witnessed. But then how could he have learnt all these things, given his lowly beggarly background?

"Well, then you shall learn, if you wish."

Oswin tried to hide a boyish beam of a smile. And so, in their few days' stay in Pan's world, Oswin steeped himself in the craft of fighting.

And if there was one to teach Oswin, it was Godwin. By dint of his lofty birth and breeding, the magistrate's son had had more lessons than he wished to recall in swordsmanship and horsemanship and every other whatmanship that belonged to manly Warcraft, all by fatherly behest. My God! What a shot he was! And what a hand with the sword! And he seemed to have been born in a saddle, such that, more than a little overawed, Oswin asked him once in funning if he could ease himself at the gallop without fouling himself or horse.

And what a quirk of happenstance it was that Godwin, the skillful warman, who in all his pamperedness had never once had to fight—outtaking the tussle with Cappella—now found himself fightmaster to Oswin, who, for all his many years of fisticuffing with fellow bumpkins, as was needful, was thoroughgoingly witless in this field, a fish truly out of water.

In marked unalikeness, Oswin had no inborn knack for any of this, but his mind was set upon mastering the craft, and so he soldiered on with his lessons. And he was most happy with his little headway. And even after his lessons, he would yet carry on for a bit, strutting—or rather limping—about with weapons in hand, thrusting with sword and swashing with wheellock, in his mindplay of bloodless bodiless fighting, tussling with windmillsails. Why, he would see himself bring whole roguish woodlands to their knees down at his feet and set cutthroat wildlife fleeing for its life. And then he would end this play with a blow to the yet smoking muzzle of his powerful wheellock, after all its bang-and-blaze.

Godwin could not help but smile, time and time again, at his friend's keenness, even if he lacked the heart to speak his mind openly when Oswin would ask eagerly about his headway. His mate was merry. Why rob him of this gladness born of harmless play? For Godwin well knew the sting of harsh words from a faultfinding taskmaster, in lesson after lesson. And it would come to mind again, as it was wont to do, and his smiles would then droop. Useless as tits on a goose! Feckless nancy! You hold that rapier as if it were a knittingneedle! The heart! The heart, you ninny! Strike at the heart! And how he had struggled hard and hotly to strike his father's heart, who masterhandedly would always ward off the thrust and somehow thwack the stumbling learnling with the side of his blade. Come on, Daisy! For Christ sake, pick up your petticoat! And unseen, the knuckles of the redfaced lad whitened in a great haftgrip. But these backglances could also be warded off, if one was nimble enough.

Far wiser it would have been for Oswin to stay off his leg altogether so as to let it heal. But all the would-be fighting notwithstanding, the leg did get better, even if it took longer than it ought to have, and every day, he came nearer his old self.

The regaining of peace, if not paradise, had brought out something else unknown to both. Godwin was rather amazed at what a good skylarker his friend was and split his sides more than once, when taken by cramping barrellaughs at his mate's wit. Even Oswin amazed himself, for how clever he turned out to be at coming up with the damnedest things, and how deftly he could word it all, without ever having seen the inside of a school or felt the caning of an angry schoolmaster. But it was—or leastwise so it seemed to him—the first time that there had ever been time for him to hold forth, and he basked therein, while it lasted, however foolish this greenthumb for the witty seemed to him. Yet Godwin said nothing of his own greeneye. If only he could likewise word and glib so handsomely!

But their time in this little paradise was now to be lost. One afternoon, while out upon a meadow at grove's edge, at the foot of a hillock, where the two were busy with their warlike play, something red dashed by, nearly within reach. A fox it was. Over the hill it had come, out-of-the-blue, and then it whisked itself out of sight. They thought nothing of it, until shortly thereafter they heard the yelping of hounds drawing near.

"Foxhunt! Out of sight!" said Godwin worriedly.

They rushed back into the grove, even as the foremost hunter overrode the hilltop, together with hounds and then other horsemen. He saw the two slip off, and turning his back on the hunt, for the nonce, he rode down to the grove and peered into the woods. Bloody poachers! He would send his men out, as soon as he was home. And off he rode again. And sure enough, later that afternoon, Godwin heard men beating through the woods. The youths quickly packed up and pushed on. They would have gladly lingered here until the crack of doom.

It came to mind again that they were outlaws here and could lose their heads if taken. They settled upon a return to their earlier forelay, to wit, havenseeking in Amsterdam. Backing to London was unwise, but surely they could find seafare from one of the lesser harbours. Ipswich seemed a good bet, and thus to Ipswich they headed.

Yes, London was the wrong place for them. They had been sighted there and nearly caught there. And since then, much more had happened, all unbeknownst to them. Most weightily, the sighting had allowed De Keyser to tighten his farflung net. Word was straightway sent to France and Spain, whither some of his henchmen had sailed, that these thugs should forthwith hasten to London. More hunters had been hired in London itself, and with painted likenesses of Godwin in hand, these hirelings were to fan out along the southern seaboard and watch the comings-and-goings in all the harbours, lest the two try to flee England. And handily for De Keyser, Leeuwenhok had strong ties already with more than a handful of businessmen in these parts, and he could look to these underdealers to teamwork readily.

And then there was the rogue's brother Charles himself, with whom De Keyser was none too happy, none too happy in the least, none too happy at all. Had not Charles pushed rather stoutly for them earlier to pass over those same buildings wherein the hunted were known to have been? Wasn't this a kind of betrayal? A withholding of seemingly hidden knowledge? And Charles had been called up on it, and he too would be none too happy therewith, none too happy at all. Charles swore guiltlessness. How could he have known who was where? Did he have some kind of wallbreaching eyesight? Or were walls perhaps glazen hereabouts?

But De Keyser was not beguiled and was given to think the worst. Before Charles knew it, De Keyser's henchmen had roughly drawn the whipper-snapper's upper body down onto the table, with his hands held down fast to his fore, facedown as if ready for some gangrape. And drawing his dagger, De Keyser cut off the youth's right forefinger. "So we know who the maid is and who the man. Do such again, and you will lose the hand."

Charles was hustled out under Spieghel's watchful eye. All he could do was whisper to himself through the pain, "The Devil shits Dutchmen! The Devil shits Dutchmen!" Yes, there was no magistrate's door to knock upon in high dudgeon, no hearing to hold forth before. But wait, there was something he could do for himself. Again under his breath, he cursed that sodomite brother of his. Why, were the rogue to hand, he would cut his bloody throat in the church! Had he not suffered enough already owing to that sad bit of Papa's wasted spunk?

But the brother was not within strikingreach. After an unhurried three days' ride, Oswin and Godwin had nearly reached Ipswich and now meant to stop at Manningtree. Near the outskirts, they met a man, one Nehemiah Hook, coming from the town and stopped to ask after waymarks for the Ipswichbound.

"Have we met before? I think I've seen you somewhere before," asked the man.

This flustered Godwin somewhat, who was fearful of being known again and found out, and so to offshrug the asking, he offhandedly brought forth the little falsehood, "Perhaps we met at Oxford" (the latter being, needless-to-say, a town-of-learning, where youths were not unlikely to meet).

Oxford?! The Puritan had never been to Oxford! What would he want with Oxford? He or anyone else from Manningtree for that matter? That was kingcountry! The king's foul lair, riddled with the popish and the ungodly. "Are you for king or Parliament?" asked the man.

"For both," said Godwin.

"For neither," said Oswin at nearly the same time.

"We brook no kingsmen hereabouts, and if you're not for us, you're against us. You'd do well to clear out. Off with you now!"

"You be off, before I knock you on the noodle!" threatened Oswin.

"You've been forewarned!" said the man and went his way.

Both youths wondered at the man's cheek. Yet, in the neck of the woods wherein they had grown up, they had gone almost wholly untouched by the great inland war, a war wherein nearly any he was ready to turn another's black-and-white into black-and-blue. And up against this war, Oswin and Godwin were set to brush roughly for the first time.

What a to-do they found in Manningtree! What throngs of folk milling in the streets! They asked a bystander what was afoot.

"Know you not?" answered one Elijah Slingstone.

"I wouldn't have asked if I knew," said Godwin.

"Why, we have witches in our midst, and today they're to be shown forth as such and to be well paid for their mischief."

"Witches?" smiled Godwin. "Some kind of play to be given then? What holiday's today?"

"No holidays here, only holy days! No play here, only prayer! As I said, we've found witches here, and today they will meet with hanging and burning for their foul ungodliness!"

The man was indeed in great earnestness, for latterly, this town and its nearlying fellows had been bedeviled by a rank outcrop of witchery, and a feverish witchhuntcraze had in upshot spread throughout this the heartland of Puritandom. And the rounds of blamestorming and backblaming made needful the calling-in of masterhands, to wit, witchfinders, who through their wizardry could betray any woman who meant to hide a hag's heart.

And what a godsend for the indwellers of Manningtree that they found within their own townwalls a witchfinder *très extraordinaire*, one Matthew Hopkins. Born in nearby Lawford, young Matthew had grown up in Manningtree, where he had heard much godly talk of misdoings in the nearby seamarshes, that misty unwholesome world lying somewhere between sea and land. The boy had seen his first devil there by his twelfth year, even if no-one bothered much about it at the time. But then the wee imp had been something of an outsider, born to the godly vicar of Great Wenham and to a Marie Roy, a French Huguenot, or "the French whore," as young Matthew's playmates were wont to call her, the mother of the "scab-of-the-French-pox," as they were wont to call young Matthew, in their play near the stinking marshes. But by 1645, those unhappy days were happily long gone.

With the coming of war, however, and with it, fear of kingsmen and popelings, Matthew Hopkins came to show his stuff. Lawyer's clerk by week, witchfinder by weekend, Hopkins, together with his sidekick Mark Stearne from Lawshall, only weeks earlier had brought a onelegged hag, one Elizabeth Clarke, to book, and to noose, for witchcraft. And he had awed Manningtree through his deftness in slickly proving her witchhood (and through his levelheadedness in asking the town for only two pounds, for all his pains in harrowing Hell). And all Hell broke loose in the wake of this hanging, when Hopkins and Stearne rode up-and-down these parts in search of those named as sisterwitches by that nasty hag Clarke, before she had given up the ghost—or the devil.

And this day, as Oswin and Godwin found inlet into Manningtree, the everbusy Hopkins and Stearne had brought to book a pawful more of witches, hence all the to-do, as folk flocked to the town—a bit of sightsee-ing—first to lockup to see others of the same ilk awaiting trial, and then for the mainshow itself, the hanging or, if they were most lucky, a burning.

"How can anyone know a witch?" smirked Oswin.

"Why, it is all written up in learned books, books that witchfinders read carefully and learn by heart. And thank God that we have such men among us in these sad times, when the world is all out-of-kilter, owing to the wickedness of kingship and popery, which hath tainted the minds of our womenfolk and turned them into hatemongering witches."

While it was indeed true that witchfinders at this time had to hand many handbooks on witchery, both older ones and newer more up-to-date ones, Hopkins and Stearne, however, had grounded their guidelines, and snarelines, upon the old *Dæmonologie* of the dead King James alone, a would-have-been beliefwright in things witchful. Indeed, for them, the king's one book was the last word on witchhunting, a holy Bible for a holy war against witch- and warlock-craft, and the king's word was as good as the king's law. In both the thoughty and thingy worlds of Hopkins' witchlore, *antiquissimum, ergo verissimum.*[*]

Slingstone had fallen speechless, as a wagon trundled into the townsquare bearing a stooped elderly witchy foursome. Only the oldest would do, for what did the young know, youth being wasted on the young? Indeed, these women looked as if they had died yesterday, only to be dug up today and

---

* 'The oldest, therefore the truest.'

brought back to underbear some wite seemingly overlooked when they were alive. And what an outcry rose up from the mob at the sight of this mouldering flesh!

"You mean to hang and burn these crones?!" asked Godwin. "Is this lawful?"

"O, yes. They've been tried before the magistrate, as is rightful, and found guilty by the law. One witch, the worst of the lot, is to be burnt and the rest hanged. We've already hanged oodles more."

"How can anyone know a witch? By a tally of her worts?" smirked Oswin again.

"The witches themselves have owned up!" said Slingstone.

"What, they come forth and say, 'Mark, I am a witch!'?"

"No, a witch will yield up the truth no more readily than a walnut its heartlet. Both must be squeezed to the breaking. Only the sternest of steps will work. They must be stripped naked and set upon a hard stool in a locked-up room, overwatched by the witchfinder and his helpmates, and they keep the witch awake day and night, ever asking her to own her witchhood. And they keep an eye out for her imps, underdevils in the shapes of cats and newts and spiders and suchlike, underlings that do the witch's evil bidding. And these imps, the witch must suckle once a day from her witchmark somewhere on her body. So if kept thus locked up and watched, the witch will be betrayed by her imps alone, or by her witchmark, but most in the end betray themselves in owning up. Look, there is Mr. Hopkins himself, our witchfinder."

Onto the scaffold there rose up a rather short awkward man of slight build, who in upping his right hand asked his listenership for hush, and spoke forth thus: "Dearly beloved! My fellow Believers! Mark! The way to Heaven High is steep and straight and narrow, most narrow indeed! And it is well bounded, and the Devil's weeds, those thornhiding rosebuds, do not grow at its wayside. And it behooves the godly to uphold the law of God, and to uproot the Devil's weeds, and the Devil's works, and the Devil's workmen, and the Devil's handmaids, who lie hidden among the godly, like thorns among roses. Oh, beware, my fellow Believers! Beware! Satan's poxy whore doth wear a patch to hide her scab. Do but scratch that scab and see what foul matter flows forth from it, as unwholesome as stale marshwater, and only fire and noose can withstand it. A woman is wise enough if she knows her husband's bed and no other's. And the husband of womankind is the King of Heaven. And a man who does not rule his woman is no more than one. We are all evenranked in the sight of God, but the Devil and his drudges would make lords of themselves and bondsmen of us all. We are all brethren, but fiendish hatemongers would turn us one against the other. Oh, turn a blind eye to the Devil's works and the Devil's whores, then see what foulness arises: your coffers lie empty, your livestock lie wasted, your wives lie barren, your daughters lie ravished, your babes lie dead. Be watchful and strong, for witches everywhere, ye Soldiers in God! For it is by such shes that evil comes into this world. My brethren and fellow Believers! O ye of the one right belief! Weak redes and weak deeds undo all! We have come together today to do God's will. Let His will be done now! Bring forth the first witch, and behold the wages of sin! See what godliness and law can do when strengthened with will and deed!"

Forthwith, the carters ordered one of the women—Magdalen Alcock was her name—to climb down, but she was too rickety and brokenbodied to get down by herself and so was manhandled down. And no sooner down but the mob fell to twitting and ballyragging and badfellowing her, spitting and cursing and striking her as she doddered by, on her way to the scaffold. But then, this onetime innkeeper, handreader, bringer-forth of misbirths for fallen women in a bind, not to speak of other former less wellmasked oddjobs, had never been wellloved in this town.

At one point, one of the crowdlings reached out and grabbed a hold of her hand, thus stopping her, and then made as if handreading, only to blurt out in a creaky highpitched voice, "Your lifeline looks awfully short, my dear!"

At this, many burst out into thighslapping laughter, although the handreader's wife, standing at his side, upbraided and warned him, "Take care, lest the old biddy hex you!"

With a worried look, he loosened his grip, and the old woman was pushed on. Yet she seemed not to give much heed to any of this. All the blackness that had once hued her now white locks—or which had filled her heart, as her witchfinders believed—seemed to have downslumped to her lower eyelids, witnesses of days and nights of sleeploss that she had been made to undergo latterly, in order to wring any selfdamning words from her lips. Onwards she stumbled to the scaffold, struck at, spit at, laughed at, jeered at, through the crush of overmany bodies busying and fidgeting. And it broke Oswin's heart to see the helpless woman meet with such a handling.

She came to stand in an upheld slump, up on the all too wobbly scaffold before the moblings. Once again, Hopkins spoke forth, "This she is guilty of witchcraft. This she hath lain with the Devil and hath suckled imps bestowed upon her by the Devil and hath sent out these imps to bring war and death to the godly. If you do not believe, hear it from her own lips." Then turning to the woman, he asked, so all could hear, "Did you lie with the Devil? Speak!"

The drooping woman was struck to fillip forth an answer, if not to waken her. "Yes, yes, even as you say," and then she slumped again.

Again Hopkins asked, "Did you lie with the Devil?"

"Yes, yes, even as you say." And then, fleetingly strengthened, she tacked on, "And he gladdened me more than you ever could."

The crowd fell to prating and hissing, although more than a few found some merriness in the answer. Not to be outdone, Hopkins went on, with even greater keenness, "Did you suckle imps at your witchmark and then send them forth to make mischief in this land?"

"Yes, yes, even as you say."

"There, you have heard it! She acknowledges it herself! A scabby witch by her own tongue! A whore of Satan! A whore of Satan! A stinking filthy whore of Satan!"

"That devils should choose to hobnob with silly old women that know not their right foot from their left is the great wonder. And that grown men should choose to set great store by such foolishness is the greater wonder! Alack that more angels and devils dance upon the crown of a nincompoop than on the pate of any pinhead! But where God hath his church, the Devil hath his chapel!" spoke Oswin.

These words trod heavily upon Slingstone's heartfelt faith, and that of many others there. But this was not the time to wrangle with any offputting outsider, and lest he miss out on any of the gawkworthy, Slingstone stalked off to be nearer the witchbaiting.

The woman was now stripped of her tattered red clothes, and oddishly enough, her wan timeworn body naked, sagging and flabbing, lined, wimpled, and wrinkled, somehow winsomed a few eyes in the crowd, and skylarks began to make the rounds about how it would be to lie with sicklywan flesh on the brink of the grave. Then the woman was smeared with pitch and halfdragged to an upright that stood midmost in a heap of things burneasy, and to this stake she was fastbound. The heap was straightway lit, and a great witch's bonfire blazed up.

In no time, fire met flesh, and the woman fell to writhing and wriggling and screeched and shrieked and wailed and wept and coughed and hacked and called upon all and any to help her, as her flesh melted and burned away before her own eyes.

Oswin fidgeted and wormed in his saddle and then said, "I will not sit by and bear this madness!" He rode nearer, and pulling out one of his wheel-locks, which had long itched in its holster, he shot the wretch in the head.

The woman's screeching stopped forthwith, and her writhing body sagged limply in its bonds. Her ghastly pain was no more. The crowd's jeering stopped forthwith, and their flailing arms wilted in the crowd. Their lively merriness was no more. All had fallen hushed and still. Heads began to turn about to see whence came the bigbang, and all eyes came to fall upon a glowering Oswin and his wheellock still smoking.

The overseeing powers-that-be, like everyone else, stood there dumbly. Hopkins halfmouthed, under his breath, an unbelieving "Why, he's killed the witch!" And then he shrieked for all to hear, fingering at Oswin, "He hath murdered the woman! He hath broken the law! Take him! Take him down!" In a deafening outburst of shouts and cries, the blindangry mob billowed forth towards Oswin.

"Fly, Oswin, fly!" shouted Godwin. The two youths madly spurred their horses. Slingstone and one other bystander had already reached Oswin and struggled to unseat him, while others picked up whatever was to hand—some boldhearts even grabbed brands from the fire—and began hurling all this at Oswin, who got more than one nasty blow under the hail of these hurlings. Luckily for the youth, his would-be unseaters were also worsted in this pelting, such that they fell back, and Oswin rode clear.

In the mad dash, the two galloped towards the towngate, and as Oswin, looking back over his shoulder, neared the opening, a halberdwielding fellow by the gate took a swing at him, only narrowly missing his leg. Onwards they rode, out of Manningtree, out of the grips of the godly, and hurtled on eastwards, hopefully Ipswichbound.

The left-in-the-dust indwellership of Manningtree stewed over the to-be-done. They had after all witnessed murder before their very eyes, and by rights the slayer ought to be hunted down and brought to book. But who wanted to ride out now and miss out on today's witchhangings? After a stint of humming-hawing, the powers-that-be settled hereupon, that they would go forward with the hangings and afterwards cobble together a manhuntparty.

By the time the three other misdoers had danced their lawless last at rope's end, and the huntingbevy had ridden forth out of the west gate in search of Oswin and Godwin, Nehemiah Hook had backed to Manningtree. The earlier runin with the two had thorned him deeply—what would he want with Oxford?!—and he could not leave off wondering where he had seen that face before, until lastly it backflashed into mind. The wanted men! And the fivehundred pounds! This was too weighty to let lie.

In no time, he found again those men who had been asking after the twain in the streets. What with all the witchfuss, and their earlier tippling, these hirelings of De Keyser had failed to spot Oswin and Godwin in the kerfuffle. But no sooner hearing of them and of their asking about Ipswich, the hirelings rode out eastwards, Ipswichbound. And Nehemiah Hook found himself not a penny richer for all his pains.

Oswin and Godwin had ridden off hard, but in time Oswin's white nag began to lag behind and falter until it limped to a halt, willynilly. Stopping, they found that the horse bore a nasty gash to its right ham and seemingly had lost much blood. The halberdswing that had missed Oswin's leg had struck his horse instead. The horse was too lame now to carry on, and unless the wound was tended to, the beast would likely bleed to death. A fine pickle this! To be unhorsed out in the middle of nowhere!

"We daren't linger here. We don't know who might be following us. We must carry on with the one horse now," said Godwin. Then stripping the jade and drawing a wheellock, Oswin shot the beast in the head.

As they readied themselves to ride on, casting aside all but the most needful things—like worried seamen tossing bodies and freight overboard to buoy up a battered ship—a head popped up over the hedgerow. The youths reached for their guns.

"No need for more shooting!" said the man. "I mean you no harm! I'll come over, and you'll see I'm weaponless. No more than a straightdealing fieldman going about his work." And once over, he went on, "But I can't blame you for being a little triggerhappy. Oh, I know about you two."

"You must be mistaken," said Godwin.

"I've seen your face painted on sailcloth, only yesterday."

"Can you tell us the way to Ipswich?" asked Godwin.

"That's where I saw your face. There were men there wandering through the street, showing your face about, and asking about you, ready to give five-hundred pound to anyone with knowledge of your whereabouts. Ipswich's likely not the best place for you, but if you wish to know, I'll tell you."

"Spare your breath," said Oswin.

Glancing at the dead horse, the fieldman went on. "Looks like you don't have many friends, if they'd do that to your horse, horses being hard to come by these days, what with the war and all. Why, everybody's all atalk here-abouts about the two wanted men and what they must have done in order to be wanted for fivehundred pound. Are you in some kind of bind? I know of a little out-of-the-way hut nearby where you could hold out for a while."

"Tongues wag until they're ripped out," said Oswin, hoping to scare him off.

"Well, don't let me keep you then. God ride with you!" said the fieldman, keen to get away now.

"Wait, man!" called out Godwin, and the man stopped. Turning to Oswin, Godwin asked in a low voice, "What now?" But Oswin only stood there wordless, gawking forlornly at his dead horse.

"Leeuwenhok must surely be behind this. Who'd have thought that a man could be so hardbitten? And if his men are already in Ipswich and London, then the whole of the southern seaboard's likely swarming with them as well. I think it best we head north. My family's got land near Chester. I know those parts. And there's a harbour there as well, and from there, we could easily ship ourselves."

Oswin nodded blankly. Godwin then asked the fieldman—he seemed harmless enough, what with his offer of help—about the best way to Chester from here, and the man readily helped, and then the two rode off upon the one horse, its black coat sweaty.

Straightway the fieldman hastened off to Manningtree. He knew where they were going! And he knew where he was going, to fivehundred pound! Hee hee! In time, De Keyser's hirelings from Manningtree came upon the footer and asked about riders upon this road.

"What's it worth to you?" asked the fieldman.

"Fivehundred pound," answered one. Whereupon the fieldman tattled. When the henchmen meant to ride on, the fieldman stood in their way and asked, "What about my fivehundred pound?"

"What about a pound on the crown?" With the end of his wheellock, one horseman struck the fieldman on the pate, knocking him down. Then three of them headed north, while a fourth hastened back to Manningtree to send word on by boat to De Keyser in London that the hunted had been sighted.

Oswin and Godwin rode for the rest of the day, unaware of any man-hunters. And when twilight fell and a cold rain began to fall, they stopped in an out-of-the-way grove for the night. As they lay upon the muddy earth before a sputtering fire, beneath dripping boughs, they had cold cheer and little talk.

How unlike those in Manningtree! What did the indwellership of Manningtree not have for talkhubs and chatnubs that day? And unflabbergastingly, there followed much chewing-of-the-fat there, well into the evening and beyond.

Some thought Oswin and Godwin to be warlocks or even devils come in all their Satanry to draw wicked necks, such as that of Magdalen Alcock, out of their rightful nooses. But alack, that those hangworthies had sideslipped a catching, for Manningtree's own manhunt had come to naught, thanks to a fieldman's nogginlump. With his pound on the crown, the fieldman had broken off his walk to Manningtree, turned about, and headed home—the nail that sticks up gets hammered down!—only to be overtaken by lawmen from Manningtree, who asked about any maybe sighting of Oswin and Godwin. But the fieldman, with his throbbing head, was too illminded now to help anyone, above all for the sake of fivehundred catchchary pounds, and so he sent the horsemen on a wildgoosehunt to Ipswich. As saddlesores set in, with the lawbreakers nowhere to be seen, the lawmen gave up the hunt. All said and done, was it truly worth it, all this racing-about over some bumped-off witch? The law would have to go abegging this time round.

But then what is hardier than weeds? In the end, the more lawminded of Manningtree could only throw up their hands, amazed how every day the road yielded forth the uneverydayest of things, outlandish codgers and untold thingumabobs of uncouthness, all kinds of vamps and tramps and scamps, all roperipe, as if the road were a great winding womb of ungodly freakish misbirths that if doggedly followed down would lead anon to the earth's smelly backside. Better that the townwall be bricked up and never more opened! Foul befall the foul!

Elsewhere, amongst Manningtree's loremasters of devilcraft, misgivings set in about whether Magdalen Alcock had truly been a witch. And in more than one snugcosy *symposium,* there followed, in *argumenta e silentio,* much dinful bitter wrangling and loggerheading, *a priori,* over whether she might instead have been a *bona-fide* devil, *a fortiori,* and then over what manner of devil she could have been, whether she ought to be reckoned amongst the *lemures, spectra, umbrae mortuorum, lykanthropoi, kakodaimona, incubi, succubi, diana,* or countless other hobgoblin- and devil-kinds that befolked the narrow pathways to godliness. But in the end, too many tankards had been emptied to allow for a thoroughgoingish underseeking into any could-be *primum mobile* for all this witchery and devilry.

And in the background to all this, unseen and unheard, De Keyser gathered together his men in London, and in the wee hours of the night, this manpower sailed to Manningtree. And by morning, when the hunted, sodden and grumpy, rose and rode off Chesterbound, De Keyser and his great band of horsemen unshipped themselves at Manningtree, ready to ride north.

SUNDERCLOVEN

WITH OPEN ARMS, ironsided Bellona ever stands, ready to squeeze all to her steely breast. Nay, she is no choosy warlike goddess, given her weakness for all stripes: blonde or black, grey or green, high or low, in- or out-law. She loves them all and loathes to leave any out. For her, there can be no greater gladness than seeing folk of all walks fall in and come together, and then fall amongst each other's arms, and then finding them, still the morning after, stripped naked of all their riving outward trappings, lying peacefully upon that bed of greenth which is the killingfield. Why, she is a true leveler in her own way. And it was into the cold enclasping of this goddess that Oswin and Godwin rode halfwittingly.

But how so? Whence this bloodiness and bloodymindedness? Why, Bellona's tarrying in England came about over a prayerbook. Well, there was a little more to it: it had to do with churchrailings as well, and a few other things of less weightiness. It all started when king Charles I—the nextbest son of James I, the same James, by the way, whom Hopkins and Stearne had followed—gave a free hand to Archbishop Laud to cleanse the church of its waywardness and bring a handsome orderliness to all things churchly. Railings to mark off the holy from the unholy, and one leading book for two kingdoms.

But oneness broke down when the Scots would have none of that English prayerbook. And war between England and Scotland ended up becoming war between English king and English Parliament, when the latter proved keener to bankroll its own cleansing of church and state. With push coming

to shove, Charles' stiffnecked nagging wife, queen Henriette Marie—sister
to Louis XIII of France and aunt to no less than the later Sunking himself—would end up skedaddling back to France, while the weak and feckless
husband Charles would end up digging his heels in and standing his ground
at all costs, and pretty much at the wrong times and in the wrong places.

The daily upshots of this war, Oswin and Godwin were now to behold, as
they rode on into the wartorn Midlands. Where once greenkind lay gridded
and patchworked by a network of hedgerows breaking down the land into
road and field and town, like a maze of Laudish churchrailings, there now
lay outburnt townlets, and fields wasted or overweeded through want of
husbandry. And the roads were now the homes of homeless warflightlings,
highwaymen, and plundering hungry warmen, and wagons bearing fresh
warfodder or the dead and the dying. What grisly comings-and-goings!
The two would need to keep a sharp lookout now, lest they were to become
Happenstance's playthings, for all manner of blackspots lay in their path.

This grimness of war and its ugly aftermath dampened the already dampened youths, who found themselves often shying away from the road and
riding over rougher ground in order to wideberth wayfarers and warfarers
who might not boggle at unhorsing them, if not worse, for horses were hard
to come by in these harried parts. Such at least was Godwin's thinking. This
roundabouting of the two upon their one nag slowed them down greatly.

But not so for their manhunters, who rode forth swiftly and steadily,
clusterwise, thickly beweaponed. De Keyser had his grounds. He illliked
the English and England, above all this wartorn England, which was as
riskfraught for him as any other. He could not wait to be home. And he had
his name to think of, for he was known back home as a salt-of-the-earth,
leastwise in his roughneckworld, and as a getter-of-things-done. And then
there was money to think of, for the longer this whole business lasted, the
more money would be outlaid and the less left for him to skim off. Well, he
wasn't hustlebustling thus out of the goodness of his heart alone. Besides,
Leeuwenhok was not looking for any costsheets, only English blood, and
for all De Keyser cared, his master could have his bloody English blood,
however worthless to De Keyser's thinking, blue or otherwise.

After a few days' ride, Oswin and Godwin reached the town of Leicester.
Sick-and-tired of lying out on the muddy earth by night, and heartsickened
by their lot, they found inlet to the town and thought they might splurge

somewhat—they were after all halfway—by having a rightwaysround lodging for the night, like anybody else, on this the twentyninth of May 1645. In their weariness, they hardly marked the edgy townbustle about them and came to stop at an inn called *What Was Once the King's Head.* (The careful innkeeper was seemingly hedging, for the town was in the hands of Parliament now, but for how long was anyone's guess.)

They sat in their shabby room, before a cold gristly porkpie, and ate little, and said nothing. But this was hardly a switch, for few words had been spoken between them since Manningtree. Godwin above all had been markedly tightlipped and was rather peeved with his friend. First Graegryck's ship—if that was the first—and who knows how many were killed then? And what a mess that spawned! And then the witch. Who knows what they left in their wake? Yet he had to yield that those wrongdoings seemed somehow rightdoings, for had they not needed some kind of redherring in order to flee? And had not the woman's painful last been ruthfully shortened thanks to Oswin's shot?

Godwin fell into a daydream wherein it was morning and he had awoken from restful slumber, in that great featherbed of his, in his old home, and soft sunlight beamed in across the still room, his own room, so handsomely trimmed throughout with red and white silk. And his door was fastbolted. He could see his books from where he lay, filled with tales of swashbuckle and faroff lands, which he had read time and time again at fireside on wintry evenings.

This dreamy tightlippedness on Godwin's part had soured Oswin somewhat, who was given to taking coldshoulder as unspoken faultfinding. But then no-one had ever understood him, it came to mind, or even tried to do so. Why should he think it would be otherwise now? And in order to busy himself, he pulled out the wheellocks and began cleaning them.

Godwin could hold his tongue no longer. "For Christ sake! Can't you leave those bloody guns alone? I'm sick of them!"

"A man without friends can't be too careful," said Oswin coldly, as he wiped away hotly.

"You're not a man without friends."

"No? Why don't you count them all for me? You'll likely need all my fingers as well, and those of everybody else in this inn, Christ no, everybody in this hole! And even then you'd have not a tenth of those who'd fawn on you. Why, your bony Dutch bride and fat father-in-law still pine away for you and clearly want you back at any cost. I'll be damned if I can make out why you hobnob with some bumpkin whose dirty hands are not good enough to clean your guns!"

"Oh, stop it! You're being foolish!"

"Forgive me, but how else does a churl from nowhere behave?"

Oswin had worked himself up into some heat by now and would have gladly gone on, but there came a knock at their door, and both froze. God-win held up a hushing forefinger to his lips. Again there came a knock, and again, until a voice without said through the door, "I know you're in there, brother. I could hear you out here. Come on, open up! I'm not going to bite! And I'm not going away until I've at least talked to you. So open up now."

Sure enough, it was Charles who stood in the doorway. "Brother, you don't know how much bother it was for me to hunt you up."

"Surely the thugs that we saw you with last were of no little help," said Oswin, with wheellock in hand and with a stolen glance windowwards.

"Still in Arcadia, I see, brother, although one that's illtrimmed around the edges. And I see the swain has not bettered his manners."

"Nor have you yours, "said Oswin.

"As to the 'thugs,' to use the swain's word, I was hardset to free myself from their clutches. They had hijacked me when you ran off in Antwerp!" Holding up a wrapped stump of a forefinger, he went on. "And this is the reward I got for the pains I took in keeping them from catching you in that whorehouse."

"Juggling liar!" snapped Oswin.

"Our eyes met, brother, when you were at the window, and you saw how I led them off! And only yesterday, I was able to give Leeuwenhok's hench-men the slip and break free. And I've ridden hard all day and night. But beware, brother, they're still after us. They know you mean to ride to Chester. It's unwise to stay here any longer. Surely they'll be here by morning, if not sooner. Let us make for home. Father'll hide us away and keep us out of all harm. How good it'll be, to be in our old home again and away from all this running-about with cutthroats on our heels. Come, before it's too late."

Godwin upped at once and began gathering together his few things almost wildly and then said, "Make haste, Oswin! We'll find a place for you as well."

But Oswin sat fast, glowering at Charles. "I'll have nothing to do with the knave who raped my sister, unless it's to cut his throat!"

"This is not the time for such things, Oswin! Come, we'll settle everything afterwards."

"In the same way the law settled things for my wronged sister afterwards and then for me afterwards as well. I'll have none of him or anything he touches, and even less so with anything of your old man!" Then to Charles, "Out of my sight, before my finger grows itchy!"

"Oswin, this is foolishness! Put away the blasted gun and come along!"

"I'm staying here, and he's clearing out before I put a ball through his guts. Your choice is clear."

"I can't stay here, Oswin! You heard what he said!"

"Yes, he's never short on words. Go with him, if you want. I'm staying put."

"Come, brother! He's not one of us."

"And bloody proud not to be!"

"Damn you and your stubbornness! I'll have no more of it!" said Godwin, who picked up his bundle in a huff and stalked out.

The stayput sat there in the stillness following, the gun still gripped. To Hell with them! To Hell with them all! It was alright. This wasn't the first time that anyone turned a back on him. He knew how to live with it. Old bloody hat! Yes, he was not one of them, and thank God for that! He did not turn his back on anyone worth standing-by. And so, it seemed, he was mistaken about his onetime friend. Better it came out in the wash now rather than later.

To have walked away so easily! Or was it rather a runaway? Over what? A bugbear of a brother! Should have shot the bastard! Runaway from the bumpkin, the clodhopper, that's what it was at bottom. Oh, to Hell with them! He would keep to his own from now on. He could trust himself, and only himself, and nobody else. Alone at last! Who needs the bloody world? An unweeded garden grown to seed.

Stillness, long stillness. O Maddy, where are you now? No more than a helpless countrywench alone in this mad world of war and backstabbers. If only he had—but what could he have done about it? He had tried everything he thought right, and that still wasn't good enough. Maybe she was somehow better off now. He would have only dragged her down more.

He would give no more headroom hereto, to this downwelling of old.

He dared not. He sat there blankminded for an hour or two, with sightless eyes to the window.

Be damned if he would stay in this hole any longer. Damn them all! He would go his way and now. He jumped up and gathered together his few havings and rushed out. The streets were wild with bustle, men and women lugging all manner of things and building up hurdles and blockers here and there in the streets. Something was afoot. Alack, no horse! Godwin must have ridden off on it. Now he had no choice but to trust to his footmanship. And how his heart fell when, reaching the towngate, he saw that it was shut up, boarded up, plugged up.

"I need to leave at once!" he said to one of the nearby troopers.

"Ay, don't we all!?" said the Scotsman back.

"What do you mean?"

"Where have you been, man, sleeping? We're beset by kingsmen, who are readying themselves to storm the town. You're trapped within these walls for the now."

"What am I to do?"

"That's for you to settle, but I can say for myself that I would sooner let my guts down about my heels than yield an inch to that bloody Stuart king! Why, you're a good strapping lad! Will you not make one with us and help us fight? We're hardset for fightingmen."

Oswin had had no mind to meddle in this war. He had long before settled upon not lifting a finger to help. Let the king and the rich fight it out amongst themselves and kill each other off! Who in their right mind needed either of them? Leeches all of them!

But everything was otherwise now. He would be fighting for his own life, stuck here as he was, as if in a great bog of quickmud, and the town was outmanned unfairly. In the end, it little mattered what became of him. He might as well die well today with a musket in his hands than be run through tomorrow while whimpering in a corner of his room, like a bitch's whelp. And so Oswin gave his yeaing word to the Scotsman, a yeaword which he meant to keep.

*"Mo ghille math ort, glè mhath!"** A laddie after my own heart, you are!" Whereupon the Scotsman, with almost motherly care, had Oswin outfitted makeshiftily and given a place by the townwall to stand his ground. And

---

* 'Good for you, laddie! Very good!'

there he stood throughout the rest of the day and the following night, for he was not such a devil-may-care slackard as to snooze away while war writhed in his lap, or so he prided himself.

Yet for all his watching and standing-ground throughout the night, Oswin failed to see how the king's soldiery made an utter deathtrap of Leicester. And it was only with sunup that Oswin and his fellow lastditchmen fully beheld the seemingly countless clusters of footmen and horsemen roundringing the townwalls, soldiery who by morning had gathered together into one great body. Pitted against Leicester's thousand or so Roundhead footmen and horsemen, eked out by a further ninehundred or so weaponbearing men drawn from the town's indwellership, stood over tenthousand.

And with sunup, Prince Rupert, who headed the kingsmen here, would call upon the Mayor of Leicester to whiteflag levelheadedly, but the holdfast latter only stalled, so that in the meantime walls might be further strengthened for the coming push-and-shove, even though the man had been told by his topranking Roundheads that any withstanding was sheer madness. By around three o'clock in the afternoon, Prince Rupert had had enough, and so the onslaught began.

The bruntbearer herein was to be *The Newark*, the strongest stretch of the townwall to the south, where Oswin had been placed, beside his stalwart Stuarthating Scotsman. It was overagainst *The Newark* that the king's fieldpieces had been set up, on *Raw Dykes*, the banks of an old broken-down waterlead, built by the Romans when they were the masters there. And for the rest of the day, the wall was stonked unforgivingly.

And what a nasty mess all those balls made! As the wall and any nearstanding buildings dwindled away under this pounding, Oswin, all kenkeen, at length popped his head up over the crown of the wall to peer through the thick smoke—a peeplet to see how things were faring—but was straightway struck in the face with a wash of blood from his friendly Scotsman, who in likewise standing tall had lost his head to a ball. And the headless body seemed to cling to life stubbornly, in its writhing and clawing along the ground as if in search of its lost head, until it lastly settled down and then, after a bit of fitful twitching, lay all meek and still, out of harm's way. Oswin had never seen suchlike before and, rather shaken, showed greater carefulness in upshot, leastwise for a while.

But when did they get to shoot back? All this blasted huddling behind a wall! Yet on boomed the king's guns from afar, and bitmeal and stitchmeal, the wall lessened until it was breached. Oswin and his fellows were ordered to block up this hole, and under the fall of further balls, the men worked away at building up a breastwork of woolsacks and other things, to forestall any foeful storming-through.

Who would have ever thought that he would spend his first day of warfare mainly walling—fussing with sheepshearings!—rather than shooting back and clubbing down? And out-of-the-blue, he wondered whether the Irishwoman, the same with whom he had stayed weeks earlier, had ever reached the end of her stonen hurdle, the one whereover he had sweated so gainlessly. But this flashback flitted out of mind as quickly as it had come, flightlingwise, and Oswin then threw himself into his work with even greater keenness.

What a toll it took, this breastworking, as balls maimed on and killed on! Oswin glanced back once and was aghast to see one of his fellows sitting upon the ground, weeping unwieldily, hugging his blow-off lowerleg, swaying to-and-fro, as if putting a baby to sleep, while the blood flooded forth, until he grew weary of it all, rolled over on his side, and seemed to fall asleep. And no-one fussed over him.

Another wretch wandered about well behind the wall, and charily so, as if ashamed of having lost face, for a ball had slickly grazed his head and indeed swept away his face: eyes, nose, jaw, and most of the tongue. Truthbe-told, Oswin hiddenly welcomed the falling darkness, which blackened out these ghastly glimpses of Mars at play, all this Rawhead-and-Bloodybones.

On boomed the guns, until midnight, when the wall was breached again, and kingsmen stormed forwards to take the town. At long last, Oswin and his fellows could open fire. It was only at the third onrush that the kingsmen broke through, and the stayputs were swept back, taking up a new line behind hurdles of pileup.

And while *The Newark* was being stormed and broken through, elsewhere, at the north and east gates, which were woefully undermanned, kingsmen laddered themselves over in the darkness, behind the backs of the fightingmen of *The Newark*. And with the north and east gates in time flung open, the king's horsemen streamed into the town.

But the fightingmen of Leicester were hardbitten and unready to truce, even if their stronghold was now but a weakhold. On they fought, from street to street, again and again pushed back, until in the end they came to make their last stand in the marketsquare, where only hours earlier cabbagemongers and their fellows had stood selling their wares. And only then did these fighters grudgingly throw down their weapons and give up the struggle.

And so the town of Leicester fell. And worse, it was set now to slip even further into a Hellish orderlessness. Thanks to the doggedness of the town's fighting-back, Prince Rupert saw himself in no way beholden to keep his men from sacking the place. And while Leicester's fightingmen were rounded up and marched off to lockup, droves of soldiers worked their way through the town, gutting it of all that was worthful, taking not only goods but also maidenheads, and further lives where deemed needful, and wasting what they could not make their own.

Numbering amongst the twelvehundred or so men taken was a weary Oswin, who had not slept for almost two days now. So great was the number of those taken that they were locked up in cellars about the town. And by fluke, by a kind of heartless fluke, Oswin ended up being locked up in the cellar to *What Was Once the King's Head*—now newnamed or rather backnamed to *The King's Head*—the same inn where he and Godwin had fallen out.

Down in the damp overcrowded pitchblack darkness he sat, and as he tried to yield to sleep and call it a day, beyond he could hear, fitfully, men laughing, women shrieking, guns firing, as the soldiery fell bloodmad. He began to doze off, and the thought padded weakly through his head that he might as well have stayed sitting up in his room all this time, for all the good his warring had done, and then he would have at least been on top of things, rather than locked up down in this cellar. Then came sweet shuteye, deep deep sleep.

The next day, Oswin and his fellow inmates were uncellared and marched back to the marketsquare, past houses burnt out here, smashed up and ransacked there, through streets still strewn with heaplets of pileup, rubble, and lifeless bodies, like washup from fleetwreckage. And along their way, they were taunted and flouted and struck by their takers. Once they had reached the square, where a further body of soldiers stood at the ready, Oswin and his mates were made to line up and then stripped of whatever worthful havings they bore, although the shabbiest, such as Oswin, were mostly passed over as hopeless, and luckily for our youth, no-one found his insewn coin.

Orders were barked forth that the bystanding soldiers were to shoulder their muskets. A firingsquad it was. So this was it, thought Oswin. Well, he could fault himself in no way. He had done what had seemed rightmost to his thinking. And now he would stand tall for the last time.

As he waited stiffly for balls to strike and his hot lifeblood to stream away, the headman ahorse spoke forth, "You have fought against your king, your lawfully Godgiven king. By the laws of God and king, you are guilty of the greatest sin and the gravest misdeed, which shouts out now for the harshest of handlings, a heavy bloodprice for lawless bloodletting. But your king is a forgiving king, even as the Lord is a forgiving lord, who enclasps to his heart his once wayward children, even as the Good Shepherd is a caring shepherd, who opens His fold again to flocks once lost. And so our king, his Highness Charles I, will stay the hand of rightdealing if you will swear now, upon all that is holy, to be faithful henceforth to him and to his rightwise struggle against England's foes, within and without. Therefore, raise your right hand now."

Most of the lined-up men sheepishly nudged up a limpish right hand, darting sidelong glances thieflike to see how their sidekicks answered this kingly call. Oswin too glanced about himself and was amazed to see these once stalwart Stuarthaters, under threat alone, crumble as if no better than stale cake, even though they had fought most manfully under a far worse onslaught of maiming and deathdealing balls only hours earlier, amidst crumbling walls and buildings.

"I said, raise your right hand!" Nearly all of those who had not uphanded before did so now. "This is the last! Swear now or be shot!"

Oswin was aghast to see that his own hand, thoroughly blackened from warfaring, had likewise upped itself, and worse, that his wayward lips began to aftermouth the oath spoken forth by the horseman, an oath not only to be faithful henceforth to the king but also to fight his war for him steadfastly. He was the king's man now, willynilly!

And off these once-lost-now-found were led, to be outfitted makeshift-ily as pikemen or musketmen and allotted here-there amongst the king's warband, as needed. So it was that in this illbankrolled strife, warfodder, living or otherwise, was hard to come by, and beggarly kings could not be kingly choosers.

With a downhung head, as droopy as a puppy's ear, Oswin trod off, and the only thing he eyed was that blackened hand of his, that dirty hand which had lifted itself shamelessly. Had he not aforegiven his word to fight against the king? Only to forget it now so as to fight for the king? What good was one's word when the following day it shapeshifted itself into a counteroath? But upon further quibbling thought, it came to mind that, truth-be-told, he had sworn only to help the Scotsman spare the town. Nowise had he sworn then to be any hardcore Roundhead. There was herein some unsameness, he thought. And then Oswin fell to wondering how many other fellow warrers, here and elsewhere, had sideswitched, and how many times. But are not the flags and fanes of warfare but windtossed vanes, the playthings of every passing gust? Alack! The lamer, the happier to limp along with the times!

Like his erstwhile mates, Oswin too was outfitted for further warfare, now as a pikeman, so that hedgehoglike he might bristle for the king. And then he made one with his new brotherhood-of-the-pike, men who would have run him through only the day before and who now took the youth under their wing and crashdrilled him, sharing all their warwisdom. And thus Oswin began in earnest his stint of warmanhood.

In his own turn, Godwin too had earlier been taken under a brotherly wing, as it were, when Charles found him out so slickly in that Leicester inn. And how deftly the brothers brought off their flight from the town, before gates were shut up, and their sideslip past the King's soldiers still drawing up. Onwards they hastened, and all the while, a prateful Charles brought to Godwin's mind their former cosy homelife, the which was not altogether irksome. Yet more than once, Godwin felt that they should turn back and get his stiffnecked friend, even if it meant strongarming him into a willynilly comealong, bound hand and foot.

But before Godwin could make the thoughtsome the deedsome, the two brothers came to a wooded bend in the road, a mile or so from Leicester, and no sooner past but a body of horsemen burst forth and rounded them. At once was heard De Keyser, who asked Charles, "Where is the other one?"

"He would not come."

"You were to bring back both!"

"I've told you, he would not come!"

"Brother, what is the meaning of all this?" asked a stunned Godwin.

"What does it look like?"

The sad truth homethrust itself upon Godwin, that his overchumsy brother had betrayed him into the hands of his Antwerp foes. Oh, Oswin, how right you were! And what a pushoverfool I've been! Godwin looked about himself for an opening to flee but could find none. Besides, his nag would not likely outstrip these thirty-odd betterhorsed bruisers.

De Keyser rattled away in Flemish, whereupon half of his henchmen hurtled off back towards the town, seemingly to get Oswin, while two others took away the reins from the brothers, bound and gag them in their saddles. Then they withdrew into the grovelet again, seemingly to wait in hiding for the others to back with Oswin. But it was not long before the thugs backed Oswinless, with news that unsettled De Keyser greatly. Godwin could only guess that, what with all the bands of soldiers gathering in the town's nearness, the gates had been shut up and that there was no getting-in or -out now.

De Keyser held forth once more, and then the same fifteen or so headed back, seemingly to lie in wait until the town opened itself up again, while the rest, with their bondsmen, rode off southwards. Godwin guessed that De Keyser meant to wait it out somewhere nearby.

The longer they rode, the more fretful Godwin grew. What were they bent upon doing? Would they drag him back to Antwerp and lock him up with his onetime bride for the length of all his afterdays? That was enough to unsettle his guts. But perhaps this was overrosy mindplay. Perhaps they had worse in mind. Was he then to waste away under Muhtmet's great Ottoman cane after all? But surely, Leeuwenhok would not have gone to such costly lengths merely to nab and then sell him off for a few pounds. Perhaps worse awaited him, much much worse. Perhaps—and now he grew most queasy.

They reached the townlet of Market Harborough and found therein only one wretched little inn. When almost upon its threshold, they sideswerved briskly, as the inndoor burst open, and a strapping thickwristed wench, with bucket in hand, tossed foul water out into the street, narrowly missing the men. As De Keyser looked daggers at her, the surly wench asked, "What are you gawking at?" then turned her back on them and went back in. Oh, these swinish English! thought De Keyser. How many more days on this middenisland?

But beggars could not be choosers, and so De Keyser held his tongue and his nose and went in. Barely through the door but Godwin, whose fears had run wild and whose guts now seethed outright uproarishly, retched and began to upspew his gristly Leicester porkpie. The wench with the bucket shrieked, "I scrubbed the floor only now, and you go and make a sty of it! Get him out of here! Out with him!"

This was not De Keyser's day! He ordered two of his henchmen to take limp writhe-and-retch Godwin out into the street to carry on there. And after another upspew or two, the weakened youth downflumped upon the bench by the inndoor, while the two heavies stood by, busy with their grumbling prate.

As he sat there forlornly, daydreaming how he would hang himself that night with his bedsheet, a small band of toughlooking troopers happened to come riding by, likely scouts, and straightway Godwin was overcome by a sudden uphearting brainwave. Why, it seemed that Happenstance had thrown him a timely bone! Before his minders eyed it, Godwin jumped to his feet, rushed up to the troopers, and asked—nay, begged—that they let him enlist on-the-spot and be one of them.

What a turnabout this! Warlords, in all their marching-plundering through towns and fields, were the ones who were mostly strained to ask— nay, browbeat and pressgang—the youth of England to take up musket or pike in this war, given the unending shortfall of manpower on both sides. And now here was one asking—nay, begging—to fight without so much as a hollow word uttered! Only a fool would pass this up.

Godwin's two bigbrothers rushed up and began to draw him back. He shouted out to the horsemen, "Help me! Spare me from these popelingspies from the Catholic Spanish Netherlands!"

As Godwin well knew, the words *popeling* and *Catholic* and *spies* were oil to the fires of the Protestant faith, which burned strongly throughout England, with its mindset of the beleaguered. Unflabbergastingly, this loaded speech filliped forth from the troopers a flurry of drawn swords and loaded guns and calls to unhand the youth. Straightway, the two men let go of Godwin, and one of them rushed inside to bring their master the illtidings, while Godwin hastened back to the horsemen and stood by them.

De Keyser and his henchmen rushed out at once. Aghast to see what had befallen, De Keyser spoke forth as smoothly as he could, with his hoarse brogue, "No grounds for any unease, soldiers. This boy has outstanding business with us."

"'Business'? What is *your* business in these parts? You don't sound as if you were born hereabouts," said the leader.

"The boy is wanted in Antwerp for misdoings. We are here to take him back."

"It's a lie! They're after my life! They hijacked me outside of Leicester! Look, see the bruises about my wrists from being bound!"

The bruises overcame any misgivings the horseman might have harboured. "Kidnapping is against the law here," he said threateningly to De Keyser. Then turning to Godwin, he asked, "You still want to fight, lad?"

"Yes."

"Do you have a horse?"

"Yes."

"Better and better. Then to saddle!" Godwin then shouted to a bystanding innhand to saddle up his nag and bring it over. "And as for you and your pack of hounds," the horseman said to De Keyser, "you'd do well not to meddle in others' business. Off with you, before the war happens to meddle in yours!"

De Keyser was no dummy. He knew that he had lost this round, and so he backed off becomingly and watched Godwin ride off with the troopers.

Godwin in no wise meant to fight in any war but rode along with the troopers in the hope that some opening would quickly arise wherein he could get away, clear of De Keyser, king, and country. He did not even know whether these horsemen were Roundheads or Cavaliers. But for the time being, the youth played along and answered all the horseman's askings freely and keenly. And soon the horseman came to say, "You're clearly wellborn. What's your family?"

"Oh, nothing great, nothing great at all. No-one, I'm sure, has ever heard of my family."

"Drivel! I know blueblood when I see it. By God, I can smell it! No need to be afraid here. I won't send you home with a scolding. We have many plucky lads among us who've stolen away from fathers and mothers in order to fight." Godwin thought it best not to trifle with this trooper and so told him his name, which wowed the man greatly and stood the youth in even better stead.

The troopers kept up a sharp lookout, for they were indeed scouts, out to gather knowledge of their foes' whereabouts, almost spywise. After about a halfhour's ride, the headman said to Godwin, "Those dogs don't give up easily, do they?" Godwin gawked at the man dumbly. "Look back. See how they're following us?"

Yes, De Keyser was no pushover. He had sent out half of his men from Market Harborough to follow Godwin and nab him should any opening arise. Godwin's heart sank as the knowledge homethrust itself upon him that it would take more than this to free himself. And even after they reached the troopers' hometurf of Northampton, the afterfollowers kept up their lurking watch of Godwin. He dared not sneak off on his own now. He was stuck! And even more so when brought before the trooper's topranker in order to be sworn in, for having offered to don the warman's weeds, he now felt somehow beholden to play the part and could not bring himself to naysay. And as he held up his right hand in the gloaming and aftermouthed the oath which wedded him to Roundheaddom, he blackguarded and horsewhipped himself within for having once again botched things so hopelessly. But then, was he not born to bungle? Godiva indeed!

NASEBY-FIGHT

W HAT IS WOTAN before hearts stirred by betrayal and loss? Oh, what does an erstwhile Valkyrie, a former chooser-of-the-slain, care about one-eyed Wotan? And one need not grub too long in ashes to find an answer hereto. Do but ask Wotan, if you can find him there, that onetime *Licht-Alberich,* and he will tell you, "Beware the wayward deeds of a self-willed daughter, for she'll blaze your way to *Hel* in a fiery *Götterdämmerung* and burn your damned hall down with you still in it!" What writhing and wriggling, what screeching and shrieking, what wailing and weeping, what coughing and hacking there will be, as fireflickers enfathom all! Oh, how it will crackle, flesh shielded or unshielded!

But what did Godwin Drighten, one of the leadingmen in our tale, know of any of this yet, as he slumbered fitfully after his flight from his foes, Leeuwenhok's men, only to be roused early in order to begin crashdrilling, for he was a fledgeling willynilly Roundhead now. And so this dull morning, he found himself led by the befriending horseman of yesterday on to meet the waiting mustermaster of today.

He came to stand before one Llewelyn ap Hywel, known hereabouts, however, as Sergeant Lionel Powell, or behind his back as Black Powell, "Black" owing partly, it seems, to his swarthiness. This newnaming, the Welshman nowise minded, for it halfhid his not-too-greatly-liked Welshness. This fellow, together with his erstwhile chum Grigor ap Rhys (known later in England as Gregory Price), had earlier forsaken his homeland, where his great unlove for the Stuart king had made him overmany unfriends amongst the mostly Stuartloving—or leastwise Stuartabiding—Welsh. And so the twain had turned their backs on their fellow *Cymry** in order to fight against the English king.

And in so doing, both Powell and Price had been drawn to the thought-stuff of leveling, which was spreading like wildfire amongst Sir Thomas Fairfax's gunpowdery soldiery, and in no time, the two Welshmen became hardcore levelers. But Powell lost touch with his Price, when the former was raised to the rank of sergeant, even if this loss left him feeling somewhat more of an outsider and loner. But such an uprising in rank nowise dampened his fullhearted belief in his own rightmindedness, that in all things, all men were thoroughgoingly the same, that is to say, altogether evenmatched and same-as.

Why, had not Sergeant Powell, more than once, held forth before his undermen that they were all brothers-in-life and brothers-in-death, that there was no tall here, no short, no high, no low, no he, no she, no English, no Welsh, that they were all one in the eyes of God and before God's law, the which no background nor breeding nor sunderly rights could other? Why, did not the smallest he have the same right to the sweets of life as the greatest he? No, no! Powell was not one to lower himself to the beastly uppityness of a Bubulcus, Statilius Taurus, Pomponius Vitulus, Vitellius, or Annius Capra of eld.

"Sergeant Powell, you have a new trooper under your wing. This is Godwin Drighten, no less than the elder son of Lord Charles Drighten, the thirteenth Earl of Etenheighte. You've some of the bluest blood in England before you. Take good care of it. See to it that his Lordship's son is handsomely outfitted and drilled."

Godwin was then left alone with Black Powell. The two looked each other up and down, or rather Powell looked up, while Godwin looked down, given that the younger wellbuilt latter was much taller than the older runty former. The two men illliked one another at first sight.

"Alright Goldielocks, let's see what you can't do," snapped Black Powell, who tossed Godwin a worn buffcoat and rusty helmet that had been stripped from a dead kingsman. Further came a chipped sword and a pair of iffy wheellocks, and lastly a stained *Soldier's Pocket Bible*, that is, a patchwork of snippets taken here-there from the Holy Writ, to be carried over the heart,

---

* 'Welsh.'

for so weakassed had the king's balls been latterly that the thick booklet had been known to stop these from reaching the heart.

The Welshman was greatly taken aback to see how skillful Godwin proved to be with sword, gun, and horse, and more than once Godwin got the better of his teacher, which nowise endeared him to his master. But no-one is flawless, and so Black Powell strove to take from this upstart any rough edges that he might find, then and thereafter.

And where arm failed the Welshman in outdoing, tongue filled the place in chiding, and a steady spate of putdowns flooded forth. "Come on, blondie, shake a legkin!" or "That was so lackgutslike that you're turned even more wanmugged!" or "What a foolish turn! So it is true that blondes are dumb!" and more of the like, not to speak of odd bits of badmouthing in Welsh, which slipped out unwantedly, and which to Godwin's ear sounded rather like Irish, but then the two tongues, after all, were kindred.

Under all this blackguarding, Godwin grew so flustered from knuckle-whitening anger that he ended up doing much worse than he should have. Seeing this, Black Powell happily ended their drillstint for the day. "Not to worry, boy. We'll whip you into shape yet." And true to his word, more of the same followed. But the youth had no-one to thank for this but himself, for he had, after all, freewilled himself into the king's warband.

It was not long thereafter that Godwin was to get his first taste of warfaring. The stronghold of Northampton was once again bedeviled with a shortfall of food, and a band of troopers was thrown together in order to go forth and gather in whatever eatworthies could be found. And Godwin found himself part of a foodgathering twelvesome.

Men of all stripes these were: Stubbes, a blankish rather shortsighted do-all; Longdale, a scamp through-and-through, pressganged; Smollet, a crooked tradesman's son a little slow on the uptake, drafted; Bigmore, a heartless cutthroat, likewise pressganged; Petty, a parson's son who ran away from home after getting the housemaid with child; Browne, a bit of a fawner; Ruddle, a beggarly fieldman keen to enwealth himself in the war; Blackwell, a frightening unknowner; Dunne, a drunkard, likewise pressganged; and lastly Grey, a man wanted for bilking and blackmailing. And the kingpin in this undertaking was to be Black Powell himself.

Before setting out, Powell gave a lofty little peptalk, then turned to the more down-to-earth nuts-and-bolts of where best to go and what best to sidestep. Above all, the men were to stay sharp, for the nearby countryside was alive with kingsmen. And if they skirmished, they were to make bondsmen of the rogues, but "if they be Irishmen, cut the swine down without a breathing!" This was no crank whim on Powell's part, for he was playing by the book here. Indeed, in the early months of 1645, the English Parliament had enlawed that any Irishman taken on English ground could be put to death straightaway, for the misdeed of being Irish on English ground.

Off the troopers rode into the thickening fog, and it was not long before they spotted a band of horsemen, standing stilly upon a hillock somewhat off. Godwin counted seven, one of them on a white gelding, not unlike Powell's. The troopers stopped, and Powell eyed them.

"Are they kingsmen, Sergeant?" asked Smollet.

"They look more like outlanders to me. Maybe paddies, or even highwaymen. Too bleachfaced for gipsies. A handsome white gelding that though. I'd gladly have him under me."

Godwin alone knew that they were De Keyser's henchmen, although he said nothing. The troopers rode on, eyeing these unknowners all the while, until the latter were fogged out. Godwin would need to be sharpeyed now.

At length they came upon a field sporting a flocklet of sheep, minded by two wee shabby shepherdboys, neither anymore than eight or nine years old. Powell ordered five of the men to gather up these sheep and take them back, while he would ride on with the other six. And as Godwin and four others rode towards the field, he asked Stubbes almost under his breath, "Who's to pay for these sheep?"

"Hey, mates! He wants to know who's going to pay for the sheep!" The men broke out into wild cackles.

"We don't pay. We barter. We show them a good time instead. You'll see!" hoarsed out Bigmore.

The two shepherds were greatly unsettled at the sight of these horsemen riding down upon them. When they saw the troopers begin herding their woolly wards off, the younger took to his heels, but the elder breasted the warmen in the hope of driving them off. Whereupon Bigmore and Blackwell took a hold of the twain, stripped them, and tied them bellydown onto the backs of two ewes caught from the flock, and now made sport with them. Whipping the ewes and the backsides of the boys, they drove off these two ewes to the end of the field. A kind of race it was to be, a game wherein these Argonauts hastened forth to fleece king Aietes of his Golden Fleece. Heartened by all this, Ruddle rode off to the nearby homestead to see what Scylla and Charybdis might be lurking there.

Godwin and Stubbes were left behind with the herd. So this was what the great war of freedom was about, herding sheep. "I thought we were at war with the king, not with the commonfolk," said Godwin to Stubbes.

"You'd best mind your words. You mustn't say *king.*"

"Why not?"

"Powell's orders."

"So what's to be said instead?"

"*Monarch.* If you want to say *English king,* or *English queen,* you have to say *British monarch.*"

"Whatever for?"

"Powell says that words like *English* and *king* and *queen* and dozens others draw lines that ain't there."

"Lines that aren't there?! Between a king and a queen?! Then Powell's never seen a woman naked!"

"Maybe so," said Stubbes, and then taken with a sudden thoughtkin of his own, and faking a Welsh brogue, "Maybe he fancies sheep more!" and he cackled. "God knows, we herd up enough of them for him."

"Why stop at that? No, let us say henceforward *ho monarkhos brettanikos.*"

"Hoitytoity with the Latin, are we?"

"Greek."

"Call it what you like. It's all the same babbling to my ears. Besides, it's not what Powell wants."

"To Hell with what Powell wants."

"Well, you've been forewarned."

With their band of few broken down into even fewer, Godwin grew uneasy, and rightfully so, for this splintering made easy pickings of them, should foe ride down upon them now. And so he told Stubbes to stay sharp-eyed, for the seven men seen earlier, those with the white gelding, might easily maul them here. And Stubbes too grew worried.

Over the cries from the ewerace, Godwin and Stubbes heard the thunder of hooves. "They're coming!" gasped Godwin. "Make ready!"

Stubbes drew his gun and squinted. Then suddenly a white horse came galloping out of the fog, and Godwin, ready to spur away, shouted to Stubbes,

"Fire!" The gun cracked, and the white horse fell, toppling its rider. Shouts followed, "Don't shoot, you bloody fool!" The rest of the galloping horsemen stopped to help the downed man. Godwin saw now that Stubbes had shot Black Powell's white horse from under him. These were not De Keyser's men after all.

What a tonguelashing Powell gave Stubbes, until Stubbes in turn blamed Godwin for telling him to fire, when Godwin had better eyesight. And then the Welshman fell to blackguarding Godwin unsparingly. But the painful stints of drill over the past days were all too fresh in mind, such that something stirred in Godwin now, and the youth found his tongue.

"Why did you come galloping down upon us out of the fog, without so much as a hailing? How were we to know who you were? And it was not my fault that you failed to set a foreman so as to sidestep the group's needless breakdown, making us all easy and edgy targets! Not to speak of the unwisdom of splitting up so small a party in the first place, above in this fog, when we know that foemen are lurking nearby." Indeed, Powell's backgallop had been spurred by a runin with a few kingsmen further down the road, although nothing was said of this.

"We don't need any slackjaw from you! Why, you think you're too good for us commonfolk, who weren't born with a silver spoon in the mouth? Well, let me tell you something, Sir High-and-Mighty, you're not in your prissy drawingroom now! By God, you need to be brought down a notch or two! On your knees! I said, on your knees! That's an order!"

And biting his wan lip, until it nearly bled, Godwin got down and knelt down in the mud, looking as if stuck in a bog, while Black Powell stood looming over him.

"Bit of a comedown, is it? For someone who never worked a day in his life or had to dirty his lilywhite hands? My goodness, you're awfully wheyfaced for all your blueblood! Wheyface lacks a hue! Oh, we'll heal you of that! Reach down and hand me up some of that mud you're wallowing in. Mud!"

Godwin reached down grudgingly and scooped up a handful, which Black Powell took and then smeared on Godwin's burning face. "Why, look here, my men! The great yellowhaired yellowbellied baby has dirtied himself! Isn't that better now?"

"Yes, yes, even as you say," was Godwin's parrotlike comeback, and the men suddenly stopped their cackling.

"Do but cross me again, and I'll tar and feather you! Now gather those sheep together, all of you!" As Godwin got to his feet, Black Powell got into Godwin's saddle, for be damned if the Welshman would footslog back. Godwin dared not open his mouth again, with the power-of-law lying in Powell's hands, who would have none of his othermindedness. And as it was, the youth had already more-or-less poohpoohed the Pooh-Bah openly.

But as he loped and trudged along behind, like a ragamuffinly shepherdboy, while someone else rode his horse, Godwin stewed and could not forget. Of all the places to be in and of all the things to do in this world, what was he doing here, doing this? He had not been born for this. This was utterly beneath him. What shamefulness! He was after all a Drighten, from a long line of Earls of Etenheighte! And he swore then and there—and he needed to make no handsome outward show by upping a right hand and aftermouthing oathy words—that he would never again stoop so low, law or no law, even if it were the last thing he did! Powell and anyone else beware! Bloody Hell! He would shout Mars!

And Mars was coming his way. The following day, Godwin and other Northampton Roundheads got their marchingorders. They were off to fight the king, who had dithered and dallied long at Daventry, but twelve miles west of Northampton. And the king's shillyshally there had allowed Sir Thomas Fairfax and his evergrowing Roundhead warband to outplot him and hardpower him into standing and fighting now. Indeed, by the evening of the thirteenth of June, Fairfax's Ireton overtook and mauled the king's rearguard.

Amongst the kingsmen at Daventry and its outliers was young Oswin Underhill, the other leadingman in this tale. He too had been busy with woolgathering, as it were, that is, sheepgathering, in the great plundering of Leicestershire ordered by the king in early June, wherein sheepen and neaten droves and other eatworthies were taken off, all to feed Cavaliers back in Oxford, the king's wartime seat. A kind of stealing from Peter to pay Paul, it was. And Oswin loathed it.

In the great flurry of lifemanship, soldiers, loot- and plunder-fattened, here-there wisped away into the fog or whisked away into the night. And more than once, an opening for Oswin arose wherein he too could have scrammed, skedaddled, with or without pockets full. And more than once, his heart egged him on to show turncoatlike footmanship, and yet he tarried, even if his wherefore had fled. Why, he was at an utter loss as to why he stayed on.

And the wherefore lessened even more, on the thirteenth, as Oswin and his fellow Cavaliers headed back north, by way of Market Harborough, the townlet which had become De Keyser's makeshift headquarters in the Leeuwenhok bywar, there where the king hoped to be shored up with Goring's men from the west. But Goring was not coming, and worse, the bearer of his letter to the king saying so was waylaid by Roundheads. The king was now outmanned. But there was enough boldness on staff to sway the king into standing his ground, whatever the odds.

The following day, the fourteenth of June 1645, the Cavaliers began to muster at Market Harborough, at two o'clock in the morning. And then at seven sharp they marched south, while the Roundheads footslogged north, reaching the townlet of Naseby by five o'clock, all as if night were day and day night. And by eight o'clock, the two great warbands, reckoned at about eleventhousand Cavaliers and fifteenthousand Roundheads, had gathered into two straightrunning lines upon two counterset hilly ridges that overlooked the yawning sleepy slump of Broad Moor inbetween, to the north of Naseby.

Neither Godwin nor Oswin had slept the night before. Nor had De Keyser's two henchbevies who had followed along behind the two warbands, like so much baggage, and who now found themselves amongst hangers-on near the laagered baggagewagons, everwatchful for a lowered guard.

In the stillness before the oncoming storm of steel and lead, while fast upon a warfooting, in all the waiting for Time's passing tread, what fighter does long for time, only to wish it cut short? And as he stood amidst the thick of fellow kingsmen and horses all tidy in rows and bunches, like fresh stock in a tradesman's showcase, Oswin strove to stay keenwitted, while yet watching his own bands of redcoat thoughts and ragged flashbacks march past and skirmish before his eyes.

On this day, which might well be his deathday, he felt what a waste it had been, all the want and dearth that had ground on, all the wrongdealing and skulduggery in the name of law and friendship, the wearying raceabout to sideslip the uneschewable, the wholesale missing of lovingkindness.

Did it all end here, to the din of shot and the shout of men that made men lose their ears? Did it all end here, to the smoke of powder that made men lose their eyes and see not light but guns, not foes but clouds? Here where men would be made as stubble to the sword, and the field would weep red for the loss of the green and the grey, where men's brains and bowels would be no more than mud and turf underfoot? Was this all? To make a heaven of a hell, and a hell of a heaven?

In his great sadness, the youth thought of home, and for the first time in his life, it seemed, he did not long to be there. Or rather he longed to be there somewhere else, such as it had been in all its flawfulness, not then but now and hencefoward. But enough. He dared not think anymore.

And there was no time for thought now, for a man-of-the-cloth came to stand before Oswin's stand of pike. As a kind of pushalong before the oncoming push-and-shove, the holyman held forth, as he read from a book thus: "The Lord giveth forth winnership, and the Lord taketh away winnership, but He taketh from the rightful at the first and giveth to the rightful at the last, for God will feed us with the bread of a foe and the body of the foe," and more of the same.

At the same hour, across Broad Moor, hemmed in by fellow Roundheads, sat Godwin ahorse, who likewise was lost in thought, no mealymouthed thought, rather altogether unsettling thought of home and bygones. And a bitter sadness also fell upon him, as he thought of brother and father. Why, if that bastardly sibling of his were before him now, he would cut his throat for him in the church without a breathing! And he thought of the loss of his mate, the like of whom he was unlikely to come across again, given what the youth had already seen of the world, if he were ever to come across anything at all again after this day.

And here too, Godwin's thoughts were broken off by the coming-forth of a holyman to uphearten any downing hearts, who read aloud thus: "The Lord is a man-of-war, who by things that are not, brings to naught things that are. For the sins of God's chosen are put into the hands of their foe. Then shall all mankind cry, 'wherefore hath the Lord done this unto this land? Oh, how biting is his great wrath!'" and more of the same.

Ready for the worst, the two youths, like nearly everyone else there, waited for things to begin and end. But not all were longsuffering. Hothead Prince Rupert, the king's darling, could not wait, could not wait for his heavyguns to reach the field, and when only a few sakers were in place, around eleven o'clock, he had had enough and began the fight.

Down the hill headlonged Prince Rupert's horsemen, on the utmost right of the king's line—for, by God, were they not in the right? Oh, now was the time to see who was keen and who was cowardly, who would run and who would stand, and which of these two deeds was keenness and which cowardliness, for in a crush of hurtling man and horse, to stop and stand was as much as to turn and run, and to run in a herd was as much as to stand one's ground.

Down the hill they were hurtled, as if a new warbride carried down the steps of a great church, down past the Selby Hedges on their right, bristling with unseen Roundhead musketbarrels, which opened fire upon Prince Rupert's right flank. However heckled and riddled they were by these hidden-in-the-greenery adderfangs, the Cavalier horsemen headlonged unworsted, onwards into the sketchy no-man's land of Broad Moor.

Overacross the Cavaliers, on Fenny Hill, on the Roundhead left, Ireton dithered a little in beholding the onrush of hardened Cavalier horsemen, until at last he spoke forth before his troopers, "Here they come, lads, rushing to their gory beds! They come before us on the field's left side, but right is on our side. Let us ride forth now and make dust and ashes of these kingsmen from Dust Hill!" Down too rode the Roundhead horsemen into the uneven slump of Broad Moor to meet the foe. And in this hurtling herd of warriors rode Godwin, swept along by time and place.

In the meeting and clashing, the orderly lines of counterset horsemen blurred and then broke down under the thrust of sword and shot of gun, as men fell and horses shied in the thick of the hand-to-hand. And as the tough got going, the Roundhead untough thought of going hence. And so it was not long until those Roundhead troopers under Butler, on the very edge of the field, gave way, some outrightly fleeing. Onwards pushed Prince Rupert, as Roundheads yielded, onwards and through until the killingfield lay behind and the laagered baggagetrain lay ahead, only a mile or so to the west of Naseby. Yes, a thousand or more wagons, stuffed with loot, ready for the taking. Gone now was the king's right flank of horsemen, turned to looting hooligans beyond the killingfield.

And bare this left the king's right flank of footmen, footmen who had likewise pushed forth swiftly to meet the Roundhead middle under Skippon, on the brow of Mill Hill. Firing no more than one round when within shot, the kingsmen did not dally there, beating about with musketballs, but rather rushed forwards, where it came to the bloody jumbled push of pike and bludgeon of musketend. In this misorder fought away Oswin, as stoutheartedly as he could, for being in the thick of it, he had to fight now, he told himself, for there was no fleeing, even if the end of his pike had been blown off in the opening hail of musketfire.

But the straightrunning Roundhead lines of foot began to break down as well under kingly brunt, above all when word afterwaved through the ranks that Skippon, the Roundhead caller-of-shots, had been shot in the ribs. And as the Roundheads brinked upon overthrow, the wind shifted, as it were, and the banners began to flutter with a new bearing.

With Prince Rupert's horsemen missing, still plundering the faroff bag-gagewagons, the Roundhead troopers that had been scattered now rallied. And in this, Godwin was brought back into the Roundhead fold, for he had hung back in the first bout of hand-to-hand fighting. Nor was he the only one. Black Powell had aftershadowed Godwin skulkingly.

Back in their lines, ready to ride forth again, Powell stopped by Godwin and said, "There'll be no time for putting blush on those lilywhite cheeks of yours. As bloodless as your weapons."

"I see no gore on your sword either."

Powell could not let this pass. It had been a hardfast law, in his thought-box, that rookies needed leaning-on, if they were ever to come out as any-thing. But Powell was forestalled now by overriding orders to gallop forth straightaway and make mischief among the king's footmen left in the lurch by Rupert's missing horsemen.

Down they rode against the footmen. And Godwin did not hold back now, could not hold back now. Away he hacked, away he slashed, away he thrust.

The kingsmen began to break up under this fresh onslaught. More than a few men near Oswin took to their heels, shouting, "Away! Away! Let every man shift for his life! You're all dead men!" But Oswin was undaunted. Fall fair, fall foul, he would hold.

It now happened that a Roundhead horseman came riding down upon Oswin, but in deftly wielding his broken pike, the youth tripped the horse, toppling its rider, who had meant to fire his wheellock at Oswin. In falling and hitting the ground, the horseman lost his grip, and the gun flew wide. Oswin dashed over to pick it up, ready to fire back at his foe. But after he had outstretched his arm to fire, an unseen horse, somewhat to his side and rear in all the helterskelter, was shot, and in rearing up and then tumbling over, it fell upon Oswin's arm, in the very timeflash that he squeezed the trigger.

What a blaze of pain shot through Oswin's right leg, with the going-off of the gun, as he himself tumbled to the ground with the horse. He had brought himself low: he had shot himself in the leg by mishap, under the weight of the horse falling upon his gunarm. He bound his leg narrowly below the knee with whatever was to hand, and then he struggled, struggled hard to limp away from the bloodbath about him, but the leg would not teamwork, and he could barely stand. He could neither flee nor fight himself free, and so, slumped down on the ground, pinned down by time and place, a bondsman to his pain, he gave up then and there. His time had come, and he made his peace. There would be no standing-tall now at the last.

Yes, his time had come, for as Oswin lay there helpless, another Round-head horsemen came upon him, ready to undo him. But then the horseman suddenly stopped short, with gunarm still outstretched, and stared at Oswin, while all about whirled slaughter.

Oswin could not make out the face of this shortstopper, what with all the wargear. The unknown rider called out, "Oswin?" And Oswin knew the voice again. Yes, it was that of his onetime friend Godwin. Who would have thought it! Yet the big wide world is all too often a small, very small, world after all. But was he friend or foe now? Would he betray him now as well? And again Godwin called out, "Oswin?"

But another voice rang out now from only a little ways-off. "Shoot him, you coward! Shoot him! He's a kingsman!" Godwin squirmed in his saddle at the sound of Black Powell's voice. Again, the same voice rang out, "Shoot, wheyface! That's an order! Shoot!" as the shouter began to work his way nearer.

From deep within Godwin, an upman of a feeling stirred, gaining speed and strength as it rose on high, taking on the shape of a onefold word. Shrieking "No!" he shifted and, jerking round his gunarm, fired, and Black Powell ran red as he tumbled into the mud. Godwin rode right up, reached down, and took a hold of Oswin's arm and pulled him up behind him. Then turning their backs on the king's killingfield, the two rode away, off into the countryside beyond.

As they dashed along, Godwin tossed off his rusty hand-me-down helmet and then could feel the sweetly toying airrush along his cheeks and through his long freeflowing hair. His heart pounded away, and his brain grew giddy as he headlonged into some heightened and timeless world.

The two saw nothing more of that killingfield, and the aftermath of the fight they had left behind, the great slaughter made there in the name of king and Parliament, the wreck of the king's warband, and the utter overthrow of the king's hope to regain power over his former kingdom. Hath God turned Roundhead after all? Or flitteth the Holy Ghost whither it listeth? But the last word is yet unspoken, for is it not written that the first shall be the last, and the last first?

STANDOFF

WHEN A FAIR LANDSPAN AWAY from the killingfield, Godwin brought their flight to a stop. He looked around at Oswin, who was a ghostly white, and then down at his right leg, which was a messy red. He needed care, and quickly. Godwin spurred on, all the while casting an eye about for a haven of some kind.

At length he sighted a hamlet nearby and made for it. *Hamlet* was perhaps too highflown a word for this wee stead, which was but a short string of linked houses along a muddy road. The place was seemingly forsaken, for not a soul was about. But then Godwin spotted a wisp of smoke rising from the house at the very end. Where there's smoke, there's fire, and where fire, folk. And hopefully a helpful somebody.

Godwin knocked wildly at the door. No answer came. He knocked anew. Again nothing. What now? His friend was wilting, and they could not keep riding about the countryside thus. Emboldened, he opened up for himself and halfdragged Oswin in through the narrow doorway.

Once inside, he was somewhat startled to see an elderly man, in an old leathern jerkin, sitting right by the door. Godwin said his sorries for their bursting-in thus and asked if the man would be so kind as to help them out. The oldster said nothing, with not so much as an eyeblink. Godwin spoke again, louder, and even waved his hand to-and-fro before the man's face, yet the greybeard sat on unshiftingly, unblinkingly, seemingly dead to the world.

Godwin was ready to scream in the man's face, even shake him into life, but then a woman's mannish voice from behind broke the stillness. "You're wasting your breath. He hears and sees nothing." Startled again, Godwin swung around, still upholding Oswin, whose blood was beginning to pool afloor. Before them stood widow Steadman, a sturdy woman with a stiff upright bearing. "Your mate won't be seeing or hearing anything either if that wound is not seen to soon. Bring him to the table."

Godwin laid Oswin out, whereupon the woman looked narrowly at the wound. Godwin asked hopefully, "Are you skilled in healing?"

"I've seen my fair share of blood and guts." Like many of her fellow women at this time, she had been not only a wife, mother, and householdkeeper but also a guide, midwife, and healer, indeed, a kind of Jack-, or rather, Jill-of-all-trades. She laid on hands about the wound, and Oswin writhed and moaned, as she squeezed and pulled and stroked.

"Men and their wars! When will they ever learn? And we womenfolk are left holding the bloody bag," she halfmuttered to herself. Then straightening up, she said hardheadedly, "This is a nasty wound. The shinebone looks like it's shattered. All I can do is take off the leg."

"No!" shouted Oswin.

"You'll die of the wound before you ever find anyone else who has skill enough to treat it. The leg must come off."

"No!" cried Oswin, beginning to weep and whimper. "Not my leg!"

"Bear up, man! We're all born to suffer. What is lost by the fife will be gained by the drum."

"No! No!" Oswin cried on.

"Oswin, you heard what she said. You have no choice!"

"Not my leg!"

Washing her hands, the woman said to Godwin, "I can do nothing more. You may stay, if you wish, until the end." Whereupon she walked off.

Godwin followed after her. "Is there truly nothing that can be done?"

"As I said."

"And there is no-one else hereabouts who could help him?"

"We're the only ones left here. All the others ran off cowardlike when they heard the guns booming out by Naseby. All afraid of being plundered by troops. Oh, this bloody war! I've lost three sons and a husband to it. A curse upon the king and his Parliament and all those lords and richmen that linger it out! Leeches all of them! I'll be bloodsucked no more!"

Hearing a call from the kitchen, Godwin backed to Oswin, who moaned now, "What a sorry wretch and fool am I! Let the knife fall! Cut it off! Take the leg!"

So, after all, the readiness was all. And straightaway, the widow, calling forth her daughter as helpmate, made ready to cut off Oswin's right leg, right below the knee. They bound his limbs fast to the legs of the great oaken table, as if he were so much shipfreight, and stopped his mouth with a strip of wood. As the three loomed over him, he lastly nidnodded for them to begin and then turned his face away. He could see the old man sitting still by the foredoor beyond.

And the pain started. Pain, too limp a word to sketch what seared through him. He thought he would go mad. And the room began to swirl about like a millwheel, until he was no longer sure whether he were alive or dead. He could not even hear himself screaming. It was as if, in bidding farewell to a limb, he had taken leave of his self.

He strove hard to block out the pain, to let his mind wander, nay, run away, far away from the now, far from all this illluck and unfairness, as the midwife's knife, long used to soft birthcords, cut away through his flesh. And before long, it somehow seemed as if the foredoor opened, there beside the old man, and he could see himself out in greenery, but a wee tyke, with a little pail in hand. And his mother was there, she too with bucket in hand and a bit of rope, and together they came to a clump of bushes to pick berries.

The berries were soft between his fingers, so soft that he could easily squash them, before eating them. Why put them in the pail when you can eat straight from the twig? His mother stopped and stroked his cheek—with a hand that had somehow never lost its softness, notwithstanding all the drudgery of her life—and told him not to crush or eat the berries. He would have to wait. Oswin began to weep. It was not the weeping of a cowardly man but the wail of a longsufferer.

The cutting and the sawing and sewing came to an end, and the stump was swaddled up like a newborn. He was carried into a bedroom and left alone. He shut his eyes and fell into the deepest of slumbers. He would need to rest now, to lie still and dead to the world, and let things run their own wendway. He had not gone mad after all.

As the widow and her daughter set about cleaning up, Godwin fidgeted and stalked up-and-down, very much in the way, until the woman said to him, "You look like Hell!" Indeed, his day on the killingfield had left him no pretty sight. "Come. I'll find you something to wear."

He came to stand before a great cupboard, which was now opened, showing forth its overstuffings. "These are my late husband's clothes. God bless his soul! What a man of a man he was! I could not bring myself to part with his things. Strong love draws a heavy load. But if he were alive now, he'd readily give the shirt off his back to you, whatever the cost. He always had a softspot for plucky youths. So here, take these. I'm sure they'll fit." And so they did.

Godwin then took his old duds and burnt them out on the muddy road. And he stood there a good while watching cloth meet fire and sag limply into flickering bonds and thence to ash. Well rid of!

There was nothing to do now but wait. Endless irksome fidgetful waiting at bedside, until Godwin himself slumbered off, only to awake still at bedside the following morning, on this the Lord's day. Oswin lay a ghostly white, in a deep sleep.

Enough of this skulking-about and idling-about! He must do something. He upped and readied himself to ride out. He ripped whatever coin was yet sewn into Oswin's doublet and pocketed it. They would need gear and food for the forthcoming ride-on, as soon as Oswin was well enough to stir again. And they needed news, news of what was afoot in the world.

As he rode off, Godwin could not help but wonder about what had become of his turncoat brother, and De Keyser and his henchmen, for it seemed highly unlikely that the Fleming would have been put off for good by the bout of warfaring of late. Indeed, he had not been. And one may well wonder if Godwin would have ridden forth so boldly into parts where iffiness only halfslumbered, had he known that his brother Charles and some of De Keyser's men were not altogether far away.

But Charles and these henchmen did not make up one chumsy party. He had proven to be all too smooth and slippery to the grasp of Flemish fingers and, when jogged unforeseenly, popped right out of grip, like a wet glass. Yes, things had gone from bad to worse for the Leeuwenhok undertaking, when the manhunters had lost sight not only of Godwin and Oswin but also of Charles.

But then, who could have kept things straight, given the great muddle following Naseby-Fight? When routed, some of the king's warband fled northwards back to Leicester, while the more holdfast or slower-of-foot had been rounded up as newmade bondsmen to be marched off. And when the following day, part of the Roundhead warband made after the fleeing kingsmen, De Keyser found himself in a sorry bind, for amidst all this wayward breakup, he himself was squeezed into further breaking up his own band into even smaller weaker scattered parties, some to follow after the fleeing kingsmen, some to tail the following Roundheads, some to scan the thousands taken, some to ride about the nearby countryside, like so much ash scattered in the wind.

In the forenoon of this Sunday, Spieghel—De Keyser's henchman that was to shadow Charles—and another lowland mate had carelessly turned their backs on their ward, for no more than a breathing it had seemed, only to see all go black, when Charles headstruck them with whatever was to hand and then wisped away, in the nearness of the little hamlet where Godwin and Oswin had found haven.

Unaware of any of this, Godwin rode on, at length coming upon another forsaken townlet, one overtowered by the belfry of its midtown church. He had not meant to stop there, but the sudden boom nearby and the downcrash of a wayward cannonball were enough to make him alight at the towerdoor and dash up to the top for an outlook on the countryside roundabout.

In springing up the winding stairs, he saw that this oldened framework, illbuilt at the outset, was now ramshackle, as the scaffolding outside had foretokened. Everywhere the air was filled with the stench of rot. Up he wound to the top, where the mouth of the bell, that rusty caller to the faithful, which had long clanged in the ears and minds of many, now hung hushed, and its pullrope dangled limply, down to the towerfloor.

A church had always stood there, ever since yearhundreds earlier a priest benamed Dunstan, a man of great faithheat and unbending willpower, had built his churchlet on this same spot, the right spot, chosen by letting God choose. For this man-of-the-cloth had blindfolded himself one morning and walked forth, with a stone in his right hand, until stopped by a cry from on high—he was sure that it was not that of a gull or any other fowl—he cast his stone, and the landingspot was to be the buildingspot. Even if Dunstan's wooden church had long since been torn down, having pretty much tumbled down, the choice arising from a blindfolded stonecast stuck fast, and another church was built there, even if there were grounds for not building upon this ground, here in the shadowland between dry and swampy earth. And dampness and sinking ground had bedeviled churchbuilders there ever after.

Godwin peered out, beyond the beams heavy with birddung. Laying a hand upon a rotten crossstave and leaning out, he nearly fell out, as the wood gave way in his grip, and pieces tumbled down, frightening into flight a flock of cowardly birds which had been dozily sunning themselves on the eaves. It was the first time that he had ever stood at the top of a tower thus. What a giddying sight! All about, he could see for miles and miles, until the landscape seemed to meld seamlessly with the sky.

But the whirr of another stray ball narrowly missing the tower brought Godwin back to the now. Nearby, upon hurst and hollow, he saw a muddled skirmish greatening itself into a small fieldfight. Which were the kingsmen and which the Roundheads, he could not make out, for how teensy and meaningless they all looked from his aloof height. And not far away, he could also see a lone horseman galloping towards this hamlet.

He thought nothing of it and watched on until he had seen enough. When nearly at the bottom of the stairwell, he stopped short, utterly taken aback by the sight of his brother Charles, keen to climb up.

"Well, the longlost brother's come to light again," said Charles. "I see you've beaten me to it, getting to the top. But that's hardly flabbergasting, since nearly everybody's looking for you high-and-low."

"Let them look until their eyes fall out."

"Well, you needn't be afraid that I've brought any fat Dutchman along this time. I was able to slip through their fingers and ride free. You must forgive me, brother, for that foulup at Leicester. I had no choice, for they threatened to harm me if I didn't teamwork with them. Threatened? Look what that blackguardly swine did to my hand!" He held up a stump of a forefinger shortened by a good two inches.

"You betrayed me over a finger? I've seen men lose much more over far less and bear it manfully."

"Have you? You're hardly the one to wag a finger about over betrayal. You're the one who left me in the lurch in Antwerp. Some kinfeeling that showed! I wonder what father will say about that. All the hardship you've brought me, and him. God only knows what's happened to the dowry since you ran off. Father was riding on that money. You were to pull us out of the red, with your Lowland wedlock. So you didn't know? You didn't know that the mighty Drighten clan, which stretches back nearly to William the Bastard, is up to its ears in hock, thanks to Papa's blundering at the bourse, over tulipbulbs."

"Well, that's his worry now."

"His?"

"What do you want from me?"

"You owe me! I've killed and been outlawed for your sake and—"

"You were never asked."

"How can a baby ask for what it needs?"

"You're the baby of this family, and it can have you."

"You, the thankless limp upshot of Papa's first lawful sweaty hump! And you're to have all only because you stemmed from the first spray of seed! How I loathe you, the dead fish that's to rise to the top, all at my cost!"

"I'll have no more of you!"

"Well, 'brother,' I mean to have no more of you!" Charles drew his sword and dagger and rushed his brother, while the latter met his kindred in kind. And thus arose a bitter struggle wherein this one blood was keen to shed itself.

On they fought, as the boom of guns grew heavier. Godwin found himself sorely hampered by his brother's nimble swordsmanship and began to lose ground, backing up the stairs. And as they wound their way up, Charles taunted again and again. "Stand your ground, you backboneless bitchdog! Think you can make off with your tail between your legs and hide away? Stuffed away like Papa's big bag of coin behind his lawbooks. Oh, you didn't know that either! No point running, coward. I'm the better swordsman."

"That's yet to be seen."

Godwin was ready to fight to the bitter end and so held out as best he could. About fourthway up, however, things took an unforeseen turn. For all his bragging, Charles' swordhand was much hampered by the loss of its forefinger, and now strain set in, allowing Godwin the upperhand, such that a worried Charles found himself beginning to back down.

But this turnabout, in turn, came to a sudden end when another wayward cannonball struck the tower's top, knocking a great hole in part of its roof and upper wall. Down came infalling rubble, which in hurtling downwards struck the rotting stairs, sweeping the two youths off and away. As Godwin began his fall, he reached out—be damned if anything was going to take him down!—and somehow was able to grasp and hold fast doggedly to the bellrope. Charles, however, fell to the stonen floor below as if so much rotting wood.

Godwin dangled there, gripping the rope which swayed wildly like a broken clockswingle, and looking up at the sunlight now beaming in, wondering if more building would fall in. Below he heard a weak moan and then a whimperish call, "Help me! I can't shift myself! Help me, brother!"

Godwin did not look down, for above he could hear creaking and snapping and could see dust and flinders falling thence. And then with a mighty crack, part of the rotting framework holding up the bell gave way, and there followed another downrush of rubble together with the great bell itself, all ready to hop and tumble upon the floor below and anything lying thereupon.

Still fastened to this falling bell was Godwin's rope, which passed through an upper pulley, as part of the works allowing the rope to hang free away from the bell. As the latter hurtled downwards, the rope shot upwards over this pulley, whisking Godwin along with it. The blue above grew ever broader and brighter as he headlonged skywards with dizzying speed, only narrowly bypassing the bell in the counterset fall and rise.

By the time the bell hit the floor, Godwin had reached a swiftness outstripping that of any horse or sandyacht, and the speedthrust bore him beyond, tossing him up through the gaping hole and out onto the churchtop. And when he thudded down, he rolled right off the steepsloped roof, and were it not for the scaffolding standing fast along the eaves, like so many warmen standing to, he would surely have fallen to the ground and likely to a muddy death. But he had stuck fast to the scaffolding. As if it had all been rain off a duck's back, he nimbly climbed down the scaffolding, ready to push on.

When the stairs had given way, he had dropped his weapons, and so he went back in to look for them. He would not give them up so easily, for he could not afford to be without. Finding them amidst the rubble, he picked them up, dusted them off, and began to leave but stopped short right by the bell. He saw that it had fallen on his brother, who was now halfburied under rubble. And he saw that the rim had come down on the neck, offcrushing the head, which lay hidden beneath the bell.

Lingering awhile, Godwin wondered what face, at the last, his brother had shown Death. Had it drawn itself into a smile or a smirk? A gawk of guiltlessness or dread? Or both or all, or something altogether other which he had never before shown forth? Which one? Well, Godwin was not going to find out now, what with that outsize bell atop, big enough for a man or two to hide away underneath.

Then whimtaken, he reached down and snatched up Charles' white hanky, which peeked out of a pocket, with *C.D.* embroidered off in an aloof corner, now halfred from pooling blood. Godwin left, taking the hanky. He was unsure why he bothered, for he had neither need nor love of it.

Outside stood Charles' horse still tethered beside Godwin's nag, and a handsome stand of horseflesh it was indeed. Godwin rose up into its saddle and rode off, drawing the other horse along behind.

How his thoughts wandered, even if he still meant to do more scouting-about. The more he trotted forth, the more he thought back, or rather the more thoughts backed to him, ghostly bits of bygone, wavering and gliding catchhard before his eyes. And slowly those loose spookish lifethreads began to spin themselves into a tough knotty yarn, a yarn that few others would likely follow or believe, it seemed to him, were he sitting-telling all to all over inntankards. And then, awestruck by the utter unlikeliness or rather the sheer madness of his life, he wondered how he had earned this, or rather how he had let himself be dragged into it all, dragged down by it all. Where had been his head? Where had been his heart?

But what was he doing gadding about here? When manhunters were still in their nearness, as his runin with Charles showed all too well. Off he galloped, back to the Steadmans' place. And Godwin had every ground to worry.

Indeed, shortly after he had left, the widow had spotted horsemen nighing. She grew worried at the sight of them, and not unrightly so, for she well knew what foulness could footslog beneath the standards of king or Parliament, with power over life and death: cutpurses and cutthroats, rogues and rascals, and other riffraff dredged up from the lowest holds of lockups or scraped forth from the grittiest of trades, in short, the very blossom, or better, the very weed of knavery. And these roughnecks, like most scavengering outriders in this war, were no guntoting toddlers.

She well knew that things would go hard if troopers were to find her harbouring a warflightling. Straightaway, the widow and her daughter roughly roused Oswin, pulling him out of bed and halfdragging him to a hole in the wall. All the while, the fretful woman told a groggy Oswin that for the next little while, he would have to stay hidden away out of all sight and make not a sound while in this hideaway, for warmen were likely to ransack the house shortly and would surely take it ill if they found him here. And before the youth knew it, he had been floored and stuffed into the hole, to take up a cramped place together with a old uprightstanding tarnished cross and a few other such things, and then shut up behind a bit of wainscotting.

In banging his head on the cross, it bore in upon him that the Steadmans must be Catholic, for he had heard of such priestholds before, those hideaways in the walls of Catholic homes, wherein a priest and the gear of worship could be hidden away, like coins sneakily sewn into lining, should the law suddenly show up witchhunting after lawbreakers, caught redhanded in unlawful worship. And so here in the pitchblackness of this priesthold, as stale and musty as an old cask, Oswin sat stilly, with ear thrust up to wainscotting to overhear whatever he could. If only the damned thing had at least a crack to peer through!

Hoping to forestall any inroad into her home, the widow had gone outside and stood blockingly on the few steps to her foredoor, even as the band drew up. Her heart fell in beholding this lot, for in all her livedness, she had never before seen a more thuggishlooking pack. But she was not of cowardly stuff—on this she prided herself—and so asked cheekily, "Are you kingsmen or Roundheads?"

"Whichever frightens you more," said the gangmaster, who stayed asaddle, somewhere between a sit and a slouch, while the henchmen behind him alighted in the mud and swaggered over.

"We have nothing left. The little we had has already been taken by others of your ilk, by one swinish robberband after the other." The widow had rightly foreguessed the wherefore of their coming, for in this cashstrapped war, looting and bullyloans were the only ways of feeding and gearing soldiery. For all her steadfast standing-blocking, a muddyfooted cluster nonetheless pushed past and in. "You'll not befoul my house!" But she found herself manhandled aside.

Once inside, they were straightaway overtaken by a kind of merriness and fell to a heavyhanded smashing-up and breaking-open of things, in their hunt for eatworthies and haveworthies. And it was not long before they came upon the widow's daughter, so prettily clad in red and white. One looter, meaning to try what flesh the girl had, met with nasty scratches across the mug and biting words to the ears. But this only nettled the man, who was not kindly given to maidenly cattiness. And so there followed a mighty bellyslug that jackknifed the girl, whereupon she was dragged by the hair into the room where Oswin had slept and thrust onto the bed.

Through the wainscotting, Oswin could hear the girl's angry cries of helplessness, the sounds of rough struggle and ripping clothes, the hooting and laughing of men, and the din of smashing beyond. It broke his heart to think how those blackguards could badfellow such a wee slip of a girl, who could not have been much older than his own sister.

But he well knew that there was little he could do, the legless helpless wretch that he was. The girl would have to make shift on her own, as best she could, he thought, for he would need to keep his wits for himself, so as to keep his own head. Good God! If they were to smash the wainscotting in and find him here, how would he ever answer? Or worse, what would become of him if no-one found him and none of the Steadmans was left alive to let him out?

The looters' former merriness had by now shifted to anger, in their failing to find much in the way of plunder or grub. As one thug headed back out to grumble to the gangmaster, he caught sight of the elderly man sitting by the door, utterly still and unshifting, blankly staring forwards. The thug wondered how this body had been bypassed unmarked. Drawing his wheellock, he went up the oldster and swung at him as if meaning to club him down but held back at the last. In seeing the old man neither flinch nor wince, the thug took another swing at him, and again the oldster sat on unruffled, making no show to fight back. Lastly, the looter merely waved his hand before the old man's blank eyes. What's queerer than folk? he thought to himself. He left the old man be and came back out into the street.

"We've found bugger-all!"

"Shake this shithole, you ninnies! Pull it apart! Break it down! I will not go hence emptyhanded!" barked the gangmaster.

"Well, you were told, were you not?" smirked the widow.

"I fear the bitch's buried it all somewhere," said one.

"Ay, the bitch's buried her bone. And if she doesn't dig it up soon, she'll have a doghouse worse than this shithole to lie in ere evening," said the headman, to the chuckles of his henchmen. "Maybe a dance in the duckpond will jog the brainlog, and soften that nasty shrewish tongue of hers," he said, fingering to a rainwaterbarrel that stood beside the house.

Up to this barrel she was halfdragged, and into the water her head was thrust and held down until her face purpled, however much she strove to thrust her head up and out. Again and again, she danced in this duckpond, as it were, and bootlessly so, it would turn out, for she stayed as stiffly dareful and tightlipped as before.

By the fourth dunk, the widow's head rose from the water to see her daughter in thuggish hands standing a little off, with all the marks of mishandling upon her body bold to the eye. "Don't you lay a finger on my daughter, or I'll bring down the wrath of God upon you!"

"More than one finger's already been laid on her, and more than once at that," smirked the gangmaster, amidst the cackles.

"Then I curse you, you and your rabble! Painful be your every breath! Black be your fall in every deed! Endless be your days in this living Hell! I curse you once! I curse you twice! I curse you thrice! Black be your fall! Black be your fall! Black be your fall!" And this dampened more than one of the men.

"Cut the girl's throat," ordered the headman. "That's an order!" A dagger was drawn, and the girl sank to the mud as her lifeblood gushed forth.

"Oh, you bloody murdering curs! Bastards!" sobbed the widow. "I would rather die a hundred deaths now than see your pockets stuffed with illgotten gain!"

"Well, you lousy bitchdog, you shall have your way!" said the headman, who, drawing his sword, rode up to her and with one swing beheaded her. And no sooner had the once proudly upheld head tumbled aground but one thug gave it a mighty kick, sending it scampering further away, thereby breaking the spell of dread that the woman's curse had woven. As the laughing and cackling grew, another rogue began to kick the head about as if it were no more than a football, and before anyone knew it, nearly the whole gang had broken into a shortlived game of foothead, as it were. Amidst the horseplay and horselaughs, the widow's once fair skin was blackened in the mud, and her once handsome face was unfaced in the kickery. There would be no sleeking-over of rugged looks for her now.

Hardly started but this game was broken off, when a head thrust itself out at one of the windows and yelled, "We've found something!" And

anon the men within herded out. The one in lead boasted, as he held up
the Steadman's cross, "See what's come to hand! This popish rattle. Must
be worth something. Seems to be of silver. And these other trinkets. All
dredged from the priesthold."

At the end came Oswin struggling on one leg and held up by two
henchmen. Yes, the priesthold had been smashed in after all, and Oswin
had been dragged forth like a helpless babe from womb to world. His heart
sank even further in seeing the lifeless leavings of the Steadman women
lying halfsunk in the mud, and it seemed to him that his unhappy time in
this world was now about to end.

Catching sight of Oswin, the gangmaster asked, "And what's this? A
milksopnancy of a Cavalier hiding from war? Or a limping rat in love with
dark holes? If that be not all one. Speak!"

Oswin knew not what to say, until in a flash, out-of-the-blue, on their
own, it seemed, his lips muttered the little lie, "A priest."

"Well, well, a man of the frayed cloth! The popish and the nincompoopish
wedded in one fell swoop, if that be not all one," said the headman. To his
smuggish gladness, this quip met with cackles from his underlings, who
began to catcall and wisecrack amongst themselves, bringing forth such merry
slights of their own as "A bugger of altarboys!" or "The Pope's fart!" Feeling
a little less bloodyminded than before, given all this funning, and marking
shabby Oswin's shortness of leg, the gangmaster asked further, "How came
you, 'priest,' to be down at the heel?" As he had hoped, his wordplay teased
forth even more merriness.

Careful of his words, Oswin again brought forth a small falsehood. "My
horse latterly stumbled under me and fell upon my leg, shattering the bone,
and I had to be unlimbed of it. As you see, I have run short on God's grace."

To see someone on the threshold of a bloody death seemingly make
light of his lucklessness in wordplay greatly tickled these thugs, such that
the headman smirked forth, "A bungling booby of Rome, yet with a little
wit to boot, even if the Pope has pulled his leg!"

"Ay, pulled it right off!" shouted one, and this too met with high mirth.
Oswin stood there shamefaced, taking all this meekly in his stride, which
in turn wrested even a few hearty chuckles from the gangmaster. "I have
half a mind, priest, not to cut your throat. Will you, to save your life, spit
upon your graven god?"

"If it keep me out of the grave," said Oswin, who, upon more than one ground, would have gleefully answered "Most gladly," but he had wit enough not to say so.

Again, his wordplay was wellmet, and the grinning headman, eager to see this lamb at the slaughter take away tarnish with his slobber, said playfully, "Then spit away!" One of the thugs came forward with the Steadman cross and held it up before Oswin, and with all the slaver that his mouth could yield, the youth spit upon the cross, and at this, the men laughed and mafficked.

But again the gangmaster upspoke crossly. "You shameful wicked heathen, how dare you scant your tawdry god!" And here, licketysplit, his merry hoodlums fell sheepishly still and speechless, dumbfounded by this unlooked-for shift, but none more so than Oswin, who feared now that he had blundered. "Take it back, I order you! Lick your foul godless spittle off that gaudy fetish!"

Slow on the uptake, his henchmen little-by-little began to see what a clever legpull this was and began to chortle and giggle anew. Heartlightened Oswin bowed his head and, as bidden, carefully licked off whatever spit still clung to this token of faith, to even greater laughter and mafficking.

The gangmaster, unwilling to forgo the last word, scouted, "Done like a true son of mother church! What lickspittles these drossy times spew forth!" His will now done and his feeling of power greatened, the headman, all asmirk, turned his horse about in readiness to leave, for he had lost all interest in the little "man of the frayed cloth."

Those still holding Oswin were bewildered by this further sudden moodswing, and one of them asked, "What do you want us to do with him?"

"Oh, string him up by the hoof and let him rot, if he be not rotten already."

The thugs bound Oswin's hands behind his back, cast a noose around his one foot, and hoisted him aloft, where he dangled upsidedown from an overhanging beam.

The ghost of wordplay having come so strongly over the men and finding itself still loath to go hence, one of them asked, "Do you think he can stand it, lads?" His mates cackled lustily at the lame wordplay.

In leaving him to himself, one of them gave Oswin a push so that he swingswanged swinglewise, with an evenness that would have shamed no craftsman of a clockmaker. "Hang in there, mate!" said the shover.

Having come with looting and hooliganry in mind, the band left in a mood of merriness, even if nearly emptyhanded. And they turned their backs on the lifeless bodies of the Steadman women lying in the mud and Oswin dangling well above, as freely as the leafy twigs of a sapling swaying in the wind.

With the world dizzily whiffling before his eyes, Oswin could hardly believe that these thugs had indeed left, and left him be, although he never found out whether they were kingsmen or Roundheads, and truth-be-told, the looters themselves were none too clear about that. But what did it matter now? They were gone, and he had skirted death, albeit most narrowly.

Even if bound, he somehow felt free, as he hung there and lingered somewhat smugly upon his sleights-of-tongue, all to pet those in a pet. And as bouts of wakefulness came and went, like so many callers at a healing man's bed, he could see now that it was all and only a matter of time.

But mistimed it all seemed to Godwin, when he came riding up to the Steadmans' house, following the runin with his brother in the belltower. Indeed, his worst fears seemed to have enfleshed themselves, when he saw there the women facedown in the mud, and Oswin upsidedown from a beam. Hardly out of the saddle but Godwin fell to his knees in the mud and stammered "No! No!" again and again. And he struck the slim with his fists, ready to curse the world, until he heard a weak voice beyond.

"Aren't you going to pull me down?" Godwin looked up. Was he going mad? "Get me down!"

Godwin scrambled to his feet and slogged over to Oswin. He was not dead after all! No sooner cut down and helped back into the house but Oswin was broadsided with many askings. In listening, Godwin's earlier thoughts that his own life had hitherto been a knotty yarn, beyond belief to all but madmen, now seemed to him a little silly, as did his outburst. It was done, and he would live it down, even if no smirkers were about.

They had every ground to fly, for they were still hunted outlaws, three times over, yet Godwin was all for staying-put, until Oswin had healed, leastwise a little. But the latter was all for flying, so great was his fear that they would be come upon yet again. And so that same day, they took to horse and pushed on.

TROMPE-L'OEIL

IN THE BLUNDERFUL BOOBYDOM that is this world, De Keyser was no fool. He knew that he—no, the Leeuwenhok undertaking—had undergone a great setback at Naseby. Lost were Godwin and Oswin, and now Charles too, as he was to learn from Spieghel, who had since backed to his master most sheepishly, and who suffered from nearly unbroken headaches now, thanks to his headwound from Charles, headaches that seemed to split his brainpan in twain, if not altogether flinder it. De Keyser could very well have picked up where Charles had left off, and pounded the blunderer into pithiness for his foulup, but to what end? Backlashing, this getter-of-things-done could not afford, unlike his master. De Keyser after all had only flawed clay to work with, and with it he would work, as best he could, hufflessly.

Spieghel was not the only bungler. Over the next few days, other scouts likewise backed emptyhanded, with no leads. And so without the slightest inkling whither the three youths might have fled, De Keyser and his band set forth once again into the unknown, unflaggingly, still with a northwest-erly bearing, in the hope that they might stumble upon if not hide then at least hair of the hunted.

How heartening to De Keyser would have been the knowledge that the bearing he followed was indeed the right one, for Godwin and Oswin—or rather leading Godwin (Oswin was too unwell for any plotting)—had not shifted their wendway. They were still more or less Chesterbound, however unwise that might have seemed in hindsight. And so it was only a matter of time before the two parties would meet again, one last bigbangful time, or so leastwise by the heavyhanded law of likelihood.

Even with their twoday lead, Godwin and Oswin made slow headway, thanks to unsureness about the right path and to Oswin's weakness, which made needful much stopping and resting, allowing De Keyser to gain on them, unbeknownst to either party. And even De Keyser was not above stopping and resting, even if only for a breathing, such as they did at one crossroad, when something oddish caught De Keyser's eye.

Scrawled on the face of a great stone halfsunk into the earth, in the crotch of the crossroad, were some chalkmarkings. De Keyser had never seen suchlike before and so asked one of the English hirelings what they might mean.

"Looks like gipsies passed this way lately. They often leave markings like that on buildings or walls or elsewhere. *Smogger* they call it, a kind of hidden writing, with words or meanings to others of their riffraffy kind about where best to get handouts or where best to thieve and where best to stay away from. Sneaks they are, ever out for themselves. Best not have anything to do with them."

"But what do these markings mean?" asked De Keyser, altogether bewitched by them.

"Beats me. You need to be a gipsy to know."

De Keyser lingered on, lost in gazing at these tokens of hidden meaning beyond his fathoming.

At length his men grew a little restless. The same hireling alighted, walked over to the stone, and rubbed the markings out. "Easy come, easy go. We don't want to be abetting such rogues. Good thing they don't carve it into the stone! But then what would be the point of that? Today's good thievinggrounds are tomorrow's wastelands."

De Keyser would have stopped the man, but before he knew it, the markings were no more than a smear of chalkdust. De Keyser snapped back to his old self, as quickly as he had been bewitched. Why was he wasting time here, gawking at scribbling? Without thinking, he spurred his horse on, and his henchmen followed.

This sudden backsnap had flustered him somewhat, and he had ridden off without carefully weighing whether the right or left arm of the crossroad were the better. But did it matter? Without any leads, one path was as good as another. Besides, and more weightily, any sudden seemingly ungrounded aboutface now and he would only lose face with his men, whose keenness for this undertaking had already begun to wane. And the last thing he needed now was more would-be-knowing looks from underlings, meant to flag up thought shortcomings in his leadership. Flawed clay it was, and onwards it would be.

But things were to pick up greatly for De Keyser by the end of the next day, when at twilight a forwardscout backed with news of a sighting further ahead. Yes, he had spotted two horsemen, one blonde and the other unsteady in the saddle, as had been eyemarked before with the twosome. By fluke, De Keyser's guess—if that be not too lofty a word for his blind groping—had proven to be right. They were narrowing in on the two again. By God! He would have them in his grasp by sundown tomorrow, for sure. Well, the two at least, wherever that smartassed younger brother might be. But De Keyser had been entasked with the hunting-down of the wayward groom and the sodomite sidekick only, and he would not lose sight thereof.

As darkness began to fall, the mastermind saw that there was little point in pushing on blindly through the coming darkness. Not to worry. They would be on the rogues' heels at dawn, and besides, he would need all his men tomorrow and thus needed to wait for the backing of other instraggling scouts. And so upbeat from upheartening tidings, the men bunked down for the night.

As he lay snug under his blanket beneath the black sky, with its own blanket of clouds, hiding from sight all those heavenly bodies, De Keyser mindplayed homing: another job under his belt, his pockets bulging below, and Leeuwenhok beaming. Life was good. He slumbered off.

Up early at dawn the following dank foggy morning, the band rode off. Within less than an hour, the scout had taken them to where he had sighted the fleers the evening before. And not long thereafter, the hunted came into sight, doddling ahead in the fog ghostily. But the two quickly became aware of their afterfollowers, it seemed, and at once spirted ahead, as did De Keyser's band, who were betterhorsed and could not but overtake them in time.

Now began a breakneck dash to flee and to follow. The scout had been right: one of the flightlings bore golden locks and the other bounced unsteadily asaddle, now short of a lower right leg. This, De Keyser could see, even through the fog. They had their men, or rather would have them soon, for they steadily gained on them.

The winding road sharply bighted and then followed along the bank of a waterstream to the right and a thickset stand of trees to the left. At first sight De Keyser thought that they were coming up to some kind of wharflet, for ahead in the fog loomed what looked like a hulk. Then the hulk shapeshifted itself into an old watermill, and beside it a cottage and a length of low stonen wall, and beyond, a bridge where the road shifted to the other bank.

The two neared the mill, but before they could ride beyond, out-of-the-blue, a tilted wagon was rolled athwart the road's bottleneck between mill and grove, blocking and thus shortstopping the riders. Suddenly out of the woodwork helterskeltered weaponbearing men, perhaps highwaymen. De Keyser halted his bevy in a clap, with a fair stretch of road still ahead.

The English hireling who had spoken of smogger earlier came alongside De Keyser and said, "Housewagons! Looks like we've caught up with those tinkers."

"'Tinkers'? What are tinkers?"

"Gipsies."

De Keyser had only ever heard of gipsies before and so watched on kenkeen now, even a little bewitched, although at first he wondered if they should rush forward nonetheless and take their men, highwaymen ahead or no. But even though De Keyser's bevy seemed to outman the lot beyond, any gunblazing rideup might prove most costly, and so he held back in order to watch and wait. He would not risk his life needlessly, and they were near enough now not to lose them again. And it felt even more rightheaded once the gipsies, catching sight of De Keyser's band, fired a shot at them.

The "tinkers," however, did not seem to be well outfitted with weapons. Some bore only pitchforks or cudgels, maybe knives, and other things De Keyser could not make out through the fog. But they were clearly bloody-minded, for the mill and cottage had been looted of late, witnessed by its smashed-in windows and strewings of inholdings upon the ground about the buildings, as well as a few bodies lying here-there, a dog, a man, and perhaps a boy. And now he could hear angry shouts from some of them, as they dragged the two down off their horses at gunpoint and began to rough them up.

The English hireling, still beside De Keyser, spoke again, "Something's not right here. This is not the tinkerway. They're thieving sneaks, not fighting heavyhands."

The shouts and shoves ahead worsened until the blonde youth angrily began to fight back, even if hopelessly outmanned, and then was soon overcome. The two youths were roughly pushed up against the wall of the building, and before De Keyser knew it or could have even foreguessed it, shots were fired, and the two youths fell limply to the ground. *Godverdomme!** They had shot his catch! De Keyser squirmed in his saddle helplessly.

He saw the thugs rifle through the deadmen's clothes, seemingly in search of money, drag all the bodies into the mill, and then set fire to the building. The ragtags hooted and cheered in seeing the quick powerful blazeup, when wayward fireflickers within seemingly met with something highly burneasy, and the blazeup came near to a small blowup. The hooters fired a shot aloft and again another at De Keyser's men. Then turning their backs on the burning hulk, in its hopeless last stand in the fog, they loaded up their loot, or whatever it was, and the fleetlet of wagons and housewagons set forth and in no time was out of sight.

De Keyser and his band galloped up quickly to the mill, which was now one hell of a blaze. Some of the roof fell in, and by fluke this freed the waterwheel, which began to turn away before the waterstream's powerful thrust. Round and round it wobbled dizzily, like a broken spinningwheel before some illlucked blind hag, drunkenly spinning itself free from its set path and narrow drudgery, until the wheel, as if long worldweary, broke free and was pulled away by the water's tow. And this was soon followed by the watersidewall, which also tumbled into the flow. No more grist for this mill.

There could be no searching of the building now, and De Keyser could do no more than gawk at the upbillowy smoke and proud blaze spewing forth from the now nearly gutted framework. He ordered his men to search around the buildings, to make sure that the two, perhaps only wounded, had not crawled out somehow and maybe were lying hidden nearby, but nothing was found, not even a droplet of blood.

The English hireling trod up to De Keyser and said, "Nobody can overlive such a blaze. I guess our hunt stops here then."

So it seemed, even to the wary Fleming. Yes, the gateway to the beyond

---

* 'God damn it!'

had proven to be too narrow to squeeze through for those hunted rogues, those cats of byword, who had come to the end of their nine lives, all through an unforeseen unashamed hijackery by the riffraffiest of cutthroats. Trust the English to harbour "tinkers" and the like!

Yes, yes, but this was all most hackleraising! *Godverdomme!* He had been entasked with the hunting-down and bringing-back of the twain, and now there would be no body—not even a bodypart—to show forth. A waterhaul it all turned out to be. How would his master take it? Well, Leeuwenhok would have to feed his dogs something other. Leeuwenhok would have to live with it.

But De Keyser could not truly fault himself. No, he had done his best with the given. And truth-be-told, he had only halflost, and so halfwon, for the rogues were out of this world at least—wasn't that the point of all this?—and so he could look forward to being halfpaid at the very least. He did have more than a few witnesses who had seen with their own eyes the two youths fall and go up in smoke and who could swear upon a stack of Bibles that the two were dead. Hopefully Leeuwenhok would not be too much of a stickler.

"Shall I have the men take horse?" asked the English hireling.

"We will wait until the fire is out. I want to see what is left."

"But we all saw the two shot. They're deaddead now. No mistaking it. No need to hang about."

"We will wait."

And wait they did. Once the blaze had burnt itself out—all fiery devils having forsaken this scorched-out hell—the men sleuthed through the ashes and rubble, looking for charred bodies. They found thirteen—a Satanish number, it seemed to some—but one of the bodies lacked a lower right leg, as far as one could tell, and this was the more-or-less clinching proof that De Keyser had wanted. So they were dead after all. The tinkering gipsies had beat him to it. Maybe he should have risked all earlier, when he could have, and ridden up with guns blazing and swords flaming and nabbed then and there. But out of all keeping, he had shillyshallied, flustered by shifting sands beneath his feet. It was too late now. Everything was cut-and-dried. There was no going-back. And so the great Leeuwenhok manhunt, which had cost so much money, which had taken up so much time, which had taken more than one life, and which had meant to right a wrong, was lastly given up, and De Keyser's bevy willynilly rode off emptyhanded, some leastwise not unhappy with their halfassed job.

Does this mean then that our tale of Godwin and Oswin has reached its sorrowful end, given that the twain had reached their sorry end, like untold others of their times and foretimes, who found themselves in the wrong place at the wrong time, on the wrong side of laws written and unwritten? So it might seem, yet flesh-and-blood things were somewhat other than those seen through De Keyser's eyes. And who knows how the heavyhanded laws of likelihood might have ended this story had De Keyser boldly ridden up to the mill that foggy morning?

And what did happen that morning, beyond De Keyser's gaze? It began the early evening before—to answer fully—when a roadweary Godwin and Oswin found themselves found-out by De Keyser's forewardscout, who then backed with all speed to his master with news of the sighting. And in his turn, Godwin had spotted the spy and knew that their afterfollowers had caught up once again. The two rode off hard, passing in their flight the old watermill where they were to make their last stand. And Godwin would have ridden the night through thus, but as twilight fell, Oswin could no more, and they were strained to stop in an out-of-the-way grove.

All this riding-about without the needed healingtime had taken a heavy toll on Oswin, who was so weakened that he could stay in the saddle only when bound fast thereto, as if so much pack. Things now seemed pretty hopeless. It was only a matter of time, as both well knew, before they would be overtaken and taken.

Godwin in time was startled by the sound of voices not too far away, and then a smudge of fiddlemusic. So they were not alone even here. He roused Oswin, but the latter seemed wholly uncaring. Godwin slipped off through the trees, to learn of the who beyond. Unseen and unheard in the darkness, he came upon a small clearing and there glimpsed twenty or so folk sitting about a campfire, ringed round by wagons and housewagons. Must be gipsies. No Flemings here, as far as he could see. A heartsoothing sigh. He slipped away back to Oswin and roused him again to tell him of his find.

"That's how we must live, if we live. Like gipsies. If only the world somehow thought we were dead. Then they'd leave us be. Need to be dead to be alive here," said Oswin, with a sorrowful nod.

"No talk of death now."

"If those Dutchmen saw us dead on the ground, eaten by worms, they'd leave us alone."

"You need to rest."

"Ay, rest in peace. Maybe the gipsies'll find us yet tonight and kill us in our sleep before morning. Sorry, Dutchmen! We're already dead."

"Enough!"

But this ghoulish thoughtstream strengthened itself into an outlandish brainwave. No, no, too unlikely altogether. But why not? "Do you think we could make them believe we're dead, even if we weren't? If we played dead?"

"Oswin, Leeuwenhok's men are not wet behind the ears! They're ruthless knaves who know every trick from every blackbook."

"What if tomorrow they saw those gipsies kill us, without killing us?"

"They'd look over the bodies and see that we weren't dead," smirked Godwin.

"But if they could not get at the bodies? If the bodies seemed to be burnt to ash?"

"And how's that to be done?"

"The eye and the mind's eye are easily fooled. Have you forgotten the trial?"

Thoughts of it now flooded back, in one heaving twist-and-turn after another: his brother's swagger, the girl's tears, the flailing mob, and his father, yes, his father. And these backthoughts haunted him until sometime later he found himself helping Oswin through the woods, to where the gipsies had encamped. And leaving the legless one somewhat further back, propped up against a tree with a stick in hand that might in the darkness pass for a musket, a wheellockwielding Godwin then went swaggering up to the camp, where he met with sudden stirup.

"Forgive my coming thus, but I would have some business with you, if you're game."

"What business?" asked one mistrustfully.

"Tomorrow morning, I would like you to stop me and my friend, who is standing a little behind me with a musket, when we're on the road and then shoot us and burn our bodies. We will be hardfollowed by other horsemen. The shooting and burning is for their sake."

The gipsies muttered amongst themselves in unbelief, and the same one asked, "Are you out of your mind?"

"Yes. But you'll be paid well." Throwing them a bag of coin, he went on,

"Here's a quarter of what you'll get. The rest you'll have after you've shot and burnt us."

A few of the gipsies upped at once and rushed over to grab the coinbag, which they tore open, spilling coin on the ground, and then nodded brightly to their speaker, who said in turn, "For money, we'll do this."

"We'll meet you then at first dawn, at the old mill by the waterstream, a few miles to the east along the road. Do I have your word?"

"Yes."

Godwin trod off boldly and quickly into the darkness, leaving the gipsies all astir. As the two youths bunked down for what hopefully would be their last night as hunted men, Godwin said, "Let us hope beyond belief they're as good as their word."

The following morning the gipsies did indeed show up at the old mill, the latter plundered only a few days earlier by either kingsmen or Roundheads in passing. And there they were enlightened by Godwin about the day's forthcoming or leastwise foreseen happenings. And there they waited away, until an hour or so later, the hunted youths came galloping up to the mill, where the gipsies were to stop and then shoot them, with a ball of soft tow rather than a ball of lead, from guns fired with only a weakish halfload of powder. The ball of tow hurt enough that the two jackknifed and writhed a little on the ground, like any dying men. And then a ballless shot or two—needfully so since the gipsies had no balls—towards De Keyser's band to keep those rascals back.

No sooner dragged into the old mill, and thus out of sight, but the youths upped and wormed their way down into the crawlspace beneath the millfloor, coming out on the unseen west side of the building, along the low stonen wall, and then up into one of the wagons left at the end. The burning of the mill ensured that the ghostbodies of Godwin and Oswin fitted in, as it were, among the dead, to wit, the bodies of the dead miller and his family and a few soldiers, one of whose legs Godwin had earlier hacked off below the right knee.

A daring foolhardy bluff it had been, one which the laws of likelihood had been deadset against. But then, had such laws not been likewise deadset against the Achaeans of eld who, stuffed into the belly of a wooden horse, ended up fordoing Troy? A tall tale, the unbeliever might smirk. But had not these same laws also been deadset against Arminius and his warbands in year 9 AD, when in hoodwinking Publius Quinctilius Varus they waylaid and slaughtered three Roman *legiones* sandwiched between bog on the right and wooded hill on the left? And did not Augustus, the *caesar* and *imperator* of the known western world, weep and bang his head against the wall in helpless sorrow upon the hearing of this news? Are the happenings of life then so greatly other than the mad makebelieve of story? Let the unsung Goliaths, those brought low by the wayward flight of a mere stone hurled from a boy's slingshot, let them come forward, back from their graves, and bear witness with their broken brows and rambling madmanly speech that even kings must pile up their broken crowns at the gates of the maggoty grave.

Luckily Godwin had learned to wield more than a slingshot, what with all his schooling in warcraft, unlike the young King David. And while the thought of playing dead was Oswin's, the bold last stand was Godwin's, for unable either to fight or flee, the two ending up doing both and neither.

And who would have thought that these gipsies would keep their word and play along so sportingly, even if for money? Or did they? Right from the beginning, that evening when Godwin broke in upon their merrymaking, some of the band thought that they should chevy after the upstart straightaway and rob him on-the-spot. Why bother trundling back to that mill tomorrow? It all seemed too fishy. And that morning, while they waited at the mill for the two to come galloping back, some had wanted to go through with only half the plan, to wit, taking them and robbing them, but then sell the two to their hunters in turn. Why burn good wares? But then who were those manhunters? Might they then be robbed in turn by these afterfollowers? All this sketchiness made for overleary gipsies.

But once the wagons had forsaken the burning mill and all breathed more easily, their former overleariness now seemed a little lackgutsy. The wagons halted suddenly, and Godwin and Oswin found themselves dumped into the middle of the road at cudgelend and knifepoint, not far from the mill. The gipsies wanted the rest of their money now, and when Godwin willingly payed up, they still wanted the rest of the money, and everything else that the two had, outtaking the dirty clothes they stood in. And so stripped of money, horses, food, and gun (even if there were no balls left)—out of a kind of roguish fellowfeeling, the robbers let the youths keep their boots, for what good were one-and-a-half pairs of outworn footwear?—Godwin and Oswin found themselves once again thrust between the beetle and the block.

As the wagons joggled off, Godwin stamped his foot and shrieked after them, "Bastards! You bastards!" But these words met only with cackles from the merry robbers.

"Don't fret. It's only money," said Oswin forlornly.

"'Only money'?! How are we to eat? And how are you to walk?"

Oswin only gawked dumbly, and then mindful of the time, said, "We'd best get off the road. We can't be sure that the Dutchmen have truly given up on us."

"Bastards!"

In a huff, Godwin helped his sidekick along. Off the road they shambled and then made their way halfhiddenly through the woods running alongside. Hard going it was, and before long, Oswin had to stop and rest.

"This is hopeless!" griped Godwin.

As the latter strode up-and-down restlessly, Oswin, seated on a dank treestump, one big enough to dance upon had it been flattopped, at length said, "I'm sorry for getting you into this mess. Maybe you should go on and leave me here. I'll find my way."

"Don't be silly! I won't leave you here."

"A lousy fighter I've turned out to be."

"Who said that you had to be one?"

"I thought, I—" Oswin stared blankly at his stub of a leg. Nothing more was said.

They trudged and stumbled on, until a lonestanding building loomed ahead, and they headed towards it. Sadly enough, it turned out to be a forsaken shell, worsted by time and war and uncare.

"This will not do. We must find an easier way, by hook or by crook." And so they settled hereupon, that Godwin should go on alone, leaving Oswin behind, and search out what help he could find and then back before twilight.

Godwin set off, and rather stormily. Bloody gipsies! He should have known better than to trust them. Backstabbers! Or rather, more backstabbers. So was this it, this world? A castle of comedown, the shoddy work of Babel's bricklayers? Oh, where in this world of shifting sands be rock hard and even enough, rock free of faultlines, upon which to build any great tower, standing high for all time, rock that does not groan and crack beneath the weight of its heady burden, out of touch and reach of the top high aloft?

And he picked up a stick as he stomped along and swung it again and again. And he sneered at the weeds growing by the wayside, with their drooping heads, like coy maidens, growing wild here-there, without the care of any gardener's hand, and with a great swing of his stick, he beheaded more than a few of them. Bastards!

In a little while, he came upon seemingly a lone homestead—or was it rather a hamlet or an upstart would-be townlet? What an endless number of squat shedlets and barnlets and hutlets stood here, like so many dumpy little Flemish burghers idling at the bourse. He looked around but saw no-one. He stalked on, past one little shed after another, as if sizing up dealers, until he reached what seemed to be a dwelling. Opening the door, which bristled with rusty nailheads, he peered in. The floor halfglistened in the sunlight, still damp from being newly washed.

But before he could do anything further, a great hulking fieldman loomed forth and said, "Took you long enough! Well, don't stand there in the doorway gawking, letting in flies! Get in and shut the door!" Godwin had not reckoned upon such a meeting, and though somewhat flustered by this oddish welcoming, he was nonetheless emboldened to tread forth as bidden. "So where's your baggage?" asked the man, bloodlessly eyeing the youth from head to toe.

"I have none now," said Godwin, nearly at a loss.

"'None'? Beats me why anyone would go about bare like that, like some rootless scamp of a tinker." And then casting his eyes up heavenwards, the fieldman moaned, "God help us! These are queer times we live in! And I take it you've eaten nothing either?"

"No."

"No, that would've been too much to look for. The young nowadays! What a feckless lot! Well, sit down. You've done not a tap of anything, and already I'm feeding you. Everyone thinks the world owes him something and stands there with hands out ready for handouts. I'll tell you now, and I'll tell you straight, I'll have no lazeabouts around here! So look to it!"

Godwin was too hungry and thirsty to turn down such a begrudging offer of food, and so he sat down at the table, as bidden. The fieldman—fieldman Lowe was his name—banged down onto the table before Godwin a great platter and lifted off its overlying cloth, showing forth the gnawed- and nimbled-at leftovers of a cold ham, with bits of limp overcooked greens to boot. Godwin's heart fell, and he sat there staring at the untoothsomelooking fare.

"Well, I'm not going to spoonfeed you as well!"

Godwin picked at the laid-before-him, while the fieldman set a wet badly cracked-chipped mug down and grudgingly poured some waterylooking ale. Before Godwin could snatch up the ale, the fieldman's bitchdog suddenly sprang up beside Godwin, to the end of helping herself to his slim pickings.

"Down, Henny! Down, I say, you bitch!" shouted the fieldman, cuffing the hound, which backed off with a yelp. The grub was bad enough without the bloody dog slobbering over him and his share! But what of it? Godwin was so thirsty that his hands shook, and as he set about greedily downing the mugful, he somehow foozled his grip, and the wet mug popped out of his hand and landed on the floor, breaking and spilling the ale.

"You clumsy dolt! I only now cleaned the floor, and you go and make a barn of it!" The roughneck stretched out his right arm and meant to cuff Godwin. But the youth was nimbler, and grabbing the man's swinging hand, Godwin pulled him off his evenweighted footing and thrust him afloor, down onto the spilled ale and shards.

"You surly little upstart! By God, you need a lesson in manners!"

"So do you, old man!"

This was too much for fieldman Lowe, who in getting to his feet meant to whip this smartass into biddableness. But Godwin would have none of it. And so the two men fell to scuffling and tussling. The fieldman was tough and wellthewed, no pushover he. And Godwin struggled hard not to let the churl worst him. And as they grappled away, they knocked all manner of things to the floor, which smashed and dinned, making not a barn but a sty of fieldman Lowe's cottage.

And the longer they struggled, the uglier the tussle got, and amidst all this, Henny strove to help out by biting and scratching away at Godwin, who was hardset to fight off two onslaughts at the same time. And things got altogether out-of-hand when the thickwristed fieldman, wrathful beyond belief now, meant to do in Godwin with a sharpedged shardlet, no wheellock being at hand.

Not too soon, Godwin was able to give the dog a mighty bellykick, which sent the beast across the room into a corner, where the whimperer jackknifed and writhed in a painful cringe. With one foe down-and-out, Godwin got the upperhand over the other, wrestling him down to the floor where he straddled him and began to throttle the life out of him.

With the worsted but still strikehappy fieldman flinging his arms about bootlessly and evermore limply, Godwin watched on, as if bewitched, while the fieldman's life slipped away under the grip of his whiteknuckled hands. He had killed before this—some nameless-faceless kingsmen at Naseby-Fight and, yes, Powell!—but those deaths had been quick-and-dirty, no outdrawn struggle, no unsureness of outcome, no frightened helpless gaze from the dying loser at the last, no great giddying feeling of power, as there was here.

The fieldman had long since dropped the shard, had long since given up flailing, before Godwin loosened his grip around the man's neck. Indeed, it was only when a handcramp had set in that the dazed youth became aware of what he was doing, of what he had done. No-one then could have deemed him guilty of underkill.

Drawing back a bit, Godwin sat beside the body awhile, staring at the fieldman's glazed eyes and gaping mouth. The look of a frightened brow-beaten boy it seemed. He lifted up and let fall one of the burly arms, arms that had nearly done him in, but the limb was limp and awkward now, as if the squishy flipper of a dead mermaid, a wishywashy mermaid who had swum away from home only to be worsted by life.

Godwin felt no sorrow, no shame, no rue. How dare the rogue make bold with him! The sight of the fieldman only sickened him, if anything. The fool had no-one to thank but himself. To have thrown away his life over a bit of spilled ale, so as to end up its blottingrag. And the oaf had not even bothered to ask him his name! But fieldman Lowe had always been thus, and be otherwise he could not. But then, was not mankind given eyes to hear and ears to see?

It was time to push on, and Godwin rose to his feet, lightly, strongly, proudly. He ransacked the place for anything to ease his wayfaring-to-come. All he could muster together was that foul ham, ale, blankets, and a wheelbarrow, and with these he made off, leaving the fieldman behind to wait out the coming of the looked-for hireling, whom Godwin had forerun.

And now where was Oswin? Peering into that ramshackle building where he had left him, Godwin saw not a soul. And it was only after calling out a number of times that he heard a mousy voice from within, through a hole in the floor.

"What are you doing down there?"

"I fell in."

"I told you not to go in."

"Someone came."

Indeed, more than one someone. After Godwin had left earlier, Oswin stayed as much as he could out of sight by the old building, which was no great hardship. Overcome with weariness, he lay down in the long grass and in no time fell asleep, only to be wakened later by the sound of voices nearby. He peered out from behind the tall grassstalks and could seen two children not far away. One, with her hands over her eyes, stood upon a knoll, while the other was heading for the building in a mad dash.

Oswin flew into a flap. What if they were to see him here? Would they run off and tell kindred of an unknowner in their midst? And would they in turn come looking and asking? But where should he hide? The one girl clearly meant to come to the building. He could not stay out like this. And so on all threes he crawled into the tumbledown framework. Was this enough? What if the girl came in as well?

He got to his foot, and with a nearlying board for a crutch, he hobbled further into the building, into a dark backroom. And the floor—or what was left of it—creaked and moaned and sagged wildly beneath him, until some of it suddenly gave way altogether, and he fell through up to his chest. And there he dangled, as if in a giant's grip. What now? He could heard footfalls already inside. He wriggled himself free, slipping down into the dark cellar. No sooner there but he heard squeaks and creaks of floorboards coming his way until they stopped nearby. The girl was almost right above him. Then hush.

The other girl reached the building and called inside, in some oddish-sounding tongue. It somehow put Oswin in mind of the Irish he heard while in Ireland. And he was not wide of the mark, for these girl were Cornishspeakers—Cornish being a tongue kindred to Irish—and English-speakers to boot. The caller freely switched from one to the other, without the slightest qualm, as she slowly made her way inside as well. A game of hide-and-seek seemingly.

The newcomer had not trodden too far within when the one above Oswin, in the dark backroom, began to moan and groan, making ghostlike sounds, as if the place were haunted. This frightened the other girl out of her wits, and she fled with a great squeal. But she did not get far before the bellylaughs of the other reached her ears, and the frightened one backed hopping mad, with Hell to pay.

The two began to run through the building, one after the other, and Oswin feared they too would fall through, and then again he might be found out. No, sit tight. They're not that heavy. But the floor creaked frightfully, and as they passed nearly overhead, another floorboard snapped. He must somehow get them to leave without his stirring. And so he fell to making the spookiest sounds that these girls had ever heard, muffled beastlike howlings and growlings. They hearkened, they squealed, they fled.

Oswin heard nothing further. But how was he to get out of this cellar now? There were no stairs, and he could not reach the floorboards above, which were a good yard or so above the hands of his upstretched arms. He was stuck. Here he would have to sit tight, in the creepy musty gloom, amidst a few broken-up barrels and smashed-in boxes, and the scurry of rats and mice beyond in the near pitchblackness. He let his mind run away, greatly gladdened as it was by the girls' flight from his fake ghosthood.

Oswin was happy to find himself soon sitting in fieldman Lowe's wheelbarrow, pushed along down the road by Godwin. Halfswaddled in blankets, he felt even a little lordly, as if he were some wealthy lazeabout borne along in a sedan, with somebody else doing all the work. Well, he hoped at least that they did not look like a hoyden of a nanny overburdened with a frightfully big ward, but then, they met not a soul upon the road for the rest of the day, apart from a marketbound woman with her elderly mother, the latter in great need of a wheelchair.

The two felt almost a giddy lightness now, as they skylarked about the children's flight, fieldman Lowe's comeuppance, the befooling of De Keyser's band, and even the gipsies' untrustworthiness. Yes, they were on their way again, even if still outlaws. Everything stood now upon getting out of England, even if they had to wheelbarrow themselves away.

It was not until the following day, when they reached another waterstream—or was it the same one where they had made their last stand?—that they gave up on trekking to Chester. This must be the Avon, it struck Godwin in time, the Avon that flows into the Severn, and the Severn into the sea. Spotting something nearby, he veered sharply towards the bank and began wheelbarrowing along the water.

"Where are we going now?" asked Oswin.

"You'll see."

They came to a sudden halt, right by a tied-in raft.

"On you go."

"On this? Why, it hardly looks waterworthy."

"What doesn't?"

"Isn't this stealing?"

"You didn't gripe about the stolen wheelbarrow."

This shut Oswin up, but he was still leary about boarding. The few times he had given himself up to a watercraft, he had ended up being tossed into the sea to be drowned or kidnapped by freebooters. And in truth, this raft was an old shoddy piece of work, the theft of which was hardly worth lawing.

A tricky business it was, trundling over the narrow springy gangplank, and Oswin nearly headfirsted into the water when the wheelbarrow lurched sharply to the side, in being pushed onto the raft, but he stayed put inside, as if bound therein. They set off, floating down the Avon, hugging its left bank, with Godwin standing as steersman and with Oswin still halflying on the blanketed bottom of his wheelbarrow, as cosy as any boatborne Cleopatra upon the Nile.

Thus they rafted on downstream, by hollows, hursts, and hillocks, until in time a wind blew up, and the water grew a little choppy and the riding a little rough. And not long thereafter, they began to near some great ruckus up ahead, near the right bank. In floating by, they saw a great throng of folk angrily pulling down hurdles and fences. The two watched keenly. But they did not need to ask for whys or wherefores, for such outbreaks of lawlessness had not been unheard-of latterly.

It was wellknown that cashstrapped King Charles had earlier sold off woods and wastes for ready money, when he had lost the goodwill of the holding-the-pursestrings Parliament. And the buyers meant to make these bought-up lands moneyearners. Trees were felled, swamps drained, fences thrown up. But these lands had long been commonland, of great weight to the livelihood of England's smallholders, for food, firefodder, and suchlike.

This loss was illbrooked, spawning in turn riots and uprisings, such as those led by Captain Pouch, a burly fieldman who carried in his pouch, so he said, a warrant from the king allowing him and his merry men to pull down fences and take back the commonlands, all lawfully Robin-Hood-like or robber-baron-like, although this letter turned out to be only a piece of green cheese. Nor had Captain Alice been forgotten, another rabbleraiser who in all the fencewrecking had stalked forth in woman's cladding, in an old motheaten red gown belonging to his wife. Why so clothed, no-one was sure, even if it was highly hootworthy, if not outrightly slighting to the powers-that-be, although the whisper went that he was but his kinghating wife's puppet and would be birched if he did not do her bidding.

With the coming of war and the weakening of the king's power, many commonfolk, hardbelieving that the former commonlands still belonged to them rightfully, even if now in the hands of a few, aped Captains Pouch and Alice of foredays, and went forth, taking the law into their own hands, to the end of undoing hurdleworks and drainingworks. By God! They wanted their old world back.

And it was one of these outbreaks that Godwin and Oswin now rafted past. Amidst the havoc, they saw some very youthful lad, a wanfaced redhead, being roughed up nastily, likely one of the lord's groundsmen, cowering upon his knees before a few of these fistuppy mobbers, begging and weeping, although to Oswin this weeping seemed somehow more and more like laughing, but then, what other comeback is there to the deadly earnest joke that is life? The two watched on and floated on.

As this sight began to pass out-of-sight, with the necks of the two all too long craned backwards, the unseen to the fore quickly got the upperhand. It was only when they heard the not-to-be-misacknowledged sound of downrushing water beneath them that heads turned forwards and downwards, only to see their raft tumble over a weir. This manmade damlet was too much for the rickety raft, which broke up as it hit the water at the foot of the weir. Tossed into the waters were the raftwrecked, and it was with some hardship that Godwin was able to fish out Oswin and his wheelbarrow afterwards. But their little food—fieldman Lowe's ham—sank wretchedly.

And so these glumsters sat down by the waters of the Avon, ready to wail and gnash their teeth, for these outlaws were without money and food and means of wayfaring and even knowledge of their whereabouts. And there they slumped away a good while, wondering how or if they would ever get off this bloody island. If only they had had the twofold gift of foresight and backsight, but then, how many wretches in this world are blessed with the twinmug of a *Janus Pater, Patulcius* and *Clusivus?*

AFTERLIFE

S O HERE THEY WERE, in the gloomy little churchyard. It was here, in that little church there, that nearly twenty years ago Godwin had been christened, had been benamed Godwin Drighten, the lastmost afterbear of one Earl of Etenheighte after another, a long line of Etenheightes stretching back into the murky yoredays when the world was filled with elves and goblins and trolls. And indeed, it was only a few months ago that Godwin had last been here, on these hallowed grounds, but that now seemed like yearhundreds ago to him, for how much water had since passed under the bridge of byword. Nothing hereabouts, it seemed, had othered itself in the betweentime, outtaking the freshly dug grave yonder, yawning hungrily for its next inmate. And here amidst the crumbling headstones, overgrown with climbing moss, the two youths had stopped for a breather.

And what a to-do it had been to get this far, or rather this near to their hometurf of Kingswood and its roundings. Hither over fifty miles of road and countryside, Godwin had footslogged, pushing before him Oswin in the wheelbarrow, all well witnessed by now blisterhardened hands. And everything that they had eaten since the Avon, days and days ago, he had pilfered and thieved, but what did he care? His misdeeds were already sundry and manifold in this land, and a few more lawless straws would not break any camel's uneven back.

Sitting stilly in the waning light, beset with jostling backthoughts, dampened by the gloomy aboutscape and the grave overagainst them, Godwin halfmumbled, as a kind of skylark, "Only Yorick's skull is wanting."

"Who's Yorick?" asked Oswin dumbly.

"A onetime fawning fool to a dead king."

Such an answer was lost on Oswin, another one of those things he somehow never got, and so he shut up and let it pass.

Then suddenly, the beams from the sinking sun burst through the churchlet's stainglazen windows, and the outshape of a crankylooking greybeard lighted up in the glass, and the words above *in nomine patris, et filii, et spiritus sancti.** Godwin held up his hand to ward off the fall of light upon his eyes.

He rose to shift himself away to a spot where he would be unbothered, but in doing so he banged his toe on a chuck of broken headstone lying in the grass and nearly stumbled over it. In anger he picked up the stone and hurled it away. But there were more bits about, for vandals had latterly fallen upon the churchyard and had smashed up a number of the headstones and holy carvings.

Then taken by a sudden whim, he picked up another and then another and then another of the broken bits and began casting them at the churchwindows, which cracked and shattered and unhanded their glazen shards. The more he threw, the more bedeviled he grew. And with each shatter of glass, he was sure that the hit smarted mightily, like a birch across a child's back. Hell, he would scatter this glass to the winds! And in no time, that greybeard's head turned into a yawning hole.

Oswin grew worried that all this to-do might upshoot in God-knows-what, and so he hobbled over and tried to soothe him down. "Let it be! Let it be!" But Godwin unheard him, and Oswin then tried to hold him back. As the two struggled, they soon heard the sound of footfalls.

It was as Oswin feared: Godwin's vandalry had been a draw, to the warmen now hotfooting it towards them. Godwin faced these oncomers and began picking up more chucks of stone. Oswin was sure that he was out of his mind and meant somehow to take on these Goliaths. And when the men were nearly upon them and Godwin had straightened up, well beweaponed with bits of stone, Oswin, fearing the worst, thrust all his weight against him, such that the two fell heavily to the ground as one.

But the men dashed on past them and rushed into the church. And as the youths got to their feet again—Godwin a little sore from the fall—the band's headman trotted up ahorse and stopped before the two. "Well met

---

* 'In the name of the Father, and of the Son, and of the Holy Ghost.'

and God bless! It is not every day that one comes across such highminded youth. Pray, make one with us as we carry on with the godly work you've begun." And thereupon the man rode his horse into the church, which now dinned from smashing and breaking.

"What's going on?" asked Oswin utterly bewildered.

"Puritans. Iconbreaking Puritans."

These were indeed Puritans, Puritans no less keen than the dead Archbishop Laud had been to cleanse the church, although these were set upon seeing burnt-out or crumbled-away the hated breaden god of Rome that still haunted these abodes in the shape of crosses, altarrailings, stainglazen windows, paintings, hangings, and other such leftovers and hangers-on of the old faith. For these Puritans were unfain to worship stocks and stones, however handsomely carved and hued. To them, godly truth was to be found in inked paper only—as good kill a man as kill the good book!

In the betumbledness spawned by this war, in the missing of a hand to stay vandals, these Puritan warmen, like others elsewhere, fell upon the helpless church to the end of stripping it of anything that smacked of greegree or fetish or popish gold. By God! They would leave it smacksmooth and blemishfree, by first beating the devil out of it.

And beat they did, some with their musketends, some with cudgels, some with fired musketballs, such that chunks of stonework hopped and tumbled onto the floor, here a hand, there a leg, yonder a head, and everywhere shattered glass. So great was the wayward flight of flinders that more than one of the men were hit by such. A few more careful hedgers, hoping not to overstep the bounds of any maybe holiness, deemed it best to give the god or gods—they were unsure how many—an opening to show themselves first, and so before bashing anything, they shouted forth, "If you be gods, spare yourselves!" But when these gods only gawked back dumbly, without so much as casting a first stone or even shifting a limb, as if stuck in a pillory, cudgels then fell and the stonen gods jigged away in their dance of death.

Some of the more reckless had gathered about the battered christeningfont, as if around some old rainbarrel, and made water therein. And when they had thus fouled it, the headman's horse was brought up, and amidst horselaughs and cackles, the steed's head was pulled down to the vatlike opening and then smeared with their salty water in order thereby to make of him the new Pope of the Roman church.

This churchcleansing, the two youths watched for a bit from their stand at the door, until Godwin, still somewhat peeved that he had been forestalled from what he had started, turned his back and walked away. And then into the twilight, the two trundled off again.

Godwin had never told Oswin why they had come back thus. But Oswin was not in the least taken aback later to find himself alighting from his wheelbarrow before the Drighten greathouse. Even in the dark, he knew where he was, for it was only a few months ago that he had stood here, at the foot of these steps, with a mob of angry townsfolk and his tearful sister somewhere behind him. And now he found himself hobbling inside, not without a little worry.

The house was in darkness, outtaking a weak light burning in the readingroom, where Lord Drighten, with a wrap over his shoulders, sat at his desk, hunched over householdbooks. The magistrate heard nothing but his own fitful coughing and the scratch of his quill, which he bit now and then between bouts of writing. He had been unwell the last while, and somewhat downhearted to boot by tidings about King Charles' loss at Naseby. But he started when he caught sight of a body standing in the doorway. Good Lord! It was the Etenheighte bequestling, Godwin Drighten!

"What are you doing here?" he asked, nearly at a loss. No answer. "Why are you not in Antwerp? And what happened to Cruikshank? He was to be back weeks ago already, with the dowrymoney." Godwin by now had reached the desk. "Why are you so slovenly, like some beggarwench?"

"Charles is dead."

"The king?"

"Your son."

Godwin drew forth his brother's bloodstained hanky, with *C.D.* embroidered off in one aloof corner, the same hanky that Godwin had taken from Charles' body as it lay lifeless at the bottom of the belltower, the day of their showdown after Naseby-Fight. He threw it into the magistrate's lap.

Bewildered, the magistrate looked up from his slouch and only now caught sight of Oswin standing in the doorway. Seeing red, he wanned and shouted, "How dare you bring that gutterling into my house! Get him out of my sight!"

Oswin began to withdraw, until Godwin countered, "Stay where you are."

"If you do not rid the house of that misbirth, by God, I'll throw him out myself!" The magistrate meant to get to his feet in order to endeed word, but barely up, he was roughly pushed back down into his chair by Godwin, and man and chair nearly fell backwards to the floor.

"It's you who should be thrown out."

The magistrate sat there dumbfounded, altogether dumbfounded. Then quickly and angrily coming to himself, he shouted, "You cheeky upstart!" Halfrising to his feet, he swung a hand at his son. But the latter warded it off and then grasped the old man's wrists and thrust them down, fastheld in a mighty knucklewhitening grip. The magistrate was overwhelmed by the strength of the youth, whom he had always thought to be but a gutless weakling, so little did he understand his own son. But was not the latter, after all, the son of a lord?

The magistrate squirmed weakly and helplessly in his seat, as if pillory-bound. "Let go of me! You're hurting me! I'm your father, for Christ sake, and a magistrate! You're breaking the law!"

"How you sicken me!" Godwin snarled and spit into the craggy face and then, with a fling of the arms, unhanded the man. The sorewristed and somewhat frightened latter sat on, thoughtfully wiping the spittle from his face, unthinkingly with the bloodstained hanky. Godwin trod to the wallshelves and began pawing away fiendishly, hurling down the dusty lawbooks, which hopped and tumbled upon the floor in heaps.

"What are you doing?"

Godwin carried on, making a barn of the room, until he found a stout bag hidden behind a shelfful of books.

"What are you doing?"

Godwin clawed open the bag, spilling a muchness of coin onto the floor, as if so many beans loosed from an old sack. He loaded his pocket with as much as he wanted and tossed the rest to the floor. Then turning his back on the old man, the robber made one with his fellow, and together the two headed for the foredoor.

The magistrate rose to his feet and shouted, "You thankless changeling! As God is my witness, I will strike your name from the book of this family! The door to this house will be forever shut to your face! Be you starving in the gutter, you will never get one farthing of my money! I will hunt you down, the dirty thief that you are! I'll—"

The foredoor slammed shut. That was the last that father and son would ever see of each other.

Now and then, as the two trundled off in the darkness, Oswin eyed his friend warily but held his tongue, for oh, Godwin, he was a stinker now! And what a rough berattling ride Oswin got in his wheelbarrow! The weary rider would have gladly stopped for the night, and it was only after a good while that he was emboldened to speak his mind, but Godwin swore he would not rest until he was off Etenheighte mould. And so onwards they trundled.

But they did stop a little later, while still on Etenheighte land, when they came upon the cottage where Oswin had once dwelt. The latter gawked for a bit at the tumbledown framework beyond, now someone else's home. What a barn it had been. And still was, truth-be-told. And it was only after they had past that his sister came to mind. Well, only a halfsister, rightly. God only knew where she was now and what had become of her. Maybe she had followed the way of much flesh and had taken to her back, meaning to whore her way through life. God speed her!

Later, much later, when they were no longer on Etenheighte land—or at least no longer upon what they thought was Etenheighte land, for few were sure where it started and ended—they stopped and bunked down for the night. Tomorrow would be a big day, for they meant to wheel into Bristol and get two places on the next outbound ship. And this was not altogether riskless, for they were outlaws, after all, and they had rather unwisely shown themselves this day to the magistrate, who had proven to be less than sweethearted towards them. If known again, and taken again, they would swing from the gallows, like clockwork. Any risk could surely be sidestepped were they to slog on to another harbourtown, but Godwin had had enough of abouttraipsing and would not hear of going elsewhere. Oswin had to soothe his own misgivings with the thought that, given their beggarly unsightliness, bearded, tattered, and dirty, they might very well pass through unmarked after all.

How heartlightened was Oswin the following morning when they reached Bristol's wharf without so much as a halfknowing look from any gawker or bystander. But how downheartening it was when the first few spoken-to skippers gave Godwin a curt brushoff, for these shipmen were not about to let aboard such a legless grubby thing as that, in the wheelbarrow yonder, who would likely bring more lice and sickness to the seacrossing than anything else.

Now, they were too beggarlylooking, it seemed, above all Oswin. Indeed, so wretched and forlorn the latter looked sitting there in his wheelbarrow, while waiting for Godwin, that one bypasser kindly dropped a coin into his lap. The youth took it not that kindly and for an eyetwink nearly tossed the coin back, but then he better bethought himself and pocketed the money. He would play the beggar after all.

After a number of such turndowns, a sour Godwin wheeled Oswin away from the wharf but stopped by an empty packhouse where he then wheeled him inside and parked the wheelbarrow behind some empty packingboxes. "I need to go and hunt you up a false leg and something better to wear. Otherwise we'll never get aboard any of these ships. Stay here out of sight until I get back."

This sat ill with Oswin, but then what else was to be done? And so he waited away on his own, lying snugcosy in the wheelbarrow. He had nearly dozed off when he suddenly heard chatter and bustle on the otherside of the boxes. He go up and peered out, where he saw that folk were streaming in. They fell to a gleeful and prateful shedding of duds, as if readying to bathe in some out-of-the-way stream. He watched on in unbelief. What in God's name was going on here?

He was at a loss about what to do. His unsettledness, however, got the better of him. With his makeshift crutch, he hobbled over to the door and slipped out. Outside, he was taken aback to see another crowd forgathering not too far from the doorway. What a grimlooking crew this, all blackclad, some with a black book in hand. Near the rear, two spinsters held up a banner which read *The Brethrenship for the Bettering of Morals*. Many of these Brethren nattered away angrily, as if ready for a row, and their number was swelling.

Oswin was again at a loss. Should he go back in and bide his time or push through this bristly mob? But before he could settle his mind, he caught sight of one busy little man amongst them, who in his turn spotted Oswin and drew near searchingly. Oswin had seen that face before. But where? Where? And the nearer the little man drew, the more he likewise seemed to know Oswin. And at nearly the same eyetwink wherein Oswin knew the man again—Richard Hooker, that bloody crownlawyer from his trial here in Bristol a few months ago—Hooker himself gasped and mouthed, "The outlawed sodomite! Here with the godless Adamites!"

Feargripped, Oswin wheeled about and hotcrutched it back into the packhouse, with Hooker rushing up to the door, shouting, "Stop, you! It is unlawful for you to be here! Stop!" But Hooker himself had to stop short when met by a pair of burly dockworkers in the buff, coming out and looking daggers at him. In untreading, Hooker shouted to the wall, as if he could see Oswin through it, "I've got you now! I've got you now!" Off he ran in search of lawmen.

Oswin was unsure which unsettled him more, a threatening Hooker without or the great naked wench who trod up to him now and said, "Don't be shy, my dear! We're all a little scared the first time. Come, let me help you strip." Oswin slipped back behind the boxes, and the amazon left him be when a raspy voice beyond called all these strippers to order. They linked hands as their spokesman rose up upon an empty box and read forth from a little black book—the Holy Writ it turned out to be—something about Adam and Eve, although Oswin little heeded the words as he watched on wide-eyed.

To the more flatminded, it must surely have seemed like some unbeliefworthy *reductio ad absurdum*, but Oswin's eyes were no liars here. Beyond stood some fifty men, women, and children, with not so much as figleafbreeches on, as naked as if straight from a mother's womb, in all their frightfully oddish shapes and sizes.

Having ended his reading, the speaker spoke on, "The prophet Genesis was naked himself when he wrote those words. Let us pray now, saying after me. I am an Adamite, the child of Adam,"

"I am an Adamite, the child of Adam,"

"Who begot me in all guiltlessness,"

"Who begot me in all guiltlessness,"

"And I follow in his footsteps before the fall,"

"And I follow in his footsteps before the fall,"

"We lay aside all clothes, the badges of shame,"

"We lay aside all clothes, the badges of shame,"

"The rags of ungodliness, the hand-me-downs of sin,"

"The rags of ungodliness, the hand-me-downs of sin,"

"And as my father Adam was naked,"

"And as my father Adam was naked,"
"Whilst in the Garden of Eden and was not ashamed,"
"Whilst in the Garden of Eden and was not ashamed,"
"So am I the naked Truth unabashed,"
"So am I the naked Truth unabashed."

Godwin had now backed, with a bundle underarm, and was no less taken aback to find the packhouse packed with the naked. And finding Oswin where he left him, he was somewhat beguiled by his mate's wide-eyedness.

"What's going on??" whispered Oswin.

"What, you don't know?!"

"I wouldn't ask if did."

"They're Adamites, or Antinomians, believers in the holiness of nakedness and the evilness of clothes. It's a splintergroup of faith."

"Good God! What will they think up next?"

"We must push on."

"But I've been spotted! That lawyer from our trial, he was here and he saw me! Outside, in the crowd. I think he's run off to fetch the law!"

Godwin peered through a crack in the wall and saw that the heap of Brethren without had swollen frightfully, even within the few minutes since his coming. And worse, there was Hooker—yes, Godwin knew him again as well—all in a flap, at the head of these Brethren, seemingly with a few lawmen.

The Adamites had by now ended their readings and prayers and whatnot-else and had started streaming out of the building. Outside, their naked white flesh, sicklywan from months of warspawned want, gleamed in the sunlight for all bystanders to behold. And the buff now came up against the blocking Brethren, these arm-in-arm blackclad Bristolburghers, who fell to a hardy singing of godly songs, in the hope of hemming in and drowning out anything the Adamites might mouth in the streets.

This faceoff, in this crossness of beliefs, now upshot in a bitter blustery struggle. The Adamites' spokesman began to bellow above the Brethren's singing, "Ye faithful of Bristol, cast aside those riggings of the body! Clothes that lead men to pride and women to whoredom! For those outward donnings match not the bodies beneath!"

Hooker, who had been scanning the crowd for sight of the outlawed sodomite, found himself hardsqueezed to answer this dare and so began bellowing back above the Adamite and the Brethren's singing, "Strip man of his clothes, and behold the beast that gnaws at the roots of Eden! Away!"

And more suchlike was bantered to-and-fro. This hardline oldline felt itself in its right to strip Eden's straightgrowing stalks of mushrooming faiths, false faiths of all stripes, above all that of these Adamites, who latterly had taken to walking forth through Bristol's streets to the end of broadcasting their belief, much to the dudgeon of Hooker and his like.

All this hubbub, Godwin and Oswin watched through a crack in the wall. There was only one outlet to this packhouse, and beyond it a bottleneck of bodies. What now? This might go on for hours! In a clap, Godwin started stripping and told Oswin to get into the wheelbarrow.

"What are you doing?" asked Oswin dumbly.

"Well, don't stand there! Get in!"

When he was fully bare, he tossed his duds over Oswin in the wheelbarrow and then Fieldman Lowe's blanket on top. And with Oswin thus hidden away, Godwin wheeled out into the street and made one with the Adamites.

The weather was a little too raw for standing outside in the raw, above all in this dingy narrow lane, and so the Adamites, keen to forward and thereby warm themselves, tried to thrust through but were withstood. Those jockeying at the forefront fell to slanging each other. "Back into your stinking hole, you heathen!" "A turd in your teeth, you old bitch!" And more of the same. And all the while Hooker kept up his outwatch for the onelegged sodomite.

Notwithstanding all the jostling, Godwin had brought off, with no little hardship, his push to the fore, wheelbarrow still in hands, and Oswin still therein, albeit tucked away like a cradlechild. And once at the head of the Adamites, Godwin too came up against the Brethren's diehard stonewalling, overagainst Hooker himself. The latter, with eyes only for Oswin, somehow did not know Godwin again. And as the hustling greatened, but without any meaningful outcome, Godwin grew evermore restless and at length had had enough of this niminypimininess. He crashed his wheelbarrow into the stonewall of the Brethren. Quick on his feet, Hooker veered aside cagily, while the two women standing behind him were not so lucky, the one being knocked down and the other run right over. With the line now broken, the Adamites troopered through in Godwin's wake. Hell, there was nothing that a good knock would not mend!

Godwin did not even look back at the hurlyburly behind, wherein an unfewness of the Adamites and Brethren came to blows. And he did not stop until he found a bustlefree bylane to wheel into, where he pulled Oswin out of his hideaway, and with a bit of fetched water, they cleaned themselves up. How happy Oswin was to don cleanish clothes and to strap on the false limb. The latter was a little on the shortside, but he was sure that he could live with the unevenness. And what a godsend, for it went leastwise a little way in masking his lack of leg.

It took over a week before they found outfare upon a ship bound for New Amsterdam—or New York, as the town would be newnamed some years later, when it passed from the Dutch to the English. And in sailing out of the harbour, standing on topdeck, above the bulkheads below inholding slaves and shipped-off misdoers bound for fields of drudgery in Virginia, they watched awhile as the shoreline dwindled away in the mist. A world well lost, it seemed. And so began their seacrossing to the New World.

In the weeks following, Oswin saw little of the sea, for he was happy to lie snug below, given that the sight of the water's toss-and-throw only unsettled him, he said. Godwin, however, slept little and spent much of the day on deck, sitting for hours at the prow, keen to be the first to sight land. And as the days passed, and as the rough and smooth came and went, Godwin at length got his wish, and he was indeed the first to spot land ahead.

"What land is this?" he asked a sailor keenly.

"It's only Newfoundland. We make a short stop here. Still a ways till New Amsterdam."

"What kind of place is it?"

"Don't know rightly. Not many folk hereabouts. Pretty much a wilderness."

Newfoundland! How the name and the misty sight of the land itself took a hold on the youth's fancy, in a kind of wizardwoven way. Indeed, the place was not without its own dreamymisty history. Unbeknownst to Godwin, it was not too far from here that Leifr Eiríksson, a great *grœnlendingr*, or Norse Greenlander, had wintered yearhundreds earlier—following a seacrossing in ships handsomely fitted out, at stem and stern, with a pair of great upthrusting carved dragonheads—before lastly being driven off by *skrælingjar*, as the unfriendlies hereabouts had been called by these *víkingar*.

By the time anchor had fallen off Avalon, Oswin had been told to ready himself for landing. Godwin was the first out of the boat and pulled Oswin down into the water after him, making a big splash. And then as the rowboats pushed off again without them, Oswin asked, "What! Are we staying here? In this place?"

"This one's as good as any other hereabouts."

Oswin found this a little downletting, for there was not much of anything roundabout. But here they were, and here they thought they would stay. And so it turned out that they fell short of ever reaching New Amsterdam, as forelaid.

And thus it was here, at the back of the beyond, on the very fraying selvedge of the New World and that of the known world, thrust up against the untamed wayward sea lying inbetween, that Godwin and Oswin meant to live out their timetorn lives in peace and unknownness. And it was here, in the months following their landing, that they tilled a hard earth and strove to earn their keep through the sweat of their brow, far from the land of their birth.

And when the day grew hotter and the work harder, Oswin would stop for a bit and for a breather, leaning on his sturdy hoe, and then at times he thought he caught sight of a ghostly dash of something bloodred struggling in the underbrush out beyond, and then he would grow oddly aware of soreness in his maimed leg. And when the day waned, Godwin would stand in the weakling twilight, lost in dim thoughts, and he at times thought he could hear something in the cool eveningbreeze, something like a laugh far off, and then it seemed he could feel a weakling of a twinge in the back, as if from the jab of an old dirty knittingneedle.

Yet however backbreaking their work and unforward their crop, were they not free at last? Did not their former hardships lie very much behind their backs now? Would a wight be foolish to think that they would always stay there?

www.edmundfairfax.com

Made in the USA
Columbia, SC
25 November 2017